INTERNET
DATING

INTERNET DATING

J. R. Niles

Library of Congress Control Number: 2011917934
ISBN: Hardcover   978-1-4653-7636-7
                   Softcover   978-1-4653-7635-0
                   Ebook   978-1-4653-7637-4

To order additional copies of this book, contact:
Xlibris Corporation
1-888-795-4274
www.Xlibris.com
Orders@Xlibris.com
106411

I dedicate this book to my extraordinary son Trey. You are the illuminator of my life and you have inspired me in so many ways that were unimaginable before you came along. I love you Son. Also, my dedication is to Beverly Flowers. This literary offering is a result of the everlasting love and unconditional support that you bestowed upon me throughout the years. You were confident in my overall abilities and you were proud of me when you left; if only you could see me now! Rest in peace my most celebrated dear. Rest in peace Mother.

PROLOGUE

Username: Trynsomnu

Introduction: Love & Music !! Explore a Possible Journey With an
Honest Man That's Not Afraid To Love!

Basic info: 38 yr. old man
Chicago, Illinois, United States
Seeking women 28-38 yrs old
Within 100 miles of Chicago, Il.

Relationships: Never married
Have kids: None
Want kids: Definitely (2)
Ethnicity: Black/ African descent
Body type: Athletic & toned
Height: 5'11" (180.3 cms)
Religion: Christian/ Other
Smoke: No way
Drink: Social drinker, maybe one or two

About me and what I'm looking for:

Describe myself. Hhmmm . . . well, I'm a hopeless romantic. A candlelit dinner at "her" favorite restaurant or "our" favorite restaurant sticks in my mind. Cooking for a woman can be even more romantic (breakfast in bed, lunch for a picnic, or dinner with my own candles to light).

I am a man who takes pride in his daily appearance. I try to look my best, smell my best, and feel my best. Exercise is very important to me, because it vastly contributes to two out of three of the above mentioned. The smell after exercise is obviously questionable; however, sweating can be sexy – at the right time.

I am a man that is confident in what he says & what he does. If something baffles me, or I know nothing about it, I will take the time to figure it out. I only have some college, but – I am definitely high on the intellectual scale. School did not give me my mind . . . God did. The Lord also blessed me with the ability to write, in which my ambition is to one day become a published writer.

I am quite versatile, unusually honest, and a very loyal man to whom ever that special woman is in my life; and to my friends. Now, why did I join this dating website? Because *I am tired of meeting, and allowing myself to be with the wrong girl!!* These playa type women with their own agendas are not for me!! Don't get me wrong, I've had a ball with a few of these playa types, but that is not what's important.

What is on a woman's mind, and what's in her heart is what's important. I need a woman that knows a good man when she sees one. She will grab him, and love him, and never let him go!! I need a *good* girl; a humble woman, that has the mindset of wanting to grow within herself and to help growth within the right man. I'm looking for a woman that knows what family is and is striving to build one of her own, with children . . . with the right man. On my mind is to be in a one-on-one, long term relationship with the right one. What's in my heart is to love, and eventually marry . . . the right girl.

The written part of Lance Austin's profile that he will be posting on the internet's dating website of his choice; his very first experience doing this . . . hence the username: *TRYNSOMNU* – "way to meet women."

CHAPTER 1

As angry as Lance is at the moment, his meticulous tendencies even now, supersedes the rage that he feels as he packs the long rectangular white box with its original contents and more. A one handed grab and one trip to the car is all he wants to do. Surprisingly he is able to secure the box shut just enough to pull the cute little handle up through the perforated slot. As he storms out the house and towards the red compact car, he scoffs in disgust and has a thought.

What a shity car!! It's a rental; and being a Friday evening after work, an hour before they closed . . . he pretty much got stuck with it. Lance knows a car is better than *no* car but he still hates it; especially considering what he needs to do in it tomorrow. He hopes he can trade it in for something else in the morning since all the affiliated car rental locations he called on the way home from work, got him no results.

The destination of Lance's first errand this evening is to drop the "stupid" white box off which is about fifteen minutes away. When he arrives, he grabs the box from the back seat like an animal. As he storms to the residential front door, he is glad to not see a certain woman's car parked out front. Then suddenly he realizes that her dad or some neighbors may be looking out the window. Lance has been working on his anger thing as of late. One thing he has learned from self help books he has recently read is to be more in control of his *reactions* to the emotion of anger. So he changes his walk in mid stride and approaches the front door with a calm demeanor – a calm demeanor that he doesn't want but a calm demeanor all the same.

Lance murmurs under his breath, "Does the fucking doorbell work!?" After another excruciating fifteen seconds, the door squeaks open.

"Oh hi Lance, how are you?"

"How are you Mr. Strong? Would you please give this to Melanie? It belongs to her."

"Oh sure, not a problem. Say, Melanie should be back shortly if you wanna come in and have a seat and wait for her."

"No Mr. Strong, that's okay but thanks." In Lance's world of make believe, the moment the door opened, he would've yelled to Mr. Strong *look out* and slammed the long white box straight through the screen part of the door. Lance tries to visit that world in his mind once more when he is behind the wheel of his rent-a-car again; but he can't seem to pull it off.

He thinks to himself, *the engine is too loud and the car is too slow for the engine to be this loud!!*

Thirty minutes later, Lance arrives at his favored destination for CD's & DVD's. After he parks, he just sits there. He reaches for his cell phone but hesitates to pull it out the holster. He starts thinking about the woman he will eventually call. Her name is Sherry. He met her on the internet about two weeks ago. When Lance first came across her picture, he was mesmerized by her pretty face and her small frame. He couldn't believe she actually resides in Illinois and not in another state like a lot of the other women he had seen on the internet he liked. He thinks of how ironic it was that he had only been on that particular dating site for a three day trial period. To be meeting someone desirable and so soon is *very* rare. The initial email to her read:

Wow! Hello Elosher36.

I am speechless right now. I will send you a better email tomorrow. For now, just wanted to say hello to you and tell you, that you look like a very special person. And I don't mean your looks either. Your beauty is obvious to me, but it's a quiet beauty that I see. It's kinda wholesome to me, and I like that. Hope to touch basis with you soon.

Lance

To his surprise, Sherry responded the next day. She was very articulate in her text, just as Lance suspected she would be. She also paid him a compliment on *his* appearance. The overall email seemed very encouraging. Because of her quick response, he answered her email later that same day. Idle chit chat ensued; where he's from, the fact that he has no children, ect. The latter of the two was something that they both had in common. With Lance being thirty nine years old and Sherry being thirty six, the aspect of no children in Lance's opinion, was something to grab a tight hold of and run down the street with – screaming for joy!

Lance's third email included his phone number and Sherry's response included hers.

On a Sunday afternoon they exchanged the sound of one another's voice for the very first time. Being born and raised in Boston, Massachusetts was the reason for her slight accent. The pace in her speech was a bit rapid for his ears but she was definitely a very intelligent woman. She even used a word or two in their conversation that he didn't quite know the meaning of. To Lance, this was a good sign.

They talked about love and life and the dating scene. She told Lance about some guy she was seeing and that she was crazy about him. Her purpose for being on the dating site was to date only; more-or-less just weighing her options. Lance appreciated her honesty, so he didn't hold it against her. Their conversation was cut short when she received another call.

Lemecallyouback is what Lance expected to hear . . . an irritating phrase people often use when their other line clicks on their Call-Waiting. To his surprise, Sherry didn't say that phrase.

She said, "Lance, may I call you back?" And not only that, she *did* call him back. This was another brownie point for the new girl who resides in Skokie, Illinois. After just the second conversation, Lance asked Sherry out and she said *yes*. Within ten minutes of their first verbal exchange, she pretty much confirmed what he assumed about her just from looking at her picture – Sherry was a good old-fashioned "girl next door" that he *absolutely* wanted to meet.

As Lance still sits in the parking lot, he decides to call Sherry after he finishes his cigarette. Then he contemplates waiting ten additional minutes after he comes out of the audio/video store. The two conversations they previously had were lengthy enough, yet seemed slightly strained. He wonders if it was shyness on his part . . . or if it was something else.

He calls her after the cigarette. "Hi Sherry, how are you? This is Lance."

"Oh hey Lance, I'm fine!! How are you?"

"I'm okay. It's Friday, know what I mean? Say, are we still on for tomorrow?"

"Oh you know what? I was wondering if we could reschedule that. I have something to do . . ."

There is an empty space of silence in the telephone that seems to last an eternity. "That's understandable . . . but I did explain my car situation to you and I told you I was going to rent a car the weekend we were going to meet up. I'm sitting in the rent-a-car right now."

"Ahhh I forgot about that! I would really hate that you went through so much trouble for nothing. Let me see what I can do to move some things around that I have to do tomorrow. But don't worry, we'll meet up."

"Okay. I'll give you a call tomorrow around noon or so, to see what's going on and we can get a definite time together," he says with relief.

"Okay, that will be good, and sorry about that."

Lance appreciates how thoughtful and polite Sherry is. It is refreshing and in some ways, well overdue for him. Without going into the audio/video store, he pulls out of the parking lot to head home.

*   *   *

Lance is so anxious to get a different vehicle before his date that he wakes up at 6:15am, well before the rent-a-car places even open. He listens to a variety of voicemail recordings to several of their facility's weekend hours, most of them being 7:00am to 2:00pm. After an intense forty five minutes, a live voice finally picks up on the other end. For the next four hours on and off, the search continues for an available car, but with no luck. Sherry won't even care about the kind of car Lance is driving and he knows this. It's the *guy thing* with cars that makes him determined to find something else; a nice car – a cool car – a fast car.

He calls Sherry at twenty after noon. They agree, apprehensively on his part, to meet at the mall in Skokie at four o'clock. This seems more like a blind date to Lance. The time . . . too early, the place . . . too lame, and mall food of course is mall food; but because it's in her area, he agrees. This is what being a gentleman is all about and he prides himself in being just that. He gets his reward for this when he finally finds another vehicle; if he can get to it before the rent-a-car place closes. Lance *does* arrive in time, normally being a fast driver anyway. He gets a brand new 2007 black sports car with a better sound system and one of those new age automatic stick shifts with an *S* gear. The *S* stands for *super turbo* and Lance had to pull to the side of the road and grab the car's manual from the glove compartment to figure that out. He now wonders if he will seriously be considering getting one of these exact vehicles next month in late May. His original plan was to get a Cadillac; the vehicle he did extensive research on a few months ago.

This vehicle . . . he thinks to himself . . . w*ow not bad!*

Lance gets to hit 90mph on the highway on his way to Skokie, before he runs into a construction zone traffic jam. However, his level of joy is so high right now, along with the volume on the music, that nothing can deter his mood. He arrives in the mall parking lot and immediately notices the difference in the people. Besides from a lot of them being Caucasian, their mannerism, the pleasant looks on their faces; kind of reminds him of the *la-di-da* nonchalant factor.

The earth is such a beautiful place to live in, and the mall is beautiful too. I cannot wait to blindingly spend a whole lot of money in these wonderful stores.

Lance thinks out loud, "I hope this girl isn't like these people!!" He cautiously approaches a store entrance with a nervous anticipation of meeting this lovely woman. As he works his way to the outside area, he checks his watch. It's a few minutes after four. He looks around and doesn't see anyone that resembles Sherry.

"Did I come through the right entrance?" he murmurs. Lance calls her. "Hi Sherry, I'm here. Where are you?"

"Did you come in through the mall's main entrance?"

"No, I forgot. I came in through a department store entrance but I'm outside now. Are you near here?"

"Yes."

"Which way are you from here, left or right?"

"Left . . ."

"My left or yours . . . ?"

"I dunno – heh-heh-heh. Hey!! Do you have on a light green stripped shirt?" Lance can hear the accent and how it stands out when she says the word *shirt.*

"Yes I do," he says.

"Then you are to my left and yours too. We're facing different ways – heh-heh-heh!"

Lance admires her cute and innocent little giggle for the very reason of what it is; cute & innocent. He turns to his left and immediately sees her. Still nervous, he approaches her, smiles, and gives her a one second hug, and a light kiss on her left cheek.

"Hi. It's really nice to meet you Sherry Anderson."

"Same here Lance Austin. Are you ready to eat? I'm starved!"

"Yes, me too . . ."

The conversation is very light on the way to the mall's food court. He can hardly think of what to say, because certain thoughts overwhelm him. Lance remembers her saying she was a *cheap date.* He wonders if the rule to getting a "cheap date" also means you get a cheap presentation of their appearance. Lance picked from his closet, probably one of his top three shirts for this occasion; and Sherry probably picked one, from her bottom three. Her hair is beautiful but in a lazy pony-tail. The sleeves on her white shirt are rolled up and so are her pink Khaki pants legs; and she has on flip-flops . . . and they *flip-flop* when she walks.

She has no make-up on, no lipstick, perhaps lip gloss . . . Lance can't really tell. He glances at her cheesy earrings and then down below her neck, trying to figure out the size of her breasts . . . but her shirt isn't tight enough. Her Khakis aren't tight enough either to hone in on her butt and the size of her hips. There were only two things about her that resembled the pictures he saw of her on the internet – her beautiful smile and her petite frame. Despite the lackadaisical first date appearance, a beautiful face and a small frame on a woman has always been two physical attributes that are very important to Lance. In his world, the questionable aspect of this scenario is a mental / emotional issue and not a physical one. The latter of the two would be a little more difficult to deal with or possibly change for the better.

Lance's thoughts continue to wander. *Well, she did more-or-less squeeze me into her day. Maybe this is all I can get because she's cramped for time or maybe there's something else going on.*

His inner inquiries cease for the time being as they arrive at the Chinese offerings of the food court. "You like Chinese food Sherry?"

"I prefer Thai food, but this is fine. It's quick and easy."

They sit by the window, which for Lance is not quite a good idea. While his single status affords him constant opportunities to look at any woman he wants, it's usually a good idea to refrain from such behavior while on a date. This is hard for him. His head does turn twice while they are eating but he at least completes his sentences while doing so. They talk again about the dating scene, this time in more detail.

"That guy I told you about, his name is Norman." Lance could care less what his name is. "We started out as friends; now we're dating but it's nothing serious . . . just casual."

The word *casual* sticks out in Lance's mind. He knows that depending on the person, the word *casual* can be used conveniently to fit whatever characteristics or mindset a person has. Lance figures that Sherry seems like the type of woman that would casually hang out with a guy, having dinner or drinks; maybe even going to a neighborhood carnival or something. *Casually* sleeping with a guy? No. Lance pretty much labeled her as such when they spoke on the phone that very first time . . . but it's always nice to detect signs of a wholesome quality in a woman face to face.

Sherry asks, "What about you Lance; are you seeing anyone?"

"Well . . . I was . . . but I haven't spoken to her in about two weeks. I think that's pretty much a wrap for her. Through life, you try and try and try again to be in a relationship with someone, and . . . I don't know . . . it just gets discouraging. We ain't gettin' any younger either!"

"Yeah, I know. We just have to keep praying to the good Lord, right? You believe in God, don't you?"

"Absolutely . . . !"

"Do you go to church?"

"Sometimes, but not on a regular basis . . ." Lance keeps his answers short concerning church. He's not ready to divulge details in his church going habits just yet; those habits being a little less than he indicated. He wants Sherry to get to know him a little better first. This will make his once a year church attendance, if even that, more forgiving to her at a later stage. This meeting though in itself, is kind of awkward for Lance. It's not the usual first date scenario that he's used to. He wonders if he was over anxious in asking her out as soon as he did. The telephone connection was never really established; the connection that sets the mutual anticipation level of meeting someone for the very first time a little higher. The situation he fears may have become more about the material on display, than about the woman delivering the material. He wants so badly for the chemistry to be there but it's not . . . for neither one of them.

Now the pressure to make something happen becomes greater, especially for Lance. He really just hopes for a miracle because deep down inside he knows there is nothing he can do. As they walk around the mall window shopping, he feels like he's following her around. Sherry is very familiar with the mall and he is not. With the situation being as it is, it's fairly simple to find a negative aspect in anything, even when nothing negative exists.

After forty minutes of window shopping in which he does at least realize she has better taste in home décor than she does in her clothing, they sit at a lonely table sipping on a couple of smoothies. The silence begins to overwhelm them both. Out of desperation, Lance tells Sherry the rent-a-car story. She *does* find the story amusing, giving him her cute little giggle . . . and she also starts to liven up a bit when he tells her how fast his rent-a-car is.

"I thought about getting one of those," she exclaims. "I wound up getting a cute little SUV. I just got it a couple of months ago."

With Sherry's certain level of interest in cars and her apparent craving for speed, it gives Lance an idea. "You wanna go for a ride?"

"Yes." Now his peak of interest is at a higher level, as hers is. They hit the highway going further north than she lives. He plays with the *S* gear, going from 60mph to 80mph in a few seconds. Lance doesn't go beyond 80mph because he's not completely sure just how *much* speed Sherry really likes. She does like *eighty* though.

"Why don't we go to Evanston? It's not that far from here!" she exclaims. They go to the beach in that area, but by now the temperature has dropped about ten degrees or so. It was only in the 50's to begin with. Just when Lance thinks the setting is getting a little better . . . he knows deep down that a proper setting without *chemistry* equals zero; only wishful thinking.

The lady is cold. Let me put my beautiful shirt around her shoulders to keep her warm, which he does. *And let me give her an extended touch of the shoulders while I'm putting my shirt on her and tell her that I know this date has been kinda blah blah, but I know we both can do ten times better. There is just something about you Sherry that makes me really wanna get to know you better,* which he *doesn't* do.

Lance even has the nerve to want to kiss her, as he imagines her face being made up a bit, a better outfit that shows her shape from top to bottom, some decent earrings and minus the flip flop sandals. This outrageous thought remains a thought when he reminds himself that this woman's heart is elsewhere right now. In Lance's opinion, she really has no business being out on a date in the first place, unless it's with the guy she's so crazy about.

Lance continues his thought, *well despite this crap going on right now . . . a man with even half the amount of common sense wouldn't just ball this woman up and throw her away. You befriend this type of woman and maybe something will give later. I wouldn't mind being friends with Sherry anyway, because she is a good girl.*

With that thought basically being his last concerning her, he mentally tries to move forward as far as the dating game is concerned. At 6:30pm when Lance accompanies her back to her vehicle in the mall's parking lot, being the gentleman that he is, he can't help but be discouraged by the mere two and a half hour meeting that they had. He can't help but wonder if she's headed home to prepare herself physically in a more proper manner, for her *real* date; her evening date – a real date time with the real guy – the guy that she is *so* crazy about.

As Lance zooms back to the south side, he makes a courtesy call to Sherry to let her know that he's near home safely. He doesn't go straight home because he contemplates going to a divorce party for one of his co-workers. He also lets her know how much he appreciated the short time they spent together. This is all on her voicemail though. Sherry did not answer; yet another indicator of the lack of chemistry between them. Lance never makes it to the party because his mood is quite low from what happened in Skokie. He wants to blame this failed attempt of connecting with someone on internet dating.

The women that men meet on the internet he suspects, are more troubled, more desperate; just worse overall than anyone that you may traditionally meet. But rational thinking and Sherry being only the fifth woman that he has met this way, convinces Lance of two main points. One: women that date via the internet are no more troubled, desperate, worse, or anything else, than the men that are pursuing them the same exact way. Two: internet dating is simply a different avenue for meeting women. It's pretty much the same game after the two people meet. As Lance drives around in his nice rent-a-car with nowhere he wants to go, he continuously tries to convince himself of these two concepts. At some moments, it all makes sense to him and the concepts are true. Five minutes later, none of it makes any sense at all.

CHAPTER 2

In the middle of June, the rural area of land and trees is vast, green, and beautiful. Once again Lance finds himself traveling in another rent-a-car on another long, endless strip of highway; this time going east along the *80/90* toll road. The scenery is refreshing to him and very seldom seen. This time the rental is by choice. His black Cadillac, with the same *S* gear he experienced before, is parked back at his house. He didn't want to put a lot of miles on his brand new car for this road trip.

Lance is accompanied by Melanie Powell, the woman that is his girlfriend one minute and wanting to be chased and begged to re-enter into a relationship the next . . . if it had ever really ended. They have gone back and forth like this a few times during the past sixteen months they have known each other. Melanie called Lance one week after the Sherry meeting, which totaled three weeks that they didn't communicate at all. This was the longest and the most extreme display of an attempt to stay away from one another. The phone call regarded something totally insignificant. It was obvious to Lance that her ulterior motive was to reopen the line of communication between them, which would eventually wind up in them hooking up again. By the way, Melanie is the second woman that Lance met on the internet.

Their eastern road trip is his latest attempt to woo her back into relationship mode. He surprised her a week ago when he revealed his plans for them to drive to New York City to see her favorite Tyler Perry movie in a live stage production format. He had actually taken the time out to make her a t-shirt that said on the front,

For my 40th birthday I will be . . . and on the back . . . *taking a road trip to New York City to see my favorite Tyler Perry play!!*

She started to cry when he presented that t-shirt to her. At the time, she did seem genuinely touched by the gesture. At other times during their on again, off again love affair, he wondered if her emotional stability was missing *a few slices of bread from the loaf.*

Driving through Indiana and Ohio was relatively simple, especially since her desire to contribute to the driving was right there along with his. But as night fell upon them, Lance realized that driving through Pennsylvania at this time can be kind of treacherous. Some of the landscape right off the toll road was very up close and personal. With only one lane of highway going east and the same going west, there was not much room for error. As Lance drives further along, the darkness continues to prevail but the roadway does widen just enough to allow side of the road access in case of a road hazard.

"You wanna stop somewhere along here, like we discussed?" Lance asks.

"Well it's certainly *dark* enough around here . . . that's for sure!" Melanie replies.

"Okay. I'll stop pretty soon." Lance finds himself paying close attention to the mile markers on the side of the road more than he ever has. This contributes mostly to the long distance driving that he's not accustomed to. He remembers the last marker was mile *116*. He decides to pull over at mile *115*; this representing the same street number that he lives on.

Lance contemplates *not* turning the hazard lights on, not wanting to attract attention to their vehicle, given what they are about to do. Then wisely, he takes into consideration how dark it is. *Better for the car to be noticed than not, in this dark area. Besides, there isn't another car going either way for miles,* he thinks to himself. "I've never quite done this before," he modestly admits out loud.

"Quite" meaning he has had a few sexual encounters in a vehicle with a few women. He recalls a back seat session in which a couple of private parts were touched and grabbed but no penetration occurred. Another encounter, penetration did occur but the awkwardness of being in a sports car made that particular incident forgettable. Lance remembers a nice sexual encounter in a front seat but with a fake prostitute – a.k.a. a crack head posing as a prostitute . . . so for him, that encounter doesn't count either. "Quite."

Melanie slips each of her shoes off by the back of the heel with each alternating foot. She then starts to let the butt part of her passenger seat all the way back and then the back part. Lance looks at her mischievously, wanting sexual pleasure. His mannerism is calm yet his anticipation is eager, knowing he is about to receive just that. He slides over to her side and tries to get on top of her as best as he can in a car's passenger seat. He kisses Melanie like he's in love with her – which he is – very slowly and passionately. He then moves down to her left earlobe and the left side of her neck, then to the front of her neck.

By now Melanie is red hot and ready for the real interaction to take place. Her getting hot so quickly is usually how it goes during their sexual encounters. Even still, Lance always takes the time to participate in a good amount of time of foreplay because that's his technique. He does move a little quicker this time around, being in a car in the middle of nowhere. Lance tries to take her pants off, but there's not enough room to do so. He moves aside briefly to let Melanie take them off.

"Okay come back on this side and let *me* get on top," she says. He quickly slips his shoes off and then his pants, then slides back over and under her with a slight chuckle. He grabs the back of her neck with his right hand and starts to kiss her again, this time with more physical enthusiasm. With his left hand, he reaches downward and goes inside her panties.

In Lance's mind, the entire area of Melanie's vagina is extremely wet, if not the wettest that he has ever touched in his life. The expression on his face during this moment makes her smile at him. He pulls her panties down quickly but then struggles to get them past her knees as she still faces him. Once he gets them down past the shin of her legs, he doesn't bother to slip them off her ankles because now his anticipation level is sky high. In Lance's mind, he is already inside of her. Obliviously, he pulls his boxer shorts down and then tries to wiggle his way out of them completely. He is not successful. Melanie chuckles as she slips her panties off her ankles. As Lance removes his shorts with his hand, he chuckles also.

In Melanie's mind, the intemperance of Lance's penis is completely inspiring, if not the best that she has ever seen. He teases her with it before he enters her . . . because this is his technique. Melanie chuckles again, this time a few seconds longer than before.

"What Mel?"

"Hhhmmpp!! Two months ago, you were probably mad as hell at me when you were dropping off my Christmas tree and stuff in that long white box. Now here you are, about to stick that big ol' thing in me." She chuckles again, "That's funny ain't it?"

"Yeah baby, it is kinda funny." Lance penetrates her. He strokes her with a kind of precision that makes every stroke count. Slowly. Passionately. Lovingly. He puts his mouth and his tongue on her large breasts, and sucks her nipples furiously. He increases the speed of his stroke.

From the moment Lance first kissed Melanie, to the increased level of their sexual intensity, is indicative of what starts as the ultimate love making venture, turned into the boisterous animalism of . . . *fucking*! Within his technique, this is how Lance views it. Melanie is sexually pleased and very receptive of the overall generous display of enthusiasm in the movement of his hips. She keeps pace with him every step of the way. Suddenly, he stops!

"Uh oh . . . I'm not ready to do *that* just yet! Let me get on top Mel." Lance is calm as they change positions, in hopes of prolonging the inevitable explosive end to their secret sexual escapade. As their transition is complete, he awkwardly yet authoritatively enters her again. This time, his thrusts are at a much faster pace than before. He can't help it. Again they are in complete unison. Every time his hips move forward, her torso comes forward. Every time he swings his butt backwards, her butt prepares for the next passionate blow. Within a few moments, the pace in which they gratify one another is so frantic, that *where* they are is forgotten, as well as the awkwardness of it all. Melanie grabs his left butt cheek in anticipation of her climax, surprisingly in this strange missionary position.

"Lance I feel it!! I'm about to come!!!"

"So am I baby!! So am I!!!" Lance grits his teeth and makes the face of a gladiator in battle. His entire body is now tensed and electrified as he ejaculates deep inside of her, like a warm, massive avalanche. Melanie makes a similar face as she lifts her buttocks completely off the car seat as if her whole body has been exposed to electric shock. He puts his right hand on the small of her back to pull her closer to him to feel this moment as one. The finality of their awesome sex explodes simultaneously. As Lance pulls out of her, they smile at one another. They say *thank you* with their eyes as they wipe the sweat from each others' foreheads.

Lance pants, "Damn Melanie . . . that was good!!"

"Yes it was Lance! Yes it was!"

Lance and Melanie arrive in New York City later the same morning; much later than they originally planned. It was his fault their departure for this road trip was six hours late. It was also his fault they somehow missed the *80/90* entrance ramp back in Chicago – another hour and a half delay. It was only fitting that Lance refrain from getting angry when they found out their hotel room was now occupied by another party. He had paid for the room in advance online but their arrival time was three hours before the checkout time of noon.

Melanie is furious. "This is some bullshit!!" she exclaims. "They're just gonna take your money and that's it?!! We gotta do something about that!! They just can't get away with that!! Where are we gonna stay and rest our heads now!??"

"I don't know. I do have these maps of the city and of the state . . . so we should be able to find something."

They drive around for a couple of hours in the immediate vicinity but all of the hotels in the city are priced on the high end. They eventually find themselves in the Queens area where the hotels are lower in price. Even there though, they experience difficulty in finding a vacancy or finding themselves for that matter. The NYC maps that they constantly refer to don't help . . . when they get lost again.

"See Melanie . . . ! I told you that street was back over on this side, and not where *you* told me to go!!"

"Well we wouldn't be going through this *mess* if you could've been ready to leave yesterday morning at the time you said we were leaving, instead of out drinking with your homie the night before!!"

"I made a nice breakfast for us yesterday morning!! What are you talking about?!!"

Now they are both angry as they go back and forth with sarcastic comments about who is right and who is wrong. The tension in the air with the constant driving around for endless hours is fatal. Lance's thoughts take him to how many times he has heard Melanie use a curse word today. Generally he goes with the flow of the woman he's with in determining the method in which he speaks. A little cursing in general conversation is not so bad to Lance . . . it's the angry cursing towards *him* that he doesn't like. Sherry didn't casually use one curse word in the few instances they made contact on the phone or in person, about *anything*. When they finally do find a room, Lance tries to calm himself down but for Melanie it is already too late. He had blamed her for being lost before and in Melanie's mind, she can do no wrong when it comes to Lance. She gives him the silent treatment as they enter the room. Lance tries to pleasantly approach her about anything from this point on but he can feel the resentment in the air. While he knows it's only momentary, he hopes it will have dissipated in time for the play tonight.

Lance is glad when she falls asleep so he can go outside and relax while he's smoking a cigarette. Melanie knows about his smoking but he doesn't do it around her. He walks across the street and sits on an elevated grassy area. He watches the airplanes as they pass closely overhead, preparing to land at the LaGuardia Airport nearby. His feeling of discouragement makes it easy to start thinking about Sherry again. He had sent her one more text message about four days after they had gone out two months before. She didn't answer that form of communication either. His phone calling power had been taken away because of that; but on this day, Lance decides to take that power back. He snatches his cell phone from the holster and dials her number. With each ring he grows slightly more nervous, not knowing exactly what to say to her if she answers.

"Hi you've reached Sherry. I can't come to the phone right now but if you leave a message, I will get back to you as soon as I can."

Lance had forgotten how cute her voice was and it was nice for him to hear it again but he was relieved that it was only her voicemail greeting. The beep sounds.

"Hi Sherry . . . this is Lance . . . we met a couple of months ago at the mall in Skokie. Every once in a while in life we come across someone that really stands out from all the rest. Despite how our meeting went back then, I never forgot about you . . . and I would really like for us to be friends. Think about that Sherry. Bye."

He has to listen to at least three prompts from her voicemail in order for his message to officially go through. Irritating. But he responds to each and every one of them to make sure she will hear his very important message. For the first time out loud, he had admitted what he knew all along . . . the chemistry was lacking when they met. Lance puts his phone away feeling confident, knowing that one: he has done all he can do regarding this situation. Two: the part about wanting to be friends is not a lie because that's what he truly feels in his heart.

He starts to silently celebrate the fact that he even made the call because in most cases he wouldn't have bothered. One thing that Lance has known for quite sometime is that opportunity doesn't always "come-a-knockin'", sometimes ya gotta go and just get it. Knowing this and actually doing something about it, as he's aware, are "two different animals." With that in mind, he decides to *do* something about Melanie's mood instead of waiting for it to change on its own.

Lance scurries back across the street to the hotel where Melanie still lays sound asleep. He stands at the foot of the bed just for a moment and watches her lying on her stomach motionless, with her face buried in her crossed arms. He stoops down and lightly touches the side of her face. As she starts to stir, he whispers in her ear,

"We better start getting ready."

"How long have I been asleep?"

"About an hour . . ." Lance gently lies beside her, placing his left arm across her back and bending it so the longest finger on his hand can touch the back of her head. He kisses her lightly on the right side of her neck; then he licks her in the same spot with the tip of his tongue, working his way up to her earlobe. Then he kisses her again in the same spot. Melanie opens her eyes and looks at Lance. The look is like "the glass is ½ empty or ½ full" depending on which way one would look at it. Lance gestures her to turn over on her back anyway, which she does. He proceeds to undress her, the way he wanted to in the car earlier that morning. He makes love to her again but this time she does not receive it as enthusiastically as earlier . . . but she does receive it nonetheless. Only his climax is reached this time around. While the force of it is usually the same, the mental aspect of it is hardly as fascinating. They both fall asleep and finally forty five minutes later, they get up to get ready for the play.

The theater where the play was held was a typical enough establishment for Lance. It is Times Square that truly grabs his attention. His comparison to it is that of the near north side in Chicago on Rush Street back in the day. Here though, everything is amplified ten times. More people, more lights, more litter on the ground, and the advertisement agenda is simply ridiculous. The lighting on some of the billboards is so excessive that you can look at a building on one side of the street and see the reflection of an ad from across the street through the windows. They walk past one famous New York City establishment after the other.

Lance looks at the vast amount of people walking the streets. Some look normal, some appear to be dazed and confused – maybe high. Some look like gangsters – some are. Almost any choice of ethnic group is down here and even a guy is dressed in a super hero costume from head to toe. They all share in this late Saturday night furor.

For Lance, the most rousing aspect of it all is the fact that they are in another state and he brought them here. He has been to New York before but as a child.

Melanie takes it all in a little differently. She *does* appreciate all the preparation and planning that Lance did for her birthday but she has been on many road trips before, mostly with her family. So the aspect of merely being out of town is not a big deal for her. The most invigorating thing for her regarding this trip was the play.

As they continue to stroll along, they stop and each take a picture of the other in front of a well known television station. Then some lady offers to take a picture of them together. The stranger takes the photo and they both thank her for being so nice. In a few days when Lance gets the pictures developed, he will scoff when he sees that Melanie is almost cut out of the picture to the left.

"Let's walk over to the Empire State Building before we go."

"Okay Lance, that's a good idea." When they see the towering structure, they wish they could go inside to the top, even though they reside where many fancy the Sears Tower. They take a rain check on that because it's now two in the morning and it's time for them to head back home to Illinois.

They head back to the car, fight their way through to the Lincoln Tunnel entrance and bye-bye to the grand NYC. As they drive west through New Jersey, Lance tries to clean the windshield with the windshield wipers to no avail. He realizes that this failed attempt is the result of extensive hours on the highway. He will have to clean it later by hand. He stops at a gift shop to purchase a coffee mug that says *New Jersey* on it. He does the same in Pennsylvania, Ohio, and Indiana to have as keepsakes. Melanie gave him the idea when she bought him a coffee mug in New York. This kind of thing is sentimental to Lance, not to mention the fact that he's somewhat of a pack-rat.

Their drive coming back, even with a one hour rest period, is a lot shorter and more to the target time of thirteen hours than the drive was coming. They both know exactly where they're going now. As Melanie approaches the last toll road in Indiana, Lance sits up from his reclined passenger seat to reach for some CD's. Suddenly she slams on the brakes to avoid someone cutting her off to get in line. Lance's upper body and neck jerk forward uncontrollably. He gives her a smutty look as if to question her driving skills, but he doesn't say anything. What he thinks is a pretty normal reaction to an unexpected, impetuous moment, turns out to be the deal breaker for their trip ending in bliss. Melanie is angry at Lance again.

Now Lance extends very far into his thoughts to try and figure out what he did wrong. He also wonders if he's even guilty of any wrong doing at all. Lance has always been known to be a bit of a nick picker, a whiny perfectionist so to speak. He has an argumentative way about himself as well. These are some of the negative traits that he has been reading about lately in his new found hobby of self help books. These are some of the negative traits he has been trying to change about himself. He figured that not saying anything was a showing of his improved attitude. However, Melanie took the mean look as condescending. This time around, Lance is not inspired to manipulate or seize the good mood back. He wasn't so confident about his success rate the first time he did it at the hotel and the trip is nearly over now anyway.

His thoughts turn to a white horse he saw walking down the street of Times Square. It was pulling a carriage ride with an empty red velvet seat. He wanted to ask Melanie if she wanted to ride on the carriage, to set a romantic tone for their evening. However he did not ask. That felt strange to Lance that he didn't. Now they pull up to Melanie's dad's house. They unload the car, she gives him a dry goodbye with no kiss and the trip is done. The fact that he didn't ask her to occupy that empty red velvet seat with him no longer feels strange to Lance at all.

His final thought as he pulls off, *Fuck it!!*

CHAPTER 3

"**H**e's a bitch!!!" Melanie exclaims over the phone to her best friend Nina, ½ an hour after Lance dropped her off.

"Why he gotta be all that?" replies Nina.

"He is such a grouch!! Every little thing he's complaining about it or frowning or fussing. It's like I can't do anything right by him. I can never relax around him cause it's always something!!"

"Like what?"

"Well, we were probably at the last toll stop in Indiana and I had to slam on the brakes 'cause this idiot cut me off to get in line. Lance was sitting up in his seat doing something, so naturally he jerked forward. Then he looked at me like *I* was crazy!!"

"Did he say something smart girl?"

"No, he didn't have to – it was written all over his face!"

"He didn't have his seat belt on?"

"Nah girl. I know that may sound minor but the thing is, when you're being critiqued all day long, when you're around a man whose mood is quite often questionable and basically always sour, the tolerance level for the little stuff is basically null."

"I can go with that girl – the big stuff is basically the set up of his downfall from the little stuff. But let me ask you, is he *that* good in bed that he's worth hanging around or keeping around?" Melanie blurts out into laughter. Nina joins her, " . . . Cause giirrrllll, I know you told me he was kinda good!"

"Oh boy . . . ! There's always a plus side to that minus side isn't it? I dunno it's like . . . when he touches me with his hands, I can feel this vibe that tells me he really cares about me. He likes to take his time – he's never in a rush. It seems like he's in it just to please me!! When Lance is inside of me – girl I'm not grossing you out, am I?"

"No, *do* tell!!"

" . . . When Lance is inside of me, it's like the whole process, the whole act – it's more mentally initiated and gratifying than it is physical for him. Do you know what I mean?"

"Yeah I know what you're saying. You're saying the man is good in bed for sure!! He sounds like a dream in the bedroom . . ."

"And in the car too . . . !"

"Ooohhh girl, no you didn't . . . !"

"Oh yeah I did. It was kinda awkward and kinda funny too but he was just as effective all the same. Now at the hotel . . ."

"Melanie wait a minute! You're giving me way too much information to process at one time!!" Melanie giggles while Nina continues, "What I was gonna say before, from all the stuff you're complaining about, it sounds to me like he's a perfectionist and that can get on anybody's nerves – but that same person usually critiques what *they* do too. If he's doing that, especially when it comes to sex, that should be working purely to your advantage!! He needs to just shut his mouth and just do what he does. Maybe that's why he didn't say anything smart to you when you slammed on those brakes. He just looked at'cha crazy."

"Well then *you* be with him Nina, since you're taking his side!!"

"I'm not taking his side – I'm trying to look at *both* sides! He's not a complete jerk I know . . . or you wouldn't be dealing with him at all."

"Damn girl, can I vent in peace?"

"Now what happened at the hotel?"

"Yesterday – well, we made love again. He only did it to me *then* because he knew I was mad at him. I wanted so badly to tell him to get off of me . . . but I couldn't!!"

"Damn girl, you were mad at him yesterday too? Anyway, you two still aren't using protection?"

"Girl you know I don't like rubbers – and he doesn't either."

"What guy does? Melanie I keep telling you and I'm not trying to jinx you . . . but you keep messing around like that and you may end up with a *way* bigger problem than the one you call yourself having now! Can you even trust this man as far as him being faithful to you?"

"Nina I've told you a million times, he's not out there like that. He's really a good guy – he just gets on my nerves sometimes!! As far as protection is concerned, most of my boyfriends I slept with the same way and I have never gotten pregnant. I really don't think I can get pregnant."

"I'm kinda getting mixed messages from you. Do you think you two guys can make this thing work, I mean the relationship – is it going to work out?"

"I don't know Nina."

The next evening after the working part of his day is over; Lance sits on the train staring out the window as he's headed home. The contemplation and the shadow of doubt regarding him and Melanie's relationship weighs heavily on his mind. This quiet moment is suddenly interrupted when his cell phone rings.

He answers, "Well hello Sonja. How are you?"

"I'm fine Mr. Lance and how are you?"

Sonja Smith is officially the very first woman that Lance met over the internet. Some of the wording in the written part of her profile intrigued him, even though the photo part of her profile – had no photos. Lance had somehow convinced her to mail a couple of pictures to his house. She was leery to do so at first, just as he was leery to give her his home address. This is a legitimate fear for some when experiencing internet dating for the very first time. On a scale of *1* to *10*, Lance gave her a *5*. He would've been a bit more generous and given her a *6* if the photos had been dated. She did tell him that the photos were about two years old, so Lance figures he'll have to add about 20lbs. to what he sees in the pictures. This is not good where Lance is concerned.

He tells Sonja about the road trip and he tells her what's on his mind at the moment.

She inquires, "So are you gonna stick with this girl or what?"

"I would like to but we argue too much and I know I'm partially to blame for that – but I have gotten a lot better since reading some of these self help books. That's an honest observation – I'm not just saying that because it's me. She refuses to read any of the books that I bought for us, so it's like – what's the point!?"

"Sounds like you got a lot on your plate – or not!! If you're done, you can always pop that trash can lid open and scrape your plate clean; but I know you're not done yet 'cause you're still in love with Melody, right? Her name is Melody, isn't it?"

"You're close, it's Melanie. And yeah, I am still in love with her."

"Is she divorced yet?"

"Yeah that finally went through this past May."

"Good! At least you're in love with a *single* woman now and not a married one. Any how, your gallant efforts to make things work will be a little more stressful than with most, 'cause you'll stick it out more. It'll be worth it in the end though, no matter what the outcome is. You know *I* know how rough a relationship can be. By the way, did I tell you I'm back with *my old shoe*?"

"Yeah you told me in your last email. How's that going?"

"Okay I guess – well more like so-so. I think he's taken my getting back with him as a sign of weakness. He's starting to act a fool again. He better understand though, if I have to throw his ass away again, that's gonna be it!!"

"Yeah I hear ya on that." The train's next stop blares over the P.A. system.

"Well Mr. Lance, I can hear you're on the train, so give me a call later when you get settled in or call me later on this week."

"Yeah Sonja I'll do that. Nice hearing from you."

"Same here – and remember my brother, if you're reading stuff to help better you as a man and to help your relationship flourish; if she won't participate, it'll wind up being y*our* gain and *her* loss."

"Yeah I'll remember that, bye."

"Talk to ya."

Lance appreciates her sound advice, her support and her friendship overall. While still on the train, he thinks back to their initial meeting on the dating website in February of 2006. It started with a couple of emails through the site, then instant messaging on their own personal accounts, then the telephone the same night. That first conversation on a Friday night lasted over two hours; they just immediately *clicked* that way. Two days later in their five hour conversation, they mutually agreed to just be friends. This agreement was based on the fact that Lance wanted children and Sonja already having two kids, did not.

On that same Sunday, Lance spoke to Melanie for the very first time. Their conversation was mutually satisfying. Just like Sonja though, apprehensiveness prevailed over the decision to include a photo with *her* profile. She initiated contact first through the dating website's traditional ice breaking technique, called "a wink." When Lance read her profile, it indicated that she has a municipal job with the state, just as he does. He felt an immediate connection because of this and decided to just go with the flow.

Usually when Lance speaks to a woman he has never seen before, he gets a deflated feeling in his gut about how she will look. This feeling started to loom over him about Melanie too, but only for the first two days of their verbal communication. By the third day he was hooked and so was she. Lance decided at that point to do something totally out of character and not worry about her physical appearance. Not only that, he had completely convinced himself that her looks would be very appealing and pleasing to his eyes. He recalls the email he sent to Melanie in response to her wink.

Hey!! How are you? Thanx 4 the wink. I appreciate it. Do you know what I'm gonna say next? 'What you see is what you get.' Okay, I did see a nicely written profile . . . but where are you? No picture = a blind date. I hate blind dates!! I bet you really don't care for them either, so share your beauty with me somehow . . . please.

TRYNSOMNU

Melanie responded by describing herself as best as she could. She even revealed what size she wears when Lance inquired in his next email. Once the telephone conversations started, they never stopped. Everyday they spoke and everyday seemed to get better and better for the both of them. Lance thought that Melanie was so sweet, very kind, and quite leveled headed. She was not as spiritually outspoken as he would later find in Sherry fourteen months later; but morally sound all the same. Melanie considered him to be very laid back and old fashioned; like chivalry wasn't dead in his book. From seeing his picture, he appeared to be quite handsome and she couldn't wait to see him in person.

After seven straight days of communicating, all questions concerning the visual aspect of their appearance to one another were answered. Melanie came to pick Lance up and at the time he didn't mind this at all. He knew how determined he was to get his financial situation in order, to make that brand new vehicle purchase in the next year to come. When he walked outside of his residence on the Saturday evening they first met, it was drizzling. Lance glanced at her through the driver side window and saw that she had a caramel complexion, maybe even a little lighter. He eagerly awaited the next interval of her wiper blades to clear the rain from her windshield because he knew the street lights above would give him a much better view. As he walked past the front of her car, the wait was over and a big smile came across his face. When Lance got in the car, Melanie smiled.

"So here I am and here you are," he said to her – his smile still beaming.

"Yes here I am Lance. Hi!" she said to him – her smile still beaming.

They arrive downtown at a parking garage several blocks away from Lance's favorite steakhouse. Now they truly get the opportunity to check each other out. Melanie purposely lets Lance get out the car first, so she can look at his butt. The designer shirt he has on is not tucked in and it protrudes slightly beyond the length of his leather jacket, so she doesn't see much. She *could* determine that it wasn't flat and this is good for Melanie. She also admired his clean nails, nice shoes and his overall stylish way of dressing. Lance checks her out from behind soon after as she bends down to get her umbrella from out the car. He determines her butt is about a size *10*, just as she had indicated in her email. Lance considers her butt to be a *very nice* size *10* as a matter of fact, though his preference is usually a size *5*. He realizes though, that being thirty eight years old is cause for a mandatory adjustment to his usual liking in a woman's physical attributes.

The steakhouse is wall-to-wall people as it usually is. It's an establishment on Rush St. well known for their steak and their top notch service. They are seated on the porch which is an area at the back of the restaurant with full length picture windows, offering an enticing view of some lavish looking women walking down the street. This is good for Lance, though he doesn't sneak to take advantage of it as often as he thought he would. Melanie's conversation is actually as interesting as it was each day over the phone. A lost for words on his part never occurs; the chemistry is amazing.

"This is really nice – do you agree Melanie?"

"Yes it is. I can say I've been to a lot of nice restaurants but never *this one*. You say you've been here before, right?"

"Yes, it's been a few years though." Lance is referring to a cold day in the middle of February 2003. The woman he was with, picked her teeth at the table with a steak knife. He stopped seeing her for good three weeks after that.

Melanie continues, "So Lance, tell me something about you that I don't already know."

Lance makes a face and puts his hand on his forehead, "Oh wow!!"

"What?"

Lance chuckles," Well, it's funny you should ask – I do have a confession to make but I wasn't quite ready to share. I was gonna do it tonight though."

"Well don't worry about it. I have a little confession also."

"Oh really, interesting. So what is it?"

"I asked you first."

Okay. Well, the truth is, I smoke."

Melanie tries her best not to be shocked but she is – she can't help it. She gives Lance the look of a chagrinned three year old.

"Cigarettes . . . !" Lance exclaims in making sure she hasn't misunderstood his saying "I smoke" to mean marijuana. Lance continues, "I didn't say I did on the website because I didn't want that one thing about me, a habit that I'm really trying to quit anyway – I didn't want that to deter anyone nice from wanting to meet me. Like tonight for instance, I won't smoke at all because I know that you don't like cigarette smoking, plus you're a very good distraction from wanting or craving a cigarette anyway."

"Well I hope you'll hold true to that."

"I will . . . and I hope it doesn't upset you that I was misleading on the website. I've been smoking way too long in my life and it's a nasty habit I do intend to conquer!"

"No I'm not upset. I appreciate you being honest with me about it. A lot of guys wouldn't have bothered to come clean about something like that right away."

Lance thinks to himself, *well, well, well, what do we have here . . . a woman that is not an advocate of "My way or the highway." This is truly refreshing.* He continues aloud, "You're very considerate and understanding. I really appreciate that in a woman." He rewords the last part to make it more personal, " . . . I really appreciate that about *you*. Thank you; I feel so much better now."

The succor is so relished by Lance that he almost forgets about the fact that she too has a confession to make – almost.

"So Melanie my dear, what were you going to tell me about *you* that I know nothing of?"

Melanie wants to put her elbow on the table and rest her chin in the palm of her hand, but she doesn't. She gives Lance the look of wanting to start her sentence with the word *well* . . . but she doesn't. The hesitation in what she's about to say is so slight, it's hardly noticeable.

"I'm still married."

Lance is shocked! He tries his best not to be; but now the chagrin occurs again on the opposite side of the restaurant's candle-lit dinner table. He acknowledges the incredulous moment with a facial expression and tries to keep his verbal fragments of disbelief to a minimum.

"Okay, that's a surprise, yes. But as you just stated about *my* revelation and I totally agree; it's admirable that you felt the need to expose this slight glitch in our . . ." Lance hesitates in searching for the "politically correct" word to label the two of them. He can't find it and so the verbal fragments increase. "I appreciate you telling me this. I will admit – I had no idea . . . there were a couple of times on the phone this past week that made me say *hhmmm . . . what da hell . . .* ? But I wrote it off as being prematurely paranoid – you know what I mean? It kept bothering me though and I'm thinking, *it's way too soon to be coming at her like that* . . . I just . . ."

"Lance its okay. I know this couldn't be any easier to hear than it was for me to say.

We're separated of course and I'm not proud of this situation . . . but it had to be said and I wanted to tell you in person."

"I appreciate that. You two still live together, don't you?"

"Yes, but I *guarantee* you, it's over between us. We had words a couple of times while I was on the phone with you, so I'm sure that's when you started having the thoughts that you had."

"Of course you two don't sleep in the same room anymore, right?"

"No we don't!"

"And when's the last time you two have done *the do*?"

"October of last year . . ." Melanie's answers are quick and definitive, though this doesn't lessen the doubt that floats around in Lance's head. There's nothing he can do about it and he knows it. He's either going to believe her or *not* believe her. There is really no in between.

"Lance . . . I really hope none of this is a deal breaker. This past week of getting to know you has really been exceptional and now that I've met you in person, I really look forward to much more of that."

Lance smiles at her before she finishes her last sentence. "It's not a deal breaker," he says calmly, " . . . but I am curious about something. Why haven't either one of you moved out yet?"

"Well . . ." Melanie can't help but starting out saying *well* this time around. " . . . This has all basically been very devastating for me, realizing that my marriage was over. It all seemed to happen so fast. Even now I'm still trying to wrap my brain completely around it. He hasn't left because he wants the house . . . I think we're gonna end up fighting over it!"

"If he won't leave, then *you* need to leave! I'm not trying to tell you what to do . . . I'm just concerned about your well being . . . you know, emotionally."

Lance is genuinely concerned about how this will affect her, how it will affect him and how it will affect the "*us*" aspect, if they make it that far. He is also concerned about her choice of words to describe her confession. Did she use the word *little* as a figure of speech or did she use that word on purpose, calculatingly downplaying the whole situation? Was Lance's confession *little*, was it smaller than hers or of equal size of significance? Did he even use the word *little*? He tries to recall but doesn't remember.

When they leave the restaurant, they take a stroll along Michigan Ave. It starts to drizzle again.

"You're not going to open your umbrella?" Lance asks.

"No, it's only drizzling," Melanie says. "It doesn't bother me." Lance seems to be slightly confused by this when he looks at her. "What?" she says. "You think opening my umbrella would be the *girly girl* type thing to do, right? Well I'm not completely *girly girl*. Don't get me wrong, I am feminine . . ."

Lance interrupts, "Oh I can see you're feminine!!" He is referring to her nails being done, her well applied minimal amount of make-up, her chest, which to Lance is just *as* nice as her butt. He appreciates this a lot because he knows that sometimes a woman will thrive in one area of her body and lack in the other.

"I told you I was a tomboy when I was little, right?"

"Yeah you told me. I do love *girly girl* women . . . but some of them *can* go overboard with it. I kinda like the fact that a little drizzle doesn't bother you." Kinda. When they get to the John Hancock Building, they stop and have a seat. Lance points to a hotel on the north side of the street.

"My junior prom was there."

"Oh yeah . . . ?"

"I didn't go to my senior prom though."

"Why not . . . ?"

"I really didn't have anyone I wanted to take – besides, I had something better to do that night anyway."

"Oh."

Neither one of them are in a rush to end the date, and they both know this is a very good sign. They both also know that the moment for the first kiss has arrived; her wishing he would make the move to initiate it and him wishing *he* would make the move to initiate it – he doesn't. Instead he makes his move at the end of the date. Melanie's kiss is perfect to Lance. Momentarily in his mind, he kicks himself for having waited so long to taste her mouth for the very first time. Then no regrets when he makes up for it by asking her out on a second date. When she says *yes* to his early afternoon brunch the very next day at his house, Lance and Melanie's roller coaster romance officially begins.

Together they explore a lot of different venues; concerts, stage plays, comedy shows, the zoo, Navy Pier, and of course the adventure in trying new restaurants never ends. Being in each other's company is overwhelming in a way that is desperately wanted and a lot less needed. Their hunger pangs for one another are different . . . but their appetites are satisfied just the same. The heart felt greeting cards to one another are plentiful and ridiculously exuberant. Lance even takes it a step further and includes original poems in some of his cards, putting his so-called writing skills to good use. His written passages in the cards he gives to her are usually lengthier than the original passage in the card.

My dear Mel,

I have never felt so secure
And been so sure
I have never been so confident
Nor has my desire ever been so dominant

Never have I gazed into a woman's eyes
And been assured of where my future lies
Never have I touched another woman's skin
To be taken to a place I have never been

Never have I been told
I need to drop certain ways of old
Never have I wanted to even listen
Or accept about myself that a quality or two is missing

When you are with me I never want you to go
When you're not – missing you is a feeling I never wish to know
When we talk I never want to get off the phone
When we're not I wonder why you are not at home

Home meaning wherever you are I want to be
Whether if we are awake or if we are asleep
It's always about you is what I mean
And never before have I had a feeling so extreme

Wanting you and needing you are both so high on the scale
I truly don't know which feeling prevails
I do know that you have a way
That requires we touch basis each and everyday

When you physically and mentally touch me
I can't put into words what I feel or what I see
I do know the place you're capable of taking me
Is a special place I never want to leave

My dear Mel this is all simply to express
That my heart is no longer in direst
Thank you for being a part of my life
And thank you for all the rest

In three months of knowing Melanie, all of that came out of him. It only took Lance a third of that time to profess his love for her. In less than *that* month, the arguments began. Their strong wills and their refusal to bend or even compromise in day to day situations that often occur with couples would prove to be a gigantic task in keeping the peace. They relied on one another too much for stability, knowing but not practicing the basic rules of self preservation and inner strength. The sex being good to both of them didn't help matters any. Melanie used it as a stimulant but like alcohol, to disguise the real issues or temporarily render her feelings of distress about them numb. His need for the good sex in his own weird kind of way was justification for how strongly he felt about her.

Melanie's feelings for Lance were of a strong nature as well. But with moving back to her dad's house in March, officially filing for a divorce in April, dealing with the emotional impact that comes gift wrapped with that and being on the rebound with Lance, would all prove to be "too much on her plate." The capacity to deal with his imperfections and admit to hers was non-existing.

They crowded one another, never letting a day go by that they didn't at least speak to each other over the phone. This didn't allow much room for continuing to look at other people on the dating website, though they both did briefly. Melanie met a really nice looking man on there who looked better than Lance to her. But he would prove to be a man not of his word, so she left him alone.

Lance met a beautiful Asian woman on the site, divorced with two children of a mixed race with African American in them. He spoke to her a couple of times on the phone and their conversations were fairly decent. She resided all the way in Crystal Lake, Illinois. Melanie would let Lance keep her car on weekends while she was at work, so he certainly thought about driving out there to meet the Asian woman; but he decided against it. Doing that would have been typical male behavior. Lance is not a typical kind of man and he prides himself in that as well as his other unique attributes. Plus he once heard a wise, older woman once say,

"If you're gonna do wrong, then do it right."

Lance understood exactly what that meant when he first heard it and he has lived by it ever since. Their being on the website from time to time felt reasonably warranted to the both of them. They were searching and wondering if there was someone on there just as appealing, but without the arguing. Melanie stopped doing so on a regular basis about two months after she met Lance and he would soon follow.

The actual arguments weren't as much torture as the long and dragged out phone discussions were in trying to make-up. These conversations lasted for hours on end, sometimes even for days. They always consisted of them both fighting to get a certain point across with neither one of them ever really winning. Her way *or the highway* turned out to be her motto after all in trying to deal with Lance. He was the same way in certain ways in trying to deal with Melanie. This is when he started buying the self help books.

For instance the *Mars & Venus* book and a book about keeping a marriage together were the two main books Lance referred to; since they practically acted as if they were married anyway. He also bought a book about anger and about dealing with divorce. Melanie's constant preaching about what Lance was doing wrong in the relationship and more importantly, him realizing that she was right about *some* things, were his inspirations in buying the books. While a lot of the reading for Lance was very informative, he needed her to also realize some of her own shortcomings and partake in some of the reading – but she just would not.

Surprisingly their first *major* lack of communication didn't occur until August, six months in. Not speaking to Melanie caused an unwanted sadness in Lance's heart, which resulted in a wandering eye and a quivering right hand as he would lightly grasp the mouse linked to his PC. When he gave in to the over exaggerated loneliness in his heart and the contemplation of considering meeting someone else online, he met *someone else* online.

Evangeline Robinson is cyberspace girl #3 and she has a picture up! She is attractive *and* she is *single* – something Lance now realizes he needs to verify before hand. She is thirty-one years of age, one three year old son, and resides in Indianapolis, Indiana just as Sonja does. This is good for Lance because if he and Melanie *do* work out, then Evangeline living three hours away will lessen the blow of no romantic link ever occurring between them. They exchanged a few emails via the website one Friday night. In an hour they are IM-ing on their personal accounts. Two more hours pass before they wind up on the phone together. Now Lance is noticing the pattern of how these interactions are occurring. He doesn't know if he should be impressed with himself, or terrified of *them*.

From their conversation, Evangeline's morals seem to be intact, though she was a bit quirky in how she typed in her IM's and how she expresses herself verbally. This is not much concern to Lance because on the percentage scale, giving up on Melanie is only at 20% at this time. He normally wouldn't even attempt to meet someone else while involved, internet or otherwise. But with the constant arguing, recent lack of communicating and the 20% discouragement in his heart, he feels he has the right. He continues to probe the future possibilities with Evangeline.

"So have you ever been in a long distance relationship before," he asks her.

"Yes I have. I was living here in Indiana and he lived in Memphis, Tennessee."

"So how did that work for you?"

"Well, it was cool at first . . . *it* always is *at first*, right?"

Lance chuckles, "Hell yeah, ya got that right!"

"I would see him normally about three or four times a month. He would fly out here most of the time. I would fly out there about once a month . . . he didn't mind that. He understood, me having a child and all. But then the visits on his part started to dwindle down and before you know it, we were only seeing one another once a month, if not every six weeks or so. I think it became too much for us both to handle . . . but I also think he started to lose interest for whatever reason."

"Well I can imagine, I mean I think overall . . . 'cause I've never been in a long distance relationship . . . I think it can be rough on both parties, especially having to get on a plane just to see your mate. Then again, me being a man – I know 'we' can start out strong in a relationship and wind up being flaky. Don't get me wrong . . . women can get flaky at times too!!"

"Yeah I agree. A lot of women now-a-days wanna be just as playa-ristic as the men that started playa-rism."

"And I agree with that statement. Now, you and I on the other hand, considering long distance . . . you're only three hours driving distance, right?"

"Yeah, how do you know that?"

"I have a friend that lives in Indianapolis." Lance exaggerates a little in referring to Sonja; them only being acquaintances and him never driving out there or even ever meeting her. "I'm kinda in between cars right now. I'm getting a new one next year. Driving three hours, to me is a lot more convenient than having to get on a plane."

"Be honest with me Lance, are you seeing someone right now?"

"Uhmmm . . . yeah, I was gonna tell you about that. What made you figure that?"

"You just sound like you're kinda planning *in the future* with me, rather than right now! If there was room for you to plan for *now*, I probably would've never met you. Are you two having problems or something?"

"The next stop is 123rd Street!!" The train stop announcement is suddenly loud enough for Lance to notice and remember that he's still on the train. He has bypassed his stop not once but twice, being so deep in thought about last year. He gets off the train and walks back to his Caddy.

Three weeks after the New York trip on one of their *good* days, Lance calls Melanie on this Saturday evening to check on her. She had expressed to him earlier how she wasn't feeling well. Unfortunately she has gotten worse.

"Mel, after you leave the drug store, if you can muster up enough energy, come by here. I'll take care of you." It's the gentleman type thing to do and not only that, he means it. As she's on her way to his house, Lance's anticipation level is just as high as it is low when they are angry with one another. When Lance opens the door to greet her, he lunges forward to give her a gentle hug and a smack on the lips.

"How do you feel Mel?"

"I dunno,"

He leads her up the stairs to his place with a slight frown on his face. He chooses not to make an issue of her answer, even though he doesn't understand it. Melanie goes straight to the bathroom with her plastic bag in hand.

"I'm going in here to take my medicine."

"Okay, but why do you have to go in the bathroom to take it?"

Melanie doesn't answer and he doesn't ask again. He simply waits. When she comes out, she has a look on her face that he's not quite familiar with. He doesn't know if the look is indicative of mirth or morose.

"What is it Mel?"

"Lance . . ."

"Yes Melanie . . ."

" . . . I'm pregnant!!"

CHAPTER 4

On Monday at noon when his lunch hour begins, Lance decides to take a walk. He walks for fifteen minutes with no particular destination in mind and no idea of what he wants to eat either. He stops on the corner of Clark & Monroe to get a hamburger, just so he can have something on his stomach. Lance is really too excited to eat, thinking about the news he got three days ago of him becoming a father. He eats the burger in four bites just to get it over with so he can concentrate 100% again on his escalated feeling of vim. As he walks half a block north on Clark St., he glances to his right and sees a bunch of people standing, sitting, talking, eating, all in a cavalier state. This is a definite area he wants to be in right now to celebrate his thoughts in peace.

Lance walks down a total of thirty three stairs that lead to an outside eating area of the massive downtown structure. He sits directly in front of the jet water fountain that shoots water vertically into the air. It is a very exciting yet calming sight for him. He stares at the white colored water relentlessly, noticing the small quarter sized droplets that extend into the air from the shooting stream. He extends his head and neck to the left so his left ear is touching his left shoulder. He imagines the water being his sperm shooting into Melanie's vagina, changing his life forever from here on out. Lance straightens his head back to normal and smiles. His 20% of giving up on the relationship is now *zero*. The circumstances at this point, legitimately warrants the sudden point of reversal on his mental scale.

Lance is absolutely ecstatic about Melanie being pregnant to a point of wanting to explode high in the sky, leaving a residual combustion to miraculously spell out his sky written message to the world – *We are having a baby!!* Suddenly an angry feeling overcomes him for agreeing to not tell anyone just yet . . . and he wonders *why* he agreed to that.

Lance thinks back to almost seventeen months ago when he first read Melanie's dating profile on the internet. The part about relationships was marked "divorced." Melanie lied. Seventeen whole months, and he is finally angry about that – because now he sees the pattern. Melanie is not a stoned cold liar . . . but she will bend the truth slightly or more so, hold back imperative information to only reveal it at her convenience. For seventeen months Lance has been dealing with this woman, sleeping with her for about fourteen of those months. She made him wait that long for the sex and he appreciated that in her; plus it helped downplay the umbrella situation.

Seventeen months together – but for the first ten months of their relationship, Melanie kept Lance a secret from most of her immediate family. He didn't meet her father until November of 2006, then her two older sisters soon after. It suddenly dawns on Lance why she had no picture on her profile. He thinks to himself, *What married woman with any half way amount of common sense would put her picture on an internet dating website?* He then questions the term *relationship.* Would he be more accurate to consider their first year together as *an affair?* He entertains that thought briefly. Now all of the anger in Lance's heart attempts to suck the positive energy out of his very being . . . but he won't allow it. He changes his thought process to contemplate who he will confide in about his good news.

The obvious choice would be his mother, but she passed away last year. Lance finds himself in another flashback memory, this time of how dedicated Melanie was to him during that time of despair and unbelievable time of grief; even though they were in the midst of one of their major disagreements that had dragged on over the course of two or three days. Then he thinks about the fact that Melanie never met his mom, even though she had a chance to before she died. Melanie had expressed a not so optimistic viewpoint in doing so, out of fear of being reminded of her own mother who passed in 2003. Both of their mothers were sickly at home before they passed on. The irony of her mother's death alone had touched Lance's heart in a way he could never quite express to Melanie in words. So when she wasn't ready to meet his at the time, it was one thing that he didn't argue with her about. But in this moment, he is furious because his mother will never know who the mother of his child will be.

Lance struggles to stay in the happy place in his mind that brought him to his unexpected destination. His mind takes him from one scenario to the next. Now his thoughts take him into the future. Will they get a place together to raise their child? Will they even still be together? Will they get married if they are? Will she sue for child support if they're not? Can he truly afford a child? Will it be a boy or a girl? Statistically speaking, most men want boys. Strangely enough, Lance wants a girl. He's not quite sure why but he does unequivocally.

The only thing Lance doesn't question is if he wants this child. He has wanted children for the same amount of time he's been smoking. Lance has been smoking for over half his life, having just turned forty years old the first week in June; one week exactly before Melanie's birthday. Now he goes back to the original question in his mind.

Why did I agree not to tell anyone yet!!? Then he adds on to that. *Why does she want to wait!!?* Then Lance asks himself the ultimate question. *Does Melanie want this child!!??*

Lance's eyes suddenly become filled with tears to a point where he can't see. He wipes them away to restore his vision. Initially, Melanie seemed very happy about the pregnancy. Now with all the questions in mind, Lance is not so sure about anything; the baby or *how* their future will play out.

Lance looks at his watch, just now realizing he has overstayed his lunch time by thirty minutes. His mind was full to begin with, now his heart is full as well. He knows he cannot return to work like this, so he grabs his cell phone from its holster.

"Hey it's me. Was anyone looking for me!?"

His co-worker responds in a whisper, "No . . . not really. Well *da warden* did walk pass here a couple of times but she didn't say anything. Then again she probably was lookin' for you . . . knowing her, the *bitch* that she is. Where are you?"

"I'm around. Look, do me a favor and put my bag away for me . . . I'm not coming back today. Tell *da warden* I can't come back 'cause I have an emergency."

"Okay will do. Is everything okay?"

"Yes and no. Well I guess *not* really . . . but it will be. Thanks!"

Lance disconnects the call and smiles from the much needed bit of amusement he just got from his phone call. A few co-workers in the office have been secretly referring to their boss as "da warden" for years. What's even funnier to Lance is when a man and a woman are in conversation about another woman, the female can refer to that woman as "a bitch" and get away with it, but the man can't. He continues to smile as he scrolls through his address book in his phone. He thinks about calling Sonja to tell her the news but then quickly thinks against it. They simply aren't close enough in the capacity of friendship, even though they have had some very nice conversations in the past. She lives way too far away anyway and Lance feels a dire need for a face-to-face. So he scrolls back to the *A*'s again and takes a chance.

"Hi Angelica, you don't have a two o'clock do you?"

"No three. What's going on? You sound terrible."

"I need to talk to you about something, in person. It's serious. Can you possibly come down here and meet me?"

"Wow it's that serious, huh? Is it Melanie again?"

"Yeah . . . it's Melanie again."

"Hhmmpp! Why did I know that? Okay, let me see if I can move my three to five. I'll send you a text in a few, okay?"

"Okay."

"And I hope you haven't gotten this woman pregnant!!"

Lance is silent and he fears that this is more revealing to her than if he had somehow responded verbally. Angelica Rose is Lance's best friend, his confidante, the person that knows him probably better than anyone else. They have known each other for thirteen years, and Lance wonders why he even hesitated to call her. Lance's phone vibrates as he continues to hold it in his hand. He reads the text message from Angelica.

O M W – meet you where?

The sandwich shop – State & Congress.

Lance stands up, walks up twenty six stairs and stops at the ceramic wall mural *Four Seasons*. He stares at it for five minutes then embarks upon the remaining seven stairs leading up to Dearborn ave.

The sandwich shop is a quaint yet trendy kind of place with its cute little kindergarten like tables and chairs. Their menu caters to the health conscious consumer; a concept that Lance is trying to partake more and more in his life. Plus he knew that Angelica would appreciate the choice because her eating habits are that of a vegetarian. Lance takes a seat by the window in hopes of seeing Angelica as she approaches the establishment. He watches the female DePaul University students walking down the street, young and slim in their tight size 5/6 jeans. They are mostly Caucasian women. In Lance's opinion, other ethnic groups like Caucasian and Asian women *now* have the bodies that African American women *use* to have. He attributes this to the obesity problem that plagues America. This makes him wonder, if he's ever in the dating game again, will he have to resort to dating outside his own race just to satisfy that particular attribute that he so desires in a woman.

None of that stuff matters now . . . I'm in love with Melanie and she's gonna have my baby!! Lance thinks this as he buries his face in his palms. When he removes his hands he sees Angelica coming down the street. It's as if the wind blows on cue so her long beautiful dark brown hair with subtle streaks can blow east, some of it blowing in her face. She flips it aside as she crosses the street in her calm, lady like stride. She has on a notch collar tweed jacket with black tipping, besom pockets and a faux-leather belt. Her size 5 black pants are wide-leg style with a black elastic waistband which makes the pants cling to her shapely hips with perfection.

Once she gets inside and approaches Lance where he sits, he realizes that Angelica in the least is as beautiful as he has ever seen her. He wonders why he isn't with *her*. They smile at one another simultaneously as he jumps up to greet her with a hug. She whispers in his ear,

"You got her pregnant, didn't you!!?"

Lance calmly pulls away from her, pulls her chair out slightly with his right hand and motions with his left for her to be seated. "So tell me Angelica, if two women are arguing and one calls the other *a bitch* . . . while I'm sure she's angry about it, it's still worse if a man calls a woman *a bitch*, right?"

"Yes it's worse because he's the opposite sex!"

"That's basically the same as a woman calling a man *a pussy*, or better yet, a white person using the word *nigger* versus a black person using it, right?"

"Lance, you didn't call me from the near north side for this I know. What's wrong!?"

"Well . . . you're right, Melanie *is* pregnant!"

As Lance explains the situation to her, they go to the counter and order something to eat. When they sit back down, Angelica offers her analysis.

"Lance you have to understand something . . . this is a huge situation for you both!!

It's big! It's bigger than big!! If she's never been pregnant before as she claims, I'm sure she's afraid. You have to give her time for this situation to sink in; three days is not enough! You both need more time and you each will deal with it in your own way. Have you considered all of the life changing questions that haven't been answered yet, on a separate basis and *then* as a couple? Do you understand that her decision making process will be ten times more difficult than yours!? Number one: she is the woman, the one that has to carry the baby for nine months!! That includes her emotions going haywire, not to mention the physical changes she must endure; and that's for a woman under normal circumstances. Lance, look at all she's going through with starting a new relationship before officially ending the old one; moving, her recent divorce. Melanie hasn't allowed herself time to heal; she needs to regroup . . . find herself. I know you've read about some of this. All I'm saying is . . . it's a huge pill to swallow!"

Lance gives Angelica the look of wondering when he would get a chance to speak, "Yeah, so I see it's a lot!!"

"I'm telling you right Mr. Austin . . . don't trip!!"

"Yes I know. I'm just teasing you. But I will admit, while a lot of what you're saying is obvious, I never thought about it because I've never been in this position before."

"I know; there's really no one at fault in the beginning phase of all of this. You two will have to be patient with one another . . . and you're *really* gonna have to be patient with her. If you're scared in your own little way, which knowing you, you'll label it as something else; you're gonna have to be strong and brave for the both of you."

"You've really got this all figured out, don'tcha Angelica?"

"Yes I do."

"That's why I called you." Lance rubs his forehead with his index finger and his thumb as if to grab the headache he feels coming on, to rip it right out of his head.

"Don't worry, everything will be fine. Her love for you which I think is questionable – well *not* questionable. She probably *does* love you, but I think it's a misguided love due to her past relationship and how it didn't end before her new one with you began. I know she cares about you. She probably wouldn't have been sleeping with you the way she was if she didn't. This woman is no dummy – she has some sense! She's just going through some things right now and they're happening one situation after another. My point is, she's not gonna let'cha down – not like that!"

"Like what!?"

"As far as maybe not keeping the baby . . ."

"I never said she may not keep the baby!!"

"Lance you didn't have to. That's the main reason why you're scared. You didn't call me over here to hear yourself say, 'Angelica, Melanie is pregnant!! Oh my God, what am I gonna do!?' You can figure out all of that stuff on your own. I know how badly you've always wanted a child. Melanie being involved as a second party and being doubtful is something you can't necessarily control. If you weren't worried about that, you would've told me your good news over the phone . . . right?"

"I don't like you sitting here reading my mind. You make me sick, you know that?"

"You're a liar. And besides, I don't have to read your mind Lance. You know I know you."

"Thank you Angelica. I don't know what I would do without'cha."

"Probably stand at the edge of a cliff getting ready to jump, then you would fall to your knees and chicken out at the last second."

"You're silly, you know that?"

Two weeks have passed since the big news overwhelmed the two parties concerned. Melanie's pride and ego will never allow her to admit that she is frightened to death. Lance feels like he's finally at the pinnacle of fulfilling the beginning stage of what he considers his life long dream in having a child. He assumed that getting a woman pregnant, a woman that wouldn't make him cringe at the thought of it happening, would've been the hardest part of the task. After these two weeks, he realizes he couldn't have been more wrong.

Lance stands in the window of his second floor residence, a two flat home in which most of the upstairs is basically his to be occupied along with his Siamese cat Priscilla. His third youngest brother Matthew borrowed his car for a couple of hours, so he waits to see the all too familiar car pull up. He and Melanie made plans to go to the shopping mall in the area and have a talk. Lance is momentarily distracted when he hears a door slam in the distance.

"Hey Bro, did you find that Kool & the Gang CD yet? Hey Brother, you in there?"

"Yeah Bro, I'm here." Lance walks away from the window and meets his brother half way. "What up Nate." They do the black man handshake; right hands held upright to tightly clasp, then a four fingered quick grasp and release, with a faint finger popping sound to complete it.

"Nah I didn't get a chance to do that yet. I'll have it for yah tonight or tomorrow for sure. You gotta work tonight?"

"Yeah I do. Give it to me tomorrow – I'm off."

"Alright, cool."

They both turn in opposite directions, Nathanael going through the so called dining room or Lance's living room; and Lance walking back to the so called living room or Lance's extended sleeping quarters/den area – hence the creative mind of Lance in occupying residential space or making due with what one has. Lance approaches the window again and pulls the curtain back to see Melanie pulling up. He is eager as always when she shows up but his slow motion like mannerism as he steps outside doesn't show it. He is nervous and he is scared of what he might hear today.

Lance glances at her through the driver's side window and notices a mean, stressful look on her face. As he walks pass the front of her car, he wishes it was February 2006 again. They don't say much to one another during the fifteen minute ride to the mall. This makes Lance more nervous than before and he wonders if any nervousness exists within her.

They sit at the centered square seating area of the mall, surrounded by a variety of shopping choices on ground level and on the second level. They discuss a few common issues concerning the pregnancy. Lance anticipated this day to be an overall finalization of the initial worrying, a ceasing of the daily anxiety and a calm to the unintended storm. One thing that Melanie says to him, echoes in his head over and over again,

"I never wanted to wind up being someone's *baby's mama*!!"

Lance could only respond in kind, "I'm not crazy about the *baby's daddy* concept either!!"

Lance often responds to Melanie with a rebuttal to anything she has to say to him. He hasn't even come close to understanding that this is the #1 culprit to why they argue so much; or why he could easily slip into an argument with any woman he has ever been with in his life. Even heated disagreements would ensue with his mother once he felt he was of age to legitimately do so. Of course that legitimacy was but a teenaged fantasy and completely inappropriate. Lance would even go at it with his present step father, Warren Foster, from time to time – not often though. Getting a marine powered blow to the chest even before he was a "legitimate" age to receive such blows, would end *that* quickly.

Needless to say, their meeting of the minds becomes a meeting of two angry people. Neither one of them even comes close to understanding or admitting why they're angry. Lance glances upward to a jewelry store and wonders if the possible solution to their problem would be to marry her. The thought of this is but a few eye blinks at the present moment because he is too disgusted with her to think about anything rationally – or otherwise. Melanie is simply furious and she wonders how many *slices of bread* Lance will need to find quickly to restore his loaf, so he can at least ½ way handle this situation.

"Stay here, let me go to the bathroom before I drop you off," she says to him in a disgruntled way.

Lance scoffs as she walks away, *"Hhmmp!"*

His disgust is now a full fledged ire after hearing the intentional condescension in her last statement. He is so far gone that he doesn't even feel his cell phone vibrate – and he almost doesn't hear it ring either. He rips it from the holster to look at the Caller ID. It says *Sherry A.* Lance is shocked but pleased. He answers the call in a subdued fashion,

"Hello."

"Hi Lance!! This is Sherry!"

Lance pretends like he doesn't remember her, "Sherry . . . ?"

She frowns at the phone on the other end, "I'm from the mall in Skokie . . ."

"Oh, hi Sherry, I'm surprised to hear from you!" He really is. "How are you?"

"I know it's been a while. I'm doing fine, how are you?"

"I'm fine." He lies . . . but not about what he says next, "To be honest with you, I'm really surprised that you called me back. You seemed so dead set on not talking to me again . . . I don't know why . . ."

"No Lance it wasn't that. I've just been so busy with work and all. I must admit to you . . . I was really surprised when I listened to your voicemail message a few weeks ago. I am impressed . . . most men wouldn't have handled our situation the way you did in wanting to be friends. You were strong and stern in your beliefs; you made me a believer! Did you really mean that?"

"Look Sherry, I know *you* know that people with a good heart is very rare now-a-days. When we sat at that table in the food court, I knew *then* that you were one of those rare people. I just wanted to make sure *you* knew – there was someone else sitting at that table that was just like you." Melanie returns from the bathroom and signals to Lance from a distance that she's ready to go. Lance signals to her to wait a second. "So yes Sherry, I *did* mean it, absolutely!"

As Melanie signals to Lance a second time, he reads her lips as she says, "C'mon!"

Lance signals back under his breath, "Wait-a-sec!"

Sherry says, "What did you say?"

"No not you Sherry," Lance says. "What were you going to say?"

"Oh. Sure we can be friends. I would like that very much. Just understand that Norman and I are exclusively dating now."

Melanie scoffs at Lance and turns around to head towards the exit to the mall. "I understand that perfectly, I figured that would happen anyway," he says to Sherry. Lance's mind tells him to start following Melanie to the exit but his feet do the opposite and he stays put. He recalls a recent email fight he and Melanie had about her not answering an early morning phone call of his because she was on the other line. Her defense was that he didn't know *who* she was on the phone with. Lance's argument was that she didn't answer because she was already upset with him about something else. Melanie denied as such so Lance simply gave her the benefit of the doubt. Now Lance wants her to give *him* the benefit of the doubt. Melanie doesn't, as she disappears around the corner.

"Lance are you busy?" Sherry asks.

"Yeah, a little,"

"Okay well give me a call sometime. Maybe we can hook up and go get something to eat again."

"Yes Sherry that would be nice. I'll talk with you soon to take you up on that."

"Okay, it was nice talking to you. Bye!"

"Bye."

When Lance proceeds to where Melanie had parked, not even three minutes after she disappeared around the corner, the parking space is empty. Melanie is gone.

Another week has passed and Lance sits away from the window of the big yellow school bus that roars down Interstate 65 going southeast to Indianapolis, Indiana. He is accompanied by his "better half," just as Melanie is accompanied by "hers." They are with most of her immediate family being both her sisters, their spouses and their children; seven of them all together. The four youngest of Melanie's three nieces and one nephew are in a basketball tournament on this early Saturday afternoon. Lance got up at 4:30 in the morning to meet Melanie and her family at 5:00am, so they could meet up with the other sixty two people that are on the bus as well. Lance *is not* a morning person.

He wants to sleep for this three hour ride, but he can't. The argument he and Melanie had about the window seat and about his lost wallet that she was sitting on, after she told him she had checked everywhere, was mentally doing him in. Lance can't help but feel a little nervous around her family, having not being around them or knowing them for as long as he feels he should have. It kills him even more that no one in her clan that he knows of, even realizes that she's pregnant. Lance literally wants to yell out loud on the bus,

Melanie is pregnant ya'll!!!

As much as it tortures him to keep this info from their families, he knows it's best to do so, given their plans not being written in stone just yet. No one wants to be a couple and exclaim they're pregnant to the world, to later have a certain turn of events. Lance knows this would make her look like the "bad guy," and him look stupid . . . and leaving him *feeling* even more stupid!

Lance does realize that they lack communication skills when it comes to one another. In other words – they are *both* uptight to say the least. Lance also knows that Melanie *does* have some legitimate concerns about their situation. She writes him in an email about two weeks ago:

You say you're 100% behind me with this baby now . . . what happens if we break up and you decide to change your mind about all of that!?? Of course I would sue you for child support, not that I would financially need it . . . but you would leave me no choice as far as getting you to fulfill your fatherly duties some kinda way. That would mean having to go through the courts again!! I've had enough court appearances to last me a lifetime!!

Lance has constantly pleaded with her in email format *and* in person to believe him when he says, "No matter what happens with us, I would *never* do that!!"

Statistically speaking however, no one can really blame Melanie for considering that particular scenario.

Lance himself has reservations about moving out of his comfort zone anytime soon and paying a full month's rent every month, as opposed to paying less than half that amount for the past fourteen years, living with his three brothers and his step father. He hasn't quite revealed this to Melanie yet because he knows it will border a question of his manhood within her. Deep down though, Lance knows that his bachelor environment and lack of space for anything else or anyone else, will pose a problem in trying to raise a baby.

Melanie does feel in her own right, that moving out of her father's house would be an absolute necessity if she's going to have a baby. Again though, no one can blame her for having her own reservations as a woman, in living alone in her own place or moving in together with a man that she basically argues with every other day. These thoughts take the place of the siesta that Lance so desperately craves.

Once the big yellow school bus arrives in the Indianapolis area, they all disperse in an orderly fashion to stand in line inside the building at the doorway of the school's auditorium. Lance imagines slipping away for an hour to go and meet Sonja or Evangeline or both. Knowing that simply won't happen, the amusing thought is brief. He decides he will try to bond with the two men that are Melanie's brother-in-laws. But with Lance only answering or making comments to what *they* say to him initially on separate occasions, makes his so called bonding efforts futile.

Before you know it, Lance and Melanie are at each other's throats again before they even get into the auditorium. It is more-or-less a silent argument that results in mean looks at one another. Melanie feels that Lance said something inappropriate in front of a couple of her family members. No one could possibly describe to anyone else, the validity of this disagreement. Needless to say, the two family members that *did* hear what they heard would never in their lifetime even try to. That's how silly their present display of bickering is.

Once they get inside and get seated, Melanie goes to the bathroom. Lance is relieved that she has left his presence. She is put at ease just as much if not more, by her departure from him. But once she arrives to the restroom, her mental celebration quickly ends as she tends to the *real* reason she came. She snatches the package of baby wipes from her purse to wipe away as best as she can, the bloody discharge from her private area. Melanie does not smile, nor does she cry . . . but her present situation is certainly a disquieted situation that she would rather not be in.

When Melanie swings the bathroom door open to leave ten minutes later, Lance is standing thirty feet away from the door with a major look of concern on his face.

"Melanie, what's wrong!??"

"What . . . a woman can't go to the bathroom . . . ?"

"Melanie . . . what's wrong dear!??"

"I've been having a bloody discharge . . . and I don't know why."

"For how long . . . ?"

" . . . About a week or so . . ."

" . . . Oh my God . . ."

CHAPTER 5

Even though Lance is worried sick about Melanie two days after her latest revelation, he looked forward to the moment he's in now *without* her. The music blares unbelievably loud throughout his second floor apartment area. The cold beer is flowing from the case in the fridge like promotional product samples being given away on a downtown street corner. The V.S.O.P. cognac flows like Jehovah Witness literature but flows all the same. The gallon of water that sits on the floor by Lance's bed is barely touched. When the felicitous feeling of intoxication arrives later in the night, this will change. Lance Austin and Kevin James as their depiction would indicate – are getting *fucked up*.

They give each other a competitive look as they take turns stepping to the line on the floor that determines their throwing distance from the dart board. Every once in a while Lance will turn down the music so they can communicate without yelling.

"Damn nigga you had that shit pretty loud!!" says Kevin.

Lance responds, "Man I ain't worried about that shit. The ol' man can barely hear it – he lives down there in that basement. And ya know none of my brothers care, especially Nate. Damn let me find that CD for him real quick. You know Melanie and I discovered she's pregnant about three weeks ago . . ."

"Wha . . . !!? Damn man, for real? That's good, I'm really happy to hear that!! I know how badly you've always wanted to have a kid . . . at least the sixteen years I've known ya anyway. Damn nigga, ya'll straight right!?"

Lance hesitates, "Man nigga, I dunno . . ." Lance uses the *n word* from time to time, mostly with his male comrades. He remembers the 70's when Richard Pryor, Redd Foxx and Sherman Hemsley would use the word and get a big laugh on television. Now with changes in society and Lance getting older, he finds himself using the word less often. Kevin being five years his junior will soon follow in those footsteps.

Lance and Kevin do a lot of drinking when they hang out together – *a lot* of drinking. More importantly especially for Lance, they do a lot of talking too. Lance always proclaims to be the certain type of man he is to his other male friends. He never says or does things out of character just to prove something to the fellas. With Kevin, the whole process just feels more comfortable. Kevin never tries to convince him to be something he's not, like a man that dates multiple females at the same time, or one that frequents the night club scene. He knows that Lance carries a strong conviction in not participating in easy sex with an undesirable woman, just because the sex can be handily gotten.

Lance is still learning the hard way that his overall feelings about love are a bit over-the-top. Ironically it is his love for Melanie that keeps him partially sane during his journey in the unfamiliar territory of her pregnancy. He thinks about the one time he probably allowed a male counterpart to be predominant in his decision making: when his step brother Warren, Jr. convinced him to sign up for an online dating service to try and meet women. Lance smiles when he thinks about Warren, Jr. being a self proclaimed playboy; the man that *thinks* he knows it all when it comes to women. He does know a thing or two about the dating game . . . but being the same age as Kevin leaves a higher point of culminating standards to be well overdue.

"Did you tell your brother Warren about the baby Lance?"

"Hell nah I didn't tell him!!"

"I was just wondering. You know how he is. When's the last time he stopped by to check ya'll out?"

"About two or three months ago . . ."

Now Lance has forgotten about the dart game and the CD. He logs on to his computer to visit a site about pregnancy symptoms. He emails it to Melanie, hoping it will help convince her to go see a doctor about the bloody discharge she told him about two days ago. Lance doesn't tell Kevin about *that* part of the situation. He wants to keep that private and he's hoping that part of the situation won't last long enough to mention anyway.

"Man Lance don't worry though. You and Melanie are gonna work that out for sure. I know she's probably trippin' right now . . . but she'll be alright once she gets use to the idea of being pregnant. You know I've seen how a woman acts right after she finds that out . . . more than once. It ain't pretty! But trust me when I tell ya, everything will be fine."

As much as Lance wants to believe his two best friends in telling him that everything will be fine, the difficulty in doing so is overwhelming. As the days go on, Lance continuously asks Melanie to go to the doctor to find out exactly why she's bleeding. The asking becomes pleading, yet her answer remains the same. She *did* speak to a nurse at a medical facility two weeks ago. They told her that normally when a woman is pregnant, their first appointment with an OBGYN is at the two month term. Melanie decides to stick with this convenient excuse in not going until then. Her real reason is fear of the situation itself and strangely enough, considering she's a woman, a fear in going to the doctor for anything.

The situation becomes a daily rivalry, especially for Lance. He can't help but think that Melanie purposely defies him in any situation just to irritate him. It angers him so much that his thoughts turn to violence. He wants to rip Melanie's head off of her neck and throw it in the garbage; ridding himself of the entire situation. If he were to carry out this grisly act or even anything close to it . . . it would be a sure sign of an emotionally deranged individual. Lance hasn't exactly been, nor has he ever claimed to be a model citizen who is emotionally intact; especially in his past. Lance smiles in amusement at the thought of taking her life though, because he knows his emotions are not *that* far gone.

Once he reinstates his rational thoughts, it becomes a medical issue regarding the woman that he cares about along with the baby. While Lance can understand to a certain degree how a person can show procrastination or neglect concerning themselves, he cannot accentuate enough, how selfish it is to do the same to an innocent, helpless second party. Out of pure desperation, Lance retrieves Melanie's oldest sister's email address from the CC'd part of an old email joke. He sends her an email urging her to call him. Four hours later, Lance answers a call from an unfamiliar number,

"Hi, is this Meredith?" he asks.

"Yes it is," the female voice says.

Lance releases a sigh of relief. "How are you?"

"I'm fine. You've got me a little worried. What's going on?"

"I certainly didn't mean to worry you. I know you don't know me very well but I deeply care for your sister and I wouldn't have reached out to you this way if I didn't. The truth of the matter is . . . Melanie is pregnant."

"Melanie is pregnant!!??"

"Yes . . . and I know . . . well, I understand why she didn't wanna tell anyone right away but the truth is, from a medical point of view, she's been having this bloody discharge for about two weeks now and she won't go to the doctor to get it checked out. It's a health issue for me . . . and I'm scared!! I was hoping you would reach out to her – maybe try to convince her to go see a doctor."

When Lance ends the call, he gives another sigh of relief. Now there is an encouraging sign of resolution in sight. He knows he has taken a huge chance in losing Melanie all together because it's a good chance she will look at the situation as him betraying her trust by telling her sister what's going on. But if something's wrong with Melanie or the baby and he can prevent it from getting worse, it will have all been worth it.

* * *

Two days later on Sunday, Lance is doing a smooth 70mph on the Dan Ryan expressway in his shiny black Cadillac with the music blasting. He did hope he would have heard back from Meredith by now but he hasn't. He hasn't spoken to Melanie today either, out of fear of how she will react to him when she finds out her sister knows the secret. It has been about a month now since they discovered they're expecting and for every single day of that month, it has been on both of their minds in some kind of excruciating way. Today on this evening at least, Lance decides to lose these stressful thoughts and have some fun.

Lance passes by the Mexican restaurant on North Ave. where he's meeting his party. It is quite lively and jammed packed with cars pulling in for valet parking. He decides to find a parking space on his own because he doesn't want a stranger rummaging through his Caddy or driving it *any* distance. After he finds one and is walking back toward North Ave., he grabs his cell from it's holster and dials a number he has memorized,

"Hey Sherry its Lance, where are you?"

"I'm about a mile away from the restaurant. Are you there yet?"

"Yes I'm here."

"Where did you park?"

Lance smiles at how she says the word *park*. "Some angled street about two blocks away. I think the street name was Concord Pl."

"Okay I'll try to find it or something close by."

Lance's sense of de-ja-vu brings a smile to his face. The last time he made the phone call to inquire about Sherry's whereabouts, he was meeting her for the very first time. The anticipation in seeing her this time is the same as before but with less nervousness. This makes the anticipation all the more enjoyable. Lance stands on the street and waits for her to approach. When she does, he can't help but smile when he thinks to himself.

What is it with this white shirt!!? I wonder if it's the same one she had on before.

He can't tell because she has something on over it, something that resembles an old jacket from the 80's. Her light blue jeans are loose fitting *again* but he knows for sure she's no more than a size 5. As he hugs her and starts to pull away, he looks down at her feet.

"What?" she says.

"Oh nothing, I thought I dropped something. Let's go inside."

Sherry has on some brown sandals and he notices that her feet and toes look very nice. Lance figures this attributes to why she is wearing a sandal like shoe every time he sees her. He decides once and for all that he doesn't like the way she dresses, though there is a slight improvement from the first time he laid eyes on her. He doesn't let it bother him though because he knows they are both committed to someone else.

Lance had mentioned to Sherry before today that Melanie is pregnant, without going into much detail. He only wanted to offer his honesty about his life to her, just as she always seems to do for him. Holding back information would be of no advantage to either one of them anyway because they are just friends . . . and he knows they are both committed to someone else. As they are seated, Sherry gives Lance a baffling look with a smile on her face.

"Lance . . . Lance . . . Lance, so your girl is pregnant huh? Wow, that's something!! That's a far cry from, 'I think that's pretty much a wrap for her.'"

Someone once told Lance that when a woman says your name three times like that, she likes you. Lance doesn't read much into it though; he knows they are both committed to someone else. Their conversation flows a lot better than the first time they met. In a sense, no one really has anything to prove to the other. This takes the obvious strain out of their meeting and their overall relationship, allowing room for them to grow as male and female companions to one another; if there is such a thing.

The Salsa tunes blare throughout the restaurant. "Do you know how to Salsa?" Sherry asks.

"Actually I was taking Salsa lessons two years ago but I never finished. I regret that I didn't . . . it's a very interesting dance. What about you?"

I'm taking lessons right now. It's kind of difficult to me but I think I'm getting the hang of it."

"That's good, keep it up. The girl I was taking lessons with . . . her and I sorta fell out, so I really didn't have anyone to continue them with."

"Were you two dating?"

"No we weren't. Actually we were good friends, like play brother and sister. In my opinion after some years, the relationship seemed to be one sided."

"In what way . . . ?"

" . . . Me being there for her and her not being there for me . . ."

"Oh well, people come and people go."

Lance thinks about that failed platonic relationship that started so long ago. He wonders if his and Sherry's platonic relationship will suffer the same fate. He thinks to himself, *well surely I'm better at picking my potential friends* now *than I was when I was twenty years old.*

About an hour later when the bill arrives, Sherry reaches for it. Lance quickly places his hand on top of hers to stop her. Lance notices how soft and feminine her hand is.

"Sherry what are you doing?"

"I'll treat you to this late lunch."

"Oh no I'll get it! I insist. You can get the next one."

"Oh okay."

Lance pays the bill and he is happy to do so. It's the gentleman like thing to do, and he always treats his platonic female friends as such. They exit the restaurant and stand on North Ave.

"That was some good food, wasn't it?" Lance asks.

Sherry quickly answers, "Yes it was!"

"Where are you parked? I'll walk you to your car."

She points north, "I'm over there."

They stand at the curb for a couple of minutes, waiting for traffic to allow them to cross the street. Lance starts to internally prepare himself for the goodbye that he doesn't want to happen. Instinctively, Lance puts his open hand out for her to grab which she does and he says to her, "C'mon."

Lance leads as they suddenly dart into the street to quickly get across. While he did think about how he had touched her hand a few moments after it happened, he did not plan to grab her hand as he did when she accepted his gesture. He does have a habit of darting into the street to beat traffic from time to time. Sherry giggles as they make it across. Lance lets go of her hand so she won't think he's trying to make a pass at her.

"You're crazy Lance!" she says to him, still smiling from the giggle.

"Yeah I am . . . but just a little bit," he replies. "What are your plans for the evening?"

"Nothing much . . . just relaxing; why?"

Lance senses a *yes* to his next question. "You know the last time we hung out, you said that since we hung out on your side of town, you would hang out my way next time around. I will admit after that I didn't think I would ever see you again; but here you are and here I am. You wanna go have a drink?"

"Yeah sure we can go do that for a lil' bit."

"Okay good." Lance's glee remains inside for Sherry not to see. He is especially glad that he didn't have to put himself out there just to be denied.

"Well here's my car. You want me to take you to your car and then I'll follow you?" Sherry asks.

"No, that won't be necessary." Lance pulls out his car keys with a Cadillac key chain emblem on it. "Leave your car here – I'll drive." He hits the remote to unlock his doors. When his headlights come on, they are shining on the back of her SUV.

"That's your car Lance!!?" I parked right in front of you!?"

"Yes."

"Wow!! This is nice. You weren't playing before when you said you were getting a new car soon!"

"Nah, I wasn't playing." Now the glee in Lance is seeping out of his pours and he can't help but let it show when he smiles; teeth showing. They're not the whitest teeth in the world but they're white enough.

Lance pulls the passenger door open for Sherry; a gentleman as usual. He swings to his side and calmly gets in. He has no idea where they are going.

"Wow, leather seats! This is really nice Lance."

"Thank you." As he starts the car he thinks about some of the neighborhood drinking holes on his side of town and they are just that – drinking holes! He doesn't want to scare her, being the type of woman she is and given the fact that she lives in Skokie. As they drive along slowly so he can think of somewhere to go before she realizes he doesn't have a clue, he pops in a Diana Krall CD. The smooth jazz isn't blasting the way he normally plays his music but it's loud enough and good enough for her to notice.

"This is nice. Who is this playing?"

"Diana Krall, this white girl. She deals with the same producers that made albums with Natalie Cole back in the day." Lance considers taking her to Hyde Park, but he's not too familiar with the restaurants in the area, though he has heard about a couple of them.

"Wow, Lance has some class!" she suddenly says aloud. Lance looks at her and smiles. He wonders why she didn't notice that the first time they met. He thinks that maybe he was too nervous to have it on display full throttle at the time or maybe she *did* notice but ignored it because of Norman.

"So how is your guy doing . . . uuhhh . . . Norman? Is that his name?" He pretends like he doesn't remember.

"He's not quite 'my guy' yet."

"But you want him to be, right?"

"Well . . . yes."

"I'm sure a woman of your caliber will have no problem in getting this man right where you want him . . . right? Right – so how is your guy doing?"

Sherry smiles, "He's doing fine."

"Have you ever been to Cuatro's?"

"No I haven't."

"It's near here, like on 20th and Wabash . . . something like that. We can go there."

"Okay."

If Norman is doing fine and Sherry had nothing negative to say about him . . . why is she letting me know she notices I have class now!? Or did she misunderstand the question. I don't care how that nigga is doing . . . I wanted to know how they are doing!! Maybe I should've been more specific. Well it doesn't matter anyway – we're both involved, especially me in a huge way!! I'm not about to create some mess that I can't clean up. Platonic – platonic – platonic!! Wow!! I'd like to hear somebody say that word ten times in a row without stuttering, jeez!!

" . . . Penny for your thoughts Lance!!"

"Okay, give it here."

Sherry looks at Lance with a surprised look, "It's probably deep in my purse somewhere. I don't have it right now."

"Oh well." Lance smiles – Sherry frowns. " . . . I gotcha! Ha ha!"

Melanie and Meredith sit in the back bedroom of their father's house. More-or-less they have just had their talk. Melanie was totally shocked when her sister came to her about her current situation. She felt backed into a corner and she felt a loss of control, neither of which she's not used to feeling often. Meredith picks up the land line to give Lance a call.

When Lance hears his cell phone ringing, he and Sherry are sitting at the bar in Cuatro's. He considers taking the call in the bathroom.

No secrets! Sherry and I are just friends anyway. He answers the call, "Hi Meredith, how are you?"

"I'm fine Lance." Melanie frowns at her sister. "I just wanted to let you know that I spoke to Melanie and while she's not giving me a definite answer about making a doctor's appointment, she will definitely consider it. You have to understand something Lance . . ."

He interrupts Meredith, "Yeah I know – Melanie is a grown woman and she's gonna do what *she* wants to do." He looks at Sherry to see if she seems deterred by the phone call. She is not.

Meredith continues, "Well yes, that's pretty much what I was gonna say . . . I can't tell my sister what to do. I can only make suggestions and love her and back her in whatever decision she makes about any of this. I think you and her will be fine if you two sit down together and seriously try to work all of this out . . . *without* all of the arguing." Melanie looks at her sister and makes a face of being in total agreement with the last part of her statement. Lance makes a face that signifies embarrassment by what he's just heard; the last part of Meredith's statement.

He answers like a child, "I know."

"Well I'm gonna let you go now . . . and Lance, I really appreciate you contacting me. Thank you, bye." Meredith places the phone back on its base, "And that goes for you too Melanie!!"

"What!!?" she says with a surprised look on her face.

"The arguing . . . ! I know carrying a child can be unbelievably stressful to say the least. I did it three times, so I know. But try to work with him. I mean . . . this man is reaching out to your family members out of concern for you and the baby. Most men not married to you would've been running the other way! He's running right into the situation!!"

"He's an idiot!!"

"He probably is but he definitely cares about you! I know you've been through a lot the past couple of years and this certainly doesn't make your life any easier. Just don't let your baggage be a carry-on."

Melanie doesn't say anything as she stares at her sister that she loves so much. She hopes the tear in her eye doesn't drop and run down her cheek – but it does.

Lance has a tear in his eye as he's placing his phone back in its holster. He wipes his eye to stop it from running then he looks at Sherry, "What are you having?"

"Lance, are you okay?"

"Yeah, thanks. I'm sorry about that. I know you know what's going on but that doesn't mean I have to bring that stress here, while we're having a drink."

"There's no need to apologize. You weren't on the phone that long and it seemed important anyway. You probably don't want to talk about it, do you?"

"No I don't, but thanks for asking. So . . . what are you having?"

"I think the Sangria sounds good."

Lance orders, "The lady will have the Sangria and I'll have that V.S.O.P. cognac on the top shelf, neat, water back."

Sherry says under her breath, "Look out Norman," then she says aloud, "You've been here before, right?"

"Yeah, once or twice . . . The food is really good too; it's Latin. We'll have to come back one evening and get something to eat." Lance loves the fact that he is showing Sherry a nice place that she has never been to before. Then he realizes that he and Melanie do this all the time, making this moment not so special and unique as he originally tried to make it in his head. His trifling thought is spoiled when he returns to reality.

"Mmmm!! This is good Lance!! Taste this." Sherry extends her drink towards Lance for him to take it. In his mind he hesitates, wondering if she wants him to put his mouth on her glass. He takes the drink from her and he does just that.

"Mmmm!! This *is* good!! I may have to have one of these later."

"What is that you're drinking?"

"V.S.O.P cognac . . . You want to taste it? It's kind of strong." Lance says this because he wants to treat her like the sweet little innocent girl from Boston that she is.

"Yeah let me taste it."

Lance picks up his drink. "Here, hold the stem part of the snifter between your fingers and bend your wrist to the left when you grasp the circular part of it, like this." As he's handing his drink to Sherry, their hands touch again. For some strange reason . . . a reason that Lance is trying his best not to succumb to, he likes touching her hand.

Sherry puts the drink to her mouth and then pulls back, "Wow, this is strong!! And that's just the scent of it!"

She pulls the cognac towards her mouth again . . . and when she places her lips on Lance's glass . . . he wonders if he is playing with the devil.

"Whoah!! That *is* strong!! I don't see how you can drink that!!" she says as she gasps slightly.

"Here, drink a little water behind it." When Sherry places her lips on Lance's glass of water, he knows for sure that *he is* playing with the devil . . . but he will not let the devil win on this night.

As they continue to mingle, they both start to wonder to themselves why this is happening and why this is happening this way. The comfort that they find in one another's company is completely ridiculous. Neither one of them expected this high level of enchantment to occur – that is the reason *why* it is occurring.

Lance orders a Sangria drink for himself and Sherry does not order another. He can see that it doesn't take much for her. He can also see that her lady-like tendencies will not allow her to over do her alcohol consumption. Of course Lance likes that in her.

But in being a man, he feels the need to make certain of his observation, "Are you *sure* you don't want another drink Sherry?"

"Yes I'm sure." Lance finds himself in a momentary trance as he watches Sherry play with the fruit and ice at the bottom of her glass with her straw. She continues, "You can give me a lil' bit of yours though." They both smile.

"Oh okay. Hey look!!" Lance brushes against her arm with his hand and points to his left. There is a Caucasian woman with a guitar on her shoulder. She approaches the wooden stool on the small wooden stage.

"Oh, live entertainment!! This should be nice. How do you know about this place!!? Sherry exclaims.

"Actually, I stumbled onto it. And I didn't know they do live entertainment. The last time I was here, my friend and I were dancing the night away right here in the middle of the floor. It was more like a club *that* night. I've never been here on a Sunday though."

"Wow, lucky you . . . !"

The blonde woman starts to play an acoustic rendition of a song that sounds familiar to them both. They look at each other in bewilderment because neither one of them can place it quite yet. The blonde woman starts to sing about a hopeless romantic.

Lance exclaims, "Oh my God!!! I've heard this before, but I can't put my finger on it!!"

"Yes, I've heard it before too, but I don't know. Anyway she sounds pretty good singing it . . . whatever song it is."

"Yes she does. She's jamming on that guitar too!" The blonde woman starts to harmonize the tune after the chorus.

"Bahh, bahh-bahh, bahh-bahh, bahh-bahh, bahh-bahh,
Bahh-bahh, bahh-bahh, bahh-bahh, bahh-bahh
Ummm . . . ummm, ummm"

Lance almost falls out of his chair, "Oh no, now it's really killing me!!!" He calms himself, as not to alienate the relaxing atmosphere they have both naturally employed. When the blonde woman finishes the song, all of the patrons applaud. Then suddenly, Sherry's left hand is on the lower part of the back of Lance's head. She kisses Lance on his right cheek.

"You are so sweet Lance. Thank you."

"A quality outing, for a quality young lady . . . You're welcome." His words are calm, cool and collective. But in Lance's mind, the atonement of the moment has him fainting to the floor.

The drive back to her vehicle on the near north side is like a blur to Lance. They continue to talk and laugh and enjoy the music he's playing in an overall friendly, platonic kind of way. He wonders what she's *really* thinking though. He wonders if the sentimental jolt is as good for her as it is for him. Sherry certainly seems excited enough when they are standing by her vehicle saying their goodbyes.

"You are *really* something Lance. Thanks again!!" She gives him a nice hug.

"Thank you for your company Sherry. We'll certainly have to do this again."

"Definitely . . . !"

He touches her hand one last time as he's helping her into her SUV. He closes her door and then finds himself still standing there, *still* having a conversation with her.

This lasts for about five minutes before he abruptly ends it. He takes a step back and is standing in the street when she pulls off. Lance stands there motionless as he is waving goodbye, then he suddenly catches himself and starts to walk towards his car. He doesn't want Sherry to look in her rearview mirror and see him standing in the middle of the street, stricken like the idiotic, love sick puppy that he is.

When Lance is certain she is out of sight, his hand is on the driver's side door handle. He doesn't pull it open, standing motionless the way he wanted to a few seconds before.

His inner inquiry about the sentimental jolt was mutual he feels . . . and this makes him wonder *why now!?*

Lance realizes at this very moment, that if Melanie wasn't pregnant, he would have kissed her; not on her cheek. The reality of the pregnancy and his love for Melanie is only part of the reason he will never even attempt to have an affair with Sherry. Being involved with a woman that is already spoken for is a situation he will not put himself in, ever again in his life. Lance considers the fact that he got lucky with Melanie in that regard – but only in certain ways. He recalls another time in his past when competing for an involved woman's attention and coming out the loser after he fell in love with her. He also knows that Sherry is not that type of girl and frankly, he wouldn't want to share her with another man anyway.

Lance gets in his Cadillac and decides to use this beautiful experience as his inspiration in how he will approach Melanie from now on; involving the baby, their relationship . . . everything. As he's driving, he recalls his purpose for this evening, *No stressful thoughts – have some fun!!* Lance got that ten-fold! He laughs out loud when he thinks of that old saying:

Be careful what you ask for; you might just get it.

CHAPTER 6

*A*ugust 2nd Thursday 2pm-94th & Western.

On this very day, time and place, Lance sits in his car in what seems like a miniature parking lot. He recalls a few evenings ago when Melanie handed him this information on a yellow post-it. She had gathered it that morning when she called the doctor's office to make an appointment. Lance has vowed for many years that whenever he got a woman pregnant, he would accompany her to each and every doctor's visit. Under the circumstances, he is really glad that Melanie made an earlier appointment and is giving him a chance to begin proving this.

Lance closes his eyes and thanks the Lord for her sudden change of heart; a small victory in his ultimate destination of "happily ever after." He doesn't pray as often as he would like but he's working on it. When he opens his eyes, Melanie is pulling up. Lance gets out of his car before she parks. Once she's out of her car, he stares at her as she approaches. His wish is to momentarily dispose of the exasperating feeling she has left inside of him as of late, especially concerning the doctor's appointment for the bloody discharge. Lance reminds himself that it's Melanie's bravery he should be admiring.

"Hi Mel . . ."

"Hey."

"Are you ready to do this dear?"

"I better be, I'm here now . . ."

"Mel . . . you are being very brave by doing this, you know that, right?"

"I'm trying."

"No dear – you were 'trying' to be brave *before* you made the appointment. Now you *are* being brave." Lance gives her a soft smack on the lips and grabs her hand into his. "C'mon let *us* do this – and get it over with!!" Melanie smiles at the last part of what he says to her.

They sit in the receptionist area waiting. Lance looks at a couple of children's books, imagining that he's reading them to his child. He hasn't picked up a child's book since he was a child himself. He remembers his mother reading the many stories to him from a children's Bible that she got him for Christmas in 1973. Lance still has that children's Bible, torn cover and all. Now he can read that same Bible to *his* child. This thought makes him smile uncontrollably.

Lance glances at a pregnant woman sitting nearby. She is very attractive to him and in his estimation she's in the latter stage of her second trimester. She appears to be very pleasant and quite content even though the father is not present. He wonders why certain situations in life often have an outcome that is opposite of what it should really be. He questions his presence here as he looks at Melanie without her noticing. She's not frowning but she's not smiling either. Lance has a thought.

If I miss an appointment somewhere down the line, will Melanie's mood go through a metamorphosis and form into something a little more positive? Lance knows that's ridiculous. He thinks on; *I wonder if she'll look as good as this lady when she starts to show. Will dealing with her pregnancy be a tougher task than raising this child?*

"Melanie Powell, the doctor will see you now," yells the assistant as she's hanging on the door that has all the answers behind it; medically speaking of course. The answers that Lance and Melanie seek, individually and collectively, will be found out the hard way. Lance frowns at hearing her last name, "*Powell*," her x-husband's name that he left her stuck with . . . like a strain that won't come out. For that reason alone he hates it and he'll be glad when she legally goes back to her maiden name *Strong*.

The nurse is extremely nice, with her superfluous smile that serves the purpose of making Lance and Melanie forget that she is but a prelude to what they will do more of . . . and that's wait! Lance knows better though, so he decides to use the time wisely.

"Melanie . . ." She looks at him but doesn't say anything. "Melanie dear . . ."

"Yes . . ."

"I want to apologize to you . . . for trying not to argue with you lately but not *trying* hard enough; for being understanding of what you're going through but not *being* understanding enough. I realize that my being here physically means absolutely nothing, if I can't mentally leave a lasting impression upon you that is positive. Being here *must* be the easy part, cause' the other stuff is really hard for me and I wish I were better at pulling off the hard stuff – I *have* been trying Melanie . . . I really have. Now, I am going to try harder!"

"Lance . . . believe me when I tell you, I really appreciate what you're saying . . . but can we do this later? The doctor might walk in any moment now . . ."

"Mel no, I really need to say this now!! This very moment, our sitting here waiting is inspiring these thoughts and these feelings in me. I just . . . Lord knows that you know how badly I want this baby! I want it so bad . . . that I think its making me forget about y*ou* . . . and you're the one that has to carry the child nine months before *he* or *she* arrives. As hard as this is for me to say but I mean it when I say it . . . whatever you decide to do concerning our child, if you have our child or if you don't . . . I will support you 100%. I want you to do what *you* feel is best in this situation . . . I have no control over that anyway. All I can do is be like your sister and love you and support you no matter what. And *I do* love you Melanie, with all my heart . . . even when you get on my nerves!"

Melanie smiles at the last part of what Lance says to her, "But Lance . . ." She starts to cry a little. Lance stands up to get tissue for her as she continues, " . . . If I don't go through with this pregnancy, would you ever be able to forgive me!?"

Lance stoops down and wipes the tears from her eyes. He whispers, "I truly don't know the answer to that. All I know for certain is that I want to plan our future together. Maybe now is a good time for us to have a baby . . . maybe later is better. Let's just try and plan our future . . . together . . . work through whatever it is we need to work through, together."

Melanie stares into his eyes. She sees better what she hears. "Okay Lance."

Melanie will never admit to anyone, not even her best friend Nina, how turned on and how sexually aroused she got when Lance delivered his emotionally charged speech to her in the doctor's office a few days ago. It made her feel like Lance *did* know how to be a man and have empathetic feelings to go along with it. His usual discourse in an uncomfortable situation was always laced with rebuttal. Melanie did receive and feel the message in a heartfelt way; but strangely enough, she felt it in her vagina first.

The doctor visit turned out to be encouraging for the both of them. Besides Melanie's condition being labeled a "high risk pregnancy" because of her age, everything medically speaking was normal. With the first doctor's visit out of the way, their health concerns and the anxiety this caused Lance, can be put behind them for the moment. Now Melanie feels like there's a bit of room in her tolerance level to talk with Lance again and at least resolve one important issue that they have – their living arrangement with a child.

Melanie's cell phone rings. She answers it, "Hey Derek, how are you?"

"The question is . . . *how are you?*"

Derek is a co-worker and a close friend of Melanie's. They have worked together for many years and they grew close platonically as the years went by. He is to Melanie what Angelica is to Lance.

"I owe you a really big thanks Derek!! I went to the doctor yesterday!"

"Oh you did, huh. Well that's good. I'm really glad you decided to go. Did everything turn out okay?"

"Yes it did. The discharge is considered normal for some women during the first month or so after getting pregnant . . . with the body more-or-less getting use to the major change that has occurred internally. The doctor said the bleeding should stop soon."

"That's good to hear but why do you owe *me* thanks for your going to the doctor?"

"It was something you said to me last Saturday. You said you think I should go to the doctor sooner than later, of course if I went sooner, you would support me, but if I *didn't* go sooner, I would still have your support all the same. Those words made me feel like I could do anything! My fear in going to the doctor . . . it felt so small after you said that to me. Meredith said something very similar to what you said . . ."

Derek interrupts, "Oh, so you *did* tell someone in your family that you're pregnant?"

Melanie snarls, "No, actually *Lance* told her. That was his way of trying to get me to go. Anyway . . . I had decided to go the day after I spoke to you and that was the same day Meredith spoke to me . . ."

Derek interrupts again, "You said 'your fear felt so small', so you are admitting that going to the doctor scared you?"

"Why do you keep interrupting me Derek?"

"Because I care . . ."

Melanie hesitates before she continues, "Well the point I'm trying to make is that sometimes it counts more *who* is saying what's being said, than just *what* is being said."

"Well you're welcome Melanie. I didn't know I had that much influence in your life."

Neither did Melanie, until this very moment. "You're a good friend Derek . . ."

"It takes one to know one." The silence afterwards is brief but noticeable. Derek continues, "So when's the wedding!?"

"That's not funny *D*!!!"

"Wha . . . ? I wasn't trying to be funny . . . well maybe just a little with the timing and all. But seriously, you guys haven't even at least talked about the possibilities of getting married one day?"

"It's funny you would ask. As a matter of fact . . . well we talked about it before, more like mentioned it. But not too long ago he mentioned it in a more decisive manner. He didn't have a ring or anything like that; he just said he would like to marry me 'before the baby is born', because neither one of us ever wanted to have a child out of wedlock. I told him *no* because I didn't wanna be standing at nobody's alter, seven or eight months pregnant!!"

"Mmmm . . ."

" . . . And I really don't, but the truth of the matter is . . . I don't wanna be married to anyone right now, especially Lance!! I don't think he's got enough backbone to be a good husband to me anyway."

"Mmmm . . ."

"He doesn't even act as if he's willing to move from his current comfort zone he calls home . . . ! So where does that leave me!??"

"Well Melanie . . . you know I'm still trying to sell this three flat I'm living in, so I can move . . . but neither has happened. Listen . . ."

Lance sits at his computer staring at the screen and playing over and over inside his head, the song that he and Sherry heard at Cuatro's a week ago. He picks up his landline to call an old friend – or more like an old friend, then lover, then old friend again after she dumped Lance and went back to her previous boyfriend and got over the guilt of hurting Lance . . . at least *he thinks* she got over it; *he* did. He asks her if she's heard of a song called "Hopeless." Simultaneously Lance is on a website where he types in that very song title and the answer pops up on the screen just as she says it,

"I know what movie that's from!!" she says in a squeaky voice. He loved her voice when he was seeing her but hates it now that he isn't. When Lance looks on the screen and sees that she is correct, he has a sarcastic thought of her at least being good for *something*. He considers her *off again, on again* offerings of her friendship after the affair to be wishy-washy at best and certainly a clear cut sign of uncertainty within herself, about herself.

Lance snatches his cell phone from its holster and activates a random ring tone to make it sound like it's ringing, "*Lemecallyouback*," he says to her.

He looks at his watch to reveal the time of eight o' clock. He and Melanie agreed on this time to meet at his place so they can talk. Lance rushes to send Sherry an email, letting her know he found the name and artist of the song they heard together and that he'll have it in a matter of days. His love of music makes this promise to her effortless. He shuts down his computer, relieved that he got that out of the way before Melanie's arrival. Lance will always maintain that he met Sherry at a time when he was convinced he and Melanie had broken up. Melanie would probably not see it that way, especially if she ever *saw* Sherry and knew that Lance was friends with her.

Lance *did* tell Melanie about another woman he met on the internet – Charmaine Williams. She was the fourth cyber-space hopeful that he encountered and she was more over-the-top and more clingy than Lance could ever be. He found this amusing and thought Melanie would too but she didn't. In fact she was jealous. He met her almost two weeks before he met Sherry in person back in April, a few days after he and Melanie stopped speaking. Emails filled with sarcasm and corny wit was the mechanism that brought the two of them together. The usual charade of visual evasion on the dating website was Charmaine's MO unfortunately. This amuses Lance even to this day. Of the three women he's met online with no picture, they each offered three different reasons or excuses as to why they didn't have one up.

Lance tries to recollect if she told him over the phone that she had three kids or if she had it posted on her profile. He can't quite remember. All he remembers clearly was that any wish he had was fulfilled at his command. Charmaine pulled up to his place less than a week after their emails first began. She pulled up in a raggedy car with her right fender hanging down to the ground but not touching it. Lance starts to giggle while he's sitting at his computer thinking about that evening.

When Charmaine got out of her raggedy car, he knew he would *never* see her getting out of that raggedy car again. Lance greeted her on the sidewalk in front of his place, wishing he was someone else. Her jeans didn't fit right, but he couldn't quite figure out why. She had so many bags in her hands that Lance almost giggled out loud as he hugged her. She had Chinese food per Lance's request and a bottle of Riesling white wine but it was from a California vineyard and not Germany as Lance instructed her to get.

As Lance walked her up the stairs, he had a quizzical expression on his face. He couldn't wait to take these stairs going down again to let her out. When Lance inquired about the other two bags, she handed them his way.

"Oh, this is for you Lance!!"

He takes the bags and hugs her again because it's the courteous gesture to make. As he pulls away, he notices the big grin on her face. When her smile leaves momentarily, to his dismay – it was not her smile that was big, it is her mouth. Lance doesn't like this, though a few of his male friends probably *would* for one purpose and one purpose only; and it's not kissing. Lance starts to have freaky ideas of his own until he realizes he's still holding the bags she gave him. In one bag is a cute little puppy dog stuffed animal and in the other bag, a card. Lance is now wondering how far he can take this woman in one evening. He feels lucky that there's a six pack of beer in the refrigerator because he knows one bottle of wine won't be enough to fabricate a delusional feeling of attraction for her.

After they eat, the wine and beer can't go down Lance's throat fast enough. He wants to hurry up and make his move and get this frivolous evening over with. Charmaine on the other hand is extremely excited to be around Lance. She doesn't seem naïve to what may happen a little later in the evening but she is oblivious to the fact that Lance does not find her attractive in any way, shape or form. At one point she stands up to dance in the mirror, as if to make a declaration of her womanhood. Lance looks at her hair that comes down to her shoulders but not enough to touch them. Her body is not as proportionate as he would like, realizing *this* to be the reason why her jeans don't fit right. He shakes his head in disgust.

Once all six beers are in his belly, Lance's goal to get drunk or even feel a slight buzz is unsubstantiated. He glances at the stuffed animal she gave him and notices something silver hanging from its neck. When he picks it up and looks at it closely, it is a small key that reads on the back, *"The key to my heart."*

Lance knew at that very moment, that while the sex would've probably been a mutual event, the understanding of it would not have been. To make matters worse for Lance, Charmaine would not accept the money he offered her for the food and wine. He ended the evening after that, without laying a hand on her. He would tell her over the phone two days later that he was not as attracted to her as he would like. And like a stubborn pecan in its shell, she was crushed.

Lance almost feels sorry for her when he thinks about how that story ended a few months ago. He gets up from his computer to answer the door.

"Hey Mel . . . !"

"Hey Lance!" He offers Melanie a cup of tea rather than coffee since she's pregnant.

When he's in the kitchen preparing it, he realizes that moving is inevitable and merely becomes a question of *when*. Lance comes back into the room wide eyed and bushy tailed, ready to come to terms with this out loud. He hopes it will cause a domino effect in resolving much more. Melanie speaks first.

"Lance, you know we were supposed to come to some kind of agreement on how we were going to do this with the baby, particularly our living arrangements. You know I absolutely *will not* bring a baby into this world in my dad's house! That's not fair to him and I would think that you know . . . your place is not exactly ideal to be raising a child in either. But you don't seem too interested in making that move."

"No Melanie, that's not so. I know we both have to move. I'm still trying to work out some financial stuff and I know we gotta do this before the baby gets here in February or early March. Early January would be the ideal time for me to actually move."

"January . . . ? That's too late for me! And no one wants to move in the middle of winter anyway. I need to be out of my father's house some time next month; no later than October!! And you'll excuse me if I don't quite believe you will actually leave this place. This is the first time you've even said anything about leaving."

"What does winter have to do with anything!? What items exactly would *you* be moving anyway . . . clothes on hangers!?? And not even that really 'cause you're pregnant!! Why are you rushing this so much?? You act like your father is kicking you out soon and I know that isn't the case!!"

"Of course he's not but it's the right thing to do."

" . . . The 'right thing to do'? Why . . . because *you* said so . . . !?"

"Oh Lance, this is ridiculous!! Why are we even having this discussion? When January gets here, you're gonna use the 'financial' excuse again to buy some more time to bullshit!!"

"'Discussion' . . . ? I thought we were arguing . . . which is what we *always* do when I don't agree to your terms!! And as usual, you don't believe in me; you think I'm lying about leaving here and you think getting my finances in order is 'bullshit'!! No wonder your credit score is 400!!!"

"You know what . . . I don't need this from you!! You talk a good game but your actions lack!! And you say you wanna be my husband!!??" She gives a smug like chuckle, "How ya gonna pull that off when we don't even go together *Mr. High Credit Score*!!' We haven't *officially* been boyfriend and girlfriend since March!!!"

"Oh, so that's why you get upset every time I mention Charmaine's name, 'cause

We *don't* go together!!? Yeah . . . that makes a lot of sense!!"

"Well if you know it upsets me, then stop talkin' 'bout da bitch!!! I think ya did fuck her!!!"

Lance is silent. He can't believe she threw the "officially not together" bomb in his face; even though he now realizes it's true. He had been so busy trying to get her back, and then the pregnancy, that he forgot. Melanie continues,

"More than likely sometime next month, I'm gonna move into an apartment with a roommate. If I'm going to have a baby, I need to start planning for that in a major way."

Lance doesn't have sense enough to embrace the fact that for the very first time, Melanie sounds assured in her decision to have their child. He is stuck in the zone of negativity concerning "a roommate" and who this person could possibly be.

"What roommate – Who . . . ?"

"A platonic friend of mine . . ."

"*Who* . . . ?"

" . . . A good friend of mine, you don't know him!!"

"I know I don't *know* him . . . that's why I . . . and why do you have to live with a roommate anyway, and how am I gonna be around my child!!?"

"Lance you can see your child anytime you want."

"'I can see' . . . oh thanks for your permission regarding my child!!! I'm not trying to 'see' my child . . . I'm trying to *take care* of my child!!!"

"You can help take care of your child Lance. I just hope you're not living *here* when you're doing it!!"

"Where I'm living next year has no bearing on when and how I will take care of my child!!"

"Then why does it matter for me!??"

"'cause you're moving in with some 'platonic' guy . . ." Lance does the quotation signs with his hands, " . . . And I don't know who da hell he is, and you're being evasive as usual!!"

"I ain't fuckin' him if that's what'cha think!!"

"I don't think you're fuckin' him!!! The first couple of years of a child's life are the most important years of his or hers development . . . and I *ain't* having *no nigga* standing over my child *grinning* and *breathing* all over *my child* and shit . . . playin' like *he's* the fuckin' daddy . . . *I'm* the child's father and *that's it!!!*"

Melanie is silent for a moment. She is astonished over what he said and *how* he said it. For the very first time she realizes that Lance has the same exact love and passion in his heart, like her own father. She has seen this display of unsurpassed protective rage in words and in actions often enough, whenever her father felt that someone or something was threatening to one of *his* kids. When she sees this in Lance, it completely inspires her, and it calms her.

"Lance . . . dear, look – January is too long to wait to be trying to move with a baby on the way. You gotta come up with something better than that."

Lance follows suite and is calmer, "You say we're not officially a couple and you're right, we're not. But I need to be around my child exclusively . . . especially for its *first* year. If anyone should be moving in under platonic circumstances it should be you and I. I would be willing to move in with you under those circumstances, because we're that child's parents no matter *what* you and I do. I love you Melanie and I do want a future with you . . . but I'm not concerned with that situation right now, not as much as I am with raising our child *the right way* . . . as morally sound as humanly possible. Let's move in together as parents and raise our child together for the first year. If we can go half on the rent, that would help me get my finances more in order. If the '*us*' thing doesn't work out after that, we can go our separate ways, okay?"

"Okay Lance, but we need to start looking for a place within the next week or two. January is out of the question."

"Okay Melanie." Lance still wonders to himself who the platonic guy is and why she wouldn't tell him who he is. He doesn't ask again because he knows he won't get an answer. Lance also knows that he has just been manipulated into moving in with her and much sooner than he anticipated. He decides to let it go just this one time, for the sake of his child. Lance now starts to take in the joy from the major plateau that has been reached on this day. It is certain that Lance and Melanie are having a child! This gives Lance another feeling beyond joy as well; he *now* knows what it feels like to be a father.

CHAPTER 7

Evangeline Robinson sits in her bedroom with a glass of Merlot. It is her quiet celebration of her four year old actually falling asleep fifteen minutes after his bedtime of eight o'clock. She has the television on but it watches her more than she watches it while she's deep in thought. She thinks about her life in general, her stressful part-time job, her stressful full time student status, her full time job as a parent which too can be stressful at times but is completely sanctioned and happily accepted. Evangeline can't help but wonder what it would feel like to have many more quiet moments like this one. The deadbeat father and ex-boyfriend whose assistance brought their child into the world has not really offered any assistance since. She wonders if being in and out of court will eventually take its toll, leaving her financially strained but stress free regarding him.

Lance Austin seeps into her thinking process; a man she was only partially lucky to have met online. He was a man preoccupied when they met about a year ago and he still is. A man that she wishes she didn't enjoy talking to so much from time to time but she does. He is a man that is obviously in love with his girlfriend.

"But ya *never* know . . ." she murmurs under her breath. Evangeline thinks about the times she has heard Lance complain to her about Melanie. She asks herself if the negative things she has heard outweigh the good or if it's merely her wishful thinking.

She thinks out loud, "Let me give Lance a call. I wanna hear some negative talk about his girl so I can get in where I fit in." Evangeline grabs her cell phone and calls him. When he answers, she has a thought.

Good he answered. Melanie's probably not there or else he wouldn't have answered.

After they trade pleasantries and Melanie's absence is confirmed, Evangeline decides to make her pitch and not wait for the negative comments about his girlfriend.

"When are you coming to Indianapolis Lance, so I can meet you in person?"

"Damn Evangeline, you say that in a tone that suggests I'm trying to avoid you or that I don't wanna meet you but I do."

"Well . . . maybe you do but what about Melanie?"

"What about her? We're friends, right?"

" . . . Yeah Lance, we're friends. But you seem like you're under lock and key when it comes to her. You're not allowed to have female friends or what?"

"Yeah I got female friends and no, I don't need her permission to have any." Lance *is* telling the truth but he *does* wonder why a situation has never occurred where Melanie was in a position to meet any of his female friends.

"I have heard you complain more than once about women on the internet trying to get it on with someone but with no pic. And here I am from day one with pictures and even more pictures when we started communicating and still no Lance!! When you first saw my picture, you told me you liked what you saw . . ."

"And I did . . . and I do. But the truth of the matter . . . I've been a little busier than usual where it concerns Melanie. She's pregnant . . . we're having a baby." Lance is ecstatic in general about the offerings of this revelation being second nature now.

"Oh Lance!!! Why are you breaking my heart like this; so soon when I haven't even given it to you yet!?"

"Given me what Evangeline . . . ?"

" . . . My heart silly!! What did ya think I was talking about . . . the *kitty kitty*??"

"There's no telling with you."

Evangeline giggles, "I thought you and I would eventually hook up and have a baby. You really do seem like you would be a good father."

"You're not happy about my news?"

"Oh Lance, you know I'm just playing with you, of course I'm happy for you . . . but I will admit it's hard to be . . . but I truly am though . . . and I *do* wish that you and I could have a baby one day."

"Wow, thank you on both counts. I don't know what to say . . ."

"Baby, we ain't 'F-ing . . . you ain't gotta say nothing."

"Girl you crazy . . . !"

"Yeah I am, *about you* . . . but whatever. So when are you coming out here boy!!?"

"Evangeline . . . I will meet you one day, I promise. But anytime soon is gonna be hard. Melanie and I are moving in together."

"Wow!! You are just full of surprises aren't you!!? You're saying a lot of *bad-good* stuff tonight!! I called to hear the *good-bad* stuff!!!"

"Huh . . . ?"

"Never mind boy!! Turn your computer on for a sec."

Lance turns on his computer and hooks up to their Instant Messaging link. They share recent photos of themselves, some of her pictures including her son. After ten or fifteen minutes, Evangeline sends Lance a strange photo that he can't quite make out at a glance.

"Girl, what the . . . ?"

"Now, you once told me that you eat the *kitty kitty*, right!?"

"Yeah, I do."

"Then you know what that is. So you're gonna turn that down and go move in with Margie . . . or whatever her name is!! You're gonna turn down the chance to be up in *that* and loving the woman it belongs to!!?"

Lance is astounded over the instant message picture of Evangeline's vagina, with two of her fingers spreading the lips open to reveal the not so attractive aspect of her insides. From an artistic point of view, he figures the picture would have been a little more tasteful, if her fingers were not hiding the lips and if she had not spread it open as wide as she did; but as is . . . not so.

Lance eventually gets off the phone with Evangeline so he can go downstairs where his three brothers are all together in one room. The time for his huge announcement has finally arrived and he eagerly awaits their response.

"Hey Brothers, what's up!" says Lance. Nathanael, Matthew, and Andrew; all given biblical names by their mother. Lance wonders where his name came from.

Nathenael exclaims, "Did you find that Kool & the Gang CD yet?"

"No Nate, not yet. Stop playing your video games for a second."

The three of them give him the look of the devil, especially Andrew the twenty-three year old; the youngest of Lance's four brothers. "Man I'm in the fourth stage!! Are you crazy!?" he asks.

"Yeah, but just a little. Stop playin' for a sec *And* . . . I got something important to say," Lance says.

"Man this better be good Brother!!" says Andrew.

"It is – Melanie is pregnant . . . we're having a baby."

Andrew drops the video game controller on the floor and gasps. Nathanael and Matthew gasp as well as they leap from their chairs.

"Oh my God Lance!!! Are you serious? Congratulations!!!" says Nathanael. Matthew is equally thrilled and congratulates his brother as well. Andrew smiles for the entire moment but doesn't say anything. He then goes into the backroom which is his, adjacent to Matthew's room. Lance follows him back there. When he looks into Andrew's eyes, they are teary.

"Man big brother, don't trip!! You know I'm really happy for ya man . . . it's just that – I miss Mom *so* much . . . and she won't even . . . she can't be here to witness this event; to share in this joy . . ." Lance walks towards his brother and grabs his hand very tightly; and for a while he doesn't let it go.

When Lance goes to the basement to tell his step dad, he is ecstatic as well but then the moment suddenly turns into "twenty questions" . . . the same kind of questions that Lance will be inflicting upon his child one day in the far away future.

When Melanie tells her dad, he is a lot more lighthearted within the parenting aspect of his concerns. Her dad is in his 70's, which usually warrants for him, the exuding of calmer reactions to most situations. Her sister Marcy, whom she told in front of Meredith to try and downplay the guilt she felt because Meredith already knew and Marcy didn't – didn't work out. Marcy could tell that Meredith already knew by her reaction. Melanie blames Lance.

"Why didn't Lance call me!?" Marcy exclaims.

"Because you told us to stop sending you email jokes – that's why!!" says Meredith, referring to how Lance found her email address.

"Wha . . . ?"

"And plus I'm the oldest anyway!!"

"Whatever Meredith; that's why you got more grays than me!!"

Lance calls his father and gives him the good news and it is received as such. Richard Austin, who lives in Joliet, Illinois is happy to hear from his son and is more than happy to have a new aspect of Lance's life that he can be a part of. Not so many years ago, Lance wouldn't have made a phone call to his dad at all, nor would his father bend over backwards to extend a phone call himself. Their relationship has hardly ever been that of a true father and son due to divorce over three decades ago, as well as other complicated issues. Their current open line of communication is pleasing to Lance because it feels more natural than it ever has before.

When Lance hangs up from his dad, he can't help but smile when he thinks about the fact that every woman his dad has married since his mom was Caucasian. His fourth and current wife Corinne is also Caucasian . . . and two years younger than Lance. He wonders if his dad is truly to blame for his lust involving women of different races. The method to his madness never being as transparent to people around him as they would like, is one thing Lance knows for sure he inherited from his father.

Sherry Anderson sits at her computer deleting emails, a common practice for many in today's society. When she gets to an email from Lance, she gets excited.

"Ooohh the song . . . !"

She opens the email and the song attachment. Norman, who is now officially her boyfriend, walks by her and stands over her shoulder.

"What are you 'ooohh'-ing about?"

"Norm, have you ever heard this song!!?"

"Of course I have. That's a recent classic! Where did you get it from?"

"My friend Lance emailed it to me. We heard an acoustic version of it a couple of weeks ago when we were out and neither one of us could figure out what it was, until now."

"Lance?? Who is Lance!!? Has he ever made a pass at you!?"

"Lance is a good friend of mine. He's cool – he knows all about you."

"Just because he knows all about me doesn't mean he won't make a pass atcha!!"

Sherry can hear jealousy in Norman's voice. She wishes she didn't volunteer as much information as she did but her honesty and her wholesome ways wouldn't have it any other way . . . but she *does* change the subject.

"Honey when are you going to take me to that Reggae club in Chicago?"

"Sherry, you know I got a lot of stress going on in my life right now!! This job isn't exactly panning out the way I hoped it would. How can you talk about us going to a club right now?"

"For the exact reason you just stated . . . *the stress.*"

"Why don'tcha have your lil' friend *Lance* take ya!" Norman walks away from her, lips pouted. Sherry ignores the intended display of jealousy in his statement and takes it literally. She emails Lance to thank him for the song *and* mentions the Reggae club to him as well, to see if he possibly would like to go.

Lance will see Sherry's email the next day. He will grin from ear to ear because no matter whom Sherry is with and no matter whom he's with . . . "Hopeless" is *their* song. He will do internet research about the Reggae club in the upcoming days . . . and in two weeks Lance and Sherry will be there.

When that day and time arrives, Lance is rushing as usual in trying to get somewhere on time. It is 10:30pm when Lance arrives at the Reggae club to meet Sherry, half an hour later than they agreed upon. He greets her with a kiss on her left cheek.

"Hey Sherry . . . ! I am so sorry I'm late – couldn't find a park."

"That's okay Lance. How are you? How is Melanie?"

"Fine on both counts . . ." Lance wonders why she asked about Melanie and so quickly. He attributes this to Melanie's condition and to Sherry's nature. He does a quick assessment of her appearance. Her hair is slightly curled and hanging down as if it *actually* took some time to make it so. Her face has just a little foundation on it, just enough for her naturally beautiful face. She has on a subtle color of lipstick and her clothes . . . though the shoes that are finally *not* sandals and her pants and top are the best Lance has seen her in yet; he still questions if the clothes are cheap or if it's the style she chooses that he doesn't quite like.

Lance reminds himself of the quality of the woman and decides to never again negatively judge her choice in clothing or appearance. "What are you drinking tonight Sherry?"

"I'll have a Cosmo."

"Mmmm, sounds good!" Lance wants the same but he purposely orders something different in hopes that her lipstick print and his lip balm print will wind up on each others' glasses. They do. When they order a second round and after that, a third drink for Lance, Sherry offers to pay for those and he accepts. Nothing turns him on more than a woman that sits back and expects to be treated as a lady in having the man pay the bill, then that same lady being woman enough to offer payment for that same gentleman from time to time.

Lance glances at three female patrons that are in the club with them. He finds one of them to be very attractive. Noticing females, particularly the ones he finds desirable, is just something that Lance does. A woman's beauty in his opinion is one of God's incredible gifts to overall existence, as some consider nature to be. *Look but don't touch* is Lance's rule when involved with someone exclusively as he is with Melanie. "Official" or not, Lance knows and so does Melanie, that *something* is still going on between them. They just won't say it out loud to one another.

His rule though, is something he considers breaking tonight – if for no other reason, to relieve some of the tension from the *exclusive* turmoil that more often than not describes the state of their current union in question. He decides at the last moment to not approach the beautiful young lady but not because of Melanie – *because of Sherry.* At one point when Sherry had gone to the bathroom, Lance contemplated making his move then. As he thought about it too long, he started to have a strange feeling of illicit guilt, as if he was sneaking to do something like a five year old.

As Lance sees her safely to her vehicle and twenty minutes later safely out the crowded parking lot, he thinks to himself, *if this evening wasn't a date, why did it feel like one??*

The months go by quickly for Lance and for Melanie. This is good for both of them; their reasons being the same on some counts and other reasons being from a slightly different perspective. They both can't wait for her to have the baby due to the ongoing occurrence of them getting on each others' nerves. Lance is simply anxious for his child to arrive into the world. He anticipates the hands on aspect will be the most exciting, while their experience together of Melanie's pregnancy is not as pleasant as he had hoped.

The anxious anticipation of the baby's arrival in Melanie's mind simply stems from the misery that she feels each and everyday. The changes in her body are weird for her and rapidly occurring to say the least. Unfortunately she almost dreads how Lance will act when the baby arrives; this coming from how she feels he acts now, which is not good.

When the sex of the baby was first revealed, they were told they were having a girl. A month later, the ultra-sound revealed a more obvious indicator of the baby being a boy. Lance was devastated for a couple of days about the error being made and the assumption being given rather than the facts. Then he realized that being disappointed about the sex of the child out in the open could be misconstrued as his level of happiness about their child in general, to be diminishing. This is simply not the case, so he lets it go.

Melanie is now in the latter stage of her second trimester. They were lucky enough to have found an apartment in a decent area with a decent landlord also, the last week in October. They moved into the apartment two weeks before Thanksgiving. Moving is no one's favorite pastime and Lance and Melanie are no exception to this rule. Two weeks ago they argued about a misunderstanding that he and their present landlord had, about *who* was to get back to whom and when. They argued about him not being able to get her items out of storage the night he had the rented moving truck because the four digit pass code she gave him to enter at the front gate didn't work. He felt that this was due to her storage fees being behind in payments; something she never admitted to but was actually so.

Lance and Melanie will argue the next two weekends in the future about him sneaking Priscilla the Siamese cat into their new apartment where no pets are allowed. The *b-side* to this argument will have Melanie questioning Lance as to why he is holding on to a cat that belongs to one of his ex-girlfriends.

They argue about everything all the time as if they hate each other. They don't – but neither one of them exercise any control over their reactions to the others' actions or words. Melanie often uses *the pregnancy card* to justify her erratic behavior as Lance sees it. He feels strongly that her "erratic" behavior existed long before she was ever pregnant. As usual he often feels that Melanie purposely tries to irritate him and it's a concept he can't quite wrap his finger around. Lance is beginning to wonder if Melanie even has any respect for him. They both had the illusions of hope that things would get better after they moved in together. Mistakenly these are thoughts that often find their way into the psyche of couples that partake in this endeavor or even the consideration of marriage.

Their first week in the new place together would find Melanie not occupying the living room area. There wasn't anything set up in that area yet to give her reason to do so. This gave Lance a chance to set up a surprise for her. He bought blue and beige ribbons, a giant card, and a big balloon that read*: It's A Baby Boy,* a teddy bear, candles and letters that he stuck on the room dividing panel near the ceiling. They spelled out*: "Thank You Mel My Dear for Carrying Our Child."* When Lance led her to the living room to show her this, the stir of emotions inside of her took over, causing her to burst into an excessive amount of tears. The stir of emotions inside of Lance led him to do this for her. If either one of them were to ever realize the potency of their emotional grandeur when negativity rears its ugly head . . . they would not argue nearly as much.

With the living room surprise fresh in Melanie's head four days prior to Thanksgiving, her thoughts about Lance are actually *still* positive when the day arrives. Their holiday for the most part is spent at Melanie's sister Marcy's house which is only three blocks away from their father's home. All of the food is very good and plentiful; so is the liquor down in the basement with Marcy, her husband and a few of the neighborhood friends. Melanie slips downstairs for a second to let Lance know she needs help carrying some of the food out to the car. She's helping her sister store some of it at their dad's house. She waves the smoke away as she enters, then she sees the cigarette in Lance's hand.

"I hope you won't be smoking around *my child* when I'm not around!!" Lance giggles and shakes his head indicating he won't. Melanie continues, "I've had enough of this food. Do you want me to make you a plate to take home?"

"Sure dear, give me the usual." The usual being everything except chitterlings. When Lance helps her load the car. He is already obnoxiously drunk. He tells her to drive on over to her dad's and to expect him in fifteen minutes to help her unload and put the food away. When Lance arrives two hours later and enters the screen door that Melanie left unlocked for him, she's asleep on her father's couch.

"Melanie!!" He shakes her, "Mel!!" She opens her eyes slowly. "Melanie – Mel dear, I'm sorry." Lance looks at the knotted plastic bag on the living room table with three paper plates of food, each plate different. His assumption is correct that it's his.

"Yeah, you're *a sorry* motherfucker is what you are . . . wit'cha drunk ass!! I didn't wanna sleep at my dad's tonight, but I was so tired from unloading all that food and putting it away . . . what am I doing wasting my time making you multiple plates for!!?"

You don't appreciate it!!"

"Would it have hurt for you to call me . . . ? Or like, maybe just wait!!? It ain't like the foo . . ." Lance belches. "It ain't like the food would perish in thirty degree weather!!"

"I'm pregnant Lance . . . or did you forget!!??"

"Yeah don't remind me!! And what does makin' me a couple of plates have to do with anything?? You offered!!! I didn't ask ya to *do* shit!! I could've done it!!" Lance grabs the bag, "I'm going home!! Come home when you act like you got some sense!!"

"I'll show you how much sense I have!!!" Melanie jumps up and grabs the side of the bag while Lance is still holding it. "You ain't taking this shit home since you don't care about it!!"

They fight over the bag. When Lance yanks it free from Melanie's grasp, she loses her balance and stumbles onto the coffee table, knocking a lamp over.

CHAPTER 8

"Was she hurt!!?" Angelica asks Lance via telephone.

"No she wasn't hurt. She was more embarrassed than anything."

"So what happened after that?"

"I helped her up, I stood the lamp back up, I grabbed my bag of food and left."

"You sound proud . . ."

"Angelica, I'm certainly not proud about what happened!!"

" . . . I mean *the food*."

"Are you analyzing me again!?"

"Yes I am."

"Well . . . okay yes. Beside from the situation, I am glad she didn't take my food. Look, I know I have issues with the dad I hardly ever knew when I was a child and being bullied and stuff. I'm a grown and a half ass man now!! I'll be damned if I let someone take something away from me . . . that belongs to me!! She gave it to me, *so* it belonged to me!!"

"Lance, your childhood issues . . . I'm not saying they're not legitimate . . . but you have to let that go right now. She's carrying your child!!!"

"Hey I already had the stupid bag in my hand!!"

"Well she obviously has childhood issues of her own – who doesn't? It seemed more important for her to *take* the bag from you, than it was for her to keep the bag – but that's not my point. My point *is* . . . anything concerning *you* right now is irrelevant. That child comes first no matter what!! Now I know you *know* this, but knowledge and incorporating what you know into your everyday life are two different things. You're certainly a lot better than you used to be; but now, especially during her pregnancy . . . you're gonna have to step it up a few notches, like right now!! In fact, probably more than that because she obviously has no self control and no line that she's afraid to cross. This has happened before, right?"

"Well, she has pushed me a couple of times, but I didn't think anything of it. Oh, let's not forget the pop she threw on me last year . . . you know, the 36oz. from the movie theater. That was kinda crazy."

"Yeah I remember you telling me about that. I thought that sorta thing only happened *in movies*. Well Lance, all I can say is that things will get better once the baby gets here. But *now* . . . I'm a little worried about now. She's getting physical with you . . . as in physical abuse. I know the machismo in you may not want to say that out loud, but that's what it is . . . and it could get worse!!"

"You think so huh?"

"I hope not!! But I have done studies on this. I know she's been through a lot the past couple of years but more than likely there is something else going on. I'm sure you're not the only person she's thrown a soda on. It sounds to me like she has unresolved emotional issues, probably from childhood. It could be anything . . . she could've been sexually violated, bullied like you were . . . and you know that's a little different for girls than it is for boys. Girls are all caught up in their looks and of course they're more emotional."

"Well, she always maintains that she was a tomboy when she was coming up! What possible female complications could she have had if *she* was bullied?"

Angelica chuckles, "Lance . . . Lance my good friend; your anger about the situation dictated what you said to me just now. Her being a tomboy strengthens what I'm saying even more. The tomboy status could've been a means to repress or overpower something unfortunate that happened to her as a child. I know tomboy status entails what a young girl was, or was *not* exposed to . . . that's part of it. But there are other aspects that cause a girl to be a tomboy as well. I don't know this woman . . . I'm just saying . . ."

"Yeah I know, and now that I think about it . . . I *am* upset all over again when I think about yesterday . . . what happened last night."

"That's understandable, but hey babe, I say this . . . *fix* what *you* need to fix, within *yourself.*" Angelica chuckles, "I'm just playin' with you, but you know what I mean. You know what I'm saying though. Fix *you*, 'cause in the end, that's the only thing you can change. You can't change her. You can only choose to deal with her, or not. At the end of the day, if you do better and she chooses not to, at least you can say . . ."

"Yeah I know . . . that I tried my best."

"Yeah . . ."

"Well ya know, I will say this. I know the drinking didn't help the situation . . . but it was a family gathering! It's not like I held a drinking session with my homies or something like that . . . but I did have *a few* too many."

"I'm gonna interrupt you now!! I am not going to sit here and let you make excuses for her!! The woman is pregnant!!! She has no business confronting you in *any* physical type of way!! She should be *more* cognizant than anyone else that she's carrying a child!! I'm only telling you to step your game up because she obviously seems like she will not take that into account!! It's a shame to say Lance but from what you're telling me . . ."

"Oh God help me!! Why is this so hard!!?" Lance blurts out emphatically.

"Lance, we both know that you enjoy drinking sometimes . . . and you're right, it doesn't help the situation any. It's funny though, 'cause even to this day it surprises me that your drinking has never seemed completely out of control . . . maybe a lil' nerve wrecking at times." Angelica giggles and then continues, "Drinking can be a vice that women would prefer *not* to have as an obstacle in their relationship but sometimes it simply is. But with you, I just don't see your drinking being a primary induction of the problem at hand."

"Thank you for saying that. I *have* always more-or-less felt the same way about myself . . . and yeah, I have had a moment or two . . . or *three*, but enough about all of that."

"Yeah, you're right. How are your brothers doing . . . and your step dad?"

"Okay I guess. Nate conveniently didn't help the day I was moving stuff outta there, while Matt & And were busting their behinds to help out . . . and you know I have a lot of stuff!! Kevin helped too. Mr. Foster was like whatever, 'Do whatcha gotta do' and that was that. I just . . . I dunno. I hope it's my imagination that Nate seems kinda' upset because I left."

"Don't be surprised if it isn't your imagination. That kind of thing happens with siblings more times than we all care to admit."

"Why is that – because I suddenly did something that seemed out of the norm?"

"Well, change is part of it. Some handle it worst than others . . . but it's also an unintended envy that occurs; you know because you have moved up so to speak. You have progressed in life and he hasn't just yet. I'm sure your brother doesn't love you any less if that's what's happening."

"Yeah I know. It's just funny, ya know?"

"Yeah, life *is*. In some ways, I still can't believe you're finally having a child!"

"I know, right? And it's funny 'cause I said to myself about three or four years ago . . . if it didn't happen by the time I reach forty, it probably wasn't gonna happen. I started praying to the good Lord to grant me the acceptance of never having kids."

"Well good things do happen in our lives. A lot of times we just don't know when, who, or how."

"I *miss* my mom *terribly*."

"I know how you feel Lance. I miss *my* mom too!!"

"I know you do. Don't you feel that void when you need to talk to someone, and a lot of times you want that person to be your mother . . . because she'll understand what you're going through, right or wrong?"

"Oh Lance . . . *don't* remind me."

"Well Angelica . . . I'm *so* glad that at least I have you to talk to. We've known each other a long time . . . and I'm glad we're friends!!"

"Lance, don't get all mushy on me, okay?"

As the days turn into weeks, the discomfort and misery that Lance and Melanie feel, turns into *walking on eggshells* with one another. As much as they both do not want to argue, they both can't seem to help it. Once one of them has mentally reached a certain measure of peace, the other disrupts it every time. Even when Lance tries to wait on Melanie hand and foot, it still never seems quite good enough for her. *Against all odds* is how he often feels when he strives for a perfect evening after work concerning her. He goes for it once again on a Monday evening as he creeps towards their bedroom doorway.

"Hey Mel, I'm gonna go and grab Kevin so we can watch this football game real quick, okay?"

Melanie looks up at Lance as she's lying in bed watching television. She doesn't answer him right away. While he patiently awaits her answer, he wonders why she very seldom smiles.

"*Yeah* Lance," she says to him reluctantly. He leaves the doorway quickly, knowing that she wanted to say *no*. He doesn't give her the chance to change her mind.

During the ten minute ride to his friend's house, Lance considers the fact that maybe he's being selfish by wanting to have company. Then he considers the flip side of the coin. The football game will last for about three and a half hours. His plans are to end the night immediately after that and take Kevin back home. Melanie was already in the bedroom and not in the living room where he wants to bring his company. Lance sees no disruption of her evening for these reasons. He also views himself as compromising with her by staying *in* to watch the game, rather than going out to do so. He figures he would've been watching the game in the living room anyway, regardless of Kevin being there or not.

Even after all of this in his reasoning, there is a main point that still remains; if the central reason of stress in his life wasn't Melanie right now, he wouldn't crave, need or want Kevin to even come by. Lance feels like he deserves a break . . . a quick break.

When Kevin gets in the Caddy, he immediately notices the somber mood that overwhelms his best friend, "Whasup dog! Damn man you straight?"

"Hoah boy . . . ! Melanie's trippin' a little bit but it's cool though."

"You sure, I don't wanna come by and end up in some mess!?"

"It's cool man." Lance ponders a thought. *Wow; I went from* 20% *down to zero with this girl! Where am I now on the percentage scale of realizing that Melanie and I ain't gonna work?? It sure as hell ain't zero, that's for sure!!* His true assessment is 60% but he knocks off twenty because of the baby being on the way. "Forty, shit!!" Lance exclaims out loud as he smacks the steering wheel while driving.

"Forty? Man what are you talking about? You wanna go get some beer? That's cool, we can do that!"

"Nah Kevin, I was just thinking about something. I got brew at the crib."

The atmosphere back at the apartment is constrained to say the least. Melanie's bad mood flows throughout the place like carbon monoxide. As Lance journeys to the kitchen for two beers, he hopes that she will stay in the bedroom, so at least the source of fermentation is contained to one room. When Lance goes to the kitchen a second time, he finds out that his run of luck would only last for twenty minutes.

"Melanie what are you doing?" he inquires as he sees her standing by the sink. "I told you I was gonna align those drawers with the cabinet liners tomorrow."

"You've been telling me that for two weeks now! I'm tired of waiting on you to do things around here!"

"How many times have I told you, that everything can't be done around here at once!? You want everything done on your time but you're not the only person involved in this situation of us moving in together!"

"I know I'm not, but I wish I was because you don't do shit except sit around witcha' homies and drink!!"

"You're exaggerating!! I don't drink everyday . . . and I haven't seen Kevin in weeks!!"

"I don't care *when* you saw Kevin last – I'm pregnant Lance!! You have no idea what this feels like each and everyday!! I don't wanna come home to you and your carousing in the next room . . . I need peace and quiet!!"

"If you need peace and quiet so bad, you should shut your big mouth!! You're the one always yelling and screaming and startin' shit!! And you make these constant demands . . . you're always telling me to jump and you expect me to say 'How high?' like I'm a child or something! I ain't your fuckin' son Melanie . . . your son is still inside your belly!!"

"No you're not a child but I'll tell you this . . . you're not a man either because a man would be doing everything in his power to comfort his woman, especially when she's carrying his child!!! *A man* would be in that second bedroom painting his son's walls blue and beige!! *A man* would be putting his son's mother's rocking chair together . . . oh I forgot, you didn't pick it up yet!!! You ain't nothing but a little punk!! All you wanna do is hang out just like a lil' punk!!"

"You with your, 'Run the speaker wire to your stereo equipment along the walls and ceiling so it's not all in the floor Lance' which I did! 'Straighten up the storage area in the back Lance' which I did!! 'Get this ridiculous CD and DVD collection in order Lance' which I have started doing . . . and if you had any idea of what it consist of to do so, you wouldn't think it should've been finished by now!!! You act like I don't do shit! I work hard everyday just like you do!! Oh and by the way you forgot something else . . . you ain't *my* 'woman', remember!?"

Melanie rips one of the empty kitchen drawers out of its slotted opening and throws it at Lance. It grazes him on his shin only because he quickly reacted when it was coming his way.

"Thanks for reminding me, you little punk . . . !! I'm glad I'm not your woman because you're not a man!! Be a man Lance!! B-A-M!!! **Be A M**an!!!"

"Have you lost your fucking mind Melanie!!?? Why are you throwing shit at me!? *Aren't you pregnant*!!?"

"B-A-M Mr. Austin!!! BAM-BAM-BAM!!!!" Lance grabs four beers from the refrigerator and he grabs the two he left on the table five minutes before. "Oh yeah, *don't f*orget the all mighty, all important liquor for you and ya lil' bitch!!" Melanie says vehemently as Lance scurries out the kitchen.

Kevin has a nonplussed look on his face as he hears his best friend's footsteps approaching. Lance almost falls as he enters the living room from walking so fast.

"Hey Kevin, grab three of these beers before I drop 'em and let's go!!"

"Damn Lance, you want me to turn this TV off?"

"Forget da TV dog, let's go!!! And grab my keys too so I don't wind up standing outside for hours, begging her crazy ass to let me in later!!"

When they get out to the car, they both shake their heads in disbelief. "Man dog, what is wrong with her!!? I know she's pregnant and all . . . but damn!!"

"And you know what's so funny about all of this? She keeps playing that pregnancy card . . . she didn't like it when you and I would kick it *before* we moved in together because I wouldn't talk on the phone with her as long!! Is it not rude to sit on the phone with someone . . . *anyone* for a long period of time when ya got company?"

"I don't mean to talk about'cha girl or nuthin' . . ."

"She *ain't* my girl Kevin . . ."

"You know what I mean . . . but anyway, she sounds like a spoiled brat!! Man I just didn't know *what* to do when I was hearing all of that commotion. I wanted to jump up and go back there and stop it, but I was frozen in my seat!!"

"Yeah, I wish I would've just stayed frozen in mine . . ." Lance says this jokingly, knowing that the ugly monster of a situation was brewing all along and would've *reared its ugly head* in one way or another.

"Ya'll still fuckin'?" Kevin asks.

"I don't see *how*, but hell yeah!! You know a nigga ain't turning down no pregnant pussy!!"

"Yeah *I know*, right!"

They sit out in the car for an hour and a half to drink their beers. After that, Lance drops Kevin off and comes back home at 9:30pm. When he walks in, Melanie is in the living room on the phone with Nina. As she talks to her, Melanie tries to instigate another argument by purposely talking about Lance out loud. It infuriates him but he ignores it and decides to just go to bed for the night. Melanie follows him into their bedroom while still on the phone. Once Lance is out of his clothes, he grabs a blanket from the closet and goes into the living room. He angrily turns the TV off and heads to the couch. Melanie follows him again like a two year old follows their parent. She turns the TV back on.

"What is *wrong* with you?" Lance murmurs as he goes *back* to the bedroom. He tries his best not to show her that he's getting increasingly irritated. The thought in his head, *if she comes in here one more time, that'll be the last straw!!*

Melanie enters and she's still on the phone, "Can you believe this Nina girl!!? He's actually trying to go to bed now, after he has ruined my entire evening!!"

Lance had hoped she didn't realize he was actually turning in for the evening but deep down he knew she did. "Melanie please, I have to work in the morning. I have a hard enough time going to bed and getting up as it is!!"

"I have to work in the morning too!!" From her side of the bed against the wall, she leans over towards Lance's ear, "Ya should've thought about that *before* you came in here witcha' lil' friend disturbing me."

"Melanie, get outta my face . . ."

She remains in the same spot still talking to Nina, "Girl can you believe this!!?"

"Melanie – get - out - of - my - face . . . !"

"Yeah I know girl. I can't believe this so-called man is about to be a father . . . a punk disguised in men's clothing . . ."

Lance quickly turns to face her with his open hand extending towards her face. He covers her face with his hand and pushes her away from him. "I told you to get da *fuck* out of my face!!!"

"Girl dis nigga din went crazy!! Lemecallyouback!!" Melanie disconnects her call. "I'm calling the police!!"

"How you gon call the police and you're throwing kitchen cabinets at me and shit!!?" Melanie dials *911*. Simultaneously Lance snatches the phone from her, disconnects the attempted call and gets out of bed to slam it on the table. "Look Melanie, I'm not about to go through this garbage with you. You're not justified in pulling this little stunt of following me around the house when *you know* I'm trying to go sleep. I never even brought Kevin to a room that you were in. Now would you *please* leave the room if you're not ready to go to bed?"

"How did you know I didn't wanna occupy the living room earlier? I'm not going anywhere, I live here too!! Let me call my girl back."

"Would you please not do that in here??"

Melanie gets out of bed to get her phone from the table that is temporarily in the room until they get a bedroom dresser and chest; something else she's been constantly inquiring Lance about. He thinks about grabbing it from her, until he envisions what happened on Thanksgiving Day. She lies back in bed against the wall.

"Melanie would you please go in the other room to make your call . . . ?"

"Fuck you Lance!!!"

The constant taunting sends Lance into a whirlwind of a flashback – the times when he was bullied in school. "'Fuck me'!? I'll show you 'Fuck me'!!" Lance grabs the mattress with both hands and literally snatches it from under Melanie while she's still lying on it, depositing her onto the box spring. He then pulls it all the way up and towards him and slams it against the wall, leaving a *45* degree angled space where she still lies. In Lance's mind, he wanted to slam it down flat on top of her – but his compunction remains somewhat in tact. As his furious moment of action is suddenly frozen in his memory bank, he lays the mattress flat again beside her and helps her back onto it.

"I'm sorry Melanie. I'm sorry!! I could've hurt you or the baby!!" Lance calmly tries to reason with her, not because he particularly wants to make-up with her . . . but because he fears what she may do to him in retaliation while he's asleep.

In between all the arguing and fighting with the obviously unhappy couple . . . or expecting parents, somehow the baby shower is planned for January 2008, a month or so before the baby is due. Even the shower eventually becomes a subject matter of arguments for them. Melanie feels that Lance made a comment about it that shows he's unappreciative of her sisters' efforts in putting it together. Lance simply shakes his head in a cavalier manner about that notion. He is more focused and truly haunted by his own actions a little over a week ago with the mattress.

He keeps hearing an echoed rendition of Angelica's words of wisdom and more importantly, words that are indicative of what a *true* friend should say . . . and would say. Lance hears his mother's voice in his head and she is appalled by his participation in their physical altercations, especially the ones in which Melanie is pregnant. He imagines sitting in a chair next to his mom's bedside; her laying there watching TV, not feeling as healthy as she would like. He questions himself about whether or not he would have divulged every single detail about what happened nine days ago. He scoffs in disbelief that he would even ask himself that question.

Of course I would've told her everything!!! What am I thinking!?

Lance's definition of a liar is one that lies more often than not in any given situation, usually for their own selfish benefit. He knows that withholding certain details about a situation is *technically* not lying, but pretending that some things simply did not occur. To Lance, this is a form of denial about one's self or whomever the story teller is trying to protect so to speak. Whatever one wants to call it, Lance has never been that way.

I would've told her I pulled that mattress out from under Melanie's butt . . . and she would've snapped!! I'm not proud of what I did but it probably would've come out of my mouth like I was. She would have silenced me . . . told me to get up and close her door so she could say something to me in private. It wouldn't have mattered though because she would've been so mad at me, that my brothers would've heard it anyway, through the door.

She would've said, "Lance!!! You know that I know about the chip on your shoulder that you've had for most of your life . . . and I take partial blame for that* *because I'm your mother! But this physical abuse towards women, the one you're with now; she's carrying your child!!! Son, I don't care what this woman has said to you or done to you!!! Your behavior is inexcusable!!! You're acting like the idiot I didn't raise!!! You know I don't curse Lance . . . but you need to get your shit together now . . . and get ready to be a father!!!"*

Lance slightly jerks as the words he imagines his mother would have spoken, sends a chill through his spine. He looks around the office to see if anyone has noticed his ascendant state of being spaced out. When he assumes no one has, he continues his thoughts.

It's funny how everyone that ever knew my mother, considered her to be so meek and so humble; and she was. But every blue moon she would snap on me like nobody's business . . . and I always hated those few moments 'cause I didn't understand it till now. Considering the few things I know about my mom in her younger life, considering all the trials and tribulations she went through in trying to be right and being denied . . . or doing wrong herself and trying to grow and do better; it's no wonder that she would lose her scruples with me if I had reminded her of a time when she was trying to grow or reminded her of those times when she was a victim of that lack of growth in a man. As a good parent . . . I guess it can't be helped at times. I don't think my mom was ever physically abused by anyone before, but I know she knows what it feels like to be with a no good man. She had to grow as a woman to the point of realizing, understanding, and applying that knowledge in finding the type of man she needed to have in her life, especially when I came along. Now here I am forty plus years later, almost twenty years her senior when she first had me . . . and I haven't figured this out yet!!? What am I doing!!? It's bad enough she won't be here to . . .

Lance's tears start to bubble over in his eyes like a boiling pot of water on the stove. One of his contact lenses falls from his eye. At this very moment he realizes . . . that he should no longer put his hands on Melanie or even initiate any physical wrong doing towards her. Lance realizes at this very moment, that he *will not* put his hands on Melanie anymore, nor will he initiate any physical wrong doing towards her.

Two days later on the last Friday before Christmas, Lance receives a distressed phone call from Melanie. She frantically explains to him that she's been in a minor car accident. Her car hydroplaned on a puddle of water, causing her car to swerve out of control. Luckily her car didn't hit anything or anyone. She's just worried that something may have dislodged from either one of the front wheels of her vehicle.

"Mel, are you okay!!?" Lance frantically asks.

"Yes I'm okay. Just gimme a call back . . . let me see what time it is now . . . almost two o'clock . . . call me back at four and I'll let ya know what's going on. I wanna get my car checked out."

"Okay Mel, I'll do that."

At four Lance doesn't call because his job is unbelievably busy and stressful. At 4:30pm he's walking to the train station down Van Buren where other trains up above constantly roar by, making it impossible to hear anyone over a cell phone. So he calls at 4:45 when he's on his train as it's pulling off. He gets her voicemail and he leaves a message. He tries two more times before he gets off the train and still no answer, so he simply hangs up both times. At 5:45 Lance pulls up in front of their apartment, hoping she's there but she's not. He calls her again; no answer and again he doesn't leave a message on her voicemail. God forbid but his mind starts to wander into the mystery and the anticipation of whom he may wind up dating in the near future. He calls Sonja Smith, who according to Lance is the originator of his internet dating endeavor gone mad.

"Hi Sonja, how are you?"

"I'm fine dear. What did *Melanie* do to you now?" Lance is taken aback to how she greets him and then suddenly he realizes he shouldn't be. His friends and even his acquaintances have grown accustomed to that certain tone in his voice when it regards Melanie and their problems. Their conversation is a lot shorter than Lance had originally anticipated.

Sonja expresses to him in a wavering type of way, "Lance my dear . . . I don't know what to tell you about this girl and I'm female myself. Men and women, you know we all have our ways . . . but damn!! She's still new to you, she's still current! Make her old-old . . . make her the past!! I know you guys are expecting but it certainly won't be the first time a child is raised single parent style. When I say that mind you, I mean the both of you . . . 'cause from what I can tell . . . I wish you were *my* baby's daddy!!"

With that comment in mind, Lance *is* slightly flattered . . . but not enough to want to call her again when he wonders who his next dating prospect will be. He goes into the apartment, turns the TV on and lies on the recently purchased living room couch that he thinks is *ugly as hell!* He briefly thinks about *that* argument; the furniture that he wouldn't help purchase fast enough for her – so she went and got it on her own.

Lance lies there for over two hours before he hears the unfortunate sound of a key going inside of their door lock. He hates that he feels that way . . . *but he feels that way.* When Melanie enters, she hears Lance talking on the phone, so she goes into the bedroom. Ten minutes pass by before he gets off the phone. What had originally seemed like an urgent situation concerning Melanie turned into a nonchalant event for Lance because she never returned any of his phone calls. When she enters the living room, all seems calm at first.

"Melanie are you okay?" he asks, half concerned and half angry.

"You don't give a fuck about me!!!" she snaps back, *more* than half angry. "You're just lying there chillin' like nothing happened today!!"

"Mel, I didn't call you at four 'cause I was busy as hell at work today . . . but I called you a total of four times – and I left you a message!!"

"I never got your message!! I'm out there in that bullshit . . . I have an accident in my car and you don't care!!" Melanie walks toward Lance as he continues to lie there, uninspired by her mindless entrance.

"Slow down on those expressway entrances . . ." he murmurs.

Melanie immediately punches Lance on the temple area of his forehead, remaining true to how their physical altercations begin – with that last enduring comment that *the other* cannot stand.

Lance surges forward like a wild bull going towards a matador with a red cape; his chest makes direct impact with hers . . . instead of her stomach where their child rests. The momentum of his sudden football like hit sends them both crashing right into his 55" projection screen TV, disabling it and obviously wrecking it for life. The few pieces of the television screen and inner mirror components of the device crack and disintegrate into hundreds of pieces beneath her head as they finally hit the floor. Despite the loss of his 55" toy, Lance is euphoric in his psychotic yet ultimate display of his *bitch fuck you once and for all* stance!!

This figment of his imagination lasts for about three seconds, as one's life flashes before them in the unfortunate moment of death. His feigning moment is tainted and it is scary to Lance because he saw the reaction in his mind as clearly as a third person in the room. When Lance's mental state thaws, he is still lying on the couch. His left hand is on their land line. Though he doesn't recall even putting it there, he knows why it's there – to save three lives on this night.

When the police arrive at their apartment, there is uneasiness that best depicts the moment. Lance is mostly embarrassed in being the one that made the call. He is also embarrassed for *Melanie* being a pregnant woman with an anger problem. Her apparent lack of remorse is appalling to him. Lance speaks to one officer in the living room while Melanie is in the dining room with *two* officers. Lance wonders why he didn't get two. When he glances down the hall at her, he can see only half of her image with the wall cutting off his full view of her. Melanie is seated and her hair is hanging down with the appearance of it being wet from the gel she had put in it earlier. She looks like a boxer in between rounds to him. Lance keeps hearing her say to them,

"Yeah I hit him . . ."

The fact that Melanie knows all of the officers because her father is a retired police officer, doesn't help Lance's situation any. However, his intent was never to have her arrested. He just wanted to diffuse the situation and show her in *this way* that the physically violent aspect of their relationship has to stop. When the officers leave, Lance leaves right behind them without saying a word to Melanie. He figures that she probably thinks he's going to get another drink.

As much as he would like to, he doesn't. He pulls off in his car and parks two blocks away because he's truly too nervous to drive. Lance calls Sherry. He needs her verbal comfort right now, so he tells her about what just occurred. He gets a certain level of comfort but also a little more than he bargained for.

"Lance, I'm sorry but I'm not coming to your baby shower . . . I don't want to meet her!"

"Oh Sherry no – don't say that!!"

"I can't be around a woman like that, you know? I shouldn't put myself in that type of situation. I don't know what that woman is capable of. I'll still get your little man a gift though."

Lance appreciates her concerns coming from a foundation of femininity but he wishes Sherry had *just a little bit* of moxie – the stuff that makes a female want to flaunt from time to time. He now fears that he has told Sherry too much about Melanie and in too little an amount of time. With their new found friendship only having a life of less than six months, Lance has unintentionally cast a certain level of fear and doubt in her heart and in her mind about his situation. When he goes back home twenty minutes later, he feels worse than he did when he left.

CHAPTER 9

Lance and Melanie's Christmas is pleasant in appearance. Even the gifts they exchange are nice. The holiday spirit in their hearts though, reeks of elephant manure. Their New Year's Eve is completely forgettable because she can't drink wine, so he doesn't either. They stay in to experience New York City again, but this time through the television. On New Year's Day most of her immediate family comes by for a nice food spread and some holiday cheer. Lance *actually* enjoys her family because they are simply nice people. He really enjoys being around Melanie's middle sister Marcy. She is crazy in a hilarious kind of way and her drinking habits that are similar to Lance's, certainly doesn't hurt.

He enjoys Melanie's father a lot too because he is very humble, very considerate, and quite sociable. He tells stories about the ol' days a lot and Lance enjoys that. Her father's mannerism reminds Lance of Melanie's ways *in the beginning*. Then after a quick reassessment of that thought, he realizes deep down that even now she is still that way . . . when they're not arguing and fighting. He had always labeled her as the sweetest person he has ever known. It's very hard for Lance to still consider her as such, but he does. He knows he's certainly no angel but he also knows that Melanie's problem is her anger. It controls *her* instead of the other way around.

If only she would read that anger book I've been reading . . . the same book I need to finish my damn self!!

He quickly lets the thought go so he can just take in the more than decent day that is happening right now. His thoughts turn to *why* his brothers and his step dad are not here with them. Mr. Foster simply *is* and will *always be* "Mr. Foster." Lance doesn't particularly care too much about *his* reasons for not being around – it's his brothers, specifically the three brothers he lived in the same house with all his life that bothers him the most.

The lack of willingness to often participate in family oriented gatherings outside the immediate family was something that Lance's mother was all too familiar with. Any intimate family congregations never extended past her own mother on a regular basis. Lance recalls those once a week visits to his grandmother's house many years ago when they both were still alive. Neither one of them were particularly close to their own siblings. Lance's mother stopped seeing her own brother in the 70's when he and his family joined some kind of religious cult. Lance wonders if he and his brothers are cursed with this family flaw that has been going on for generations. If so, it will be that much harder to get them to come around Melanie's family in the near future, not to mention Lance himself.

He shakes his head while he's thinking. *Nah!! Surely an innocent little baby boy can change all of that . . . or at least put a dent in it!*

Nathanael's absence on this day is more of a nonchalant lack of interest than anything else. He *does* socialize with many different crowds, when he feels like it. Matthew and Andrew on the other hand could be considered to be socially deficient. Shyness usually looms on the forefront of their excuses for not being around, but it's *more* than that. They don't work – they don't drive – they don't date. Their high school diplomas were obtained through home schooling for the latter part of those years. Matthew and Andrew basically have *no experience* in socializing in society. Basically they don't know any better.

All of this weighs heavily on Lance's mind with a son on the way. As he tries to concentrate once again on the current day at hand, he can't help but ask himself one question over and over again.

Is there anything I can say or do to change this if it continues after my son is born or will my son's birth be the injection needed to diversify all of this??

As the New Year's Day gathering draws near an end, Meredith and Marcy's husbands, Mr. Strong, and Lance all pose for a picture together on Lance's new digital camera. After the picture snaps automatically, Lance walks over to the camera which is set up on a tripod, to see how it came out. When he views it on the display screen, he can't help but smile because *soon* he will have in common what the other three men in the picture already do; they are all fathers.

When all of their company leaves, Lance dreads what will happen next. Usually Melanie will initiate a verbal analysis of what Lance *said* wrong or *did* wrong in front of her family members . . . which of course always turns into an argument. To Lance's surprise, he gets the alternative,

"Lance, I really had a nice time today with you and my family – thanks!!"

They pose for three pictures, one in which Lance stoops down and puts his right hand on Melanie's stomach while it is elongated towards his profile. When he checks the picture, they are *both* smiling. This leaves a glimmer of hope for the future in the both of them. In the back of Melanie's mind though, she wonders when she will have to pay the price for a day in which Lance did nothing wrong to leave her perturbed. In Lance's mind, he wonders how high the price will be in the near future for Melanie's rare offering of positive encouragement where he is concerned.

The eight unit apartment where Lance and Melanie live with the established rule of no pets being allowed doesn't bode too well for Lance or Priscilla the Siamese cat. Matthew and Andrew aren't taking care of her properly, even though they said they would. When Lance stops by his old place to check on his cat, he discovers the food in her bowl to be hard as a rock, not having been changed in days. This sends Lance into a frenzy . . . not because they're not caring for the cat but because they *said* they would and are doing the opposite. After Lance yells at his brothers at the top of his lungs about this and leaves, he realizes that he is going to have to give the cat up.

Lance had touched basis with his ex about the cat a couple of weeks ago regarding a medical bill from a recent vet visit. While she didn't mind *that,* she did mind his criticism of her regarding why she cannot care for the cat. They argued over the phone that day . . . and they argue again on this day when Lance contacts her to tell her he has to get rid of the cat. When he goes to the Animal Humane Society facility located on Southwest Highway to drop Priscilla off, he finds the task at hand to be more difficult than he thought. As the clerk hands Lance the receipt, he takes one last look at the cage the cat is in and he's glad that the cage's opening is not facing him so Priscilla can't see him.

When he gets back in the car, he starts to cry. *Wow,* Lance thinks to himself, *I can't believe I'm sitting here crying over a silly cat!! I* did *live alone with that cat for five or six years . . . but still! Wow! I thought only white people felt this strongly about their pets.*

Lance compares the bond that he surprisingly developed over the years with his cat to the bond *he knows* he will share with his son. He wonders if his tears are for *that* reason, or if it's something else.

January 19, 2008 is the date of the baby shower. It turns out to be a wonderful winter day celebrating a new life coming into the world. A lot of peoples' opinions about the event is that of perfection. The planning of it was excellent, the food is very good, the turn out is great and the gifts are excessive. Lance calls a mental strike *#1* for his step father and his three brothers for not showing up. His stepbrother Warren, Jr. *did* show however. Mr. Foster had the audacity to lie about his starting time at work for that day, saying it was two o'clock. He thought he had cleared himself from stopping by briefly before work until Lance told him the event started at noon. His step dad then stuttered something about not wanting to show up in his police officer uniform.

Lance did call and invite the big mouth cousin of the family, her phone number being the only one he could find since moving. He asked her to tell her parents and the rest of the family that lives in Illinois about the shower. Most of them live about two hours away. Only the big mouth cousin shows up, without her parents; her dad being the brother of Lance's dead grandmother. Sherry holds true to her word and doesn't show. Even a couple of other close friends surprise Lance by not showing. The female offered her excuse the day of, not really being ecstatic about meeting Melanie. The male simply didn't care about the shower; another nonchalant male attitude – and he didn't want to buy a gift.

"He never bought our children anything!!" he said to his wife one day recently; the children that Lance was never told about until years after the fact.

Angelica shows up but sits outside in a taxi when she calls Lance to let him know she's there. When he goes outside with no coat on, he is shivering as he slightly bends down to look into the cab's backseat.

"Hey pretty lady! When are you gonna learn how to drive?"

"*Hhmmpp*! Anyway . . . happy babyday!!" Angelica hands Lance an envelope.

"Are you sure you won't come in for a moment?"

"Nah, I really have to be somewhere, like right now. You know I will talk to you soon though."

"Okay and thank you sweetie!"

"You're welcome."

Lance watches the taxi pull off. He no longer shivers as he shakes his head negatively, knowing that Angelica will reveal to him soon enough her *real* reasons for not coming inside. Those reasons are similar to Sherry's but slightly different in a feminine type of way.

As the festivities start to wind down, Lance gets a chance to talk with Kevin for a few moments.

"Wassup Dog!!"

"Wassup . . . ! You da man . . . !" Kevin says. "Looks like a really nice turn out . . . and all those gifts! How ya'll gon get all that stuff home man!?"

"We got about three or four cars and a couple of SUV's going our way luckily. Say dude come here. You see that guy over there talking to Melanie . . . the one in the black furry hat?"

"The one lookin' like he's R & B's hottest singing sensation?"

Lance chuckles, "Yeah him. Look how he's looking at her while he's talking . . . probably about nothing. When he first came in, I noticed how he was looking at her . . . like he wanted to eat her pussy right then and there while we were sittin' up there opening the gifts!! I'm thinking to myself, *who is* this *mothafucka*!!? I think something's going on with that!"

"It might be – sheee-iitt! The way ya'll argue . . . if somebody else hasn't *hit it* yet, they *will* after she drops that load. I know *you* gotta be working on something else on the side by now . . . with her throwing kitchen drawers and knives at'cha!!"

Lance smiles at Kevin's exaggeration of that particular incident. "I've been out to lunch with a couple of beautiful prospects, but I ain't trying to have nothing jump off right now with Baby Boy on the way. Plus you know I learned some years ago that playing on your girlfriend is the *easy* solution to relationship problems. The more *difficult* path in actually trying to work it out is usually the way to go *if* ya still care about her.

Ultimately in the end if it doesn't work out . . . *then* I'll officially move on."

"I thought you two *weren't* going together anymore."

"Well, we're not . . . but there is a certain level of tact I'm trying to have here. I mean, we are about to have a baby together."

"The way she's acting, it's unwarranted. Forget dat! Say, who is ol' girl with her titties hangin' out?"

"Oh, that's Melanie's co-worker Shanna and yeah you're right . . . that's not cleavage hanging out, those are titties!! Man, I would *hit that*!!"

"Sheee-iitt . . . not if I *hit it* first . . . ! *You* got a baby on the way, remember!?"

"Man Kevin, did I tell you what happened Thursday with ol' girl I met on the train about two months ago?"

"The one you had the *$20.00* lunch with?"

"Yeah her . . . Well we went to lunch again last week . . . *$18.00* this time around."

"Oooohh, big difference . . . !"

"Anyway, next thing I know, this woman was cussin' me out on the train Thursday morning! Turns out she has a boyfriend and I think someone that Melanie knows, told *her* guy that we were socializing. It *had* to be someone on the train 'cause Melanie mentioned some shit to me yesterday about her . . . by name! Whoever spoke to Melanie, *had* to witness whatever they told her!"

"She cussed you out!? Was she loud?"

"Nah, she did it low key if you can believe that. She said to me that I was trying to mess her thang up with her guy. I was just being nice to her. I never came to her like that!"

"C'mon Lance! These women know that when we're being nice to them over and over again, we're trying to get in those panties!"

"Okay, I'll give you that, but give me this: a woman needs to actually hear a man declare some type of courtship or interest in order for it to become official."

"Yeah, in *some* cases . . ."

"Man I ain't talkin' about the *quick fix* woman that gives it up like rain in Seattle . . . I'm talking about a *real woman* . . . a woman with some class. Yeah I flirted with her a little bit, but she was acting like a silly high school girl . . . she was flirting back!! She was trying to reel me in slowly . . . get *something* from me, till she got caught!!"

"Man that's crazy!"

"Man I forgot where I am! Let me start loading some of this stuff in the car. Are you coming by her sister Marcy's for the *after* shower?"

"Yeah that sounds like a plan. How is her sister?"

"Crazy and cool . . . you'll like her!"

Even Lance's father and Corinne, his "millennium mom" whom he refers to his dad's wife as, come to Marcy's house. Lance gets good and drunk in celebrating the new life that is due in this world about a month from now.

When the late night transitions to early morning, Lance stumbles through the front door of their apartment behind Melanie. With another gleeful day in the books, Lance wonders if he can knock 10% off the forty. As much as the alcohol in his system tells him to do so, he decides to wait until he's sober. He also wants Melanie to earn her merits on his self made internal percentage scale on her own without her family's presence.

Melanie sits at her computer at work. She stares at the screen as if she's hoping the cursor will start to scroll solutions to all of her problems; to provide insightful input to her doubtful thoughts and her repetitive questions. Her January doctor visit revealed that certain medical complications would require her to have a Cesarean Section. It is scheduled on the 25th of February at five o'clock. Melanie is scared to death! She has expressed this to Lance but not in detail. She feels that it would make her seem vulnerable and Melanie does not succumb to any emotions involving weakness; at least not in front of anyone. The pretty picture she paints of her life is comparable to a teenaged boy that stuffs everything in his closet to make his room look clean.

Melanie thinks about an incident that occurred with Lance three days after the baby shower. She had wrestled him to the living room floor after one of his sarcastic rebuttals as to why he hadn't cleared the living room of all the gifts yet. Lance let his body go limp when she did this, so he wouldn't hurt her or the baby. 20% was added to the forty right after that. She doesn't know why Lance is able to get to her the way he does. She told him in the beginning after their first argument,

"Just don't make me angry, *especially* on purpose!" Melanie is fully aware of the rage inside of her and what it's capable of; but she blames the source of her feelings instead of blaming the source of her actions. She pulls up her email and starts to type,

Some Things To Think About is the subject matter of her thoughts. Lance is constantly telling her that he doesn't have time to call her like he use to or he can't always answer her emails right away. Melanie thinks he's exaggerating but he's not; though another reason *is* the obvious dwindling state of their union in question. Certain issues that she brings up in her electronic letter will have Lance wondering why she's *still* talking about things that happened weeks ago. What Lance often forgets about women – when they bring up the past in an argument, this is caused by their emotions.

Melanie types,

I know we didn't agree to this, but I have been trying to get our relationship back to an official status . . . I hope you have been attempting the same. When we moved in together, it put my feelings about you on a different level.

Melanie then goes into the intimate area of their unofficial relationship and how the sex has tapered off as of late.

How do you think it makes me feel to find a sex tape in the VCR and know that you've been jacking off to it instead of making love to me.

The feminine part of her along with being pregnant, yearns for much more attention than usual; the compliments, wanting to be touched, wanting to feel desired, needing to feel adored by Lance – all seems to be in a state that is lacking fulfillment. She mentions subtle changes she has noticed in him, as if he is preoccupied with something else, or s*omeone* else. Melanie reveals in her email that she had assumed things would go back to the way they were before, a pattern that had developed from them going back and forth so many times in the past.

I still love you Lance and I really do want things to work out between us, especially now with our son on the way.

She expresses graciousness in the event of Lance *not* wanting things to work out between them. When Lance receives the email and opens it, he prints it. It is three and a half pages! He knows he cannot possibly address her feelings at work, so he types a quick reply.

Melanie, we'll talk about this later.

After he reads the email, he can't help but notice that *not one time* does she say *I'm sorry.* This makes Lance think that she thinks she's justified in her physically abusive actions. This makes Lance think that she doesn't care about his feelings but only her own. This makes Lance feel like she doesn't respect him as a person or more importantly, as a man. The worst feeling *of all* for Lance is that her physical expressions of anger seem more important than their son, the child she is carrying inside of her. He wants to accept Melanie's so-called *pregnancy card*, put it in his wallet and consider it valid – but he cannot. Unfortunately, the strong, negative thoughts and feelings that exist in Lance now have existed in him *long* before Melanie was ever pregnant.

Lance knows it wouldn't have hurt to compliment her more than he has over the months. He also knows that lying next to her at night and not touching her lately has never had anything to do with him finding her hideous because she's pregnant – something that she implied in her email. Lance told Melanie two years ago that he *adores* the concept of a pregnant woman. Months ago, he thought his efforts of a higher level of intimacy, mentally and physically towards her, reflected this. He cherished those love making moments with her, more so than he ever had before – *because* she is carrying his child. From what Lance has read in her email though, it obviously wasn't enough. In Lance's mind, he's afraid *it never is*. He adds 10% to the sixty, then out of pure arrogance adds another 5% so that his internal scale tips at an even three quarters.

Throughout the rest of the day, Lance tries to find the words he will say to Melanie when he gets home. When he arrives, he gives her this explanation,

"I still love you too Mel, but as much as I would like for the '*us*' thing to work out, I just don't see it happening." Lance then proceeds to soften the blow, "We still have ten more months on our lease and I don't know what's gonna happen in the future. Maybe that door of possibilities will open again. That's just how I see things at this very moment."

Without paying any attention to Melanie's immediate reaction, Lance's mind suddenly drifts back to the Friday evening before Christmas. For two days after that, Lance could barely chew anything he ate. She had punched him directly on the nerve of his temple, the nerve you feel when you grit your back teeth. Lance adds five more to the 75%.

There is an obvious nervousness in the air the night before the expecting parents are due in the hospital for their son's arrival. Lance and Melanie lie in bed in the dark, both with their eyes wide open. Melanie exhales an occasional grunt from an excruciating pain in her side. The baby is ready to join them in this world and they are anxious to see him as well. Lance lightly touches her stomach. He whispers,

"You're hurting Mommy lil' boy. Go to sleep." He rubs Melanie's side where the baby is kicking.

"That doesn't really help," she says to Lance.

He doesn't respond. He feels flustered when he thinks about their discussion over a week ago, the part about his recent lack of sexual desire for her. Lance is not bothered by the fact that their sex went cold because of her anger and her physical abuse. He is bothered because it was *him*, the male in their situation that initiated the sexual cold shoulder; something the female usually does in a situation like theirs.

Lance begins to slide his hand down her pajama pants. Despite his male ego, he still deeply cares for Melanie and it bothers him more that she is in pain. He touches her vagina the way she likes him to touch it; the way that gets her really wet. He then exerts those juices onto her clitoris – until she comes like a banshee. Lance looks at her smirking,

"Did *that* help?"

In the months ahead, Lance will come to realize *this* sexual relation, as their last.

The sound of a telephone ring can generally become irritating after the fourth ring when one anxiously awaits the party to pick up on the other end. In this case, it only takes three rings. A connection is established after the seventh ring.

"Hello."

"Hey Mom . . . ! What were you doing, jeez!? I didn't think you were there! I was about to hang up!"

"My coffee pot was over flowing. I may have put too much water in the coffee maker!"

"How are you?"

"I'm fine Richard. What's going on?"

"I called to tell you that your great grandson will be landing here on earth sometime this evening!!"

"Boy what are you talking about!!?"

"Lance's baby boy is going to be born today."

"Oh! Oh!! Melanie, bless her heart! Are you guys going to the hospital!?"

"Yes, Corinne and I will definitely be there."

"I want to be there too Richard!!"

"You want us to come and get you on our way to the hospital?"

"Oh yes, yes!!"

"Okay. Their appointment is at five o'clock. I'm sure they'll be there a couple of hours before that for prep time. We're leaving at two."

"I'll be ready a quarter to three. Come get me Richard, okay? I knew something was going on – you never call me this early."

"Okay Mom, I will. You be ready, okay?"

"Yeah boy, I'll be ready."

"Okay bye."

Corinne sneers at Richard, "Richard Austin!! Give your mother a break! She *is* eighty years old!"

"I know she's eighty and I'm sixty two! Besides, her place is no bigger than a female movie star's closet! Her phone can't be anymore than three footsteps away." Richard smiles at his wife.

"We'll see how long it takes *you* to answer the phone when *you're* eighty!"

"Two rings tops!!"

"You know what Melanie?" Lance says as they prepare their departure.

"What?"

"This is kinda weird but it's really funny though. We have a five o'clock appointment to have a baby!!"

"Yeah Lance you're right. That is funny! When we come back here together, there will be three of us instead of two."

They take pictures of one another before they leave so they can show them to their son later in life when he understands the concept of his being born on this day. When they arrive at the hospital, the small family entourage is already there; this being Lance's three family members and Melanie's sister Meredith. With this significant event on the horizon, no formal invitation was necessary for any of them.

Melanie is use to family comradeship being on a voluntary basis; Lance of course is not. It is he that is particularly glad to see them there. He gives his brothers and his step dad a mental strike #2 for their absence when it is needed most. He knows if they aren't there now, they won't be later.

When Lance and Melanie wait in the hospital room together, the nervous anticipation is mostly silent. When the nurse comes for Melanie, Lance kisses her like he's in love with her. He says to her,

"Everything will be fine dear. I'll see you shortly." Lance takes a picture of himself in the mirror with his hospital garb on. He wants his son to see the goofy, happy look on his face about two hours before he was born.

In the operating room, the silence of the moment is more intense than either one of them have ever felt before in their lives. With Melanie lying on the table, a light blue curtain hangs down right below her chest to conceal her stomach area. Lance wonders if they would let him take a peek beyond the curtain if he inquires; *only* wondering though because he knows he won't. The anesthesiologist administers the epidural before they begin the procedure. Melanie is groggy but still awake. Lance holds her hand with a tight grip, never letting go to reassure her – and to reassure him. He looks into her eyes and whispers a prayer,

"God, please watch over us and make this moment a successful moment. Amen."

Just then Melanie starts to twitch, "I feel a little pain . . ." This scares Lance a lot but he doesn't show it on his face. He knows his show of support has to be firm, solid, and unyielding. He says the same prayer, this time to himself. The doctor gives Melanie a minor dose of anesthesia to ease her pain. Now she starts to fall in and out of consciousness until finally, the drugs take their toll.

While she's out, a slight complication occurs. Lance can be silent no longer,

"Doctor what's wrong!?"

They explain the situation to Lance in a way that is medical jargon to his ears. But when they tell him that another specialist is needed in the operating room . . . a specialist who is *not* answering his cell phone, his lack of comprehension is no more. Now Lance is *really* scared and yet his incurable sanguine will not allow him to show it. He knows if he *shows it*, reality will *know it*.

God will see us through this storm that is brewing – the storm that has not yet arrived, Lance says to himself. When Melanie awakens for a moment with her hand still in his, he says to her,

"Not yet dear, they're still working on it. Not yet baby . . . almost." Her siesta supersedes once again.

After fifteen minutes of futility in finding the specialist, the woman that is Melanie's doctor, *the woman* that has been the proctor of their child's development for the past seven months – *the woman* whose colleagues' high regard for her in her field of expertise is *not* a fluke, is the one who figures out how to medically handle the situation. Fifteen *more* minutes pass and God's will is done. The room is satiated with a baby's cry.

Lance thinks to himself, *Faith is magic and magic is faith!!*

He squeezes Melanie's hand even tighter than he thought possible but she is still asleep. When the doctor brings the baby to the front area where Lance can see, Melanie miraculously opens her eyes and smiles,

"My baby . . ."

LJ is born.

CHAPTER 10

The first five weeks of parenting as expected, comes with a little bit of everything to behold. It is happy – it is sad. It is easy – it is difficult. It is exhilarating – it is tiresome. Melanie constantly thinks about the day after LJ was born. This is when the anesthesia had truly worn off and it dawned on her that she is *now* a mother. That was the day she hoped some major changes for the better would occur in Lance. *Maybe* their current union in question could reach the relationship stage again. Unfortunately the life changing event of a baby isn't enough to douse the flames of their fire. She's not sure if things have actually gotten worse since LJ's arrival but there is one thing she's certain of – she's not happy with Lance! In Melanie's opinion, he is nothing more than a selfish jelly fish with good intentions. As much as she fiends for his sex, she knows *that* alone can no longer keep her afloat; especially since they haven't engaged in months.

The influence of other men swoops down on Melanie like hungry vultures, especially Derek. She finds herself communicating with him over the phone more and more, particularly in the morning before work and in front of Lance. While she hadn't planned it that way, she does hope that the daily morning calls irritate him. She figures if *that* doesn't, then the dozen red roses that Derek recently sent to her *will*. They are sitting in plain view in the center of the living room table.

Melanie's apparent lack of respect for Lance is unfortunately something that she no longer bothers to deny. Her reasons are plenty to a point where she *truly* knows there's no turning back. When Lance left her alone in the hospital for twelve hours on her second day there, it infuriated her. The drinking with his friends that day was the last straw for Melanie. When the three of them came home from the hospital together on the third day, the occasion was joyous. It was also recorded on Lance's camcorder. But when the camera stopped rolling, it had all gone downhill.

As Melanie looked at the walls of their son's room, it reminded her of how long it took Lance to paint them. Even though the room was finished before they brought the baby home, it still wasn't soon enough for her. She expected him to paint within the first four days he had moved into the apartment before she actually did, so she wouldn't have to smell the paint fumes throughout the apartment or when fixing up LJ's room. He hadn't put the small shelves on the wall for LJ's stuffed animals until much later either. The rocking chair that Lance picked up about a week before she gave birth is still not put together. The dirty dishes in the sink are the same dishes that were there when she went into the hospital.

The first Sunday after coming home from the hospital was when Melanie had to take their one week old baby out into twenty-five degree weather. They went to her sister Meredith's house to host a visit from Lance's father and Corinne. That visit was originally set at their apartment but Lance had not cleaned the living room *for that visit* as he said he would. The next time she had to take the baby out into the cold was two days later at five in the morning. This time *Melanie* had to call the police to make sure she got out of the apartment with no conflict from Lance. She had to go to her sister's house this time around to stay there for a week because Lance wasn't doing enough to help out with the baby. She wonders why he took a week off of work without pay for maternity leave.

Three weeks after that incident, Melanie found herself angry enough at Lance to once again put her hands on him. The disagreement this time was her feeling that he had no business leaving the apartment for two hours to attend a female friend's birthday party. She had hit him in the face with her right palm . . . *while* she was holding the baby on her left arm. She never considered that Lance might return the physicality, especially while holding their child. He didn't. He simply just left the apartment and stayed gone for much longer than two hours.

The first five weeks of parenting as expected, comes with a little bit of everything to behold. It is happy – it is sad. It is easy – it is difficult. It is exhilarating – it is tiresome. Lance constantly thinks about the day LJ was born. It was the happiest day of his life. It was also the day that Lance looked at Melanie in a different light, hoping that their son would ease some of the emotional disruption in her heart. Maybe the door to their previous relationship would creep open again.

Unfortunately the life changing event of a baby isn't enough to calm the storm of their season. Surprisingly, things haven't gotten any better but Lance assumed it would. In Lance's opinion, Melanie is a selfish brat that wants to "wear the pants" in their relationship – *but* she has good intentions in her heart. When he watches her breast feed their son, it turns him on as it would any typical male – but not enough for him to want to make love to her again.

Even though Lance's loyalty has never officially faltered, he imagines more and more what it would be like to be in another relationship – a *true, loving* relationship. His thoughts are very brief in considering Sherry for obvious reasons but a little more intense when he imagines Evangeline being his woman. He finds himself speaking to her over the phone more and more, particularly in the morning before work and in front of Melanie. If Derek may call Melanie every morning, then Evangeline may call Lance just as often – two can play at that game he figures. One of the unspoken rules of a man in Lance's opinion is: If one of the first things a man does in the morning is call a woman, he is trying to get close to her in one way or another. Also if that same woman welcomes his calls or even starts to call *him* early in the morning, then he is succeeding. Lance thinks about Sherry's *before work* phone calls last year when he lived alone but that time was unfortunately very brief.

Lance assigns a specific ring tone to Evangeline in hopes of irritating Melanie – "Sexual Healing" by Marvin Gaye. He doesn't do this out of jealousy; he does it because he suspects Melanie is trying *to get to him*. He suspects the same with the dozen red roses *without* a card, sitting in the living room as the current centerpiece on the coffee table. Lance also considers this situation to be plain ol' disrespectful. In his mind, if a man's attempt to woo his *baby's mama* can arrive on his front doorstep and be displayed in the residence in which he lives, then *the man* may as well be sitting in his living room on *any* given evening when he arrives home from work.

Melanie was very disgruntled when Lance left the hospital at one o'clock in the afternoon and came back "drunk as a skunk" at one in the morning on her second day there. He had gone home to tidy up the place and to receive the bedroom chest he had his friend Carl James pick up from the furniture store in Hoffman Estates, the suburb where he lives. The furniture store had also made a delivery that day of the bed post, frame and dresser that he purchased. Lance knows that when the liquor gets in his system, he tends to lose track of his priorities and lose track of time. When Kevin joined them, Lance did just that and the evening became more of a celebration of his son's birth, than an evening to clean the apartment.

Lance figured that nine o'clock probably would have been a *more* reasonable time to arrive back at the hospital that night; but he thought Melanie would have been a little more understanding to a certain degree. She was not and to Lance; this always seems to be the case in *any* error he makes, even when he admits it. She had even once expressed disgust in not receiving flowers from him while she was in the hospital.

"You didn't care about the fact that I had *just* had your baby!!" she said to him. Lance found this statement startling when he thinks about the hours he spent decorating the living room for her when they first moved into the apartment. He thinks that maybe starting the paint job in LJ's room that day would have been more pleasing to Melanie. He wonders if she is forgiving of anyone's imperfections or tendencies . . . or if it's just him.

Lance thinks about the paint fumes that Melanie complained about being exposed to and how the majority of it was easily blocked off from the rest of the apartment by closing both doors to the room or by simply staying *out* of the room for a day or two.

He thinks about the *cheap* shelves he spent half a day trying to put on the wall. Melanie had spoken of them as if he didn't try at all. He did eventually get them up but then she complained about the positioning of them. She said that even though she agreed to it when Lance suggested it, she didn't want to. He did eventually put the rocking chair together . . . the same rocking chair he *never* saw her sitting in. The dishes . . . well as much as Lance likes to cook is how much he doesn't like to wash dishes. He knows it wouldn't have hurt to have had them cleaned on the particular day of their homecoming though.

Lance was furious when Melanie took LJ out into the cold because she was mad at him. This was completely selfish, childish, and irresponsible to him. It took him fifteen minutes to clean the living room after she went to Meredith's house. The night before when he didn't clean it, Lance had put the baby to sleep, massaged Melanie's swollen feet and fallen asleep at the foot of the bed. When he woke up, it was morning. She could not understand why he was so tired that night after caring for and interacting with the baby all day long.

The second time her anger was influential in her feeling the need to leave and go stay with her sister for a whole week was when he told her,

"You're not taking my one week old child out into that cold again for your own selfish reasons!!!"

That's when she called the police. Lance knows she only did that to show him tit-for-tat; again quite childish in his eyes, not to mention inconsiderate – given the fact he took that whole week off of work *without pay* to care for them.

When the one sided physical altercation occurred again while she was holding the baby, Lance just stood there for a moment and stared at her. He felt sorry for her in that moment. Deep down he knew that somewhere down the line when she least expects it, she will pay dearly for these actions. He simply left, never even making it to the party; but he stays gone six hours longer than he had originally discussed with her.

The first five weeks of being LJ's parents with LJ's part in all of this being excluded, has been total hell! It all comes to a head for the both of them on one Sunday afternoon. Lance actually starts the argument on purpose because he is mad about the flowers. They go at each others throats for about half an hour. Surprisingly they both seem cognizant of their son sleeping in the bedroom so they are not as loud as they *usually* are.

"I'm tired Lance!! I simply cannot depend on you anymore! I may as well be raising this baby by myself!!"

"Why do you exaggerate everything negative you say about me!!? You're just a spoiled little brat that expects me to jump every time you say so! I should've left you da fuck alone when you wouldn't open your umbrella two years ago!!"

"Yeah you're right . . . then it would've saved *me* a whole lotta trouble!! Hell, I see why your family never comes around . . . it's *you*!! Even *they* say you and I are on completely different levels!!"

"Who told you that idiotic shit, my step dad!!?" Melanie gives Lance a look that basically confirms his suspicion. "And you bought into that!?" Lance chuckles, "Wow, if you only knew!! You're a pretty dumb bitch, ya know that!!?"

"Yo mama was a bitch and she gave birth *to a son* that's a bitch too!!!"

Lance doesn't say anything right away; he is too shocked to respond. He thinks to himself, *100%!!* Then he disposes of the scale in his head once and for all because he no longer needs it. Lance is through with Melanie – and he knows at this very moment that he will never ever again in his life, lie next to her in the nude with an erect penis.

"Okay Melanie Powell . . . let me say this to you . . ." Somehow his words are calm, "Tell your new boyfriend that if he ever sends anything else like flowers or anything of the such to this address where *I* live too . . . you will find whatever it is out front in the middle of the street. And . . . if you ever put your hands on me again, you know, like initiate any kind of physical altercation with me – I'm going to knock you the fuck out. If you're holding our child when you do it – as soon as you put him down, I will knock you the fuck out. Your father can be a retired cop all he wants – it won't matter. If you ever touch me again as long as you live – I will knock you the fuck out."

Lance walks out of the living room. Melanie remains on the couch massaging her breasts, disgusted from how they feel from breast feeding. She doesn't turn her head one time to see if Lance will enter the room again but she does posture in a way that indicates her non-concern about what Lance just said to her – just so he can see it in case he does return. But on the inside where it *doesn't* show, his words are taken slightly more into consideration.

The shiny black Cadillac zooms down the highway in the middle of the week in the middle of April. As the music blasts through six premium speakers and a high powered sub woofer in the trunk, Lance tries to recall if he has ever played his music low while driving alone – he can't say that he has. The beat of the music surges through him and the long distance driving calms his nerves.

He thinks back to almost three hours ago when this stolen moment first began. Lance put his portfolio strap on his shoulder, said, "See ya later" to Melanie, and walked out the door as if he was going to work. By not volunteering any information, it technically meant he did not lie about driving to Indianapolis, Indiana instead. The "two can play at that game" scenario had come into play again. Besides that,

Melanie has walked out the door more than once before, saying nothing and leaving Lance at home stuck with the baby all day long.

Lance makes a call on his cell phone as he nears his destination, "Hello Evangeline, what's up baby!"

"Hey Lance darling . . . are you almost here?"

"Yeah, I'll be there fifteen minutes sooner than I said before as a matter of fact."

"Okay I'll be waiting!"

When Lance parks in front of her house, he can't tell the front door from the side door. As he dreaded when he saw this, he winds up having to knock on *both* doors. Now the nervousness begins because she takes too long to answer either one. Lance walks back to his car and rests his arm on the open driver's side door. As he's dialing Evangeline's number again, someone comes to the door.

"Hey what's up?" she says while hanging out the door.

"Hey baby!" When Lance gets close enough, he realizes it's not Evangeline he's talking to.

"*Hey baby* yourself! Who are you?"

"I'm . . . I'm sorry, I was looking for . . ."

"You're 'sorry'? You don't look sorry to me! You look quite handsome as a matter of fact! And what kinda name is 'Sorry' anyway?"

"No I meant . . ."

"That's okay hon, I'm just playin' wit'cha. You're Lance, right? You must be lookin' for Evangeline. C'mon in . . ."

Lance can't tell if the woman is her mother or her older sister. When she talks to Lance non-stop for what seems like ten minutes but is really only half that time, he can't help but get the feeling one gets when they're being flirted with by someone they don't want to flirt back with. When Evangeline comes downstairs, she introduces the woman as her mother. Lance imagines having a few drinks in him and being left alone with her mother in the near future. He wonders if he would have to perform copulation with her in order to keep the peace between him and Evangeline – or disturb it. Either way seems plausible in his mind.

Lance looks at Evangeline up and down as she walks back and forth like a waitress in a diner. Her jeans are nice and tight but her butt is a little flatter than he would prefer. Her chest is better, especially the rose tattoo on the upper part of her right breast. She has a light complexion like Melanie – and Sherry – and Charmaine. A coincidence. She has a diamond earring stud above her lip on the right side and a very light mustache on her cute baby face. Strangely enough, Lance finds *both* to be sexy on her – as he does on some women. Compared to the other three women, her hair length is longer than Charmaine's only.

Evangeline had once told Lance how she and her mother have a relationship as if they are best friends. Now he understands where her quirkiness comes from. Along with that, her estimated size *6* frame and her other physical attributes, Evangeline will do. When Lance meets her son who is almost five years old, it doesn't excite him anymore about Evangeline; nor is it discouraging. He just thought a child his age would be a little more curious and a little more sociable. Lance assumes the little boy is just shy or maybe it's something else.

Evangeline finally gives in to her nervous anticipation of meeting Lance and sits down to talk face to face. When he watches her express herself in person, in particular how her mouth moves and how it smiles, he is suddenly intrigued about her sexual prowess. No sooner than his male like thirst begins to get mentally quenched, is when Evangeline reveals,

"My Son has a pediatrician appointment at one o'clock. I'm sorry I forgot about it. We can do a little something after I do that. So how do you wanna do this?"

"I can take you to the doctor dear – I got all day! But it's only noon now, so what do we do till then?"

"Well, I do have to drop some homework off to my professor at school. You feel like rolling that way – it's not far?"

"Evangeline look, I drove three whole hours . . . well, two hours and forty five minutes just to get out here and meet you. If you got a couple of things you gotta do, I'm not just gonna let'cha go and tell you to call me in three hours when you're done. I ain't got nothing to do out here anyway."

"Go visit your *other* friend you said you have out here."

"Please . . . and besides, while we're out running errands, it'll give us a chance to talk . . . get to know one another – in person!"

"Okay, cool. Gimme ten minutes."

Lance is no longer interested in meeting Sonja because their communication habits tapered off dramatically a while ago, to a point of nonexistence. What he can possibly form with Evangeline is much more solid and definitely more consistent in nature. One thing that really surprises Lance though is his reaction to Evangeline needing to run errands. There was a time not so long ago in his life when an argument would have ensued because the plans that were made concerning him coming to visit were altered.

His experiences with Melanie in similar situations actually helped him to realize some of those nick picking tendencies. What Melanie had constantly pleaded with Lance to change, he felt like he did – but this enabled her to inflict some of those same tendencies on him and receive less resistance. It's discouraging to him that Melanie didn't embrace his calming down and it angers him that she chose to take advantage of it instead. His reaction and response to Evangeline felt strange and new but surprisingly natural. He only hopes to reap the benefits of this newfangled behavior.

The length of time the three of them spend at the pediatrician's office is typical of any doctor's visit. Lance thinks to himself how irritating it can be at times to be a gentleman. He can't wait for them to drop the kid off, hoping that they *even* will. Lance finally gets the little boy to speak to him. He finds it strange that it took so long because kids usually take to him quickly. He can feel in his gut that the interactions and relations with his own son will be a lot different.

When Evangeline tells Lance to take her back home for a moment, he has a thought that makes him smile. *Good!! Finally she's leaving the quirky kid with his quirky grandmother so I can be with the quirky mom!!*

"What?" she asks.

"Oh nothing . . . Say, where is a good place to eat out here?"

"I know of an Oriental place that has some pretty good food."

After they drop her son off and are on the way to their destination, Evangeline starts to smile. "What?" Lance says.

She laughs, "Oh nothing . . . not really important. I was just wondering if you were *going downtown* today."

"Here in Indiana? Don't you mean *us?*"

"'Us' in the sense of the word . . . but I really meant *you* going downtown *on me!*"

"Mmmm . . . well is your mother planning on going anywhere . . . and taking her grandson with her?"

"No silly, I meant right here, right now! You were so adamant before about liking to do *that* and I know it's been a while for you – living with a pregnant woman and all. We could pull over right here on the side of the road!"

Lance hesitates; hating that she's right about him not performing cunnilingus as of late. "*Evangeline* . . . we'll get around to that."

Lance *does* think about the IM picture Evangeline sent to him last year but that's not what deters him from pulling over; it's the lack of romance. She had once been *adamant* herself, about not liking to kiss. For Lance, kissing is the *#1* mood setter in a physical sense. Besides that, having a sexual adventure on the side of the road is only reserved for a *pre-existing* romantic establishment with someone. Doing this with Melanie was one thing – starting a sexual relation with Evangeline this way is something else.

Their time together in the restaurant is quite amusing in a comfortable kind of way. The appetizers are good and Evangeline's entrée is good as well; but the noodles in Lance's dish are over-cooked. This is one of two things he hates most whenever he goes out to eat, the other being bad service. The first time he sends the dish back, he is cordial when he complains about the scorched noodles. The second time Lance sends the dish back, this time via the manager, he tells him *not* to send it out a third time. The manager insists upon making a third attempt anyway and not charging him for it.

When the food finally arrives, it is packaged to go as Lance instructed at this point. When the bill comes shortly thereafter, Lance's tolerance level and humble demeanor are *not* packaged to go – they're already gone! Lance jumps up from the table and goes near the kitchen doorway where he saw the manager disappear twenty minutes before.

"Tell *your manager* to come out here please!" he says to a busboy passing by. When he comes out, Lance ignores the colorful name tag pinned to his chest even though he looks straight at it, "Excuse me uhh manager . . . let me show you something on my bill!"

Lance summons the unfamiliar calm that he had put on display with Melanie two and a half weeks ago, "You told me I wouldn't be charged for the noodle dish but on my bill, it says minus *$18.95*, then there's a plus *$18.95* on here, twice. *That* means I was charged for the dish and I need you to readjust this bill."

"No sir you are incorrect. For purposes of inventory, the food item has to be documented on your bill and *then* taken off, in which case that was done."

"Okay *manager*, I'm gonna say this to you one more time and after that I'm done. My dish was not listed near the top with my date's dish because there was conflict with it in the beginning. Your so-called adjustment starts with a negative *$18.95*, the second *$18.95* being a positive takes the amount back to zero. The *third* *$18.95* being positive takes the total back to *$18.95* which means I *was* charged for it. Your restaurant inventory concerns are legitimate, but *how* you record them concerning the customer is not."

"Sir . . . there's nothing wrong with your bill! All adjustments were done accordingly!"

"I *don't believe this* . . ." Lance says under his breath before he continues, "*Manager* – I have a feeling you *think I'm* a fucking idiot." Lance remains calm throughout, "One positive number and two negative numbers would correctly document your inventory – something the customer shouldn't see on their bill *anyway* 'cause it's confusing to most. But *I know* . . . and not to mention the total of the bill . . . I'm not most and I am not a so-called typical ass nigga that you probably assumed I am. Now . . . you take this bill to the back, throw it in the garbage and calculate a new one. Otherwise the same internet that brought me out here to your establishment will be the very source that closes this *rat trap* down . . . or at least have *your* job by the time I get through with all of this."

The manager snarls at Lance as he's holding the bill in an upright position, pointed at his chest but not touching it.

" . . . And *don't* snatch it from me when you take it out of my hand," Lance grumbles back.

On his way back to the table where Evangeline waits, Lance wonders if she thinks he's crazy. "Just a couple more minutes, then we can go," he says to her.

Evangeline's original assumption was that Lance would pay for her meal. Now she's not so sure. She wonders if he's crazy or just cheap.

"Uhmm . . . how much was my food?" she says as she fumbles through her purse looking for a twenty dollar bill.

"Oh no dear, I got you! Hey, I know it's not always about who is right and who is wrong – but in this case . . . *it's about* who is right and who is wrong!"

"Oh."

When the bill comes back, it is arranged and totaled just as Lance said it should be. As he leads Evangeline towards the door, he pulls his container of food from the brown shopping bag. When she's out the door, he turns the container upside down and squeezes it so the lid pops off, spilling the entire contents onto the floor.

"There's a spill at the front door *manager*!!" Lance yells as he's walking out the door, hoping that Evangeline didn't see what he just did. He continues to carry the brown shopping bag by its handle, pretending like there's still something in it besides napkins, plastic utensils and a menu.

When Lance takes pictures of Evangeline, he notices she has a cute little dimple on her left cheek just like he does. He also likes the way she poses for a couple of pictures, laying on her stomach on the concrete area of a monument for Indiana's fallen soldiers in various historic war battles. In the background of those pictures it says, *Keep off the wall.* Lance likes the slight bad girl in her for doing exactly the opposite. A stranger takes a picture of them together, looking like they're a couple in their similar black leather jackets. Evangeline is sitting in front of Lance and both his arms are wrapped around her and they are both grinning from ear to ear.

Their day together is a good one and the chemistry . . . though it is a tad bit awkward, is definitely there. When their date comes to a close a couple of hours later, Lance gives Evangeline a quick smack on the lips. He wants more but he keeps reminding himself that she doesn't like to kiss.

He wonders if he will ever get pass that or be able to get her to like it. As he's driving on the dark stretch of highway that is Interstate 65, he looks at his cell phone clock to make sure it's an hour ahead of the clock in his car. 7:30pm is the *correct* time.

Lance is glad to be in the Eastern Time zone because this will get him home at a reasonable time of nine o'clock.

He and Melanie verbally agreed recently that she would not fulfill her part of the year long lease agreement and move out of the apartment at the end of May. With that and all respect for one another basically being out the window, Lance *still* tries to keep the peace to a certain degree.

When he gets home and enters their bedroom, Lance doesn't acknowledge Melanie until he has looked down in the bassinet at LJ first. A big smile forms now and whenever he looks at his son and then it is gone when he looks at Melanie. Lance doesn't give her *true* eye contact out of guilt. This doesn't bother him much though because he no longer wants to give her eye contact regarding *anything* anyway. What Lance doesn't realize is, Melanie called his job on this day and Melanie knows what he did on this day.

Two and a half weeks later on a Monday when Lance comes straight home from work, he walks into an empty apartment. The living room furniture is gone! He bursts into LJ's room; all of his stuff is gone! When he hits the bathroom, only the bare tub, sink and toilet remain. In the master bedroom, the furniture remains. He then storms to the dining room – it is empty! In the kitchen, the stove is gone, the refrigerator is gone, the table is gone and the microwave is gone!! Lance's first thought is that someone has broken into their apartment; until he sees two coolers in the middle of the kitchen floor with perishables in them and a note lying on the floor in front of one of them:

Please return this cooler to my dad when you're done with it. The keys are in the mailbox.

On this Monday while Lance was at work, Melanie moved out – *Tit-For-Tat!!!*

CHAPTER 11

"**O**kay, so is everything in place for now Melanie?"

"Yes Derek, thank you for all of your help today and thank you so much for getting me in this apartment so quickly! Thank Antonio too!"

"Well that's not a problem. Just because I'm the *previous* owner of this building doesn't mean I'm not good for a big favor or two when it's really needed. Besides, Antonio and I go way back."

"Well as stressful and difficult as it is, LJ and I got outta there; fresh new start!"

"Yeah that's for sure; say, don't worry about the rent for the first two months until you get back on track. Antonio and I will work something out."

"Oh no Derek, I can't let you do that! I would have to at least give you *something*."

"*Give me* some imperative information . . . are you really through with Lance!? I got the impression one morning we were on the phone, that maybe you weren't . . ."

"I *guarantee* you it's over between us. We had words a couple of times while I was on the phone with you, so I'm sure that's when you started having the thoughts that you had . . ."

"Yeah, but I believe you though. Let's go out on a date one evening very soon."

"Excuse me . . . ?"

"*I said* let's go out on a date one evening very soon."

"Oh! I just wanted to make sure I heard you correctly."

"Yes you did. And I think it's been a long time coming."

"Yeah Derek you're right. Okay, we will do that one day soon. I'll let'cha know."

"Okay cool."

The simultaneous moment that Melanie has verbally confirmed her inner desire to move on, is the moment Lance is coming down from the rage that hit him in the face the moment he arrived home. *Now* he sees the items throughout the apartment that belong to him. His computer, desk, big screen television, his stereo with surround sound speakers, his five CD players – each player holding four hundred CD's and his two thousand plus CD cases – most of them being on CD racks. All of these items including his treadmill are all still in the living room; something he initially didn't notice when he saw the living room furniture was missing.

Lance says a silent prayer to thank the Lord that he *does* own a refrigerator. He also thanks the Lord for the old furniture he still has. All of these items are still at his old place and it's obvious to him that one more truck rental will be needed to retrieve these necessities. He does have a microwave but the stove, a kitchen table set and some new living room furniture are items he will have to purchase.

Lance calls Melanie to scream at her, letting her know that he doesn't appreciate how she's doing things. He immediately makes an issue of the baby's items, the gifts that came from *both* of their co-workers. He wonders how she feels she has the right to claim it all. He also makes an issue of her leaving with their son and not telling him where she has taken him.

"Where do you live *now* Melanie? – What's your new phone number Melanie!!?"

Lance's newfound calmed anger doesn't occur this time around and he doesn't care either. The very next day he calls her again, this time on her new phone number to make sure it's legit . . . and to scream at her about wanting to spend time with his son.

"I'm not coming by there to *visit* my son – I'm coming by there *to pick him up*, so have him ready!!"

Lance talks to Melanie like she's nothing now because he's angry about her actions and how they basically say to him – he *is nothing*. That's how he takes it anyway. It will be years before Lance makes a logical deduction that his secret Indianapolis trip inspired her sudden move without telling him. Thinking of that in the future will be mere amusement. In the present, he is too angry to even wonder why . . . and he is no longer trying to figure Melanie out anyway.

Lance is also not wondering why she easily agrees to split LJ's gifts, though it does cross his mind that she simply wanted to control the situation to fulfill an outlandish need for a feeling of empowerment. He's certainly not complaining that the arrangement to pick up his son the next day is drama free. He does find this strange but he definitely appreciates it though. Melanie does threaten Lance that she will sue for child support and this is not the first time these words have come out of her mouth. Lance pleads with her once about this.

"Melanie, please don't do that. If you do, I will not be able to afford to take care of my son."

With this hanging over his head, Lance quickly realizes that he can no longer call this woman and scream at her about anything. Her moving out the way she did is done and Lance has to let it go and move on – so he does just that. When they verbally agree to a weekly schedule of caring for their son, Melanie decides to hold off on initiating legal documentation to see if Lance will hold true to what they have agreed upon.

Every other day and every other weekend is how often Lance sees his son. He picks him up immediately after work and drops him off to the babysitter in the morning before work. The joy that LJ brings to his father's life is ten times more than he could have ever imagined. It's all the more reason why emptiness resides in Lance when it comes to not having a special woman in his life to share this joy with. He regrets now and always will that the traditional *Mommy/Daddy* scenario will not play a part in Lance, Jr.'s life.

When Lance considers the future as such, it is not surprising to him because he knows how he is. He has only *once* rekindled a relationship that had reached that certain point of *really* being over – a mindset that seemed desperate when he looks back on it. While he had never made an official proclamation of never doing that again; it has more-or-less been his MO ever since. Lance thinks about the word *traditional*.

That traditional Mommy/Daddy stuff always starts as such!! How many times does it end as such!!? Maybe my son will be better off with Melanie and I beginning his life with us being apart.

Statistically speaking, Lance's way of thinking makes *some* sense. But he realizes that the convenience of what his son is introduced to in life in that regard will only last for so long. Deep down though, there is one thing they both dread and that is the mystery of what the current society's label of single parenting will bring – *baby momma drama* and *baby daddy drama*!!

In the meantime Lance makes the decision to go back to the very source that put him in the situation of winding up with a child – internet dating. The reasons behind meeting women in this manner were nowhere near as logical over two years ago as they seem to be now with a child in his life. This gives Lance the expectation of finding more encouraging results in his cyber space endeavor this time around. But when his quick and easy new found line of communication begins with Anitra Downing, the de-ja-vu monster makes an encore appearance. Miss Downing doesn't have a picture on her profile! She is thirty-five years old, no children and resides in Chicago.

Once they exchange personal email addresses, she easily agrees to send Lance a photo of herself. The price he pays for her cooperation is a blurry picture. When he zooms in on it, it gets more blurry and when he zooms out, it's too small to get a really good look at her. From what he can tell, she has a nice smile – kind of jolly in a way. Lance hates that the word *jolly* first came to mind; this word generally being associated with the word *fat* more so than not. The *Is She Too Big for Me* game in his head starts all over again. He also wonders why she has an *r* in her name.

Lance tries to concentrate on more important issues concerning her or *any* woman he will eventually bring around his child. He figures now that there are three types of women he will encounter in his life: the woman with a grown child or children, the woman with a young child or children probably three to eight years older than his, depending on her age, and the rare woman without kids. Lance still finds it astonishing from time to time that he no longer belongs to *that* exclusive club of *not* having children.

Lance wonders which type of woman would be best suited to have around his son. He weighs the pros and cons of each. The woman with grown-up children will understand what he's going through with raising a toddler in a reminiscent kind of way. By her going through it so long ago though, will probably be an indication of her not wanting anymore children. Lance hasn't ruled out the possibility of having more children, in the right situation of course. She will be more available to spend time though in having offsprings that are capable of taking care of themselves.

The woman with the younger children will certainly be understanding of the constant demand of parenting a toddler – it being a lot more fresh in her memory. She will be more likely to want more or be willing to have more children with the right guy. Statistically speaking however, her single parenting status may prove to be even more demanding than his, with her baby's father probably not being around or not assisting as much as she would like or need. Stealing some alone time will be *quite troublesome* to overcome.

The woman with no children does have a lot of obvious advantages; but it can be kind of tricky with her. If she wants children, anything that Lance goes through in the aspect of parenting will be thrilling to her. The anticipation of going through her *own* child raising experiences will be the primary reason for this. If she *doesn't* want children, it will be difficult if not virtually impossible to win her over. She may try her best to be patient and understanding but her overall enthusiasm of the situation will be fleeting.

Lance leans a little bit towards wanting the latter of the three to be a part of him and LJ's life. If he finds that *this* woman doesn't want children, he can easily eliminate her from the already extremely short and selective list of potential step moms for his son. With Lance being a father now, he has no problem with LJ coming first in *any* situation that presents itself – even the potential woman in his life. Lance doesn't know if Anitra likes kids or not and he doesn't care either. With the borderline idea of her being overweight, she is excluded from the *step mom* list before she even makes the list.

Their telephone conversations are very nice and frequent enough – at least once a day, always after work and usually after 9:00pm. In Lance's opinion, Anitra seems kind of clingy but in a cool laid back kind of way. His own clinginess concerning her is just as evident but he suspects that his differs from hers.

Lance thinks of an old college professor of his that often used a metaphor for doing something just for the hell of it – *shits and giggles*. Even though his communication with Anitra is quite consistent, he leans more towards the *friendly terms* side of things instead of a true potential love interest. In the end, Lance is *really* talking to her . . . just for *shits and giggles*.

Memorial Day weekend has arrived and Lance is free of his parenting duties until Monday evening. His step brother Warren, Jr. is having a bar-b-que in Merrillville, Indiana right near the Illinois border. Lance decides to go since its close. While he sits and waits for Carl to arrive from Hoffman Estates so they can ride together, he thinks about Sherry Anderson. Besides from emailing her pictures of LJ and a few text messages, Lance hasn't communicated with her since early February. With Melanie gone, it is *now* imperative that he hold on to their friendship and get it active again from its dwindling state.

Lance calls her. "Hey Sherry, long time no hear!"

"Hi Lance! How are you? Your son is simply adorable!"

"Thanks, I'm doing fine – busy of course. How about you . . . ?"

"I'm fine and busy too. I'm still working a ridiculous work schedule but I manage. So tell me about fatherhood. Is it everything you ever hoped and dreamed it would be?"

"*That* and more . . . ! It's very time consuming . . . and it's detailed. I enjoy ever minute, every second of it though!!"

"That's good." Sherry doesn't ask about Melanie because she's afraid of what the answer might be – that he is still with a woman that is physically abusive.

"Sherry, you know what . . ."

"Yes Lance . . ."

"We haven't spoken in a while and it kind of feels like you're slipping away – you know . . . your friendship. I don't want that to happen. You and I are still friends, right?"

"Yes Lance we are."

"Okay Sherry, I just wanted to make sure. So what do you have planned for this holiday weekend?"

"Well actually Norm and I are *supposed* to be on our way to a bar-b-que gathering. I wish he would hurry up and finish getting ready."

"Yeah so am I, in Indiana – its close though." Lance notices that Sherry says her last statement under her breath – just enough for him to assume Norman's presence there, which in turn can also leave him to insinuate that Norman lives there with her now. Lance doesn't ask though because he's afraid of what the answer might be – that he *does* live there and their relationship is getting more serious.

"Hey here's my homie pulling up now; I gotta go. Don't forget Sherry, keep in touch!"

"Yeah Lance, okay." As they're hanging up, Lance has a quick thought.

Norman's there with Sherry and I'm not. Lucky bastard!!

He scoffs as he opens the door for Carl.

"Whasup dog . . . !"

"What up! Damn man what's wrong with you!?"

"Ah nothing; just got off the phone with this female. She's got this guy . . . I think that fool is living with her now!"

"Well everybody's gotta fuck up and do that sometimes, right? You just got through doing it again! That was like the third woman you lived with, right!?"

"Whatever!!"

"Forget him dog! If she's hanging around *you* at all, it's for a reason. It may not be the reason you want; she may be using you to try and make dude jealous. But trust me . . . she wants *something* from you."

"Oh so you're an expert on women now . . . ?"

"Hey, you want advice from me or you want advice from your brother Warren? You know what he'll probably tell ya! What's up with that fool anyway? Are there gonna be any women at this bar-b-que?"

"He said there are a few fine women there right now. We better hurry up 'cause you know if we get there and they're gone, he's gonna say, 'Oh they *just* left.'"

This is exactly what happens when they do arrive forty minutes later, making the get together a fulfillment of food only. The only woman that *is* there is the owner of the house; the woman that Warren, Jr. is living with. She is 5'7" and 280lbs., putting her in a category of being nowhere near his type. When Lance first lays eyes on her, he can't believe what he's seeing. The woman is quite paunchy, though her face isn't hard to look at; but her arms in her short sleeve blouse remind Lance of Christmas ham before the glazing. He looks at her hairstyle and the fact that it's a *Bob*.

Nice choice of a hairstyle but maybe not for her.

Lance can't help but wonder what the method to Warren, Jr.'s madness is. When the five fellas *only* sit in the backyard to talk about things that women shouldn't hear, Lance gets the answer to his question. Warren, Jr. has placed himself in the position to partake in one of society's latest dating scenarios: an African American man being involved with a financially secure African American woman for the sole purpose of that female taking care of that man. Lance finds this latest dating trend to be ridiculous; though he wonders how morally sound *he* could remain if he found himself in a financial stability mishap like his step brother. Warren, Jr.'s viewpoint is – desperate situations call for desperate measures.

"Hi Lance! I was wondering why I hadn't heard from you today. How are you?"

"I'm fine Anitra. There wasn't anything really going on earlier . . . you know for the holiday, but now there is. I know this is extremely last minute but do you wanna meet today?"

"What time hon?"

Anitra's quick answer is a turn-off to Lance. "Uh . . . kinda like right now; my brother is having a bar-b-que. We're not too far; we're just in Merrillville, Indiana."

When Lance ends the call, he is confident that he has solved the fellas' Memorial Day doldrums. He gives the other four guys in the backyard a look that indicates as such.

"She's gonna try to round up one of her home girls and come out this way," Lance says.

"Man how you think you gon get some females out here at the last minute?" Carl asks.

"They'll be here dog!" Lance says, reaching for that sense of male attainment if he can pull this off.

"I hope so 'cause a couple of ol' girl's friends showed up 'bout fifteen minutes ago . . . and they ain't lookin' like nothin'!!" one of the guys says, referring to Warren, Jr.'s girlfriend without calling her by name. In fact, none of the fellas care about what Warren Jr.'s girlfriend's name is; and Warren, Jr. doesn't either.

Carl suddenly starts to complain about having to be somewhere else since he rode with Lance. He calls one of his friends in the area to come pick him up since Lance is stubborn about leaving before he has heard back from Anitra. An hour passes and the drinks continue to flow but the confidence level of Anitra showing up with someone does not. Lance has heard back from her twice but only to announce that she hasn't found anyone to hang out with yet.

Lance thinks that if he asks her to just come alone, she probably would. Though this would seem to be an ultimate showcasing of his power over females to the fellas, this is a level he will not stoop to. He wants her to be a lady and have a friend accompany her, whether or not she has sense enough to do so. As Carl is headed out the door with his ride, he scoffs and frowns like a disgruntled female.

"I'll see ya fools later! Ya'll waitin' for nothing!!"

Anitra's third call comes right after Carl leaves. "Hey baby!! My girl Mia is gonna roll with me! We'll be there shortly!"

"Okay, you know where Merrillville is, right?"

"Yeah, just give me the address." Lance gives her the address and ends the call.

"Oh well, I guess Carl is gonna miss out," Warren, Jr. says.

"Man fuck Carl!! He was carrying on like a lil' bitch anyway!! If he had somewhere else to go, he should've told me that before he got in my car and just drove himself!" Lance says.

"Man dude chill out! You talkin' about that brother like you think he's gay or something!"

Lance gives his brother the look of wanting to continue their conversation about Carl – but he doesn't. Instead he goes to the refrigerator for another beer and to eagerly but silently await Anitra's arrival. Any nervous aspect of meeting her for the first time is easily masked by the amount of alcohol in his system already; mostly beer. He also knows that this meeting will be much easier than the other meetings with internet women because he already suspects Anitra to be overweight. One thing he's sure of though . . . she won't be as big as Warren, Jr.'s woman.

Anitra and her friend Mia finally arrive. As soon as Anitra enters in the doorway, she makes her presence known.

"Hey ya'll!! Happy Memorial Day!! Let's party!!"

Her apparent zest for life and her obvious zeal for the party/get together setting will serve Lance well for tonight. But it will contribute to her downfall in the overall of things – *that* and the fact that she *is* overweight in Lance's eyes; though he will admit he has seen worse. Her excessive weight appears to be toned and her choice in clothing is more than complementary in camouflaging her obesity – though the scarf around her neck reminds him of Bea Arthur's character in the 70's sit-com "Maude."

Lance looks at her face. He doesn't think she's very attractive at all – but he doesn't think she's ugly either. *Plain* he thinks to himself, though he can see the efforts in her make-up to *not* be considered as such. He then looks at her hairstyle. It is a *Bob* like the one on Warren, Jr.'s woman.

What is it with these big ass women with these Anita Baker haircuts!!?

When Lance looks at Mia to check her out, he hopes he *won't* find her attractive. The awkwardness of trying to woo Anitra's friend after spending the past two weeks over the phone with Anitra is an understatement. Even though nothing potentially intimate ever occurred in their telephone conversations, Lance knows that she has labeled their phone time together as slightly intimate in the least. No worries though; Lance doesn't find Mia to be attractive – neither does Warren, Jr. *or* his two friends.

As the evening progresses, the liquor flows more than before, even the premium gin for Lance. The two female saviors of the evening did *just that* when they arrived – saved the evening. Both of their personalities and natural people skills makes the late evening a blast. They all drink, talk, laugh, and play board games; making the big hand on the clock turn like seconds instead of minutes. When Lance is at the refrigerator again for beer, an unexpected male bonding session occurs with one of Warren, Jr.'s married friends.

"Whasup Lance. Whadaya think about ol' girl Myra . . . ? Is that her name?"

"I think it's Mia and even though I *remember* her name, I ain't thinking about her at all! Gon head dog!"

"Nah! I'll pass on dat. But hey I forgot, Anitra is your girl anyway, right?"

She ain't *my girl*!" Lance answers in a tone of disgust.

Warren's friend chuckles, "You know what I mean dog . . . Anyway, you gon holla at her?"

"Nah dog, I'm straight! Gon head man, you're more than welcome to make that move."

"I ain't trying to risk my marriage . . . not *for that*!"

"She dresses nice though," Lance points out.

"Yeah, like an unknown stage actress!"

They both chuckle as they walk back to the front room where a card game is going on now. With a smirk on his face, Lance shakes his head at the reality of people not respecting the sanctity of marriage the way they used to. He's glad he's never been married before because he knows if he had been in his twenties, it would have been a complete farce. He even realizes that for the majority of his thirties, he wasn't ready then either. Lance wonders if he's even ready now.

When 6:00am arrives, Lance insists on driving himself home until Anitra insists otherwise. She had her share of drinks too but not nearly as much as Lance did. She offers him a ride home and even tells him that she'll bring him back to get his car the next day. Lance's intoxicating thought process is strange, like being logically illogical.

But somewhere deep inside, Lance *does* consider that experiencing one less doubled vision *90*mph shot across the highway, to not be such a bad idea.

While walking with a slight stumble to Anitra's vehicle, Lance notices that she drives a black SUV. As the three of them get in, Lance frowns because he finds her choice in the vehicle she drives to be a turn-off. He quickly doses off with that thought in mind. As they ride along the highway, Anitra turns her music up just a little bit.

"Mia girl, I'm gonna drop you off first," she says sheepishly.

"Girl *you know* you're going out the way to do that! You gon give him some, ain'tcha!?"

"Nah girl . . . !"

"Oh so you're just gonna go in and have a cup of coffee wit him, right!?"

Anitra puts her index finger to her lips, "Sssshhh!!" and points to the backseat.

Mia points to the CD player, "Wait a sec, turn that down and watch this girl!" She turns around in her seat to face Lance and then she starts to reach for him. "I want a piece of that too!! Pull over girl – I'm gonna pull it out and get started on him right now!!" Lance doesn't blink, flinch, or even move. Mia turns back around in her seat smiling. "See, he's really asleep girl."

Anitra returns the smile. "You crazy Mia . . . !"

Forty five minutes later the black SUV is parked in front of Lance's place. "Hey sweetie, we're here!" she says to him. "Wake up Lance!" He doesn't move so Anitra gets out of her vehicle to open the door where Lance is leaning. She shakes him vigorously. "Hey baby wake up, we're here!!"

Lance starts to slowly stir. "Whoa . . . !" The first thing he notices is that it's daylight. He looks at his watch, "It's five after seven! Wow that was some party!! Where's your girl?"

"I dropped her off already."

"Oh . . . I had the weirdest dream . . ."

"About what Lance . . . ?"

"Uhmmm . . . never mind . . . you wanna come in for a cup of coffee?"

Anitra smiles, "Are you trying to be funny?"

"Funny about what . . . ?" Lance says with a serious look on his face.

"Never mind; I'll come in and have some coffee with you."

Somehow Lance feels refreshed from his one hour of back seat siesta but he knows the coffee will still do them both some good. He wonders where the unexpected horny feeling came from as he opened his eyes. He reminisces of better times when he would wake up next to someone who was much more desirable than what he sees before him. That morning sexual fever was cured with open arms back then . . . and of course he appreciates it more *now* since it's gone.

Oh well . . . I guess Anitra will have to do.

When Lance brings the coffee into the living room, he makes his move. "Here ya go sweetie." He places the coffee mug and saucer in her hand, puts his on the table and then leans over to put his lips on hers. His tongue soon follows . . . and so does hers.

Anitra suddenly stops. "Uugghh! You want me to spill this coffee all over me sweetie?"

"Yeah I do, 'cause then you'll have to take your clothes off for sure." Lance smiles as he takes the coffee from her grasp and puts it on the table.

"You don't waste any time do you?" Anitra asks.

"I try to never let a good moment go to waste," he replies.

As Lance reaches over to kiss her again, he closes his eyes and pretends like she's Melanie, to mimic the passionate foreplay *they* once shared. It works, but only to a certain extent. While he *does* feel the heat when kissing her neck and undoing her top, he wonders why he is engulfed in this make believe moment of intimacy.

Lance removes Anitra's bra to be delighted by the sight of her breasts; not because they are exposed but because they are perky and more toned than he had imagined. His technique is on display as usual when he slowly works his mouth down to what he considers *the prize* of a woman's chest – the nipples. The gratifying sensation Lance gets from a woman's hard nipple in his mouth is short changed with Anitra though – hers are not big enough to extend outward enough when hard. This takes away from the already sham of a moment of amorousness. Anitra is hot and bothered in a good way nonetheless.

"Ooohh baby that feels good how you do that . . . !" Anitra slowly and reluctantly pushes Lance away. "Baby . . . as much as I wanna give you *this* right now – you're not getting' it just yet . . ."

Just yet he thinks to himself. "Okay Anitra," he says to her calmly and convincingly. Lance's honest sincerity is indicative of the gentleman in him. Unfortunately though, when Anitra stops this moment from going all the way . . . he is also relieved.

CHAPTER 12

On Memorial Day early afternoon, Lance lies in bed still weary from his Saturday night / Sunday morning drinking binge. His system doesn't rid itself of the ethanol in alcohol like it used to in his twenties and thirties. He peels himself out of bed to use the bathroom and then he slowly works his way to the living room. Anitra's full cup of coffee still sits on the table where she left it yesterday morning. Lance leans over his couch where they sat and shakes his head with a smirk on his face.

He tells himself that her vagina scent should be present instead of the stench of her "so called" sexy perfume scent. He looks around the room for his can of air freshener but doesn't see it. Lance can never find anything right away when he's looking for something. With that and being in what is now *his* apartment for over six months, is a sure sign of his pitiful state of disarray when it comes to his belongings. Even after his emergency truck rental after Melanie moved out, he *still* has a few things back at the old place that need retrieving. Perhaps one day . . .

Having the luxury of a babysitter that watches LJ on most holidays gives Lance the option of not having to pick him up until six o'clock. But he misses his son terribly. He hasn't seen him in a couple of days. He texts the babysitter to let her know he will be there at three o'clock to pick LJ up. While Lance enjoyed drinking with his step brother and their friends on Saturday, it pales in comparison to his *#1* desire of staying home and caring for his son. Not every single mother is as lucky to have what Melanie would appear to have regarding child care where the father is concerned.

"What are you doing Lance?"

"Nothing Evangeline, just lying around. I'm getting ready to pick my son up in about an hour or so. I didn't get a chance to talk to you again late last week. How did court go?"

Evangeline scoffs at the phone, "It went okay *I guess*. Needless to say, his father is full of it like always!! I don't even feel like going into detail right now!"

"I'm sorry to hear that. Oh no . . . !"

"What . . . ?"

"I was just sitting here watching TV and it reminded me I had something to do tomorrow evening! Even if I didn't pick LJ up at three o'clock, I couldn't do it today 'cause everything is closed."

"His mother doesn't get him tomorrow evening?"

"Normally yes – but she asked me if I would watch him tomorrow 'cause she has something to do. We switched days basically. I don't know if I can get this done during work tomorrow."

Evangeline snarls back, "What difference does it make if you can get *whatever* done or not!!? *My* child basically has to go everywhere with me, everyday!! You got some nerve complaining about not having a free day without your son!!"

"*Whoa*, where is this coming from!!?"

Evangeline is angry that her son's father is a deadbeat and she's jealous of Lance's neatly packaged verbal agreement he has with LJ's mother. Basically it's hard for her to know any better when she hasn't experienced any better. Once Evangeline calms down, she surprises Lance again.

"You know if I was to get married and have my new husband legally adopt my son – it would eliminate *Mr. Asshole* from the picture all together."

"Oh really, I didn't know that."

"Yeah, I think he would have to consent to it. He basically is consistent in showing me and his son that he can't or more so in my opinion, *doesn't want* to have anything to do with his son. Would *you* marry me and legally adopt my son Lance?"

"Who . . . ?" Lance is dumbstruck by Evangeline's unorthodox proposal, even though he heard her loud and clear.

"*You*, silly man . . . ! We should get married and then you can adopt my son! You're such a dream in the fatherhood department. As far as a husband, don't trip . . . we wouldn't have to live together if you don't want to. I would come out there on weekends and fulfill my wifely duties among other things."

"Evangeline . . ." Lance almost falls off the steps of the back porch he's sitting on . . . and he almost burns himself with the cigarette he's smoking. "Sweetie . . . you're playing with me, right?"

"No Lance I'm *not* playing, I'm dead serious! Your relationship with ol' girl didn't work out and I'm not with anyone at all right now. I know it would be a marriage of convenience, mostly on my part . . . but it would have its advantages for you as well."

"Wow *Evan* . . . I'm speechless right now!!"

Not only that, Lance is also confounded by the fact that he just called Evangeline a short version of her name. He only does this with family and women that he's deeply involved with mentally and physically. He wonders if the fondness in his heart for Evangeline is a little more immersed than he originally figured.

Lance gracefully turns down Evangeline's proposal, knowing that an arrangement as such would wind up being something he wished he had never done. The three hour distance between them is an issue that he never really stopped struggling with internally, just in considering her to be his girlfriend – let alone his wife. Evangeline's proposal was strange yet kind of admirable to Lance when he considers the lengths she would go to as a mother regarding her child's well being. He was even somewhat flattered. And strangely enough, when the words first came out of her mouth . . . Lance actually considered it.

As Lance is at work in the midst of an all too familiar workforce shortage in his department, his mind starts to drift. He wonders how long it's been since he has communicated with someone that has actually turned him on mentally. He searches in his mind for a woman that has brought a big smile to his face when he hears her voice on the other end of the telephone. Sorry to say for Lance, but the only woman that comes to mind is already spoken for – Sherry Anderson. He doesn't think of Angelica or any of his other long time female friends because the mental thrill he's looking for is lustful.

Lance's constant reminder to himself that Sherry is *just a friend* is truthful . . . but a certain intuition in his gut tells him that a legitimate opportunity to advance their friendship will present itself; meaning *no* Norman. He doesn't know how or when this will happen and he doesn't wish for Sherry's relationship to not work out either. He just feels that nature will take its natural course and the wind will blow his way. Lance and Sherry have never talked on the phone during working hours. Her job as an Administrative Director in the medical field is a very busy and demanding job title at best. Working in Human Resources for Lance is not exactly a cake walk either. He tries his luck instead with a text message.

Hey Sherry! *Buenos tardes, como le va seniorita. Que tengas buen viernes.*

To peak her interest during the busy work day, Lance includes the Spanish language in his text to almost guarantee a response, no matter how busy she is. As he continues his work, he often looks at his cell phone lying on his desk waiting for it to light up. After twenty minutes it does so he grabs it to read it.

Hey Lance! *Como estas?* You know how to speak Spanish? *Que tengas buen viernes tambien!!*

The fact that a portion of Sherry's text is in Spanish intrigues Lance. He had only learned the phrase, *Happy Friday to you* in Spanish out of a recent frivolous curiosity of the language. He briefly explains *just that* in his response. Sherry on the other hand is actually learning the language from a friend, as she states in her response. Now he wants to test her just to see how much of the language she knows. Lance quickly leaves his desk to go to another area of his department's office facilities on the same floor; the source of information about the Spanish language.

The Hispanic woman is Lance's co-worker. She is a very sweet lady that he likes to talk to from time to time. Their many conversations about the heart and how it works emotionally are exchanges that he takes in whole heartedly. He asks her how to say another phrase in Spanish. She writes it down for him. He then scurries back to his desk to copy the Spanish she has written for him in his next text message.

Sherry, I just wanted to let you know *tu esta bien Buena!!*

??? What are you trying to say exactly?

You are so hot!!

Oh!! *Mucho gracias senior!* How did you come up with that way of saying that?

One of my co-workers told me how to say it. She's from Mexico.

Oh – from what I've learned from my friend from Mexico, I would've said it differently.

Now Lance wants to call Sherry but he doesn't. The time intervals between each text she sends are about five minutes apart. The fact that she is responding to his spontaneous, frisky text messages is more than sufficient for him; for now. Lance's cell phone lights up again. He snatches it off his desk.

Eres tan catiente tu tambien!!

Not knowing what it means, Lance pratically runs across the huge office space area to confer with his Hispanic co-worker once again.

"*Please* tell me what this means . . . !" he frantically inquires.

"Oh . . ." his co-worker says, " . . . I see what she's saying. You have to understand something Lance; the Spanish language is very diverse. There are a lot of variations of how to say something. A lot of that has to do with what region of Mexico a person is from."

The suspense is killing Lance as he waits for the translation. He patiently let's her finish her explanation though because he likes how she sounds when *she* speaks English. He only struggles in comprehending a couple of words in her speech, yet her accent and the mere fact that she sounds different from what he normally hears is reason enough to peak his interest in wanting to learn the language. His co-worker continues,

"It can also have to do with different lingo or slang in saying the same thing . . . you know, like in the English language. But anyway, basically she's saying here that *'you are so hot also.*"

"Really . . . ? Wow! Thank you." Lance walks away with a smile on his face like a six year old on Christmas morning. He sends Sherry a response.

Mucho gracious seniorita bonita!!

On the other end of this text conversation, when Sherry reads his response, her face shines with a similar Christmas morning smile. The unexpected texting back and forth with Lance is a moment in her day that she savors a lot more than she knows she should. She sends another text to state the obvious in the form of a question to downplay the situation.

Lance, are we flirting with one another?

Yes we are my dear!

We better stop. You are committed to someone and so am I.

Correction Sherry . . . you are committed to someone. I on the other hand am not.

You're not with your son's mother anymore?

No I'm not.

Lance originally included three explanation points behind the statement in his last text. At the last second however, he deleted them and used a period, as not to make such a big deal out of his revelation to her – even though his revelation to her *is* a big deal.

When the busy work day reclaims its territory in their lives on this day, the texting exchanges come to an end. The fulfillment for Lance was tantalizing, even in text message form.

Ta hell with Norman – seems he's slipping anyway, Lance thinks to himself.

On the other end of their recent technological connection, Sherry searches for the logical reasoning behind *why* she let herself go so far with Lance in their texting exchanges. When she finds the answer, she ignores it – leaving room for the inner voice she just ignored, to ask a question.

How long are you *going to keep ignoring the obvious in your present situation with Norman?* She doesn't answer.

Later that evening as Lance sits at his computer while he's on the phone with Anitra, he says a silent prayer of thanks to the Lord for whomever invented the baby monitor. The constant care and attention his three month old requires is never a faltering issue for Lance but as a parent he is certainly appreciative of the breaks in between, especially in another room where he can roam freely.

The telephone presentations that Anitra gives him, every since their slight sexual encounter, indicates to Lance that their "pilot" will soon become "a series." Surprisingly though he could care less. His right ear being free of the phone is in a constant fixation of hearing a possible sudden infant outburst. The secondary contentment Lance's free ear receives is the music playing, much lower in volume than usual. His left ear, in which Anitra is offering her sweet nothings and "so called" sensuous tone for free, is muffled in Lance's point of view. The dissonant sound in his left ear would be otherwise if it were Sherry's voice or even Evangeline's at this point.

The phrase that once irritated Lance, *Lemecallyouback,* is *his* MO as of late. The phrase is effective too when he says it to Anitra. After he disconnects the call, he tries to decide on the excuse he will offer her tomorrow more than likely, for not calling her back *this* evening as he said he would. Now his eyes can give their full attention to the many women he had been viewing on one particular dating website while he was on the phone with her.

At this point of the internet dating fiasco that started over two years ago, Lance has lost count of how many different sites he has ventured. His usual pattern in trying them out was at least one at a time before. Now he finds himself linked to three different sites at the same time in some way, shape or form. Some of them offer a limited access for free while others will not even let a person view photos unless a fee is paid. Lance is quite aware of the little gimmicks a.k.a. marketing strategies used to get a person's attention, draw them in and suck them dry. He doesn't give in to it most of the times – but every once in a while he does.

Lance has recently made contact with a couple of desirable women through the dating service's email. One woman lives in New York City and the other in Houston, Texas. With the obvious distance barrier of ever meeting these women in person and caring for his son every other day which doesn't allow time for traveling if he decided to, makes it easy for Lance to keep their communication level limited to email only. He tries his best to keep his selections to a local area only, but it's difficult because most of the time the local women are not that attractive to him.

Lance checks his personal email account and notices that someone has sent him an email through one of the sites he's linked to.

Probably no picture is the first thought that enters his head as he clicks the email alert to investigate. When her picture pops up he is surprised but not moved. The woman reminds Lance of a poor man's version of a local television station's news anchor. Her screen name is *Alluredbymybeauty. How presumptuous of her,* he thinks. She is twenty-nine years old and lives in Calumet City, Illinois. Her short email reads:

Hello, I was captured by your words and wanted you to know you had my attention. Take a look at my profile and see if you find it as interesting as I found yours.

Belinda – email address: Ichooseyou@belinda.com

As if she's doing me a favor by choosing me – jeez.!! Lance clicks the "view profile" option just for *shits & giggles.* Belinda is 5'9" and 240lbs. When he reads this, a sudden uncontrollable frenzy begins on his computer keyboard.

Oooohhhh baby!!! You're too much for me!! I just gotta be honest. I have never been with a woman that weighs what I weigh and certainly not over that. And that's not to offend, for real! I'm just a little guy and I like being a little guy, just like I'm sure you like being the voluptuous woman that you are. My homie Carl would like you though. He's 39 yrs. Old, lives in Hoffman Estates and no kids. Let me know what's happening.

Lance

Her response is almost immediate.

Oohhh something is wrong or something on your page!! You have on there that you desire a few extra pounds or plus size women. Do you have it there so you can send noooooo way to those whose interest you catch? I am not offended because darling I am all good!! And if your friend has a page, feel free to send him my ad . . . take care dear.

Belinda

Lance laughs out loud at her response. Her email makes no sense because in his mind, *only women* sometimes turn down potential suitors on purpose. He doesn't check to see if he has the wrong preferences marked on his profile; he knows he doesn't. He looks at her picture one last time to be reminded of *an Anitra* with long hair. The wishful glitz and glamour in Belinda's appearance is evident and definitely overstated in her username, her email address, and her email response. Lance saves the emails for amusement only. Other than that, he never wants to see her face on his PC monitor again!

*   *   *

"Hey Mr. Lance, how are you?"

The voice that Lance hears on his cell phone is the very one he wanted to hear just yesterday, thirty hours ago. "I'm fine Sherry. To *what* do I owe this pleasure?"

"My best friend is in town from Boston. We were looking for something to do. What are you doing?"

"On my way home from Joliet. I was hanging out with my dad and his wife."

"Oh well, we were thinking about going out dancing and maybe having a drink. I don't know where to take her. Do you know of any decent clubs?"

"Well you know I'm not too keen on the club scene but I certainly know where you two can get a good drink. You've been there before."

"I have . . . where?"

"Remember Cuatro's . . . ?" Lance hates that she doesn't recall on her own, their evening at Cuatro's. He blames Norman for her slight memory lapse. He blames Melanie for the many months that have passed since he has seen Sherry at all. His son on the other hand did no wrong by coming into the world when he did. It's easy to blame Melanie for a*nything* at this point because they didn't work out.

Sherry continues, "You know what, I think we *will* go to Cuatro's. That was a nice place now that I think about it. Will you meet us there? I'm trying to show my friend a good time before she leaves town to go back home tomorrow."

"Yeah sure I'll stop by. I can just stay on this highway and swing back around." As Lance disconnects his call, he wonders where Norman is and why *he's* not with his woman on a Saturday night, entertaining her best friend as he should be. He doesn't wonder too long though. He's glad to have received the unexpected call from Sherry and more than happy to oblige. He wonders if the Spanish text messages from yesterday resonate in her somehow.

When Lance arrives, Sherry and her friend Tammy are already seated at a table on the outside patio. Their smiles at one another are unrelenting as Lance greets her with the usual kiss on her left cheek and what has progressed over time, to a *three second* hug. Though the nervousness is minimal, having diminished more and more with each time he has met up with Sherry, it is *still* present. Lance thinks he knows why this is so but decides to analyze it later.

Tammy is light skinned, appearing lighter than Sherry at some angles in the restaurant's lighting. Her hair is black with a centered part and laying flat on each side. The lack of length makes her pony tail disappointing to Lance. Her top is a pretty colorful light blue simple offering. Yet when she removes her sweater, the top appears to be either too big . . . or her breasts are too small to fill it. *The itty bitty titty committee . . .* he thinks to himself with a smirk. While his criticism of Tammy seems mean, it is merely an observation in comparison to Sherry's top which is very similar. Hers is beige and it fits her very snug, indicating to Lance finally – that her breasts are a little bigger than he had guessed before.

The fact that Sherry is *actually* showing some skin is surprising yet pleasing to Lance, though her cleavage line is only two centimeters in length. Her khaki jeans are black and not tight, which gives Lance the impression that his gorgeous platonic friend might be one of those *church girls*. As the three of them order Sangrias, Lance thinks back to Memorial Day weekend when he first suspected that Norman now lives with Sherry. As if on cue, Tammy starts to talk about her boyfriend back in Boston and Sherry soon follows.

"Yes Tammy, I know exactly what you mean. Norm leaves the toilet seat up too! Why do men do that . . . ?"

They both look at Lance, suddenly expecting an answer to Sherry's rhetorical question. He gives them both a confused look, "I wouldn't know ladies . . . I don't do that."

"*Ooohh* look out Michael . . ." Tammy says under her breath, referring to her boyfriend back home. Sherry frowns, wondering why she would say that out loud for Lance to hear. She elbows Tammy in the arm, "Tammy . . ."

"Ahhh Sherry girl, you know I'm just playing. You know Michael ain't going no where!"

Lance chuckles in response to camouflage his true nature of mentally analyzing situations at times as they unfold before his very eyes or in this case, his ears. *"Norm . . ."* he thinks, *" . . . leaves the toilet seat up."* Lance hates her reference in shortening Norman's name. It reiterates that she's deeply involved with him mentally and physically.

He continues his thoughts. *The fact that she mentioned that probably means it has happened enough times for her to find it significant – which means he lives there. If a man is visiting his woman, he would put the toilet seat back down . . . but if he's at home – I dunno! Us men, we're soooo stupid – we do all kinds of crazy stuff!!*

"Lance . . . !" Sherry exclaims. "What are you thinking about?" She grabs a quarter from the table that's there from the change left from their drink purchase. "A quarter for your thoughts . . ."

"Oh, you have the money this time for that . . . ha ha!! Well since it's a *whole* quarter, I guess I have to tell you . . ." Lance hesitates, "Are you and Norman living together now?" Lance tries his best to sound as if his question has no pertinence to it.

"Yes we are. We've been living together for the past four months now. I didn't tell you?"

"No you didn't." Lance quickly gives *her* an excuse for him not knowing, even though he really doesn't want to. "That was probably the same month my son was born, so that's understandable."

Sherry gives a slight chuckle to downplay the fact that she *does* realize she never mentioned her current living arrangements to Lance. She thinks she knows why she didn't but decides to analyze the reasons later.

Lance continues his thoughts as they get a table inside.

Oh well, so much for that . . . for now anyway. But what's up with this Tammy person? Her personality is just as colorful as what she has on. She's not as laid back and relaxed as Sherry is. They do say though – sometimes people befriend those that are the opposite of themselves so they can live certain parts of their lives vicariously through them. I wonder if their friendship is a coincidence or a subconscious occurrence. Tammy ain't all that cute neither – again the opposite of Sherry. There are theories about pretty girls hanging with ugly girls too! She's got a lot of nerve talking about some man "ain't going nowhere" – especially when she resembles the mother on "The Addams Family*!!"*

Lance chuckles mostly to himself, not realizing that he is a victim of his own game – being observed on the sly by Sherry. She silently wonders to herself.

What is this man thinking about? I hope he's not upset that I brought Tammy. She can be a little obnoxiously silly at times. I kind of hate that we both wore our tops! She looks a little different in hers than I do in mine. I like that shirt Lance has on. He's always so well groomed when I see him, even though I'm not a big fan of facial hair. I wonder how Norm would look with a goatee and a perfectly trimmed beard like Lance's. Mmmmm . . .

Tammy suddenly blurts out, "Why is everybody so quiet!? Are we getting something to eat or what!?"

"The lady that seated us forgot the menus Tammy; they're bringing them over right now," Sherry says in a slightly irritated tone over her best friend's senseless interruption of her thoughts. "I need to look at one – I've never *eaten* here before."

"I'm just enjoying the music," Lance says calmly.

Sherry can't imagine what Tammy will say next, nor does she wait to find out, "Lance I see you brought your camera."

"Yeah, today is my millennium mom's birthday."

"Millennium mom . . . ?"

"She's younger than I am."

"Oh . . . !" she says, understanding the logic behind the term.

"How much younger . . . ?" Tammy blurts out.

"Just a couple of years . . ." Lance says calmly.

Sherry imagines a muzzle on a dog. "I'm sure you have plenty of pictures of your son on that camera, so hand it over."

Lance is thinking about gray tape as he hands the camera to Sherry. "*Si, Correcta!*" he says.

"Oohhh Tammy!" Sherry grabs her arm, "Yesterday Lance and I were sending text messages back and forth in Spanish! It was kind of interesting. We were almost flirting with one another."

Lance thinks to himself, *"Almost"? And what was "interesting"* . . . *the Spanish or the fact that we were flirting??*

"LJ is *simply* adorable Lance!!"

"Ooohh *he is* cute! Let me see!" Tammy says, putting her hands on the camera before Sherry can hand it to her. Lance starts to get nervous about his camera.

"I like your shirt Lance," Sherry blurts out, to overcome her nervousness in wanting to say it. "You *always* have on a nice shirt."

"Thank you Sherry." Lance smiles because Sherry has complimented him, and because he is fascinated by her Boston accent when she says *shirt.*

"So what are you getting to eat?" Sherry asks Lance.

"I don't know but the lamb chops sound good. What about you . . . fish?"

"Of course – you know I don't eat meat."

"Yeah I know – your figure." Sherry smiles while Lance continues, "Are you still exercising?"

"I must admit, not much lately. What about you . . . ?"

"With a three month old in the house . . . ? Not a chance!"

"Oohhh Sherry, look at this picture!" Tammy exclaims as the camera slips out of her hand and hits the table.

Lance throws a fit . . . internally, but says calmly, "Uhhh, do you have *$350.00* on ya? Lemehavethatback."

"Sorry . . ." she says regretfully. Lance doesn't respond to Tammy but he does look at Sherry to receive a *sorry* gesture with her eyes. He acknowledges with his eyes and a slight nod. He checks the camera to make sure it isn't broken.

"It's okay," he says with a sigh of relief. "You two want to take some pictures?"

"Yeah sure . . . !" Sherry says with relief in her voice also. Lance and Sherry pose for a picture first. He hates that *Butter Fingers* has to handle his camera again. *But a beautiful woman that doesn't know how to dress is still a beautiful woman nonetheless,* he thinks to himself. His very first photo with Sherry is worth the risk to him. Afterwards, Lance poses for a picture with Tammy. Of course the opposite preference defiles him in his gut – Sherry still has her jacket on in the picture and Tammy has her sweater off in hers.

Lance takes the last two pictures of the ladies sitting together and then standing together after dinner. Lance is thankful that Sherry had finally taken her jacket off in the last picture. When they are reviewing the pictures on his camera, Tammy doesn't like any of the pictures she took.

"This one looks pretty good Tammy, the one with your mouth closed," Lance says. He will notice in a few days, that Tammy's teeth are big. When her teeth are showing, it makes her smiles a little less attractive than when they are not. He will hope that his comment on this night did not offend her because it was not his intent – even though he wishes Sherry had come alone tonight.

When they move from their seated area that is closed off from the bar, the partying crowd has begins to show up. They have a seat around the corner from the bar and order more drinks. Lance does eventually switch to drinking his favorite cognac but there is no expectation of him and Sherry swapping drinks, thanks to a certain third party with a mood spoiling presence. They did swap plates during dinner, all three of them; not forks – just plates. What seemed a bit intimate and personal to Lance before now has him wondering if it's some kind of *Boston thang*.

"So how did you two meet?" Tammy asks.

Sherry hesitates in answering as she looks at Lance whose answer is also wavering.

He stumbles, "We met uhhh . . ." Sherry gives Lance an affirmative nod that is hardly noticeable. He's not sure if this means to make something up or if it's okay to reveal how they really met. He considers Sherry's overall demeanor when he answers,

" . . . We met on an internet dating website."

"Oh, that's interesting!" Tammy exclaims.

"Yeah, we went out on a date last year right before I met Norman. Lance and I didn't really hit it off but we became really good friends," Sherry says.

Lance recalls the story a little differently, knowing that Sherry already knew Norman when they first went out.

Is this a typical human error, her slight lapse in memory or is this a mental barrier that has conveniently constructed these turn of events in order to justify how things turned out and who's lying in her bed with her now??

He silently wonders in what context was Sherry using the word *really* which she used twice.

Is there any emphasis on either "really" *she used?*

While Lance continues to socialize with the ladies, he can't help but wonder why neither one of them seems willing to dance.

What, are they waiting for me to ask one of them to dance? I don't dance that much! And why did Tammy ask that question about how we met anyway? Usually two people that are dating or officially together get that question posed. What did Sherry tell Tammy about me . . . or was it Tammy's own observation that led her to ask that question?? What is going on . . . ? And where is Norman!!?

CHAPTER 13

Usually on Sundays, Lance will sit around his apartment all day long *thinking* about the errands he needs to run. When the evening arrives as it has now, his thoughts turn to ironing at least two days worth of clothes for the coming work week. "The errands" part of his day *did* get accomplished on this particular Sunday – a conscientious effort on his part. Lance was suppose to watch LJ this weekend but Melanie agreed to watch him for a second weekend in a row so he could attend his step mom's birthday gathering the day before. The many errands he needed to run on this day was another reason for asking Melanie to step in.

The lack of conflict in their relationship as parents is a little scary to Lance – but he embraces it nonetheless. While anything regarding Melanie is basically a non concern at this point for Lance . . . he still can't help but wonder if she has a bipolar disorder.

If she is . . . I hope it doesn't effect our son's well being 'cause that's all I care about now!

As he smiles at his own personal thoughts, deep down he knows he cares about Melanie's well being in the capacity of being his son's mother. He never has anything negative to say about her to anyone . . . because he knows that their situation in trying to raise their son together could easily be ten times worse.

Now what about these clothes . . . ? He scoffs, "To hell with it . . . !" He picks up the phone and dials a number he has memorized, though he doesn't know why he did.

"Hello . . ." the female voice says on the other end. With her Caller ID indicating it was Lance calling, Anitra decided to play it cool and not address him by name.

"Hey Anitra! How are you!?" The enthusiasm in Lance's voice when he addresses her is the opposite of how he really feels – he is bored.

"I'm fine Lance. I haven't heard from ya in a couple of days – what's going on wit'cha?" Anitra indicating not hearing from Lance means the coolness in her clinginess is slipping. She quickly catches herself in mid sentence and asks how he's doing instead of asking why she didn't get a return call Friday night.

"Nothing much . . . Sorry I didn't call ya back Friday – I ended up in Joliet at the last minute that night." Lance voluntarily offers his *made up* excuse about the phone call he didn't return Friday night. He detects that she really wanted to know.

"Oh that's okay. So what are you doing?"

It's not *okay* he thinks to himself. *She's trying to play it cool. It's okay though, I'll make it up to her.* He answers her question, "I was just ironing some clothes for next week and I was thinkin' about'cha. I wanna see you. Why don'tcha get in that big black truck of yours and come over here."

"Tonight . . . ?"

"Yeah . . ."

"Well . . . let me finish up something I was working on, then I'll be by there, okay?"

"Yeah Anitra, sure – that will give me time to finish my clothes."

"Okay, I'll call you when I'm in my big black truck!"

"Okay, bye!" Lance doesn't even start to iron the clothes he claimed to be ironing already. He opens a bottle of premium whiskey instead. He doesn't want to be "three sheets to the wind" when she calls back – maybe just *one sheet*.

When Anitra steps foot into Lance's apartment, the living room is dimly lit and a strange yet relaxing tune plays at a low volume. There are four candles lit but they sit in the far off corner of the room. Lance did this on purpose to remind himself that he really doesn't like this woman the way she thinks he does. His buzz is just enough to claim and have her believe that he's only had *one* drink when he's really had *three*. He would hate to have her think of his alcohol consumption to be a necessary mood getter for him.

Lance opens a bottle of red wine and pours Anitra a glass. He expects her to wait for him to pour his glass so he can make a toast. His first disappointment occurs when she takes a sip before hand. His second disappointment is when she picks up her wine by the body of the glass and not the stem. And his third,

"Lance, this is *not* cold! Do you have any red wine in the refrigerator?"

"You're *supposed* to drink red wine at room temperature," he says in a snooty tone. I usually drink white wine during the summer months, but I haven't gotten around to picking some up yet. So sorry but no, I *do not* have any cold Pinot Noir."

"Well that's okay – this will have to do." Lance is kind in not taking any points off for her not sniffing the wine's aroma and twirling it around in the glass before she tasted it.

While Anitra reluctantly sips on her wine, she considers the fact that Lance is trying to seduce her. The very next thought she has, is if she will give him the sex in the living room or in his bedroom. By the time Lance is on his second glass of wine, he decides to not waste anymore time and pick up where he left off with Anitra exactly one week ago today. Even though Lance offers a few select soft spoken words before he kisses her, they are not sentimental words from his heart. He hopes this will give her some kind of a hint that their "thing" will *not* progress into something special or meaningful to hold on to.

She'll probably ignore the hint, he thinks to himself as he nibbles on one of her excessively pierced ears.

Lance follows his usual technique of intimacy to the letter, leaving no stone unturned. It's really the only way he has ever gone about pleasing a woman and making love to a woman, though he *certainly doesn't* consider this night of potential sex to be the latter of the two. He lightly touches her breasts in a circular motion, working his way to the middle of one of them. He teases her areola with his middle finger, attempting to stiffen her nipple so he can feel the imprint of it through her bra and her top. But once again her nipple, even when hard, is a disappointing thrill ride for Lance – he can't feel it! He tries the other nipple just to make sure . . . he can't feel that one either.

He gets on top of her and starts to grind her. The scope of his penis is very long and not centered, thanks to his boxer shorts and his loose fitting jogging pants. As he continuously rubs it against her inner left thigh, a zenith is suddenly reached and Anitra can't take it anymore. She yanks his jogging pants down to just above his knees and grabs the black silk extension she sees before her. In this moment, Lance knows he will have his way with this woman.

The moment suddenly stops when Lance lunges away from her and stands up. He extends his hand for her to get up and follow him to his bedroom. He considers carrying her there but doesn't want to chance it being a struggle to do so, with her being overweight. When he swings the door open, he allows Anitra to enter first so he can slip out of his house shoes and jogging pants in the hallway and to be a gentleman of course. She sets eyes on a queen size bed with a deluxe black comforter, six maroon colored pillows – three of them prints and three of them enclosed in one tone silk pillow cases. Two more pillows are in black silk pillow cases.

Lance tosses some pillows aside to pull the comforter back to reveal black silk sheets. He usually doesn't take the time to make his bed in the morning when he's rushing for work. One thing Lance *will* take the time to do though . . . is put on a presentation when it is needed. Anitra gives him a look of animated surprise,

"You're a freak, aren't you!?" Lance shakes his head *yes* while clasping his lips together to give Anitra his serious, sensuous look. It would appear he's holding back a smile as well. He can't help but feel that typical yet questionable male sense of achievement in sexually conquering a new woman for the very first time. What amuses Lance even *more* is that Anitra doesn't seem used to a man going all out or showing her a bit of class. This makes his presentation seem extraordinary to her, whereas it being nothing special to him.

Lance slowly walks up to Anitra. He starts to kiss her and undo the zipper on her size *16* jeans. They fit her so tightly though, that he can't. He chuckles and he wonders why big women wear tight clothes. When she unfastens her jeans and takes them off, Lance is once again amazed at how toned she is for her size. As he slowly unbuttons her top, he suddenly starts to embrace even more notable qualities about her. Not only is Anitra a good kisser; she is very effective in how she expresses her sensuous side to Lance. Her sexuality is puissant yet charismatic . . . and she is comfortable within it.

Lance allows this to settle on his brain like a mental imprint. As he enters her, he is glad about not having to pretend she is Melanie because if Anitra's sexual prowess is capable of mentally sending him to another place, he doesn't want to *forget she's not* Melanie, and perform cunnilingus on her. Lance is fully aware that his own discretion in determining who is privy to this act is risqué – however, where Anitra is concerned, he simply *will not* do that to her. He hopes she won't try to perform fellatio on him either because this will put him in a place of guilt in not returning the favor.

As they transition from the traditional missionary position, they can't help it when they share a quick laugh about the comforter being so slippery on the silk sheets. When Lance slides it completely off the bed, it looks as if it's moving by itself. They continue their sexual act in the *doggy style* position. When he feels like he's ready to come, he stops to change positions again. With over four months of not being sexually active, it surprises Lance that he has lasted this long without exploding.

Anitra lies flat on her stomach with her legs spread apart. Lance then vertically lies in between her legs to enter her from behind; now they are *forking*. When they change positions one more time, she is lying on her side with her back to him again, legs pinned together. Lance lies behind her and only has to lift her left leg slightly to enter her again; now they are *spooning*. They both *really* like this position, especially with her thighs being close together. There is more friction in his thrusts for her *and* for him – and Lance doesn't have to look at her face as her internal vicissitude goes from *I like this man* to *I* really *like this man*.

Three days later, Lance sits back in his recliner trying to stay awake so his free day without his son isn't wasted. He had him yesterday and will have him tomorrow and then the weekend – the weekend of his birthday. He doesn't care that this will minimize his choices in how he can celebrate. LJ is Lance's daily celebration within itself! With no special lady in his life and Anitra, who doesn't even measure up to a quarter of what "special" means to him, are two reasons enough to really just let his special day on Sunday, come and go without making a big fuss over it. If any of the fellas want to come by in the evening after LJ is down for the night and have a birthday drink, that would suit Lance just fine.

The only definite plans he has on this upcoming Sunday is for Melanie and LJ to take him out to dinner. Lance and Melanie surprisingly share the magnitude of their child's first holidays in his life, including *their* birthdays. Lance took Melanie out to dinner with LJ for Mother's Day, even though it was a mere two weeks after she moved out the way she did. What Lance will do for his son's sake is unyielding. Melanie shares these sentiments as she plans to acknowledge Father's Day just the same.

When Lance's cell phone rings, he is half asleep. He fumbles to grab it and sees that it's Sherry calling. He wakes up in a matter of seconds, clears his throat and answers the call,

"Hi sweetie, how are you!?"

"I'm fine Lance, how are you? Were you asleep?"

"No! Well . . . maybe just a lil'bit. What's going on?" he says while trying to clear his throat again. Sherry immediately goes into an apologetic mode about her friend Tammy on Saturday night. Lance had figured *that* was the reason for her call, though he didn't expect a call. He is gracious in accepting her apology and acts as if it was nothing, which it really wasn't to him – at least not after the fact.

"You know what Sherry . . . speaking of Tammy, I hope you didn't mind me telling her that we met on the internet. Not everyone is as open about that as others. She completely caught me by surprise when she asked that question . . ."

"Yeah she caught me a little off guard too and I hesitated because I wasn't sure how *you* felt about that. I'm fine with it, but thanks for acknowledging that."

"You're welcome. Thank you too! I figure like this . . . some people use the internet to meet people and some don't. Not everyone that does is willing to admit it out loud though."

Lance is referring to Melanie who would always tell people that her and Lance met at a grocery store. He couldn't figure out why in the beginning but he went with the story to appease her. The reasons are crystal clear now, but irrelevant. He's just relieved that Sherry is as upfront as she is, basically about everything it would seem.

"Lance!! I have some exciting news to tell you! I'm going to apologize in advance for not telling you sooner . . . I'm sorry Lance!"

Lance chuckles, "That's okay sweetie . . . what is it?"

"Norman and I are engaged!!"

"Oh that's wonderful! When did *this* happen!?"

"About a month ago . . . ! I was so excited when it happened and then with work and all . . . I got so busy; I guess I just didn't find the time to call you and tell you . . . again I apologize."

Lance responds but his mind begins to drift, "That's okay dear." – *No it's not!! And why did I just call her* dear*!?*

"I can't believe I didn't tell you this past Saturday when we were out . . ." she says.

"Yeah, shame on you. I could've given you a big ol' congratulatory hug" – *and squeezed the fuckin' life outta ya!!*

"I really want you to meet him one day!"

"Yeah sure, we'll do that one day" – *just so I can see if he's one of those pretty motherfuckas . . . I bet he is!!!*

Sherry's kind and honest nature of being upfront about things is suddenly not appreciated by Lance. When they hang up, he is thoroughly disgusted. He then considers the fact that *if* any glimmer of hope exists in finding his way into Sherry's life on a more personal level; at least he'll know what he's up against. Her announcement does deflate the internal inspiration in him though . . . but only for a couple of minutes.

Lance jumps up from his recliner fully awake to grab his digital camera and hook it up to his computer. Even though the pictures on the memory card can be viewed on the camera's display, he wants to make sure he doesn't miss what he's looking for by viewing them on his PC monitor instead. When he looks at the pictures from Saturday night, this is the moment he notices Tammy's teeth.

Oh my . . . he thinks to himself. More importantly, when he looks at the picture of both the ladies sitting together holding their Sangrias, Lance sees what he needs to see.

On this date forty one years ago, Lance was born. He stands over his son lying in his bassinet sound asleep. He thanks the Lord for this day's arrival and for being included in it. He also thanks the Lord for his beautiful son and asks for forgiveness for having him out of wedlock.

"*I'm sure I went about it wrong in the beginning . . . when I entered into a relationship with Melanie. But I think in the end Lord, I tried to make it right – amen.*"

Lance has always been a spiritually conscious individual; acknowledging it more could always use some work. When he looks down at his precious son, he realizes the gravity of prayer and the urgency of a more spiritual demeanor within himself.

When Lance's doorbell rings, he frowns because he is not expecting anyone so early in the afternoon. He looks out the window first to eliminate any surprises. He sees a black SUV parked out front.

"What is *she* doing here!?" he murmurs. Lance buzzes Anitra in. When he opens the door, she has a big smile on her face and a small plastic jeweler's bag in her hand.

"Happy birthday Lance . . . !"

"Oh, uhmm . . . thank you! You didn't have to . . ."

"I know I didn't . . ." Lance accepts the gift. He is totally surprised that she actually went out and bought him something for his birthday. When he opens the small jewelry case to reveal a pair of diamond earring studs, he wants to faint.

"Oh wow . . . !"

"I thought those might look good in your ears! I left the receipt in the bag just in case you don't like 'em and wanna exchange 'em."

"No these are fine." If Lance had picked them out, the diamonds would have been a little smaller. He sits the case of earrings on the table. He pulls out the receipt and glances at it while he's folding it; *$500.00*. His status in wanting to faint is suddenly upgraded to cardiac arrest. He wonders why Anitra didn't follow proper etiquette and obtain a gift receipt instead. Lance thanks her again and kisses her, practically putting his tongue down her throat because of the price of the gift. "I was just about to prepare myself a late breakfast – you want some?" he asks, even though he really doesn't want to. In accepting a *$500.00* birthday gift though, he feels it's the very least he *should* do.

Anitra accepts his offer so Lance goes to the kitchen to prepare breakfast; sausage patties, eggs, and shredded hash browns. He puts the frozen patties on a cast iron skillet and puts the fire on them low so they can cook slowly. For the hash browns he wipes his griddle surface with olive oil so it's not excessive. He then heats it and melts a smidgen of butter over the entire surface. He puts the potatoes on and then goes to check on his son. Little LJ moves around a lot in his sleep but he is still resting comfortably. Lance closes the door behind him and goes back to the living room to check on Anitra where he left her.

Anitra doesn't know that LJ is present, nor does she ask. Lance doesn't volunteer this information either. He doesn't want her to know that his son is home with him; he doesn't want her to see Lance, Jr. Instead of inviting her in the kitchen, he turns the television on for her and runs back to the kitchen to tend to his normal weekend ritual of the preparation of a big breakfast.

Lance sprinkles a small amount of cayenne pepper on the hash browns. He then dices some fresh garlic and green peppers and adds it to the potatoes, distributing it evenly. After he turns them he sprinkles seasoned salt and pure ground black pepper on them. He slices half an onion and distributes it atop the hash browns. He then turns his sausage patties to brown on the other side. Lance grabs half a tomato and a lime from the fridge. He dices the tomato, cuts the lime in half, and squeezes the fresh juices and pulp atop the tomatoes.

When the hash browns and sausage are done, he puts it all on two plates and covers them with cake lids to keep them warm. He quickly cleans the griddle and distributes olive oil and butter on it again. He cracks six eggs on the griddle, busts the yolks and spreads it around atop the egg whites because he likes egg yolks more than he likes the white part of the egg. He seasons them with a pinch of kosher salt, flips them and seasons the other side with coarse ground black pepper. Lance has never had to explain why he uses two different black peppers; pure ground and coarse ground. He smiles when he thinks of how gladly he would, to any inquiring mind that wants to know.

When the eggs are ready he puts two eggs on her plate and four on his. Anitra's plate has less an amount of sausage and hash browns as well; this being Lance's way of distinguishing between a plate for a woman and a plate for a man.

She probably can eat as much as I do . . . but whatever, he thinks to himself. To top it off he puts the diced lime flavored tomatoes atop the hash browns and a little on top of the eggs. He includes a few chopped pieces of green onions also on top of everything, mostly for a color effect and yet another flavor all the same.

"I hope you like tomatoes . . ." Lance says to her. Anitra gives him a look of astonishment when he presents the breakfast plate to her. He hates it when women seem struck with amazement over the fact that he cooks on a regular basis. "I need to eat just like everybody else does and *I like good food,*" he says to Anitra. It is something he often finds himself saying, mostly to some of the women on his job when he's eating leftovers for lunch.

Lance mentally reaches deep inside of himself – the part of him that very seldom tells a lie . . . and lies to Anitra to get rid of her. She tries to get Lance to agree to letting her take him out for dinner or drinks or whatever he wants within the next few days.

"Okay I'll let'cha know," he says to her as he's seeing her out. He knows he will probably have to lie to her at least two more times before the inquiries eventually disappear into thin air. When he closes the front door behind her, he goes to the picture window and opens the blinds to give her the illusion that he is seeing her off. He rushes back to his bedroom where Lance, Jr. is and he is beginning to wake up.

Just in the nick of time, he thinks to himself.

A week has passed since Anitra's immoderate display of endearment. Lance *did* manage to avoid an outing with her for his birthday. The fact that *she* would've paid doesn't entice him at all because the *quality* of the company he keeps is more important than *who* is paying. Lance knows he could have and should have avoided another sexual encounter with her as well. The second time he touches her that way *is* partially a selfish desire to feel her insides again, but it feels more like the easing of his guilt over the earrings and another way to thank her for them.

In the week to follow when Anitra goes out of town with some family members, Lance is relieved to be getting a break from her. When she calls him just as often as she does when she's in Chicago, he starts to wonder if he has created a monster.

"I miss you Lance," she says to him in a voice that *now* sounds whinier than ever before.

"Oh that's sweet Anitra," he says, hoping *that* response will be enough.

"Do you miss me!?"

Lance hesitates, "Yes, I do." Now the final straw has occurred in that one little question. It shows signs of her desperation and neediness for the most part. It is also indicative of controlling and manipulative tendencies in order to fill some kind of void in her. Anitra has compromised her integrity more than once in a feeble attempt to claim Lance as her own. She has even made statements to Lance about how she tells her friends and family, *"My man knows how to cook!"* Her expensive gift and her quick and easy sex are no match for the *true* desires deep within Lance's heart. While her sex *is* good to him, there is nothing to savor after the act is done.

Lance doesn't deny his own fairytale like disposition when it comes to love and relationships – but he would like to think that he's not as insane as Anitra. He thinks about Melanie when they first met and how she had set out to find a remedy to the emotional distress of her failed marriage. While Melanie's relationship goals with Lance were pure, Lance's goals with Anitra are nonexistent. But in the end the situations mirror each other in being too soon to partake in them – being on the rebound!

This is why Lance is fooling around with Anitra; not to mention the fact that he is also trying to fool himself into believing that something substantial can eventually develop between them. His thinking was the same when he drove out to Indianapolis two and a half months ago to meet Evangeline in person. At that point he knew that Melanie was due to move out soon anyway.

Lance thinks about the incident with the manager at the Oriental restaurant in Indiana. While his demeanor was refreshingly calm, some of his words and actions especially, were crazed. The lack of control of his anger, or those angry thoughts that *become* actions rather than remaining thoughts . . . reminds him of Melanie's behavior. Lance is *also* trying to deal with an emotional distress of his own by taking the quick and easy way out and finding comfort in another . . . just like Melanie did with him.

Subconsciously, Lance has the audacity to do this with someone undesirable; trying to fool himself into thinking he's not on the rebound, but just being a typical guy and "getting his."

It is easy for Lance to see these faults within himself only because of the comparison to Melanie – someone he definitely doesn't want to be like. The inner voice presents Lance with a question.

How long are you going to keep ignoring the obvious in your present situation with Anitra? He doesn't answer right away.

A couple more weeks have passed by and Lance somehow continues to find himself sitting at his PC monitor looking at women's pictures on internet dating websites. He's not quite sure what it is he's even looking for anymore. He knows deep down what he wants but fears that he won't find it on the internet. His doubts have become frustration which makes him weary of the concept all together.

Lance keeps looking at one particular Caucasian woman on one of the sites, trying to make her cuter than she actually is. She had winked at him more than a week ago and Lance did not respond. He knows what will happen if he does – he will wind up with another *Anitra type* female on his hands.

On this particular evening, Lance decides to change his mindset regarding any woman he meets from now on, internet or otherwise. He will make the concept of *friends first* his priority and his MO from here on out. He thinks that women will have a hard time believing this – and so will *he* if any woman he meets is beautiful enough and intelligent enough to penetrate the terminus of his true aspirations.

Lance decides to respond to her wink with an email *just because* she is Caucasian. He knows what many, especially African American women, would think in his reasoning behind this – that he wants to convert to dating *white women* because he thinks they are better within the concept of dating. Lance has always preferred to replace the word *better* with the word *different*. In his mind, while people in general do share certain attributes and personalities no matter their ethnicity; the flip side of the coin can offer differences as well. With that in mind and his *friends first* philosophy in place, he will argue and fight with anyone to his grave regarding his stance on this matter.

The woman's name is Trisha Sampson. She is single, never married; thirty-seven years old and lives in Joliet, Illinois. She has six children.

Damn she's a freak!! As Lance reviews her profile, he looks at photos of her being at a baseball game. It reminds him that he really doesn't like Caucasian women that like baseball because it makes them seem a bit tomboyish. He reminds himself of the *friends first* policy or in Trisha's case, *friends forever.*

"*So* Lance, what have you been up to?" Angelica asks over the phone.

"Nothing . . . and *everything,*" responds Lance.

"You're not still having unprotected sex with that woman from the bank, are you?"

"Who, Anitra . . . ? I only did it to her twice."

"It only takes *one time* my friend."

Lance chuckles, "Well I pulled out before I . . ."

Angelica interrupts, "Oh I forgot, *you are* the 'pull out king!'"

"Well to answer your question, the answer is *no* . . . I had to let her go. She was too much!!"

"Ooohh Lance, you ain't no good! I'm sure *you were* thinking '*she was too much*' every time you were putting those diamond earrings in your ears."

"Well actually, yeah I was. The gift *was* excessive."

"Yeah I know – I'm just playing with you. And being a woman myself, it's a shame that I can't take her side. Not only was the gift excessive, it was stupid!"

"I thought about giving them back – but I decided against it. Anitra played her hand the way she saw fit. If she feels like she has to do that to land herself a man, then that's *her* business."

"I wouldn't have accepted such an expensive gift to begin with – but since you did, you're right, that's on her . . . and why does she have an *r* in her name?"

"I dunno . . ."

"You know me . . . it would've taken me at least *two years* to spend that kind of money on a man! How did you break it off with her?"

"Before I tell you that story . . . did I tell you that Sherry is engaged!?"

"Oh really – all of a sudden, huh . . . ! Did you see the ring?"

"That's funny you should ask. I was looking at some pictures we took the last time I saw her, and there was no engagement ring on her left hand."

Angelica almost drops her cell phone, "Wait a minute Lance . . . the woman is engaged to be married but she doesn't have an engagement ring!!? Maybe she put it on the other hand."

"She didn't have one on her right hand either!"

"Where are you meeting these women Lance . . . !?"

"On the internet . . ."

"Let the internet dating go!!" Angelica laughs as she continues, "You know I'm just kidding, right? Most people are crazy now-a-days, no matter where you meet 'em. You know there's something wrong with that picture, right!?"

"Absolutely . . . ! I don't wish any bad luck on her but if that situation blows up in her face, I'll be there to comfort her."

" . . . How noble of you Mr. Austin. You like Sherry a lot, don't you?"

"Yeah, she does affect me a little more than I would like right now. She has *really* gotten to me since the second time we hooked up last year. To this day I still get a little nervous around her and that's because I like her so much – she really matters to me!"

"Well that's fine and all, but be careful with *that* one – don't fall for her too hard. She *is* spoken for, even if their union doesn't sound like it will last. And if it doesn't, *still* be careful with her. As you have probably learned first hand, Sherry won't be emotionally equipped to enter into a new relationship right away – not until she's gotten over the old one. Hint hint . . . *Melanie.*"

"Uhh . . . *yeah*!! Lord knows I learned a valuable lesson from *that* experience. I think too many of us in society have gotten away from being friends first anyway. We all keep hopping into bed with one another . . . way too soon; like Anitra and I."

"From what you've told me about Sherry, she won't jump into bed with you right away but still take it slow. *Anita* with the extraneous *r* in her name on the other hand . . . sounds *GH* anyway. That's the oldest trick in the book; for a woman to try and influence a man into being her boyfriend the way that she did it! At least Sherry has sense enough to allow a man to take her out to eat before getting involved in *any* kind of way."

"What's *'GH'*?"

"Oh . . ." Angelica giggles, "That means *ghetto.* That's a code I use when I'm talking on the phone on the train. I've used that term before . . ."

"I must have missed it before; that's funny though."

"So she must have told you about the engagement *after* you saw her?"

"Yeah and at first I found that weird but now I see how smart it was."

"Yes because the first thing a woman does when she announces that she's engaged, is extend her hand to show off the ring. She knew she didn't have anything to show off, so she waited and told you over the phone. I bet she was excited when she told you, wasn't she?"

"Yeah she was . . ."

"Yeah, you be careful with her. She sounds a tad bit silly. An engagement with *no ring* is nothing to be excited about. So how did you get rid of Anitra?"

"I took her to Cuatro's and broke it off."

"Lance, *you* are terrible! Angelica laughs, "And what is it with you and this Cuatro's place?"

"That's my spot! I like the place. It has a nice ambience to it. As far as taking her there, I felt so guilty about not taking her out *anywhere . . .*"

"That's a shame! This woman gave up her sex without ever sitting across a dinner table from you – you didn't even take her to a greasy spoon diner before she laid down with you! She gave you some twice, huh?"

"Yeah, and the second time was really just a *thank you fuck* for the earrings!"

Angelica giggles, "Did she spend the night?"

"No she did not! I figure if a woman can come out the house at midnight for sex, then she can go home at 2:00am after she's gotten it. I had to work the next morning anyway!"

"Lance, *you are silly!*"

They both laugh as Lance continues, "I also took her there to see how it felt to take someone out to dinner to break up with them. I'll tell you this – I'll never break up with anyone *like that* again! And it had to be a major let down for her, especially *it* being our first time ever going anywhere."

"She drives a black SUV, right?"

"Yeah, why . . . ?"

"You better make sure there isn't one following you around after this. She could be a stalker!"

"I know right! And please don't mention the black SUV; I hate it when some black women drive around in these big ol' black trucks. It's like they want to take on a semblance of male role playing and indulge in certain male tendencies; it's just not feminine to me!"

"I know exactly what you mean. Some women just don't know *how* to be women anymore – because they're *GH!!* So what did you say to Anitra? How did she take it?"

"Well . . . I did the 'it's not you, it's me' thing . . . and she was devastated. She didn't even order dinner; just a salad. It was *really* difficult to do – especially in the atmosphere we were in. I do take part of the blame for letting things get out of hand. I really hurt her feelings and she didn't see it coming."

"You told her *before* the two of you ordered – that's why she only got the salad?"

"You're so silly Angelica. I don't think I told her before that . . . I really don't remember when I said it."

"So you broke up with a woman that you never even referred to *as* your woman and you never treated her like your woman either. That is pitiful! A woman *is* responsible for setting the pace of a developing relationship but only if one *is* developing. Regardless of that, her pace was rampant and out of control. By the way, your rendition of black women and black trucks reminds me of something funny you once told me about white women and baseball."

Lance laughs, "You remember that!? That was years ago. Speaking of which . . . there's this white woman on the internet . . ."

Angelica interrupts, "Ah! You're looking to diversify now, huh?"

"Well, yeah . . . but I'm gonna take the pressure out of the dating game and do the friends first thing."

"Oh really . . . ? Interesting . . ."

CHAPTER 14

L ance stands by his desk at home staring at the calendar on the wall. He is on the phone with Kevin.

"Man dog, I can't believe its August already! Looks like it's gonna be another dead summer!" Lance says.

"Yeah I know 'cause it's too late to meet anyone now. We needed to bump into some decent women in May or June in order for anything to be jumpin' off by now. What's up with that white girl you were telling me about?" Kevin asks.

"I dunno . . . I'm gonna call her when I hang up with you. I just met this *other* female on another site though; her name is Jim."

"Her name is *Jim*!?"

"That's the name she had on her profile. I'm sure it's short for something; either that or she's a transvestite!!"

"For *real* . . . ! What does she look like?"

"I dunno dog – *no picture*!!"

"Aahhh man, what is it with these Chicago women being so scared and secretive about putting their picture up on a dating website!? What's the point in them gettin' on there in the first place!!?"

"I dunno dog – but she gave me her phone number just like *that*!"

"Hhmmpp!! That means she's probably ugly but I'm sure you know that!"

"Nine times outta ten she probably *is* . . . but what about that *one*!?"

After Lance hangs up with Kevin, he calls Trisha for the first time. Their conversation is easy going and typical. They swap short stories about the declined quality of the dating game. They speak of how misleading internet dating can be in most cases, according to their experiences. They talk about how stressful their jobs are and they talk about movies and music. Their conversation is *now* comfortable enough for Lance to explain his *friends first* mindset. He goes into this whole schmeal about how the dating process can be made less complicated and more relaxed. Only time will tell if Trisha actually buys into it. Only time will tell if *Lance* can actually buy into the concept himself.

Trisha tells Lance some amusing stories about her and her girlfriends going to different clubs and bar spots. She likes to drink and Lance likes this about her – something in common. He pictures himself being out with a bunch of drunken Caucasian women and it makes him smile.

White women are so fun to get drunk with. I don't know why but they are! With the constant background noise of six children on Trisha's end of the phone, Lance wonders how she even has a chance to go out at all. He figures that exhaustion should take its toll on her if nothing else, as it often does with him in raising just *one* child.

Lance had considered calling the young lady with the male's name after he got off the phone with Trisha; but their conversation lasted for over two hours. He decides to wait a different day to venture into the unknown with the woman with no picture on her profile. Lance also has to remind himself that he and Jim's email exchanges occurred just hours earlier.

The male rule is – never call a female the same day you met 'em . . . wait a few days he thinks. *That fits perfect with my* friends first *policy. No neediness – no clinginess – and no desperation!!* However, he *does* read her email and his reply once again.

Hi Lance, how are you? You seem to be an intriguing person, according to your profile. I know that most people would like to see a picture first. However, I really don't know how to download or upload pictures on the computer. I can honestly tell you that I am an attractive lady by most standards. I'm 5'5", size 3/4, brown eyes and brown hair. I'm not big on emailing but I would love to chat with you. I'm going to share my # with you if that's ok. I look forward to hearing from you.

Jim
(773) 555-1234

Hello Jim, I can't wait to hear what your full name is. Anyway, I am speechless!! The reason being – in most cases; and I'm being honest here, so keep an open mind . . . in most cases a woman that will give her # out so easily usually doesn't possess the physical attributes that one would consider "easy on the eye." However, I am going to give you the benefit of the doubt and call you. Part of me is saying, "Why would she lie?" So do expect to hear from me soon. And thanx for checking me out.

Lance

*   *   *

On a Saturday night Lance decides to do something he very seldom does and go out to a club. While he's on the highway on his way out to Hoffman Estates to meet Carl, he thinks about what he has to do in the morning – meet Sherry's boyfriend Norman. Lance finds himself in an uncomfortable predicament of meeting them both at 11:30am for brunch. He knows he agreed to it because Sherry is his friend and nothing more. He still can't help but wonder though, *why* he agreed to it. He then recalls how determined Sherry was over the phone a few days ago to set this meeting up and how important she made it seem. Of course Lance couldn't say no, even if he wanted to.

When Lance arrives at Carl's house, they drink a six pack and a couple of shots before they head out. By their standards in the old days, the amount of alcohol they consume now-a-days exhibits consumption in moderation. Lance misses the old days but he doesn't miss the recklessness that came along with them when he considers the fact that he now has a child.

When they get to the club, Carl is totally taken by the party's atmosphere. The alcohol flows steadily for the both of them as they take turns buying each other drinks; but the atmosphere is a struggle for Lance. He is reminded of why he doesn't frequent the club scene. The music is obnoxiously loud and he doesn't mind this; only the selections that are played. This calls to mind how music in itself has changed.

The group of patrons is what plagues Lance the most. The establishment seems to be a party going haven for thirty-somethings – but these thirty-somethings seem to be the twenty-somethings of Lance's hay days. The way they act and interact with one another is immature. The way they dress is juvenile; especially the men. A lot of the women, no matter their race, seem snooty and unapproachable. A lot of them seem to already know many people in the club also, which makes this place feel more like a neighborhood bar than a "happening" club spot.

The only taste of the old days that Lance can take full advantage of is the number of drinks he has on this night – so many that he loses count. He blames the excessive alcohol consumption on the late morning brunch with Sherry and Norman that he has on his mind. He tries to deny it at first but then quickly gives in to the fact that he can't wait until it's over and done with.

Lance continues to order drinks, even after he's reached the point of knowing he should've stopped. He spins his bar stool away from the bar and spots Carl on the dance floor having a ball with some woman that looks like an amazon. He quickly turns back towards the bar, hoping to find himself in an uncoercive conversation with a woman that is at least half way decent at this point. Lance is quickly deterred of that thought when he thinks of Anitra.

The next morning Lance rushes to get on the Dan Ryan expressway entrance ramp. At 11:45am he calls Sherry and tells her that he can't find a parking space near the restaurant, even though he's still on the highway. Needless to say, his hangover is determined to ruin his entire day. He knows he won't be giving the best self presentation to Sherry that he normally does and he's okay with that. It's more important to Lance that Norman sees him in tip top form. He wants this man to see with his own eyes and hear with his own ears, that *there is* a quality man in Sherry's life who will have her as his own if he doesn't do right by her.

When Lance quickly finds a parking space near the restaurant where they're meeting, he tries to shrug off the torpid feeling of his hangover while he's walking. He is not successful, so he doesn't worry about it because the damage is done. As he arrives near the front of the crowded restaurant, he sees *more* than a few classy and desirable women.

Wow I need to hang out here more often!! As he tries to spot Sherry and her boyfriend to no avail, Lance almost drops his cell phone when he snatches it from its holster to call her.

"Hey Sherry I'm here. Where are you guys!?" The phone call reminds him of the day they first met at the mall almost a year and a half ago. Lance thinks about that day and wishes he could have it back to do all over again. He would have planned their one and only date better than he did. He tried to do some research on the restaurants in her area back then . . . but he wishes he would have done *more* research. He never considered until now that maybe he should have taken a rain check and gone on a date with her on a different day – on a day when he didn't have to be squeezed into her schedule. Lance stops thinking about it because again, the damage is done; and it distracts him from being able to locate his party.

"You guys are outside on the patio, right?" he asks.

"Yes . . . and you're on the sidewalk right in front of the place?"

"Yes."

"Okay, I'll get up and meet you," she says. Lance can't help but smile when he recalls the *left/right* exchanges that he and Sherry shared over the phone before when they first met. When Lance sees her approaching, the smile that appears on his face is under its own power.

"Wow! No wonder you couldn't find us . . . this place *is* crowded!" Sherry says as she returns his smile with one of her own. Lance is glad that she left Norman at the table to get up and meet him. He doesn't have to contemplate the kiss he gently places on her left cheek or deduct any seconds away from the four second hug that he gives her.

"How are you?" He then blurts out before she can answer, "Sherry you look nice!!"

"Thank you Lance, so do you . . . as usual," she says blushing. Lance cannot believe that this is the very first time he has complimented such a beautiful woman.

Her clothing is different this time though; dressier. The previous offerings of her cheap fashion statements didn't warrant any compliments in Lance's eyes.

"C'mon, we're over here *somewhere* . . . it's so crowded, I can't find the table now."

Sherry says accompanied by her cute little giggle. When she finds the table, Lance gives Norman a slight smile as his initial greeting. He gives Norman a very quick "up and down," to not be mistaken for showing signs of a homosexual male – staring at another male too long.

"Norman, this is Lance – Lance, this is Norman . . ." Sherry says in her introduction.

"How ya doing man . . . ?" Norman says.

"Whasup man . . ." Lance says as they shake hands in an old fashioned, traditional way. *Hhmmpp! His handshake is firm – that's good but the white boy part of it has gotta go! Preppy motherfucka!!*

Norman is 6'2", well toned – not extremely muscular; but enough to be more muscular than Lance. His tight beige pullover ribbed shirt does nothing but help his cause – and Lance knows it. He is slightly lighter in complexion than Lance and he is completely bald and clean shaven.

Okay, he gets one point for having a better body than me; half a point for being taller and half a point for his face – only because I have a hangover, Lance thinks as he quickly drinks his water.

Norman has a thought. *Hhmmpp! His handshake was firm – that's bad! It eliminates the possibility of him being gay. He's hanging around my woman for one reason and one reason only . . . but it shouldn't matter though. It seems like he likes to use slang by his greeting – probably one of those uneducated motherfuckers! Sherry wouldn't go for that type anyway.*

As the three of them look at their menus, the usual icebreaking subjects are discussed between the two men. When Norman reveals that he has a Bachelor's degree, Lance notices a certain braggadocio in his statement. He then reveals that he is currently in between jobs by choice. Lance doesn't relate to this too well because if Norman *didn't* need a steady income, Sherry would have an engagement ring. Lance has been on his job for seventeen years and he is internally ecstatic when he reveals this.

Ha!! One point for me, Lance thinks to himself.

They talk about different restaurants and whose food and service is favorable and whose is not. "I will admit, I've never been *here*," Lance says.

"Yeah they're pretty good here, though I will admit the service is usually a little better," Norman says as he stops a busboy that's passing by. "Excuse me, may I get water refills for him and I and tell our waiter we're ready to order now."

"Oh sure no prob . . ." the busboy replies.

Norman chuckles, "Hhmmpp! He didn't speak very good English, *did* he?" Even though it is an observation that Lance himself would have made and commented on, he looks at Sherry and detects that she didn't appreciate the smugness in Norman's comment. Lance gives him a slight nod as not to show too much encouragement in his so called joke.

The conversation then turns to the club scene; something Norman seems to know a lot about. Lance assumes that he no longer has to wonder where Norman was on the night Sherry needed someone to entertain her out of town friend.

Not spending enough time with his woman . . . I now have two points – we're tied!

Sherry sits at the table as if to bask in the sunlight over the fact that her boyfriend is so knowledgeable. In reality, the disdain fills her insides completely. A lot of the venues that Norman speaks of, Sherry has never ventured. She knows better deep down inside, than to think that a lot of these experiences occurred *before* they met.

"Excuse me busboy!" Norman says with authority. "I asked for water refills ten minutes ago and why did I even have to ask!? Also, we were seated twenty minutes ago! Would you *please* find our waiter and tell him that we have *been* ready to order!!"

"Sure sir, I'm sorry sir!"

"My goodness, what is wrong with these people today!?" Norman says as the busboy walks away.

Hhmmm . . . interesting, Lance thinks to himself. He is all too familiar with the arrogance and disgust that Norman has willingly put on display, especially regarding the food quality and overall customer service of a restaurant. What he has learned and started to live by in recent years though, is *not* to display it in front of a lady.

I'm way ahead of this guy on the realization of needing an attitude adjustment! Another point for me, Lance thinks.

The conversation finally turns to Lance's son when he conveniently uses him as his excuse for not getting out often enough. He wishes it was really the reason and not the fact that he's just not enthusiastic about going out anymore, especially with no special lady to do so with. This slight exaggeration does serve as the perfect excuse as to why Norman knows about more venues than *he* does.

"I love being a father!!" Lance proudly says.

"Sherry and I have talked about having a little one," Norman adds. "That would definitely be different but it would be nice! No definite plans as of yet . . ." Norman grabs Sherry's hand and looks at Lance when he does so. He then squeezes it as if to give her reassurance that they *will* talk about it again soon. Sherry realizes this and squeezes his hand also, but just to humor him. She had expressed to Lance in their very first conversation last year that she would like to have children. With the timing of them technically not becoming friends until after LJ was conceived, it never gave Lance a chance to be internally excited over her revelation. She was into Norman since day one anyway.

Lance mentally prepares to give Norman his third point. He knows that the eye contact Norman gave him when he grabbed his woman's hand was a silent signal to confirm,

"Even though she is *the girl next door, I'm sleeping with her and you're not!!"*

Sherry asks, "So Lance, if you were to meet someone *really* nice – you know, a woman that you *really* like . . . let's say you two get into a serious relationship and she wants to have a child; would you have a baby with her?"

"Absolutely . . . !" Lance says without hesitating. "Now all I need is *the woman.*" He looks at Sherry for a few moments longer than he should. He forgets momentarily that Norman is even there.

"Yeah that's the easy part, right?" she says jokingly. They both give a slight chuckle. Lance can't help but wonder why she asked him that question, especially in front of Norman. He then questions the validity of his thoughts.

Is she talking about me? Or maybe she isn't 'cause surely the overall good nature that rules her demeanor wouldn't allow her to say something so rude or callous, indirectly or otherwise towards her guy on purpose. But what if she's so painfully honest that it slipped out before she caught herself and she is *talking about me.*

Lance goes on and gives Norman the third additional mental point because no matter what, Norman is waking up with Sherry every single morning and he is not – at least he *hopes* it's every morning. He is ready to deem their unspoken male battle a draw, and then the bill arrives. Lance offers to pay.

"Oh no Lance, I'll get it," Sherry says with her credit card already in hand. Norman doesn't even offer to pick up the check.

. . . Another point for me! Your gentleman's etiquette is lacking Mr. Norman . . . *and I get another half a point just for your overall manhood now being in question! There is one of two reasons why you didn't offer to pay the bill – my presence here today bothered you to a point that you didn't wanna pay . . . or you couldn't pay!! Either way I win!!!*

*   *   *

Lance and Sherry have only spoken twice in three weeks since their brunch outing. He had hoped that she would start to give him small increments of information to confirm the uneasiness that resides in him about Norman. Instead he gets the,

"*Oh, everything worked out so well that day for brunch"* speech.

Yeah right he thinks. *I would've loved to have Sherry get up from her seat and come stand by me so I could've flipped that brunch table upside down and dropped it on top of Norman's head!!*

Lance smiles at his own outrageous thoughts as he tries to focus on the task at hand. He and Kevin are on their way to his old residence to finally pick up the remaining items he still has there. Most people would consider these items to be junk but Lance doesn't consider anything as such – not until he's had a chance to sift through it for final consideration.

Once they arrive, Lance tries his best to make their visit brief by quickly gathering his belongings in one room to be carried out. When he comes across an entertainment center and a pulley weight bench system, both of which need partially taking apart just to get through the front door, their visit becomes longer. Against his better judgment, Lance knocks on Nathanael's door to borrow a flathead screwdriver. He remembers how his brother refused to help when he initially moved out almost a year ago. He's not holding a grudge but he's not bending over backwards to socialize with any of his brothers or his stepfather, given the current circumstances of the lack of family comradeship where his son is concerned.

Surprisingly, Nathanael decides to assist Lance and Kevin move some items without being asked. When they are almost finished, all three of them give a sigh of relief as they're sitting at the back of the rental truck having a cigarette break. Lance truly appreciates the spontaneous bonding that occurs with his brother on this evening. They both know it has been too long since they last did so. During their final break about an hour later, Lance receives a text message.

Lance – Norman and I broke up! When I told him I had been out on a date, he got really upset and broke it off. I really hurt his feelings!!

The mixture of emotions that overtake Lance are extreme. He is saddened by her news but he is happy as hell! The anger he feels towards Norman is equally divided with gratitude that he did the right thing and stepped aside to make room for a man more deserving of having Sherry as his mate. Lance asks himself if he's dreaming, yet he knows he isn't. He had always anticipated this day would come but not as soon as it does. He smiles while he types the words in his response.

I'm really sorry to hear that. Are you okay?

No not really – but I will be.

Okay, I will call you soon.

Lance wishes that Sherry was referring to him when she indicated having gone out on a date with someone. He assumes that she meant within the past week or two, making it virtually impossible for her to be making reference to anywhere *they've* been before then.

Lance does get around to calling Sherry, not really knowing what to say except for how sorry he is. He wants to choose his words carefully and not be judgmental of anything regarding her situation until it has started to sink in for her. As a friend who is genuinely concerned, he graciously invites her to come to his apartment so he can cook dinner for her to help her feel better. With Sherry feeling out of sorts, she doesn't hesitate in accepting his kind gesture. But when Lance starts to reveal in detail what his presentation will consist of, she starts to wonder what she may be getting herself into.

"This sounds like a date! Is this a date!?" she asks inquisitively.

"This can be what ever *you* want it to be." Sherry can hear the calmness in his voice and yet, his tone also sounds coy to her. She reneges on accepting a home cooked meal from her male friend with an apparent agenda. When they get off the phone, Lance has to re-evaluate what would seem to be a classic case of,

Me and my big mouth!! Oh my God!! What did I just do!? One statement and the whole thing is out the window!!? I can't let that happen!!

Lance calls her back fifteen minutes later. "Sherry!! I'm sorry I said that to you!! I'm sorry if that made you feel uncomfortable!"

"Why did you say that!?" she anxiously inquires.

"I don't think that came out right! But I said it because I'm not going to sit here and pretend like I wouldn't mind going out on another date with you but I know that's not what you need right now. I'm still a man though and I can't pretend that isn't so either – so I called myself just leaving it up to you."

"Well I'm not ready to date anyone right now! My whole world has just been turned upside down!! Going out on a date . . ." Lance interrupts her,

"*Did* you hear what I just said to you Sherry? And I told you before that I was concerned as a friend. My gesture was, and *is*, purely based on our friendship."

"Okay Lance," Sherry says calmly.

They end their call after that exchange. "Jeez!! And they say that *men* don't listen to women . . ." They set their meeting up for Friday after work and Lance is just as anxious about cooking for his female friend, as he would be if he *was* cooking for a date.

When their significant day that means *nothing* arrives, Lance *tries* to maintain that exact attitude. Of course he won't tell her that he purchased new plates and glasses and some other minor home decor items just two days before her visit. While this does coincide with the new furniture set he purchased a few weeks ago, Sherry's visit on this evening *did* slightly influence his additional purchases as well.

Lance doesn't change his routine where LJ is concerned; he simply includes Sherry in it. He drives out to Skokie to pick her up *with* his son who is seven months old now. LJ's social skills and overall sense of awareness are keener than ever before, making him almost feel like a second passenger that Lance can communicate with.

He can't wait for his son to *really* start talking. He also can't wait for Sherry to meet him. By the time they arrive, LJ is asleep.

"Oh he's so cute!!" she exclaims before she gets in the car.

"Thanks. He'll say hi to you later when he wakes up; but in the meantime, 'hi' from his father!!"

"Hi yourself . . . ! Lance is my homie, wow!! This is wonderful. Thank you!"

"Don't thank me yet, I haven't done anything," he says.

"You wouldn't let me ride the train out to your place; always *such* a gentleman."

Lance thinks to himself, *"Lance is my homie" . . . what does that mean? Maybe she's excited about being able to relax in a man's presence for once. I hope so 'cause that's what I want her to feel . . . that's how I'll get her in the end.* He smiles when he thinks about how "my homie" came out of her mouth – like she had just learned of the word and used it for the very first time.

By the time they arrive in front of Lance's apartment, they are in a deep conversation about relationships. It's so deep that they sit in the car for about ten minutes before they get out.

"Lance, in your next relationship, what is the main thing you would do differently than you did in your previous relationship? Like, would you *not* move in with that person or would you wait to have sex or what?"

"Wow, that's a long question Sherry," he says with a surprised look on his face. "I know the answer though. I don't think the *moving in together* part is as much of an issue as the two people's mindset that are doing it."

"You mean like if they're really ready for it?"

"Yeah and their personal plans for the future and if the person they're moving in with *really* fits into those plans. Me personally, I'm going to be more empathetic towards that woman and know when to zip it up at times; not be so nick picky and bitchy, be calmer and just realize that I will not *always* get my way and to let certain things go instead of harping on them."

"Wow that's a long answer Lance," she says while smiling.

"Yeah I know. *Empathy* is the key word though. No matter how many times I may tell a woman how much I care about her . . . if I'm always fighting with her over stupid stuff, she's going to start to feel like I *don't* care about her."

"Mmmm, that's a good point . . . I take it you're one of those guys that likes to argue?"

"I *used* to, but now . . . I realize most of the time it's not worth it."

"What about waiting for sex?"

"'Waiting for sex' . . . well, I have been with some women where I didn't have to wait that long for sex; and I've been with others that made me wait for a long period of time – we're talking months. I prefer the woman that wants to wait. She's usually a woman with more substance and the relationship is usually filled with more substance. I respect a woman more that will make me wait, though my problem in relationships has always been a lack of respect on my part. It never came from a place of not liking women, but a place of no empathy for them. Do you know what I mean?"

"Yeah, I think I do. I guess when a man doesn't care about his woman's feelings, it can be considered a lack of respect. Have you ever considered waiting until marriage for sex?"

"Oh! Is that what you meant when you said, 'waiting?'"

"Yeah, pretty much . . ."

"Well I've never done *that* before; but at this point in my life with my next woman, it's definitely something I would consider. Lance thinks for a few seconds, "You know what, if I care about her enough, I probably *would* go for that. We better go in the house if we're going to eat tonight."

"Okay Lance . . ."

CHAPTER 15

When Sherry walks into the apartment behind Lance and LJ, she gasps when she sets eyes on the living room. "What . . . ?" Lance inquires.

" . . . This is *nice!*" she exclaims.

"Thanks!" Lance takes a lot of pride in his apartment's set up. He will admit to anyone that *it does* look nice, even with this being his very first apartment ever. He wonders about Sherry's compliments overall though; if they are truly filled with praise or if they embody awe over the fact that *he* is capable of reaching such heights of status quo.

Lance is a true advocate of "you can't judge a book by its cover." But in his opinion, most people do, so he uses that to tease people with and throw their perception of him off a little bit. He attributes this so called cleverness to his Zodiac sign of a Gemini. The dual personalities that one of *this* sign is often described as having is a trait that Lance used to find fascinating in himself. The realization of his argumentative ways in recent years however, drastically changed his viewpoint of this trait. In regards to the self indulging mind games he plays with people in having them think he's hard to figure out; Lance has kept these games to a minimum where Sherry is concerned. Therefore he thinks the time is well overdue for her to have figured out what he's truly made of.

Lance takes Sherry's jacket and lays it on the arm of his black leather sofa. He uses hand and head gestures to have her follow him to his bedroom so he can lie LJ down in his bassinet, hoping that he won't wake up. Lance also hopes that Sherry won't think he's up to something within the male, masculine aspect of *I'm showing this woman my bedroom for future reference* – though as a male, the thought does cross his mind. They enter his bedroom and Lance takes LJ out of his infant car seat, removes his blanket and small jacket as he places him in his miniature sleeping quarters.

Almost melodiously Sherry says, "Wow you have a beautiful child and no mate and I have neither . . . I don't know which situation is worse!"

Sherry starts to cry. Lance immediately rushes over to give her a hug; much longer than he ever has before. When he pulls away from the hug, they remain standing close to one another. As he places his hands on each side of her, right below her shoulders, he feels a tear forming in his left eye. Lance hopes it rolls down his cheek because this will show Sherry his sensitivity towards her and her situation. He slowly moves his hands up to each side of her face. As much as he wants to offer her words of encouragement, he knows the moment has arrived in which nothing needs to be said; something needs to be done.

Lance's feigning moment is interrupted when Sherry calls out his name for the second time. "You didn't hear me?" she says.

Lance turns away from LJ, "No, I drifted for a moment. What did you say?"

"I said, so this is your bedroom huh?"

"Yes . . ."

"You're *always* drifting off. You're a thinker, aren't you?"

"Of course I am – I'm a Gemini, remember?"

"Oh yeah, that's right." Lance turns the baby monitor on before he leads Sherry through the bathroom and then to LJ's room. He'll show her the dining room on their way to the kitchen. He knows that leaving her in the living room while he cooks is *completely* out of the question.

Lance wonders to himself, if Sherry were emotionally weak enough to want to have sex, would he take advantage of the moment. As much as he would want to, he wouldn't because he cares about her too much. If an inevitable kiss were to occur however, he would prefer it be followed through with sex, instead of the awkwardness of having to apologize for just a kiss alone. Lance's mental struggle with these two scenarios is minimal though. He doesn't anticipate either one of them occurring. He takes his thoughts back to the aspect of their friendship, as not to stress himself out on this evening; or give himself away.

When they are in the kitchen twenty minutes later, Sherry sits at the table with a girlish grin on her face. Her shoes are off and her feet are up on the chair. Lance is happy that she asked if she could take her shoes off; this being indicative of a comfortable atmosphere for her to do so. Though she doesn't admit it out loud, Sherry is also starting to realize more and more, just how sweet and thoughtful her platonic friend really is.

Lance is preparing chicken breasts cooked atop the stove with sautéed green peppers and onions in an olive oil base. He is also baking some catfish, tilapia, green and yellow bell peppers also in an olive oil base with fresh lime to top it off. This is the first time he has ever prepared fish like this. After this evening, it will definitely not be the last. He steams some whole green beans and also makes herbal styled rice. Lance even thinks to prepare them both a salad ten minutes before dinner. He uses Romaine lettuce, red onions, and thin slices of both colored bell peppers, tomatoes, cucumber slices and egg whites with Italian dressing.

Even though Lance will eat an *8oz.* filet mignon at the drop of a hat, he does try to indulge in healthier food choices from time to time. These carefully picked food items were also with Sherry in mind because she is a vegetarian. She *is* impressed with the food spread.

"Lance you really went all out!! This is a lot of food; I hope none of it goes to waste!"

"It's no big deal; I like to cook. And no, it won't go to waste because I like to eat too! So what went down with you and Norman? Did he kind of find out you went out with someone else or did you volunteer the information? Knowing you, probably the latter of the two . . ."

"You're funny Lance . . . yes it was 'the latter of the two.' I guess it was my way of letting him know that things just weren't quite right in our relationship. I just wanted to wake him up a bit; I didn't expect him to break it off with me!"

You probably hurt his poor little ego. What did he have to say about me?"

"When, three weeks ago after brunch . . . ?"

"Well . . . anytime for that matter?"

"Well, he just kind of brushed the whole situation off . . . though I think you bothered him a little bit. He seemed a little jealous when I would mention you *before* you two met. I guess that's why he wanted to meet you."

"*Norman* wanted to meet me!? I thought *you* wanted me to meet Norman," Lance says in a startling tone.

"Well I did in some ways . . . but he *insisted* upon it. He may have thought I was trying to make him jealous when I would mention you, but I really wasn't. I talk about all of my friends."

"Yeah but most of them are female friends I bet! Well, he did seem a little uptight to me and a lot of *arrogant.* I knew that nigga wasn't right for you!!"

"Ughh!! You use that word!?" she says with a frown.

"What word?" he asks innocently . . . even though he knows what word she's talking about.

"*Nigger . . .*"

"Yeah and you sound funny saying it." Lance chuckles. "It's okay for *him* to be a *nigga* in my book 'cause he did you wrong!"

"Of course you know the history of that word in our culture. I just think it's inappropriate."

"Well I tell you what . . ." Lance lowers his voice to be humbling towards Sherry,

" . . . I knew that *motherfucker* wasn't right for you . . . and please excuse my French on that one."

"Whoa!! Why don't you tell me what you *really* think about him," Sherry says jokingly. Yet there is something in her voice or maybe it's just something in the air that makes Lance think that maybe she's not ready to be through with Norman just yet.

He did dump her, so that doesn't help!!

Lance doesn't dwell on it because like mostly everything else in his life, he understands that whether or not she's ready to be through with Norman, *it is what it is.*

Lance knows that only Sherry can make her mind up about her situation and be final with it; he can't and won't *try* to change it for her. He does however continue to dwell on Norman from a negative point of view.

"I bet he frowned when I rolled past in my car that day while you two were walking after our brunch. Did you know that was me rolling past with the music blasting?"

"You know, I kind of figured it was you; I knew it was your kind of car. I *frowned* too! You had that music going *awfully* loud – but I *did* like the song you were playing."

"Uh huh see, that's my whole point!" Lance says excitedly. "Besides from the fact that I drove around looking for you guys and blasting my music on purpose just so Norman could hear it . . ."

"Why . . . ?"

"Well you said you think I bothered him a little bit; I suspected that all a long. What man *wouldn't* be bothered by another man that's been on his job for seventeen years while he's fumbling around with his Bachelor's degree under his arm and *no* job!!? So after that it's like . . . give this nigga . . ." Sherry frowns. Lance frowns back at her and then continues, " . . . Give this *silly man* a false sense of hope and make him think I'm ignorant! Anyway, back to my main point . . . I know that playing loud music in the car is an ignorant thing to do, but just because I do it, doesn't mean I'm ignorant. Same with the *n word* . . . just because I use the word *nigger*, mainly with my male comrades, *doesn't mean* that I am one or act like one consistently enough to be legitimately considered as one."

"You are *truly* crazy Lance . . . in an interesting kind of way."

"Yeah, but like I told you last year – just a little bit . . . An even better response would be, no I'm not crazy at all . . . I'm just a Gemini!" Lance smiles, "And you said, 'but I *did* like the song you were playing.' I know you like the song 'Hopeless.' I have a pretty decent idea of what you like music wise. Method to my madness baby – method to my madness . . . !"

Sherry giggles, "You are something else Mr. Austin!"

"Hey it's okay to be a little wild and loose sometimes and I'm not criticizing you and how you may do things . . . I'm talking about how *I* do things sometimes."

"Oh okay," she says hesitantly.

"Dinner's ready," he says in a proud tone of voice. Lance makes a plate for a lady and he makes *his* plate; twice as much. He smiles to himself about his subtle attempt to get Sherry to loosen up from time to time in her life. Ultimately though, he knows that only *she* can decide once and for all, to do that.

Sherry and Lance go back to his living room to eat dinner. She chooses the lonely recliner to sit in and Lance allows it even though he lets *no one* else sit there. He has a couple of DVD movies in mind for them to watch in case she's in a movie watching mood. Sherry raves over the food and the overall thoughtfulness of his gesture. Lance is just happy to show her this side of him, as a caring friend and more importantly to lay the groundwork for future reference on a more personal note if needed.

"You're still not drinking?" Lance inquires.

"No I'm not. I told you, I don't like the way I act when I drink alcohol," she says in a girlish voice.

"That's okay, I got you a non-alcoholic Spumante; its almond flavored."

"Wow you think of everything, don't you?"

Lance knows what she means regarding her statement about alcohol, so he doesn't ask. The uninhibited and sometimes aggressive nature that alcohol can conjure up in many people is something Sherry seems to be afraid of in herself. He thinks about their first visit to Cuatro's last year and how she had kissed him on the cheek and told him how sweet he was. Lance knew how "all of a sudden" that seemed on that particular evening; but he never attributed alcohol being the force behind it . . . not until now.

He drinks the non-alcoholic Spumante with her.

Drinking Riesling alone with a lovely lady present is no fun. He can recall a few times in which alcohol gave *him* a little courage in a nervous situation; like a first kiss. Lance doesn't anticipate anything like that happening this evening with Sherry, so he won't need any alcohol to save him so to speak.

They find themselves in another conversation about relationships. Lance can tell how saddened she is over the recent turn of events in her life. He tries his best to comfort her with the only thing he has in his arsenal – words. What he *really* wishes he could use to comfort her with, are both his hands to touch her and to hold her in his arms. When Sherry inquires *again* about his willingness to have a second child with a potential new girlfriend in the future, it surprises Lance. He gives her the same answer he gave her about three weeks ago.

"Absolutely . . . ! Why are you asking me that again?"

"I just wanted to make sure your answer didn't change," she says.

Lance isn't sure what she means specifically by her response; if she is referring to the length of time that has passed since she asked that question the first time or Norman's presence then versus now. He doesn't ask nor does he worry about it because he assumes that any mysteries that may exist now concerning Sherry will eventually come to light and the time will probably be more appropriate to ask.

Lance puts a movie in the DVD player for them to watch. It is somewhat of a love story but with a twist. Sherry criticizes the content as if she doesn't like it. Lance takes offense to this, though he doesn't let Sherry know. The internal affects of certain movies and certain music is something Lance likes to share, particularly with certain women. When they don't quite take to it, he is usually disappointed and attributes this to a lack of open mindedness of the different expressions of *true* art and what it stands for. Lance is one that can be described as having impeccable standards in most areas of his life. When anyone, especially a woman, can relate to that or even match it, he feels that it puts them on *his* level of intelligence.

"It's getting late, we better go," Sherry says. Lance is *really* uptight now because she says this before the movie has ended and eleven o'clock being late for her is early for him. He goes into his bedroom to get LJ ready for their long journey back to Skokie. Having to risk waking the baby up to go anywhere at this time is extremely rare next to non-existent for Lance. In this situation though, he feels that it's worth it. He wants to see Sherry interact with his son anyway; an analyzing of future reference material for himself this time around if ever needed.

LJ *does* wake up as Lance prepares him for their excursion. "Sherry *this* is Lance, Jr.!!" Lance exclaims as he walks out the bedroom with his son in his arms. As he places LJ in his infant car seat, Sherry walks over to see him up close.

"Aawww! Look at him!" she says. Lance stands away to watch the interaction between the two of them. LJ is wide eyed and fully awake and *always* takes well to the pretty ladies. He gets that from his father and his grandfather. Sherry starts to talk to LJ in baby talk instead of using real words. She doesn't seem to be as much of a natural as Lance thought she would. He wonders just how much time she spent around her nieces and nephews when they were coming up.

They drive back to Skokie to drop her off. "Thank you Lance . . . it's really nice to have a friend like you in my life. I really appreciate it."

"You're welcome Sherry."

"Do you still want me to go to your co-worker's birthday party that you mentioned earlier tonight?"

"Absolutely . . . !"

"It's next Saturday, right?"

"Yes I'll pick you up about 8:30pm, okay?"

"Yes okay . . ."

A few days later, Lance decides to follow up on his email response to the female named Jim and call her. When he reaches her and they are talking, one of the first things he asks her is what her full name is.

"My name is Jymilia," she says in a tone not so solicitously.

"And why do you use *Jim* besides from the fact that it's short for *Jymilia?*"

"I dunno . . . I just do," she says in a dull timbre. Lance can tell by her manner of speech that she is at least as intelligent as the text in her email would indicate, but . . . he doesn't like her answer to his question. He wanted her to say something like,

"I use the male version as a short for my name because I'm pretty enough to do so." He's looking for the method to her madness; that interesting twist in how she expresses herself about certain things. He doesn't get it. In fact, their short conversation lacks the zealous flow that Lance has grown accustomed to experiencing with most of the previous internet females.

Lance immediately knows that the only way he will find Jymilia remotely interesting would be to meet her and she be cute. When Lance tells her where he works, she inquires about him knowing anyone from a different municipal department than his. He tells her that he does and his lucky break arrives.

"I was coming downtown tomorrow morning to try and obtain some information about a particular apartment building dating back to 1999," she says.

"Yeah that info would probably be in the archives but I certainly could find out for you. That department is just across the street from where I'm at. I can probably avoid you having to stand in a long line too. What approximate time were you coming down?"

" . . . About ten-thirty; I have an appointment in the area at noon also."

"Okay, well give me the specifics of what you need and I'll get it for you; that way we can meet in person and I get to see what a *Jim* looks like," he says.

Jymilia laughs, "Yeah sure okay and I can just text you when I get downtown."

The next day at his job, Lance gets bogged down with a lot of work first thing in the morning. He speaks to his friend in the other department and tells her about Jymilia's request. His original plan was to meet up with his friend at about 10:15am, grab the information and hopefully run into Jymilia fifteen minutes later. With his relentless work load staring him in the face, it is practically not feasible for Lance to leave his work station for anything. He does anyway at 10:45am because he told Jymilia he would do this favor for her.

A person's word being their bond is something that Lance believes in, deep in his heart. If a person says they're going to do something and it involves someone else or others, they should do it. If they can't, then a person should be man enough or woman enough to offer a reasonable explanation as to why whatever they said they would do, wasn't carried out. This is what *loyalty* is to Lance . . . and this is what *honesty* is to him. There are too many people in the world now-a-days that don't care about what *he* considers common courtesy.

Lance obtains the information from his friend and checks his phone to see if he somehow missed Jymilia's text message. He scoffs when he realizes he didn't. He decides at this very moment that if he doesn't hear from her by the end of the day, he will not call her anymore.

What type of potential date would she be to leave me hanging like this and not call or text me, after I took the time out of my busy work day to do her *a favor? Yes I did want to meet her but still.* When the day comes to an end – so does his interest in Jymilia.

With the recent demise of Sherry's relationship, it is obvious to Lance that her availability to hang out has increased ten fold, working to his advantage. He feels that the birthday party he invited her to this Saturday will work to *her* advantage as well. It is an opportunity for her to be with some quality company and to help get her mind away from the misery that Norman has caused her. When Lance's cell phone rings and he sees its Sherry, he smiles. Her tendency to pick up the phone and call him has increased as well.

"Hi Lance, how are you?"

"I'm fine but the question is . . . *how are you?*"

"I'm a little worried. I think Norman may have access to my voicemail on my cell phone!"

"You mean as in stealing your access code and listening to your messages?"

"Yes!!" With Norman being the enemy in Lance's eyes, even before the break-up, its not hard for him to quickly offer resolution to her concerns, from a negative spin.

"You two broke up, right!?"

"Yes . . ."

"So what does it matter . . . really? I don't mean any harm. Excuse my French Sherry but I say *F him.*" Lance says it in a normal tone so she's no more offended by his choice of words than she has to be. "Are you still going out with the guy you initially told him about? Don't get me wrong . . . I know you don't want Norman all in your business regardless of you two being together or not."

"No I'm not. From us going out just that one time, I could tell he and I wouldn't work out – too much pressure!"

Lance pats himself on the back mentally for not being overly anxious in pressuring her for his own desires. "If it bothers you that much Sherry, then change your number."

"I've had this cell number for years – I would hate to change it at this point. I'm surprised he hasn't called yet!"

"Wow, what did this guy *do* to you!?" he asks. The translation in Lance's mind . . . *Wow, this guy musta really beat that pussy up good!!*

"You know what Lance; you're being a little insensitive right now. I care about the man!"

"You're right Sherry, I'm sorry. I'm a guy and I know how guys are. My opinion is just a little hardcore about him. I kind of wonder how you ended up with a man that wouldn't go out and get a job just because it wasn't to his specifications, to help you two out." Lance doesn't mention the non-existing engagement ring. He knows that would be the ultimate insult.

"I will admit that I kind of got caught up in his looks – but he *is* a nice guy though.

"Aawww . . . the knight in shining armor – the fair maiden princess . . . ! I'm not making fun of you Sherry; believe me when I tell you – I have heard about and *actually lived* that fairy tale stuff a time or two!! As I get older though, I'm starting to realize that fairy tales don't exist!!"

"I know what you mean Lance. I'm starting to think the same thing."

"Relationships are just hard, no matter what point of view you look at them from."

"He's trying to make me call him . . ." she says under her breath.

"Uh uh Sherry, *don't* call him!" he exclaims.

"I'm not . . . but I wonder why he hasn't called me yet; that's so unlike him."

It suddenly dawns on Lance that Sherry and Norman are not done yet. "You know what Sherry . . . I'm going to say this to you as a friend – from what I've learned myself. A person, man or woman, is truly not done with the other in a relationship until they get tired – completely exhausted within themselves. You're saying a lot of the right things that places doubt in your mind about Norman . . . but you're still wondering and you're still inquiring. When a person is *really* tired of the other, they don't care – they don't ask – they don't wonder . . . about anything!! You're not tired yet Sherry . . ."

"It's over Lance, he said so . . ."

"But you haven't . . . and it's okay. You may not realize it yet within yourself just yet but you exhibit all of the symptoms." Sherry doesn't respond. Lance continues, "I'm not trying to be harsh dear. I'm just telling you what I know about human nature . . . from what I've seen in others and what I have seen within *myself.*"

"I just need time to adjust Lance – I'm just . . ."

"It's okay Sherry – *believe me*, I know. Say, are we still on for Saturday?"

"Oh, you know what . . . I intended to tell you, I'm going to pass on that. If this party is at your co-worker's house, I'm sure there's going to be a lot of drinking going on. With where I'm trying to be right now, spiritually, I don't think I would feel too comfortable at a party like that."

Lance wants to pressure Sherry but he doesn't. "Are you sure Sherry – my co-worker is pretty cool?"

"Yes I'm sure but thank you."

"You're not upset with me about what I just said to you, are you?"

"No I'm not *really*! I called you to listen to what you had to say. You *can* be a little bit over the top, but it's okay. That's kind of the reason *why* I called you."

When they get off the phone, Lance is discouraged. He's not angry though because he truly understands what she's going through emotionally. His own experience with Melanie and his empathy kick into high gear to keep him calm about Sherry – even though she's not saying *anything* that's pleasing to his ears right now.

*   *   *

Sherry is quite understanding of Lance's point of view; a *male* point of view. But a lot of times a woman finds another female's point of view to be *more* comforting. So she calls her best friend Tammy in Boston to get her take on the situation.

"Hey girlfriend, what's going on? How are you Sherry?"

"Oh Tammy, what is going on in my world!? Why is this happening to me!?"

"You know Sherry, it just wasn't meant to be. You need time to get over it – either that or you two are just taking a break."

"What do you mean Tammy . . . ?"

"Give Norman a little time to tend to his wounded ego. After that, he'll take you back."

"'Take me back?'"

"Oh girl who do you think you're foolin' – you ain't through with Norman yet!"

"Oh no, you sound like Lance! What did I call *you* for!?"

"Who . . . ? The guy that met up with us the night before I left Chicago – *Tasty Lance*!? I'm surprised you still talk to him – he likes you!!"

"He may have a little crush on me but I don't think it's anything serious. He's a good friend – he even cooked dinner for me last week when I told him about what happened."

"Wait a minute . . . he did *what*!?? Sounds like a really nice date! Maybe that was just what you needed to help take your mind off of Norman."

"That's what I told him, that it sounded like a date – he assured me it wasn't though."

"Did he make a pass at'cha?"

"No . . ."

" . . . And you say he 'may have a crush' on you? Nah girl, that man *adores* you! Most men don't just *up* and cook dinner for a woman – and between 80 and 90% of those few men that do, won't do it unless they think they're getting *something* in return! What did he make?"

" . . . Chicken breasts, baked tilapia and catfish; some kind of herbal rice, and string beans. He even made a small salad before we ate. He also had apple pie for desert and a non-alcoholic almond flavored Spumante."

Tammy pulls the phone away from her ear and stares at it with her mouth open, "Sherry . . . ! Are you *kidding* me???" You got *a keeper* on your hands!! I knew there was something weird about him, in a good way though! My advice to you because you *did* call me for it . . . keep hanging around *Tasty Lance* and let him do what he's trying to help you do . . . get your mind off of Norman!!"

"I'm not ready for a relationship right now Tammy!"

"I didn't say anything about a relationship! I said let nature take its course. You like him too . . . you just got Norman all on your cranium right now."

"Lance is a really nice guy but I don't know about him . . ."

Tammy interrupts Sherry, " . . . You 'don't *know* about him'!? *Please* . . . you practically ripped my arm from outta its socket when you were telling me about the text messages!" Tammy does a little girl's voice to imitate Sherry. "'We were texting each other in Spanish . . . it was kinda interesting' . . ."

"I don't talk like that!!" Sherry snaps back.

"Let me tell you . . . I saw something and felt something in the air between you two that night. And I *swear*, I don't know what came over *me* that night . . . but I was trying to figure out how to get him in one of those bathrooms so he could eat my pussy and maybe let him stick it in me real quick! No telling what I would've done for him in return!! *Tasty – Tasty – Tasty*!!"

"Girl, why are you being so *vulgar* . . . ?" Sherry asks in a concerned voice.

"Sherry, you know I don't play on Michael like that but I was *so hot* that night, I coulda' crawled under the table!! But when I noticed the connection between you two, I left it alone. Don't get me wrong, you two weren't playin' footsy under the table . . . it was an unspoken chemistry going on in the air."

"That's fine and all Tammy but why do you have to be *so* nasty about the other stuff!?"

"Sherry, grow up!! You're my best friend . . . I'm just telling you what I was feelin' that night. You know I don't talk like that in the streets."

"You just caught me off guard a little bit . . ."

"Girl we're almost forty years old – the libido is changing for us now; it's gettin' better! That don't mean it has to *always* make sense! You mean to say, your vagina has *never* gotten wet before when you least expected it!?"

"No, it hasn't."

"Well I don't believe you Sherry. I think it has – that's why you stopped drinkin'!"

"You know Tammy you're really starting to . . ."

Tammy interrupts her again, " . . . And what's so wrong with *Tasty Lance* anyway?"

Sherry hesitates, wondering if she even wants to continue her conversation with Tammy. She does answer, "I think Lance is a little too worldly for me! He rolls down the street in his car playing his music real loud for *everyone* to hear!"

"So . . . ! Everyone's got at least *one* thing about them that another person doesn't like! I wouldn't concentrate on his bad habits or every little crazy thing he does; I would concentrate on what he's doing *for you*!"

" . . . And he uses the *n word*!!"

" . . . He uses the *n word*? And how often have you heard him use this term Sherry?"

"Once, maybe twice . . ."

" . . . In a year and a half . . . ? You know what Sherry, you need to quit!! What are you lookin' for in a man . . . some face and body picture perfect heart throb from a Hollywood movie with four or more years of college!!? Let me answer that for you – *yes*!!! In fact, you *just* got through with one of those . . . *Norman* – and look where that got you!! He uses the *n word*, so what!! You need a man that will piss on the side of the road every once in a while!! 'Fantasy Island' was a TV show – it doesn't exist in real life!!! Hell, at least *Tasty Lance* knows how to cook five course meals!"

"Norman knows how to cook!!" Sherry says in a defending manner. "He was cooking for me two or three times a week!!"

"Hell he better have been, while you're out working a full time job six and seven days a week!! How many months has he been out of work? He knew he could've taken that job with the law firm you were telling me about, until he found something better in his field . . . but he didn't, 'cause he's a snob!! *Tasty Lance* is cookin' and workin', Norman was cookin' and lookin' at TV!!!"

"I *wish* you would *stop* calling Lance *that* name . . . !"

"You know what Sherry . . . you know what your problem is . . . ? First of all, *we* are both fully bloomed, grown women, mentally and physically!! I shouldn't have to walk on eggshells like I've been doing most of my life when I talk to you!! All your goodie-two-shoe ways and church going efforts are fine and all . . . but sometimes you *miss* the obvious when it's *right* in front of you!!!"

"Tammy . . . letmecallyouback!!"

CHAPTER 16

As the weeks go by in the season of autumn 2008, the wear and tear of meeting women in cyberspace is reaching its final point of exhaustion for Lance. The many obstacles of dating; anything from lack of attraction, lack of control of one's attraction, emotional issues, personality mishaps and of course caring for his son who is starting to develop a personality of his own, is enough to throw in the towel.

Lance can't imagine giving it up completely because it has become an addiction. An analogy of that is every time he has tried to quit smoking *for good* or eliminate drinking alcohol for a week or two, he always ends up going right back to his bad habits. He knows he'll eventually revisit internet dating but it won't be in a week or two. The overall dating scene and even his sexual desires have become a distant priority for him.

Lance calls Evangeline Robinson just to see how she's been during the many months they haven't spoken. She describes herself as being one that crawls under a rock when things get too bad for her to handle. At one point during their constant communication before, she had really started to like Lance, more so than she let on at the time. He's not surprised when he hears this but it does surprise him that she thought that he and Melanie would eventually get back together. This was another one of her reasons for why their communicating tapered off.

Evangeline knows deep down though, that the three hour distance between them will always be a hindrance to any possible relationship they could've had. Lance knows that the occasional strangeness in her demeanor or making any sense of it will always hold *him* back. He has never been able to quite put his finger on it. Today, she reveals why.

"I have bipolar disorder," she says to him.

"You have wha . . . ?" he asks, even though he heard her.

"I have bipolar disorder."

"Oh . . . it's not that serious though, is it? I've never suspected or noticed that in you." Lance is being kind when he tells her *this* lie.

"It *can* be serious enough if I don't take my meds!" Lance recalls one of the last times he spoke to Evangeline, when she had snapped on him about him needing time to run an errand without his son. This was the same day she proposed a marriage arrangement to him. Now he understands her quirkiness. He adds *medical issues* to his list of dating obstacles. Lance doesn't know why she chose to reveal this about herself on this day but it definitely reiterates why a dating sabbatical is needed and fully deserved.

Lance thinks about his co-worker's birthday party at her house a few weeks ago; the one he had invited Sherry to go with him to. Instead he was accompanied by Renee, another platonic friend of his, since Sherry decided not to go. They didn't stay at the party very long because it was nearly over by the time they got there. They went and hung out at Cuatro's for about an hour and had a couple of drinks. After that they picked up some rib tips and went back to his place.

Renee spent the night at Lance's place that night. It had been the plan all along since she lives all the way in Roselle, Illinois and needed a ride home. The thing that is so amusing to Lance about that night is the fact that there was *no* sexual tension between them nor was there any wondering if there would be in comparison to Sherry the night he made dinner for her. The history of dating between Lance and Renee was brief years ago. Afterwards they became friends just like Lance and Sherry did.

In society's rules, if a man doesn't get his way within the dating aspect of a relationship with a woman, he's usually not interested in the platonic aspect of it thereafter. Renee had no problem in believing that his friendship was a genuine rarity to be honored and accepted. The obvious question to Lance is, why did Sherry seem to have a problem with it?

Lance can only assume once again that the doubtfulness and the emotional turmoil exists within Sherry herself and not anything that he did to trigger it. Though the situations differ slightly, whereas Lance not being interested in dating Renee a second time but with Sherry he is, he doesn't think he has been too intense in letting his feelings show for her.

If his theory about Sherry is correct or not, he really doesn't care too much. Lance hasn't heard from her in several weeks, which indicates to him that she has probably gotten back together with Norman. He refuses to call her and find out for certain because he simply doesn't want to hear her say the words. He also knows that the more time that passes by without hearing from her; the more correct he is about her and Norman.

Lance talks to Trisha Sampson every so often but they can never seem to get on the same page as far as hooking up whenever her and her girlfriends are going out. He can tell that she likes talking to him and that she probably has a thing for him. She does on both counts but she won't give in to her overall attraction to Lance because she wants him to ask her out on an *official* date. Lance won't do this because he refuses to find himself in the all too familiar and unfortunate situation of going out with someone he's not attracted to. He *really* doesn't want to have sex with anyone like that either.

With a new outlook on dating and how it should transpire if he does decide to officially date anyone, it also brings about a transformation in how Lance spends his free time. He lowers his expectations of the club scene so he isn't thoroughly disappointed when he doesn't meet anyone there. He doesn't start going to clubs a *whole* lot, just a little more often than before. Lance continues to see his father a lot more than in years past. This first began a few months before LJ was born. When he thinks about his dad and how often he has seen him this past year, given the hour distance in which they live, he can't help but scoff at how often he has seen his brothers excluding Warren, Jr., who are only ten minutes away.

Lance calls them because he knows how important it is for LJ to get to know his uncles. This is the *only* reason why he makes the first move. They set up a visit at Lance's place, particularly because the two youngest brothers, Matthew and Andrew have never seen his apartment. He will have to pick them up and take them back home, but he doesn't mind too much, considering the cause.

It is a football Sunday on TV when they get together. Lance makes plenty of chili for the occasion in trying to accommodate their hearty appetites. Unfortunately the opposite occurs and the two youngest brothers are not that hungry. Lance knows it's shyness that causes this and they're not entirely to blame. He knows they're social deficiency comes from a lack of exposure to socializing situations.

At least they're here today! I'll worry about later . . . later, he thinks to himself. Nathanael is simply not in an eating mood due to one of his usual nonchalant attitudes.

Lance doesn't let their somewhat ill behavior overshadow his enjoyment of their visit. LJ being as surprisingly sociable as he is enjoys their company also. They take pictures, each of them holding LJ and then they take a group picture, all three uncles and their little nephew. As much as Lance wants to offer his opinion about their absence in LJ's life among other things, he knows today is not the right day to do so. He wonders if the so-called *right day* will ever truly present itself or will he have to force a chosen day in the future to be as such.

When the broadcasts of pro basketball games are in their first full month of the new season which is November, Kevin starts to come around more. Lance doesn't mind him or anyone coming around for a visit; as long as they call first, not overstay their welcome and just realize and respect the overall fact that his apartment is just as much LJ's residence as it is his own. This basically means no smoking in the house and keeping the noisy outbursts to a minimum when LJ is there; also no walking through LJ's room to get to the bathroom if LJ is there or not. Kevin has had his share of drunken mishaps around Lance over the years. There's always the occasional broken wine glass or the felt tip pen he left the top off of which caused the ink to stain his new living room sofa, luckily in between the pillows where it's not visible. This time Kevin introduces a new twist to one of their drinking sessions.

"Kevin!! Kevin get up!!" Lance exclaims, shaking Kevin frantically as he lies in the middle of Lance's hardwood floor face down and unconscious. "Kevin!!!" Lance turns and looks at his landline on the end table. He stands up to go and grab it so he can dial 911. As soon as the phone is in his hand, Kevin starts to wake up.

"Oh shit!! Man what happened!!?" Kevin asks, still dazed and confused.

"Dude, you got up from the couch and you were laughing at something silly I said. You took two steps and then fell flat on your face. I was just about to call an ambulance; I didn't know what was going on!!" Lance says.

"I passed out!?"

"Yeah and I know you're not drunk 'cause we're still drinking our first 40's – unless you had something else before you got here!!"

"Nah man – I ain't had nothin' before I got here. Damn man; get me something to clean this up; I got a little blood on the floor!!"

"Has this ever happened to you before Kevin!?"

"Nah man . . ." Lance goes to the kitchen to get an old rag and a mop to clean up the spots of blood on the floor from where Kevin slightly busted his lip when he passed out unexpectedly.

Right after Kevin hit the floor like a rock, he started to shake a little bit before he went completely unconscious. Lance doesn't know if his blood sugar is too high, causing him to loose consciousness or if he perhaps had a seizure. Kevin doesn't know *either*. As scary as this incident was to Lance, he manages to shrug it off. But when it happens again three weeks later, Lance knows that beside from his best friend's health, there is another significant issue he will have to address.

"Say dog . . ." he says to Kevin over the phone a few days after the second incident, "You need to go to the doctor and get that checked out! Besides your health and your well being, I got a ten month old in the house with me. I can't have that type of thing going on around him if it can be helped. You do what you want 'cause you're a grown man . . . but you can't come back over here until you get that checked out. I gotta look out for what's best for my son you understand . . ."

Kevin is appreciative and understanding of what Lance says to him. It will be months before he visits Lance again. With Kevin being his main drinking buddy, the doldrums will get worse. The only excitement that will occur while Lance is drinking alone will be the drunken phone calls he makes to people that he really doesn't want to talk to. The #1 priority since day one, of caring for his son, is his *only* priority and the only thing that keeps him going each day.

On the last day of February 2009, Lance sits in his computer chair on this early morning. LJ's first birthday was three days ago and his birthday party is this afternoon. He looks at all of the commemorative photos of his son's first holidays from the past year. He smiles as he sifts through hundreds of pictures he has taken. It warms his heart when he considers the *most* unexpected turn of events in his life, besides having a child in itself – he and Melanie no longer argue . . . about anything. Any disagreement or misunderstanding they *did* have, which was twice in the past year, was resolved so quickly and so peacefully, that he doesn't even remember what they were about.

"Lord, thank you for Melanie! I know that this single parenting situation with her is something that is usually not a peaceful or easy going experience. I thank you for the strength and endurance you instilled in each one of us to help make that possible. I thank you for the moral foundations that we each possess in making us what I think are good parents – and I ask that it may continue. I thank you Lord for her family – the people that never make me feel like the ex-boyfriend when they open their homes and their hearts to me on holidays or on ordinary days that we may cross paths when LJ is involved. I know that through her family, my son will get most of his knowledge and hands on experience of what family is all about. My own family members that are consistently involved in LJ's life are but a few in numbers. It angers me Lord that I am aware of the fact that my three brothers that I grew up with and my step dad, will not be at my son's first birthday party this afternoon. Three strikes and you're out!!! I'm trying my best not to keep count of how many significant events my brothers and my step dad have missed . . . but it's hard not to. Lord, help me to find peace with this situation as it is now – help me to reduce my anger so that I am able to approach them about this, without conflict. And watch over them Lord – help them to find some of the strength and endurance within their own hearts . . . the strength and endurance I am so thankful to have bestowed upon me and within my own heart. Without it, I know I would've never been able to financially maintain living in this apartment alone with my son. I feel like I completely reached the threshold of manhood when I became a father . . . and I thank you Lord, conclusively for that – Amen."

The Memorial Day holiday seems to arrive once again in the blink of an eye. This is particularly true for Lance when he considers the fact that he is a father watching his helpless little toddler become a little boy. Lance, Warren, Jr. and Carl are throwing the big bar-b-que this year at Lance's place; *$350.00* worth. The three of them had been planning this get together for weeks.

Unfortunately the expected turnout is no where near the number they thought. Again Lance is reminded of how times have changed. In the 90's he could pick up the phone and call five people and have ten or twelve at his door that evening.

Now . . . he thinks . . . *you have to call thirty people and hope for twelve to show up.*

Carl is the first person to show. No sooner than he gets through the door, he is handing over the cash amount they had agreed upon after Lance went and picked up most of the food and some of the items for the bar-b-que. Lance's *big mouth* cousin from the baby shower shows up next. The verbal exchanges between her and Carl are interesting at best. Her personality is best described by others as being electric. It gets even more verbally interesting and humorous when Lance's gay friend Robert shows up soon after. Lance's skirmish attitude about homosexuality is not with any men or women that are gay. It's just the idea of the same sex copulation of it all; especially men, that makes him want to internally scream in agony over the thought of it.

Lance expects Warren, Jr. to arrive next because he agreed to have the remaining essential items for the gathering, including beer. He is already two hours late.

"I really don't wanna bust this cognac open until I've had a couple of beers first," Lance says. "Really, I should wait till later this evening after lil' man goes to sleep!"

"Man, I'm gonna go ahead and grab a case!" Carl exclaims. "If Warren should've been here by *now* and he's not . . . well I don't wanna jinx us . . . but he might not show at all!"

"I really didn't wanna say that out loud but . . ." First and foremost, Lance keeps an eye on his son, who is with his father this year for Memorial Day weekend unlike last year. It's a lot easier to do so now since he's over a year old and walking around pretty good. It's amazing to Lance to have witnessed first hand, the independent part of his son's personality develop – at least when he's in the same room with him.

Usually LJ can find himself mesmerized being held and spoken to by a beautiful woman. Lance had hoped that his cousin would be able to stand in as Lance, Jr.'s mesmerizer, even just for ten minutes. The level of difficulty to multi-task in the kitchen, even *without* a child present can be somewhat overwhelming for Lance. While his cousin *is* beautiful to behold, unfortunately LJ doesn't take too well to her. The term that Lance uses to describe her – *big mouth*, is not only indicative of her tendency to gossip; it is also literally accurate in describing the high volume of her voice. This scares LJ.

Lance does get a little relief when Valerie finally shows up, after calling his cell phone four times for directions. Valerie is one of Lance's platonic girlfriends and she is accompanied by her sister. When she complains about getting a speeding ticket ten minutes before her arrival, Lance can't help but wonder to himself,

How does a person get a speeding ticket while driving around in an unfamiliar neighborhood . . . ? If you're lost, wouldn't you drive slowly??

Valerie is meeting LJ for the very first time. When she picks him up and starts to talk to him, it is love at first sight for both of them. Lance notices her natural communication skills with a one year old and can't help but wish that Sherry could've had those same skills when she interacted with LJ last year. His second thought is,

Well hell . . . who cares at this point – I haven't heard from Sherry in seven or eight months! She's got da Norman virus no doubt!!

Lance's next thought is why he and Valerie are not together as a couple or why they never even went out on a date during the ten year tenure of their platonic relationship.

I could easily label her as having emotional issues like a certain someone else I know or knew . . . or know – whatever the case! But truthfully, Valerie just more-or-less chose the wrong guy to be with!! I think she had just met her guy back then when we first met. But just because she broke up wit' him about two years ago certainly doesn't mean I was 'bout to come chasin' after her like I'm somebody's left overs!! She should've chosen me to begin with!!

Lance smiles at her while he's thinking and she smiles back. "Thanks for coming!" he says to her. He is quickly reminded of how beautiful Valerie is while staring at her – face first and then her delightful pair of breasts with a nice cleavage showing to top it off. As she puts LJ down, Lance looks at her butt as she turns around to go into the other room with her sister. She *is* slim the way he likes in a woman, like a size *3/4* but he has always wished she had more hips and more butt. This slight imperfection in her lower body frame is truly *not* a deal breaker for Lance. Unlike a lot of African American men, he judges women by their face first. A nice body is a bonus that goes along with a beautiful face in his opinion. He *still* wishes she had more hips and more butt though.

Because Valerie and her sister are ladies, he extends a courtesy and offers them some of his premium cognac. They both accept as he seats them in the living room to watch TV until some food from the grill is ready. He goes back into the kitchen and out the door to check on the meat. LJ frowns in the doorway at his father, wanting to be outside with him.

"C'mon out here lil' boy!" he says to LJ as he holds the door open for him. Carl comes outside right after him.

"Your brother ain't comin,' is he?" Carl asks.

"I dunno . . ." Lance says. "He keeps calling with these flimsy ass excuses for why he isn't here yet! You gonna be out here for a minute with LJ? I gotta run back in the house for a sec . . ."

"Yeah go ahead." Lance goes back into the kitchen to open two cans of tomato puree, a can of whole peeled tomatoes and to start the linguine for the noodle dish. A minute later lance happens to look up and see Carl in the kitchen. Lance loses it,

"Carl!! You left LJ outside on the back porch by himself!!? What da fuck are you doing!!?" he says as he slams the pot of tomato sauce on the eye of the stove, splashing it all over. Lance's cousin and Robert are suddenly silent.

"I can't find my phone . . ." Carl says.

"*Fuck* your phone – That's *my son* out there!!!" He says emphatically as he rushes towards the back door. "He still wobbles when he walks – he could fall down the stairs!!!" Lance calmly opens the door so he doesn't startle LJ and brings him in the house. He wanted to hit Carl in the head with the pot of tomato sauce. Of course he didn't – but he *wanted* to.

*   *   *

At six in the morning, Lance calls Renee to make sure she drove home safely from his place. She showed up for the bar-b-que much later that evening. The gathering ended just one hour ago. Renee, Carl, Robert, the cousin and Lance found themselves in the kitchen for the better part of four hours, *still* drinking and talking about l*ife* – a topic of conversation with *no* ending in sight – then or now.

"Wow Renee, I'm gonna be tired as hell trying to take care of LJ today!! Gotta do what I gotta do though . . ."

"I know that's right – *you* go Daddy!! I wanna know what's up with the light skinned girl you showed me the picture of at the gathering tonight. Are you gonna handle your business or what?"

"You mean Valerie – no, I'm not. Any woman that will leave a third of a snifter of premium V.S.O.P. cognac on the table when she leaves is *not* the woman for me! Her sister did it too! I could understand if it was *cheap* liquor."

"Oh well, so much for that! Carl is a trip, and the gay guy was funny; what was his name?"

"Robert . . . but we call him Bobby. Yeah, he's a real comedian."

"Well 'comedian' is *not* the word for Carl! What was his problem? He walked in on me when I was in the bathroom! Was he drunk!?"

"Renee, you're kidding me right!? He did the same thing to Valerie's sister . . . and we didn't tell you that he told Valerie *to her face* that she was too skinny for him! How rude was that!? It's not like she asked him!!"

"Lance he didn't do that! Please tell me you're making that up!!"

"I wish I was . . ." Lance says in a disgusted tone. "He even kept yelling out my name from the living room, for *stupid* stuff, when I was in LJ's room trying to put him to sleep. He came *in* the room at one point . . . and he kept going through LJ's room to get to the bathroom instead of going through my room after LJ fell asleep!! I don't think one has to experience parenthood to know better than that!"

"Yeah that is common sense; at least you would think it is."

" . . . And I *told him* which room to go through before hand! I've known Carl for many years; we've been gettin' drunk together for as long as I can remember. We use to go on club hopping sprees almost every weekend and be drunk as hell riding around in our cars and stuff! I've seen Carl meet women left and right, then turn around and avoid 'em afterwards! Whatever the method to his madness is concerning that is *his* business! Carl can get wild and act a little crazy when he's got a lot of liquor in him – just like I can. But never have I known him to be flat out disrespectful towards women. If a woman goes to a man's house, no matter what the level of friendship is, and she doesn't feel comfortable, she's not gonna want to come back! It's almost as if he set out to do something crazy as hell to each one of *my* female friends, to turn them against me . . . so he can have me all to himself!!"

"You're definitely right about a woman's comfort level in a man's house! But 'have you to himself' . . . what do you mean by that exactly?"

"That's some gay shit – *that's* what I mean!!"

Renee falls back on her bed from a sudden outburst of laughter. "Lance you are crazy!! That's deep!! *How* did you ever come up with that!?"

"You know last Memorial Day we were out in Indiana at Warren's girlfriend's house . . . oh wow. I can't believe I just mentioned *his* name! I can't believe how he faked yesterday . . . and left Carl and I stuck with the bar-b-que bill."

"Yeah that's kinda rude too! Did he at least offer to pay his third of the bill since he verbally committed to contributing . . . or even a portion of it?"

"No he didn't . . ."

"Oh well, so much for that!"

"Well anyway . . . last year's bar-b-que, everything was cool with Carl when a bunch of men were sittin' in the backyard lookin' stupid. As soon as I tried to get some females to come out and join us, he started complaining about how he had somewhere to be and he didn't have his car because I drove!!"

"But you said he meets women left and right or at least he *used* to?"

"And he still does!! He has the gift of gab but that could just be a front!"

"Hhmmm . . . that's a little weird but what guy isn't? I'm still not convinced though."

"Well try this on for size . . . Bobby is *my* friend. I don't say that to mean that I dictate who they can or cannot hang out with . . . but Carl met Bobby through me and then they started emailing one another, then they started hanging out together. Guys usually don't do that unless it concerns business."

"Well maybe they *do* have some kinda business venture going on . . ."

"Yeah, the business of . . . damn let me shut-up! Now, guys *will* do that if a female is involved. It's just like my homie Kevin. He met Bobby through me too . . . but he never wants to hang out with Bobby unless it's through me."

"Hhmmm . . . maybe I'm a little convinced . . . and you know I know men. A man will go out of his way to get next to a female but not another male."

"Exactly . . . ! And don't get me wrong, if he is, it doesn't bother me *that he is . . .* it bothers me that he is and he's pretending *not* to be!!"

"Oh well, good luck with *that* one."

"Oh no baby . . . I don't need any luck for that situation. I don't give a fuck which gender he wants to fuck . . . just don't be mistreating my lady friends when they come around!!"

"I heard that!! Speaking of your lady friends, any prospects for something beyond friendship with anyone?"

"Yeah Renee, I confess . . . I'm in love wit'cha girl!! Let's get married this afternoon!!"

"Lance you are silly!! Seriously though . . ."

"No . . . *no* sparks with anyone right now. I may go back to internet dating . . . I dunno."

CHAPTER 17

In 2008 Lance had a ball on his very first Father's Day. Melanie and her sisters put together a backyard bar-b-que that probably saw forty people pass through before it was all said and done. The gathering was exclusively for their own dad and included Lance, his dad and his wife, a few of Lance's male friends and a whole lot of *dads* from the neighborhood. The festivities were held at Melanie's sister Marcy's house; so the alcohol was flowing profusely.

The same type of celebration transpires this year for Father's Day; just not as extravagant in the number of people. Lance is more than happy to take part in a smaller gathering which includes his own dad and his wife only. His other immediate family members and his friends are simply getting on his nerves. Lance's stepfather and his brothers Nathanael, Matthew and Andrew still lack socializing etiquette which hinders their acknowledgement of Lance, Jr. The more Lance considers the things that have been said when they *do* talk, lets him know that all four of them are suffering from a deep seeded form of depression over their wife and their mother's death in 2006.

The way Lance sees it, Mr. Foster and the brothers in particular, take the grief of her death and hold on to it tightly, as if it is theirs alone to own. This angers him because he knows they are not the only ones that lost a loved one. Lance has had plenty of quiet moments where he will suddenly burst into tears over the endless grief from missing his mother. It is an emptiness he feels in every fiber of his being – but he uses it as motivation to move forward in his life. It would seem that his brothers use it to move in the opposite direction.

The stunt that Warren, Jr. pulled on Memorial Day still lingers in Lance's mind. A person that doesn't take care of their business, especially when money is involved, infuriates Lance. He knows for sure now that he will *never* organize anything with his stepbrother again.

Lance then thinks about his best friend Kevin, who did eventually make it to the county doctor to inquire about his passing out episodes. They couldn't find anything obvious to be the cause of it. Lance thinks that a personal doctor and a referral would've been more in order. *But to each his own,* Lance thinks. According to Kevin, he passed out once in January and hasn't passed out since. Lance has seen him by his place a couple of times since then but is still a little leery of doing so.

With his other best friend Carl and his *possibly gay* issues, along with everything concerning everyone else leaves reason to believe that a change of priorities is in order. The refuge that Lance sought through all of them from cyberspace women and dating in general seems to need just that.

Lance gives in to his manly sexual desires and admits to himself he *is* human after all, when he glances at Melanie's butt while her back is turned in the backyard at the Father's Day bar-b-que. His mental montage is swift when he remembers how good her sex was, how often they argued, and their physical altercations. He almost wants the two of them to reward one another sexually in a sense, for their drama free parenting efforts during the past year. Deep down though, Lance knows this would be considered *typical* behavior – something that he usually has no interest in taking part in. He also knows that at least one of them would let the emotional aspect of sex supercede the physical part of it and the arguing would start all over again. Lance will not allow anything to interfere with raising his son effectively – *not even that.*

With sex on his mind now, Lance turns to what he considers a more logical source of possible fulfillment – a *new* woman. He snatches his cell phone from its holster to connect to the internet and login to one of the dating sites he has recently revisited. As he scrolls through different prospects, he comes across a familiar screen name. When Lance pulls up her profile, he is surprised when he realizes that it's Jymilia from last year. The infamous female that goes by the male version of her name *Jim,* has *a picture* of herself on her profile now.

She is beautiful . . . in such a way that Lance really likes. She is slim and with a nice feminine shape . . . in such a way that Lance really likes. He goes to the archive of the website's original emails to retrieve her phone number once again. When Lance bought a new cell phone four months ago, Jymilia's phone number was one of the few that he decided *not* to keep in his memory bank, electronically or otherwise. The small amount of alcohol in his system gives him the nerve to call her without hesitating. When she answers, he tells her who he is and reminds her of the emails they exchanged last year.

"Oh hi, how are you!?" she says in a pleasant, high pitched tone.

"I'm fine, how are you?" Lance says with relief.

"I'm good!"

"I see you finally put a picture on your profile; you look really nice!" he says anxiously.

"Oh thanks! Say, may I call you back in about ten minutes?"

"Yeah sure . . ." Lance explains the situation to his dad who is sitting in the backyard with him. Mr. Austin is amused by his son's overall dating dilemma, being reminded of some of his *own* dating adventures in years past; some in between his many marriages and some during.

When Jymilia calls Lance back, her high pitched tone is gone. The flow of their conversation is like trying to stay afloat in quicksand. And then finally she offers,

"You know, I don't think this is gonna work out too good between you and I. You're a nice person but I just don't see you fitting into my spiritual path."

"Your 'spiritual path' . . . ? What are you talking about!? We've never even discussed anything concerning spirituality."

"You don't remember when . . ." She hesitates " . . . This is not the guy from the coffee shop?"

"No it isn't!!"

"Who is this? What did you say your name was again . . . ?"

"You called me!!" Lance suddenly recalls her greeting when she called back; no name, just *hey.* "Do you even know *his* name!? You know what . . . if you've given your number to that many men on the website, then why bother even telling you *my* name!! Good luck with that 'spiritual path' of yours . . . 'cause you're sure as hell gonna need it!!" Lance disconnects the call without saying goodbye. "Unbelievable!!" he says aloud.

Surprisingly, Lance doesn't drink as much at Marcy's house as he normally does. But when he, his dad, and Corinne leave and go back to Lance's place, the drinking continues at a much faster pace; especially after the botched love connection with Jymilia. Lance burns a few CD's that his father hand picked to add to his own collection. It's refreshing to Lance that his father is a fan of rap music. Overall, his father exhibits a personality of one that is much younger than his actual age. Lance hopes when he reaches his father's age, that he has even half of the energy and passion for life that *he* has.

The more alcohol the three of them drink, the more interesting their conversation becomes. They talk about little LJ and how much of a life changing concept he is, now that he's in the world. Establishing a relationship with his son from day one was *always* a concept filled with passion for Lance. The actual hands on experience of fatherhood in itself has made his feelings even more powerful; so does the buzz from the alcohol.

"I love raising my son!!" he exclaims. "It's very challenging, yes . . . but I love every minute, every second of it and I will *always* be there for my son!!"

Corinne shakes her head affirmatively, feeling very proud to hear Lance say that. She knows that the situation could have easily turned out to be the opposite, given the fact that Lance didn't have *his* natural father around that much when *he* was coming up.

As if on cue, Richard Austin offers *his* version of what happened in Lance's early years as a child. He speaks of how he financially helped Lance and his mother out, even when he wasn't around. He speaks of how Mr. Foster was a hindrance of his coming around when Lance's mother remarried.

"I can appreciate the financial part of what you're saying Dad, to a certain extent . . . but that other stuff sounds like an excuse . . . you fucked up."

"How . . . ?" Mr. Austin inquires, surprised without showing it, that his son has just cursed at him.

"You weren't around nearly enough when I was coming up . . . and I needed you!" A tear rolls down Lance's right cheek. The damage in his heart regarding his father has been present a whole lot longer than he originally realized; all of his life. He's not sure of the exact order of how he displayed these emotions throughout the years but his quick assessment is – oblivious to his feelings as a child, angry feelings as a teen, denial in his twenties, and ignoring his feelings *and* his father in his thirties.

Now Lance is in a place where he understands the power of forgiveness and he realizes the unyielding force that exists within a person when they *do not* forgive.

"Son . . ." Mr. Austin says hesitantly as he grabs Lance's shoulders. "I'm sorry . . . I don't know what else to say . . ."

"That's okay, but I can't forgive you today . . . I already did that years ago . . . that's why you're here in my life now," Lance says as his mouth forms a soft smile. He had often pictured him and his father having a heart to heart about this very subject. Never in his wildest dreams did he imagine his verbal declaration to come out of his mouth the way it did. Lance had always possessed a certain level of fearful respect for his dad, as he should and he still does. But on this very night only . . . Lance did not fear his father – and Richard Austin allowed it. Lance will thank his dad for just that in a text message an hour after he and his wife leave. On this unexpected yet memorable Father's Day, all seems right in the world.

Lance doesn't allow his recent experience with Jymilia over the phone discourage him into thinking that more of the same will occur with his internet dating rebirth. He reminds himself that *she* was a cyberspace girl from last year. A whole new abundance of righteous females awaits him this time around – he knows it; at least he *hopes* he knows it.

Lance tries a dating website that he's never been on before. It takes him over three hours to answer the different format of questioning in order to complete his profile. Word of mouth about this particular site is that it's of a higher standard than most of the other ones, so he feels the time spent is worth it. Once his paid membership begins to unfold, one aspect of this website's protocol sticks out like a sore thumb – you cannot browse through different members profiles; only a select few are emailed to the member each day based on the answers in each of member's profile questionnaire.

That's kind of a good idea, he thinks. *But what if I want to choose someone that has some differences in their personality? Who says that good relationships* always *consist of individuals that share a lot of the same qualities!? I should be able to decide that for myself! I'm paying them to think for me!!*

Having paid already, Lance goes with the concept. He does admit to himself that the quality of women emailed to him are unexpectedly more pleasing as far as their looks than before; a little bit. Unfortunately though, as weird as it seems to Lance, most of the appealing women are 5'8" and taller. He really doesn't prefer women 5'8" and over because when they put on heels, sometimes they become taller than he is. Having paid already, Lance goes with it anyway.

He comes across and links up with a single African American woman, thirty-eight years of age, no children, and resides in Chicago. Her name is Lynita Everstall. She is a very attractive woman in Lance's eyes – in a Linda Carter kind of way . . . and she is 5'9". When they speak on the telephone for the first time, she is just as intelligent as he had hoped.

"So Lynita, what made you decide to try internet dating?"

"Well, I thought it would be a new and interesting venture into this thing we call *dating.* And even if an alluring mate doesn't come about through this endeavor, it's still an excellent source of networking."

"'Networking' . . . I like that word. But the networking part of it can only truly work out if you come across someone that is genuinely nice."

"Yes you're right about that. Any negative aspects of networking are certainly not for me . . . especially at this point in my life."

"I know what you mean. Be careful with the dating part of the internet though . . . I mean, it's no different from conventional dating . . . just a new avenue. You'll meet some men that are only interested in their own agenda . . . and they'll say or do whatever it takes to get you to give in to it or fall for it so to speak. Once they get a hold of you, they'll spit you out like you're . . . well, like you're spit! As far as networking, if it's on a friendship level or business or whatever . . . from a man's point of view, remember that *a jerk* will wanna date ya first, before he's trying to be a part of your networking."

"Whoa! It sounds like you have a little experience in internet dating! I do understand what you're saying though. It's the same 'ol song in dealing with men as far as I'm concerned. You've come across a *female* jerk or two from the internet, haven't you?"

"*Please* . . . the internet, a downtown submarine shop, the work place, the club . . . you name it!"

Lynita laughs, "Oh my God, don't get *me* started!"

"Yeah I know, right? Let's talk about that a little later. That subject sounds like a very long conversation in the making," Lance says as he chuckles. "So what do you do for a living?"

"I'm the head nurse at a very elite hospital."

"Ahh, that's interesting . . . but you can tell me which one; I'm not a stalker."

"I will determine *that* in due time, okay?"

"Fair enough . . . You're smart, aren't you?"

"Well yeah, I would like to think that I'm somewhat intelligent."

"Don't think it baby, know it! I'm intelligent . . ."

"Oh okay . . . and aren't you a *Mr.* Smoothy . . . smooth and devenaire! So what is *your* agenda with me?"

Lance answers quickly, "*Friends first* – with you or *any* woman I meet from now on! When you talk about being at a certain point in your life, believe me, I can relate!"

"I know! The priorities in my life right now are my health, my career, and my dogs. When I get home from work everyday, my dogs bring me peace."

Uh oh . . . ! A black woman that loves dogs . . . that's strange! Then again, I did grow close to my old cat . . . but I would've never gone out and gotten that cat on my own accord; that was my ex's doing.

With that in mind, her 5'9" frame and her *happy go lucky* type demeanor which Lance usually labels as *goofy* – is enough to leave no room for temptation in breaking his own *friends first* dating rule. He scoffs when he considers all of this but then he smiles because he *does* enjoy talking to her. Lynita scoffs to herself when she considers the fact that Lance is too short for her and too full of himself – something she usually labels as *conceited*. She then smiles when she takes into account the amusement in his conversation and the enjoyment she gets from talking to him.

Two women sit in the back of a club on the near north side, both with Dirty Martinis in hand. Their bodies sink so far down into the black leather chairs they sit on, that it makes them think they're at home. One of them can't wait to get home to check her email for the new batch of male prospects that the dating website she's on, has sent to her – so she checks it *now* on her cell phone.

"Arlene Jansen!! Are you scrolling through those guys on that website again!?"

"This is a different website – ooohhh girl, look at this one!" Arlene frantically hands her phone to her friend.

"Girl this man is ugly!" she says.

"I don't think he's cute . . . I think he's sexy! There *is* a difference you know . . ."

"Not my type . . ." she says as she hands the phone back to Arlene. "And neither is being on the internet trying to meet someone! That type of thing is for the youngsters – we're forty years old!!"

"That's *your* opinion . . . hey!! Okay, look at *this* guy." Arlene hands her friend the cell phone again.

"*TrynsomnuPt2* . . . Hhmmp!! That means he has messed over some unexpecting female on here before; now he's back for more!"

"How you gon read all into *that* through his username!?"

"Yeah he's cute . . ." her friend says. "Looks like he's stuck on himself though . . ."

Arlene snatches her phone back, "Cute . . . ? Girl, he is *fine*! I would eat him up and down and all around!!"

"Girl, you are dirty just like these Martinis we're drinking."

"You got that right! I like my drinks the same way I like my sex – rough and dirty!!"

Arlene sends *TrynsomnuPt2* an icebreaker indicator to show her interest. Meanwhile Lance sits at home on his computer, trying something new again by searching for love on the internet – hence the username *TrynsomnuPt2*. He is on the same site that Arlene is on. When he opens her icebreaker email, he immediately screams at his computer monitor,

"*Unbelievable* – no picture!!!"

Within a mere week Lance can't wait to call his best friend Angelica Rose and offer her his beguiling cyberspace stories. A couple of incidents stick out in his mind as he dials her number. When Angelica answers, she smiles, already knowing that Lance will probably make her laugh with his animated story telling tendencies.

"Hey Angelica – what's going on!?" he exclaims.

"Hey, what are you up to?"

"Nothing . . ."

"Oh there's *something* Mr. Austin – I can hear it in your voice!"

"Well . . . you know I'm back on the internet craze and it's either gotten crazier since my last venture . . . or I'm just *jumping the gun*!"

"Okay, but just don't have me laughing *too* hard; I'm at the library."

"Well it was my fault for letting this *one* female slip through the cracks – a woman with *no picture*!"

"Let me guess . . . you read something in her profile that you really liked."

" . . . Whatever . . ."

"I mean, that's how Melanie slipped in and the rest is history, right!?"

"Whatever . . . anyway long story short, her name is Arlene . . ."

" . . . GH . . ."

" . . . And yes, she *is* single . . ." Angelica chuckles as Lance continues, "She is a self proclaimed *diva*, works with a public relations company as a consultant.

They do a lot of business with different professional sports teams and other major corporations, so she travels a lot."

" . . . A *diva* with no picture . . . hmm . . . interesting."

"Even more interesting, when she finally *did* text me a picture of herself, she looked more like a *beava* than a *diva*!"

Angelica has a quick outburst of laughter. "Lance, why are you soooo silly . . . !? Now everyone in the library is looking at me!"

"Well of course the other two females in the picture looked better than her – I hate when females on dating websites do that! The picture was small too! I tried to zoom in on it, but . . ."

"So you tried to make her cuter than she actually was!"

"And get this – the day I was talking to her, one evening when I was on my way home from work, I ran into an old female friend of mine. I hadn't seen this woman in over twenty years. I told Arlene I would call her right back."

"Who was this old friend of yours?"

"Someone I used to date, a lifetime ago but the timing was off."

"Any chance of rekindling that level of friendship with her . . . ?"

"No . . . long story – I'll tell ya about that later. Anyway, she texted me her picture while I was sitting on my friend's porch. When I showed my friend the picture and said she reminded me of a male 1950's blues singer with a weave, she almost fell off the porch from cracking up. You remember those old black and white pictures of the blues singers; you know what I'm talking about?"

"You know what Lance . . ." Angelica says while laughing with her hand over her mouth. " . . . I'm about to get off this phone with you! I can't leave the library right now; I'm doing some important research."

"No wait! Arlene sends me a text message twenty minutes after that and says . . . here, I'm gonna read it to you; it's still in my phone.

You and your old friend must really have a lot to talk about – you haven't called me back yet. Are you sure there isn't more going on with her than what you're saying!?

"Wait a minute, what am I missing here!? Did you commit to this girl in *any* kind of way? You skipped *that* part of the story, right?"

"*Commit* . . . ? I've never even met this woman in person! She is clearly the jealous type; not someone I'm anxious to develop a relationship with – even if she was cute! It's funny when you get older, how the indicators to *not* get deeply involved with someone are ignored less and less!"

"Yeah I agree; that's what life is all about – living, learning, and growing. How did she know you were talking with an old friend; you told her!?"

"I kinda said it all out loud when I first saw her. It had been so long since I'd seen her . . . I couldn't believe it. I was surprised."

"You need to stop *that*, thinking out loud."

"Why . . . ? I have nothing to hide. Well I guess in certain situations, I shouldn't."

"Are you going to ever meet this woman in person?"

"I doubt it. I know they say that beauty is skin deep but let's be realistic here – if one is not physically attracted to the other in a relationship, how long can that person fool the other or more importantly, fool themselves when they touch that person? It is truly a recipe for disaster! We both know what one of the first things a man does when he has problems in his relationship, not attracted to his mate, or finds himself bored in a relationship – is to look for excitement elsewhere."

"Yes, and nine times out of ten it's sexual!"

"True, so why even put myself in that situation. I think if a lot more people, *men* and *women*, would look at themselves more closely, especially emotionally, there would be a lot less broken hearts in the world."

"My . . . aren't you the consummate believer of thinking logically. Put that in a bottle and sell it; you would be rich!"

"Ha-ha-ha . . ." he says sarcastically.

"Seriously though Lance, you know I have known you for a very long time . . . and you have come a long way. I'm impressed!!"

"*Why* thank you my dear friend. About what I was saying though, I'm gonna give you the perfect example. I met this other girl on the same website about four days ago . . ."

"The site *I* told you about, right . . . ?"

"Yeah . . ."

"Uh huh, they do have a reputation of being one of the top notch dating websites . . . though according to you, that opinion may differ I fear."

"Well, it remains to be seen . . . they're definitely different though. Anyway, this woman and I were having really nice IM exchanges and I was just about to get her phone number and move forward into getting to know her. She had mentioned initially that I looked a lot like her ex-husband; then suddenly *that* became the ultimate excuse for why she felt like she and I would not work out."

"Did the woman have a picture on her profile at least?"

"As a matter of fact she did; about fifteen of them! She looked like Jane Kennedy. She was a little taller than I would prefer but beautiful nonetheless. Even though I thought her reason for not proceeding forward was a little silly; from an emotional point of view, she put it out there upfront basically, rather than waste anymore of my time. She realized it was something substantial enough to bother her. In the end, I really appreciated that."

"Wow, her ex must have really done her in! That's a shame though because from a mental point of view, she needs to figure out how to get over that. I'm sure she hasn't been hurt anymore than anyone else in this life; she's spoiling whatever future chance at happiness she could possibly encounter or have! Now if her hurt was *physically* induced, of course that's a little more difficult to emotionally resolve."

"It's funny you should mention that, because as I sat and thought about it and kept looking at her pictures thinking to myself *'what a shame, she's so beautiful'*. I started to notice white blotches in some of her pictures. I had noticed them all along but assumed they were bad reflection angles from the camera lens. When I realized they were on the same parts of her body in *different* photos, I thought *'Wow! These blemishes are on* her *and not the photos!'* She could be a burn victim and maybe her ex is to blame for that! Maybe that's why the sight of me resembling her ex-husband was so terrifying to her! Completely understandable . . ."

"Wow, that's far fetched but certainly not impossible. You just never know what a person has gone through or currently going through in their lives. But yeah you're right, if she's not emotionally healed from whatever her ex did to her, it's good for you that she laid that on the table ahead of time. I think in a lot of ways that's what that other girl did for you in her own messed up kind of way; the one you met online a couple of years ago. What was her name, *Sharon*? Have you spoken to her?"

"You mean *Sherry* Anderson. No, I haven't spoken to her since last fall. She obviously got back with her ex, you know *Mr. Pretty Man!*"

"Hhmmm . . . sounds to me like you haven't quite resolved that situation within yourself. Are you going to eventually obtain a bit of closure and give *her* a call one day soon?"

"You know what; you really get on my nerves!!" Lance says jokingly. "How is it that you know me so well?"

"That's a rhetorical question, right?"

"I suppose it is. But to answer your question, I guess I *have* been thinking about Sherry a little more than I prefer; especially lately. I really don't want to call her but I guess I should. Hopefully she'll say to me, 'Well Lance it was nice hearing from you but I have to go – my husband and I are on our way out' meaning she married da motherfucka! I really don't feel like being bothered with her wishy washy feelings that seem to be swirling around in a blender when it comes to deciding if it's okay to be *just friends* with me or not."

"You don't mean that Lance. You're just a little angry right now because she hasn't picked up the phone in so long. If she did get back with that man, I don't think it worked out! Human nature dictates that she would put *you* in an uncomfortable state of mind before she would do that to herself. If it *was* working out, you would've heard from her by now. If it didn't work out and she picked up the phone and called you, she would be *eating crow* . . . having turned down a chance with you, friends or otherwise, to go back to him."

"In some ways, I do hope it all worked out for her . . . in other ways, I hope it didn't – I dunno."

CHAPTER 18

A nother week passes Lance by; another week of his 2009 summer gone – another *boring* summer where women are concerned he fears. He decides not to put it off any longer and call Sherry. He goes through his address book on his cell phone to retrieve her number having forgotten it; even though deep down he didn't want to. When he gets to her name, he hesitates before he hits the "send" button, wondering what he will say to her. Then suddenly he wonders no more and hits "send."

When she answers, she is pleasant and welcoming as usual. Lance can't tell if she's truly glad to hear from him or not. Then suddenly he realizes that it doesn't matter because the damage is done; the phone call has been made. The first thing she reveals is that she and Norman *did* get back together as he had suspected all along. The second thing she reveals is that Norman told her to stay away from Lance because he suspected that Lance liked her; a conclusion he came to after their brunch together last year.

"I've been through that before – given up a friend of the opposite sex just to please my mate," he says to her. "In the end, the relationship didn't work out and I wound up crawling on my knees back to the friend I had given up. That didn't work out either; you know the female I told you about that I was taking Salsa lessons with. My point is, at least I ultimately found that out on my own without an outside force to manipulate the outcome."

"Hhmmp, what a coincidence . . . Norman and I didn't work out either . . . well that's not *exactly* what happened. His mother died a few months ago, so he moved to North Carolina to be with his father."

"Oh, I'm really sorry to hear that . . . *but*, he left you here in Illinois!?" Lance cannot believe his ears at first. Then he considers the fact that it *is* Norman she's talking about.

After meeting the man himself, hearing that he did something as extremely selfish as moving out of state and leaving a good woman like Sherry behind seems like the typical, self centered thing for *him* to do.

Sherry provides more details concerning her circumstances involving Norman. He suspects he will move back to Chicago one day, depending on how his job situation turns out. His current state of grieving over the family dilemma doesn't particularly help matters either right now. He leans more towards the idea of her leaving Illinois and joining him in North Carolina. Neither idea seems feasible to Sherry as she expresses to Lance. She finds herself in the undesirable position of being in a long distance relationship.

"I'm going to call Norman very soon and tell him that this isn't right for me and I can't do this!" she says candidly. Lance offers his condolences to her just as he did about ten months ago. It disgusts him that his *sorrys* concern the same guy as before. He quickly goes into explaining to her how other peoples' jealousy is really discomfort within themselves.

"Norman needed to control you and what you do to make himself feel better about his own shortcomings and *you* let him . . . and look what he did to you in the end."

Lance reminds Sherry of how they stopped communicating after their first and only date in 2007 and how he called her and asked if they could be friends. She said *yes*. He then reminds her of how their communication tapered off in the beginning of 2008 before his son was born. Lance called her again months later and made an inquiry about their so called existing friendship. Again her answer was affirmative.

"Yes we're friends," she said back then. Lance offers a little advice and a bit of concern about their current communication gap.

"Sherry, don't ever let anyone tell you what to do just to satisfy their own inadequacies. I *do not* want to lose your friendship and I hope you feel the same way about me!"

"I do Lance, I really do. I'm sorry Lance."

"Sherry, you truly have nothing to be sorry for; you did what you thought was right at the time and you were just trying to make your relationship work. I respect that. I just hope you learned a valuable lesson from all of this."

"Oh believe me; I learned a *few* valuable lessons from all of this . . ."

"You matter to me Sherry and as far as how I feel about our friendship . . . this is the last time I'm gonna tell you this."

"Okay Lance, I hear you."

On an early Saturday morning, Lance is awakened by the whirring sound of his cell phone vibrating on the surface of his night stand. The first thing he does is look at the clock to reveal the time of 8:50 in the morning. There are less than five people in his life that he'll welcome a wake up call from. When his Caller ID reads the name *Arlene Jansen*, he scoffs. She is certainly not one of the few allowed to call Lance so early. He now realizes that she has gotten completely out of hand.

"Good morning Lance my darling. Did I wake you!?" she says in a voice that reminds him of Anitra, the last woman he had sex with.

"Yes you did," he says in a reluctant tone.

Arlene ignores it, "Good! I wanted to be the first person to say *good morning* to you. You don't have anyone lying next to you, do you?"

"Of course not!" he says emphatically.

"Good – I *am* the first to do the honors. Who knows, maybe the next time I'm first to do so, *I'll* be lying next to you . . ."

"Maybe . . ." he says.

Surely I'm not awake for real – this has to be the TV I'm hearing in my sleep! Rip your vagina off, put it in a FedEx box and mail it to me why don'tcha! I knew this girl was GH . . . jeez!!

"You know I have an early morning flight to the west coast tomorrow – got business out in Cali! She says. "I would really like to meet you in person *today* before I leave!"

"You must have read my mind, I was gonna say the exact same thing," he says, lying. The truth is in his thought.

. . . 'cause this nonsense has got to end . . . today!!

They agree upon a mid afternoon meeting to have a cocktail or two at his favorite place, Cuatro's. Lance purposely schedules it as early as possible because he and Sherry made plans to have dinner this evening. He doesn't want this woman to be conflicting with that, even though he feels in his gut that Sherry will call him later and cancel.

Later on that day at four o'clock on the dot, Lance is standing in front of his sparkling clean black Cadillac. He is parked directly across the street from Cuatro's. He arrived a few minutes early to claim their meeting place as *his* territory and to prepare himself for the unexpected, good or bad. He frowns as he calls Arlene because now she's late.

"Hey girl, where ya at . . . ?"

"I'm getting off the expressway now, so I'm at Cermak."

"Okay good – You're just a few minutes away. I'll see you then."

"Okay bye." Lance disconnects the call and brushes his shirt off in the front. It is a short sleeve button down designer shirt. It is a thick *100%* rayon material and light metallic blue in color.

Sherry will like this shirt . . . and when Arlene sees it, hopefully she'll realize that I'm completely out of her league!

Lance had been trying his best to maintain a positive attitude about meeting Arlene all day long. But truthfully in his heart, a mere "pin drop" can change that perspective. Her tardiness *and* her getting lost a few minutes after they hung up, is already one "pin drop" too many.

It is twenty minutes later when Lance crosses the street to stand in front of Cuatro's. With the establishment being two blocks north of Cermak, he expects her to approach from the same side of the street he's parked on; that way she will have to cross the street by herself instead of him walking her over. Lance knows this is arrogant and not like his usual *gentleman* like way of thinking . . . but at this point he really doesn't care.

When Arlene calls Lance a second time while she's *still* trying to figure out where she is, he tells her what he has on and where he's standing. A few minutes later she arrives in a raggedy light blue car; and automobile not fit for a self proclaimed *diva*.

"Hey Lance . . . !" she yells from her open car windows as she passes by. Lance gets a good look at her because she approaches from the wrong side of the street. This is evidence that she bypassed the place when she was lost.

Oh no . . . she looks like the black woman version of that green cartoon character's wife with the red hair!!!

Lance looks behind him with a feeling of embarrassment, as if every single Cuatro's patron seated outside on the patio is looking at him. He sees a beautiful African American woman among the people that are seated. He wishes he was with her instead of *Da Beava*. As he turns back and watches Arlene make a u-turn, he suddenly rips his cell phone from its holster and calls one of his best friends.

"Kevin!!" he says frantically.

"Whasup man, you straight . . . ? You sound like you in some trouble!"

"I am man – this girl is a *dog*!!"

"Who . . . ?" Kevin asks with a slight chuckle.

"Arlene . . . ! Look, I only got a second 'cause she's parkin' her car right now! Do me a favor; call me in forty-five minutes and just kinda go along with whatever I say! I know . . . you'll be my brother and a family emergency has occurred!! I gotta get away from this one – she's *too* far gone!!!"

Kevin is on the other end of the phone cracking up. "Lance, you are crazy as hell!! Alright man, I gotcha!"

"Hey man . . . don't take a nap a half hour from now and wake up two hours later talkin' about, 'damn . . . I didn't call Lance!'"

"I'm straight dog, I gotcha!!" Kevin says, still laughing uncontrollably.

Lance disconnects the call and tries his best to readjust his animated demeanor and the overall look on his face. After Arlene parks, it takes her about two minutes to get out of the car.

"Oh my God . . . is she putting on make-up!!?" he murmurs under his breath. At this point, Lance is afraid to turn around again and see if any of the patrons noticed what's going on. He doesn't recall talking in a low volume when he was on the phone with Kevin. When she finally gets out of her car and starts to approach, Lance suddenly feels nervous jitters – not because he's meeting Arlene for the very first time but because he *doesn't* want to meet her *at all*. How he will convey a reasonable level of social etiquette towards her is beyond him.

"Hi Lance. Sorry about the delay; I don't know what I was thinking when I was looking for Wabash."

"That's okay – c'mon, let's have a seat right here outside," he says pleasantly.

If anyone out here does know what's going on, I may as well face it head on instead of hiding at this point! If you're from Chicago and you don't know where Wabash avenue is . . . you're stupid!!

They have a seat right next to the beautiful woman he spotted a few moments ago. She is sitting at the table with a man that *looks like a subdued Hip Hop rapper.* When the waitress stops at their table, she exchanges quick pleasantries with Lance by name. Arlene orders a Dirty Martini and he orders the Sangria.

"Extra fruity . . . and extra liquor too sweetie!!" he says to the waitress, smiling.

When she walks away, Arlene attempts to conceal the fact that their knowing each other by name has irritated her. "You've been here before?"

"Yes . . . why?"

"Oh no, nothing . . ." Arlene hesitates to formulate her lie. ""I just like a man that knows his way around when it comes to recreational activities."

"Oh," he says. *She's a liar* he thinks. Lance recalls the last time he was at Cuatro's last year, when he had cut the pseudo umbilical cord of him and Anitra Downing's relationship. Now the establishment feels tainted to him. It suddenly dawns on him that he can never bring Sherry back to this place.

He gives Arlene a five second stare, to her face in particular, while she fumbles through her purse. He can't fathom the idea of how she considers herself *a diva*, unless the declaration was indicative of her overall personality and not her looks. Arlene's complexion is dark, her eyes have bags under them and her hair is stringy, with no body to it . . . and it barely touches her shoulders.

Lance has often been accused of discriminating against dark skinned African American women versus women that are light skinned or have a brown complexion. He considers this accusation to be false and simply believes in his mind that women he usually finds attractive, just so happen to be light skinned or brown skinned the majority of the time. He has often defended his belief as simply being his preference and not an intentional discriminatory credence.

No matter what complexion this woman is that sits before him, Lance simply does not find her attractive; not even a little bit. He doesn't even try to look at her body because he already analyzed and determined he was displeased with it when she was crossing the street. Within the fastidious nature of his preference in a woman, her blue jeans were either tired or incapable of properly fitting her outlandish shape and her purple blouse resembled an article of clothing that he saw his grandmother in twenty five years ago.

Lance struggles to find a topic of conversation. Arlene notices. "Cat got'cha tongue Mr. Lance?"

"No not really. I just have to warm up to people when I first meet them, that's all. It's kinda like a tad bit of shyness . . ."

"Shyness . . . ? You're not shy!"

"It's complicated . . ." Lance doesn't feel like explaining it to her. He can only wonder how he will look at his watch without her noticing and how he can steal a quick glance at the pretty young lady that they're sitting next to. Lance certainly knows that this is not a date and he wouldn't want it to be even if it was. He knows that Arlene thinks otherwise.

"So what do you think?"

Lance hesitates, not because he doesn't know what she means but because he can't believe what he's hearing. " . . . Think about what?"

"What do you think about me?"

"Arlene . . ." he says. *I think you're ugly – seeyalater!!!* Lance continues, "I can't believe you're asking me that question!" he says. "What does it matter what I think about you!? I explained to you more than once that I'm not diving into a dating situation with *anyone* right away . . . talk about pressure!"

"That's not pressure, it's just a question," she says innocently.

"I beg to differ. Let's talk about something else." Lance looks at his watch and then he looks at the desirable young lady seated next to them and smiles at her. Her smile in return is accompanied by a small giggle, as if she heard him and Arlene's exchanges. In many ways he hopes she *did* hear them. Somehow in his mind he feels obligated to offer the other patrons and *especially* her, some kind of explanation as to why he's sitting there with Arlene. If Lance was a good liar, he would've lied to her and said she looks nice. He's not though because his thoughts, good or bad, always show up on his face. He can't pinpoint one thing about her that he likes anyway.

They each order another drink as Lance awaits the phone call he's suppose to receive from Kevin. He looks at his watch again, not even concerned about what she may think at this point.

I wish I was drunk right now!! Jeez c'mon Kevin . . . ! Oh that's right, I can't get drunk now; I'm meeting Sherry in less than two hours. I haven't heard from her, so she's not canceling – good!!

"You know what sweetie . . ." she blurts out suddenly, " . . . I'm feeling deliciously tipsy right now – you wanna go skating!?"

"Do I wanna go skating!?" Lance repeats the question to waste time. He doesn't know what to say. He knows what he *really* wants to say. He just can't think of an alternative response.

Wow! Just what I need; a pregnant elephant on roller skates, he thinks. Suddenly he snatches his cell phone from its holster, hits a couple of buttons on it and then stares at it as if he's reading a text message.

"I gotta go – my brother is stranded in Harvey!!" he exclaims.

"I didn't hear your phone ring . . ."

"You've heard of a vibrator, right?"

"A rabbit . . . ?"

"Never mind . . . !" Lance vigorously waves his arm back and forth to get the waitress' attention.

This girl must want my arm to fall off!!

After he finally gets her attention and has the check sent over, he suddenly realizes he should have asked for separate bills. Lance never does this with a lady, platonic or otherwise. Today he wishes he would've made an exception. When Arlene doesn't reach for her purse, it infuriates Lance.

Ugly ass purple purse . . . ! Hhmmp!! A supposed platonic meeting turned into "I'm gonna have this man pay for my drinks since he doesn't like me." At least he *thinks* she knows he doesn't like her. *She did ask me to go skating with her. Maybe that was her way of confirming the obvious . . . I dunno. Whatever!!*

Lance let's her slide just this once; knowing he will never ever have to see this woman again.

"Damn dog, you left before I called!? I was only fifteen minutes late calling!!" Kevin's voice blares through Lance's cell phone.

"Man I left probably twenty five, thirty minutes ago. I'm at the mall in Skokie now!"

"Damn dog, she was *that* bad!?"

"Put it this way . . . there was *nothing* good about her! I don't even think I hugged her when we parted ways . . . I truly don't remember."

"I think maybe you need to stop fooling with those girls with no picture on their profile! I think that's kinda shady anyway. You may as well just go to a club where all the women are walking around with black garbage bags over them and a brown paper bag on their heads with two holes in it for the eyes!!" Kevin and Lance explode in laughter. "They can call it *The Here Ya Go-Good Luck Club!*"

"Yeah you're right! It's just like only hearing *Droopy's* voice over the phone and knowing nothing else about her – all talk!!"

"*Droopy* . . . ?"

"Yeah, her eyes were droopy or she had heavy bags under them or something . . . I dunno!"

"Man you are crazy as hell!!" Kevin laughs out loud again. "Now you're about to meet up with that Sherry chick, right?"

"Yeah at seven o'clock. I got a little extra time; it's only 5:30. I'll probably walk around the mall for a minute."

"You're talking about 'ol girl . . . I don't know about Sherry *either* to tell ya the truth! I know she's cute and all and I'm sure you'll tolerate her garbage just a little while longer than say . . . a *'Droopy.'* Just be careful with her. Don't spend all your money on her just to get nowhere wit her!"

"It doesn't matter . . . we're friends anyway."

"Friendship – friendshit!! I know you still like her, even after all this time. Just watch yourself wit her, that's all."

"Yeah you're right man. Fourth quarter in basketball for her as far as me liking her; I hear ya!"

Lance sits on a cream colored bench watching the spiral staircase of the same color, waiting for Sherry to arrive in the lobby area of the high end restaurant they agreed to meet at. He prefers to see a person before they see him in situations like this, good or bad. In the not so favorable situations, he feels this gives him the advantage over them, especially if he may have to pretend like he didn't see them.

Because it is Sherry that's running a little late, Lance doesn't mind. His main concern was receiving a cancellation call from her. That was put to rest once and for all the moment he spoke to her an hour ago, when he told her he would see her at seven o'clock and she said *okay.*

As he continues to watch the stairs, he notices that the majority of patrons coming in are mostly Caucasian women. He sees *one* in particular that basically blows him away with her appearance. She has on beige stilettos with two inch heels. Her dress is exactly the same color as her shoes, medium length, perfect fit all the way around. Her calves and her thighs are that of a figure skater. Her panty line through the dress is nonexistent and her butt is a size *6.* Her breasts are thirty six inches in measurement; her cleavage is excessively revealing, yet classy and tasteful at the same time. Her hair is jet black, straight, and hangs in length to the small of her back. Her tan is subtle and not over done. Her face is that of a beauty contest winner and her stride reminds Lance of a sexy underwear model on television.

Lance looks at her and frowns. It's the kind of frown a man's face makes unconsciously when a woman's beauty in person is too much to believe and behold. He imagines himself walking up to her without thinking and saying,

"Hi, how are you?" Her demeanor is serious looking, mostly confident, yet she seems pleasant and approachable. He imagines that she bestows the radiance of her smile upon him during her response.

"I'm fine, how are you? Beautiful shirt by the way . . ."

"I'm doing good; in fact I'm doing very well after receiving your compliment about my shirt. Thank you for both!"

"You don't have to thank me for the compliment – thank your mirror at home . . . and as far as the small extent of my contribution to changing your already good mood for the better . . . happy to oblige!"

"Okay, you're sharp. Let me guess . . . you have arrived here by yourself because you're running a little late in meeting two of your girlfriends here that are already seated inside. When I ask if I may join the three of you for one drink, you'll ignore the obvious indicators that I am sitting here waiting for someone and say 'yes.' One of your girlfriends will be disgruntled when you bring me to the table but she'll begin to get over it the more and more she keeps glancing at my shirt." At this moment in his imaginary conversation, Lance chuckles because he can no longer keep a straight face.

The perfect 10 young lady says, *"Okay, you're a little* sharp *yourself. Are you a writer or something? You have a colorably detailed imagination."*

"Yes . . . and I will reveal more while the four of us are having our drink."

The perfect 10 young lady chuckles, *"Well unfortunately you are only correct about my tardiness and my party already being seated. However, my party only consists of my boyfriend."*

"Unfortunately' meaning that there was a good chance that you and I sharing a quick drink together could have occurred?"

"My boyfriend and I have been dealing for about a year now." She leans closer to Lance and whispers, *"Darling, if I had bumped into you six months shy of that in this situation, I would have given you my number and told you to give me a call tomorrow."*

"Men never call the next day."

"Okay, Monday . . ."

"Darling . . . it is now January of 2009 – what's the problem?"

"Sorry intriguing stranger; you are six months behind in ripping those pages from your calendar," she says with a smile.

Lance chuckles, *"Well . . . you can't blame a guy for trying, right?"*

"Not at all . . . and thank you for trying . . . it really means a lot to me. Take care, okay?" Lance nods his head affirmatively and gives her an acceptable smile of rejection.

When he snaps out of his chimerical moment while waiting for Sherry, the beautiful young Caucasian woman is still standing by the hostess' podium. As the hostess motions her to follow her to a table, Lance jumps up from the bench without thinking and gets her attention.

"Wow!" he says to her while giving her a look of admiration. "I just had a dream!"

The young lady gives Lance a look struck with wonder, "Wow, so did I; *but . . .*" She throws her hands up in a supine motion and twists her mouth sideways to indicate the timing of sharing their thoughts and their "dreams" to not be such a good idea at the moment. She takes two steps forward and then turns around one more time and says, "Nice shirt!"

If only my personality had a bit of an edge and my approach in meeting women was a little more daring. I may have actually gotten her number! Now, what do I do to get Sherry to look like that *whenever we meet up to do something!?*

It is now seven-thirty and *still* no Sherry coming up the spiral staircase. Lance doesn't panic simply because he spoke to her a little over hour and a half ago to get a final confirmation of their meeting. He now starts to worry because he knows the woman's character would not have him sitting there waiting for so long, unless something was wrong. He calls her.

"Sherry, is everything okay? I was getting a little worried . . ."

"I am so sorry Lance . . ." His heart is ready to drop to the floor from the sudden anticipation of her canceling at the very last minute of their 7:00pm meeting. "One of the tires on my car is *really* low and I've been trying to find a gas station in the area that could hopefully look at it in case I need to get it fixed. I let the time get away from me without calling to let you know what was happening. Again I am *really* sorry."

"It's okay Sherry. Is it a slow leak or are you on a flat by now?"

"I'm not sure but I certainly hope it's not a flat. If it is . . . I'm in trouble!"

"Not with me around you're not! Pull over to the side of the road Sherry. Get out and check the bad tire. You've been riding around on it for a little over forty minutes now, right?"

"Yes that's right."

"Well if you still have air in it, then it's a slow leak and you should be okay tonight – probably until tomorrow."

"Yes, it still has some air in it. It looks about the same as it did when I first noticed it."

"Good! Go and put some air in it now and try to put a little more in it than you normally would. That way it'll definitely be okay to drive home later; unless you want to take it home now and I come and pick you up?"

"No Lance that's okay, thank you. I'm only a few blocks away from the mall already."

"Okay, so I will see you in a few minutes and don't worry, everything will be fine, okay?"

"Okay Lance . . . thanks again."

He disconnects the call and smiles about her lack of knowledge about her apparent car trouble. *How feminine of her – I love it!* Lance begins to look around the restaurant and notice how nice it is. He can't believe he couldn't find this place on the internet over two years ago, with it being in the mall where they first met. He considers the irony of the *mall* being the place where they first met.

Lance assumes that their one and only official date not taking place at this place must have been for a good reason, probably having a lot to do with timing. Even though this meeting with Sherry is not a date, he does consider it to be a "starting over" point for them regarding their friendship. The timing now, seems as if it will be a little kinder to the both of them as far as Lance is concerned.

When Lance turns right and sees Sherry finally coming up the spiral staircase, his enthusiasm is aroused. "Sherry Anderson!" he exclaims before she has even approached him. "It's *so* good to see you sweetie!" Lance holds both of his arms out. He would have her do nothing less than greet him with a magnanimous hug, given the many months that have gone by without them communicating.

Sherry is happy to oblige as she extends her arms forward a couple of seconds before she gets to him. "It's good to see you too Lance!" Their hug is more than amiable and their smiles are quite relentless. Sherry realizes at this moment that she is truly just as excited to see Lance as he is to see her; especially after he talked her through her car trouble moments ago. "Thank you so much for helping me with that tire on my SUV; I was *so* worried about it before I spoke to you!" she says.

"Oh it was nothing. C'mon let's go inside, I'm starved!"

"Yes, me too . . . !"

CHAPTER 19

Lance is unusually mesmerized with Sherry on this night. He doesn't know why but he can't stop staring at her. He knows it's not because her jeans are a little tighter than he has ever seen before, though he is surprised by it . . . and pleased by it. Her black top is nice too and he can tell she spent some time in the mirror with her hair. This pleases Lance as well because her hair has always been long and beautiful to him. He figures this night to be her second best fashionable appearance next to their early afternoon brunch last year.

There's something about Sherry and not what she may or may not have on, that throws Lance *for a loop*. And he doesn't hide it either.

"Sherry, it is *really* nice to see you again," he says in a calm, cool, yet pitiful voice. "I missed you . . . I miss this – sitting down with quality company and having a good conversation along with a good meal."

"You know what Lance, I kind of missed you too and all of the above. Truthfully, I didn't quite realize it until I laid eyes on you. I've been so busy with . . ." she hesitates, " . . . other things, ya know . . . and to no avail."

"Did you make that phone call yet . . . to Norman?"

"Yes I did. Do I have to tell you that it didn't go too well?"

"No . . ."

"You know, I just don't get it! No matter what the situation is . . . or was, it always winds up being about him. I can never win with him! I feel so silly for going back with him last year! You're silent . . . you're probably thinking *I should* feel silly."

"No Sherry, I'm not. I'm just letting you vent. It's good for you to do so right now because you're hurt. Please believe me when I tell you, I understand completely."

"I thought things would eventually change for the better . . . instead things just got worse. I thought he loved me!!"

"I'm sure he does. I really can't imagine any man dealing with *you* and *not* falling in love. The first thing about love though . . . a person can only love you with what they have and/or what they're *willing* to give. It's just like the book I was reading a few years ago – it taught me that love is never enough!"

"What was this book about exactly . . . relationships?"

"Yeah . . . In summary it talks about how to *maintain* a good relationship. It consists of more than just saying *I love you* and feeling that love. It states that one's actions and how they handle their own emotions are keys to a successful monogamous relationship."

"Sounds like a really interesting piece of reading material."

"Yes it is and as you know, it's a lot harder to pull it off than it sounds."

The waitress comes by to take their drink order. She is African American, a little bit on the heavy side but very cute.

"I'll have a glass of Riesling please," Sherry says to Lance's surprise.

"Is your Riesling from Germany?" he asks.

"I believe it is. I'll check and make sure. You will have a glass if it is?" the waitress asks.

"Please . . . thank you."

Sherry smiles at Lance. "Well that's certainly one thing I know I missed about you; how you order your drinks!"

"There *really* is a difference in the taste."

"Hey, if you say there is, I believe you. The fact that you're even capable of noticing . . . I like that."

"*Why* thank you. Now, let's talk about the surprise of the evening . . . you're drinking again?"

"Yeah, every once in a while; not a whole lot . . . I'm trying to be more in tune with my spiritual path, especially more than before."

Lance chuckles, '*spiritual path', I've heard that somewhere before,* he thinks.

"What's so funny, you don't agree?"

"Oh no, no . . . I was just thinking of something else. I'll tell you about it later."

"Well I just figured that since my recent relationship seemed as if it *would* work out and it didn't, is because I wasn't in it under God's terms – you know, having premarital sex and stuff like that. That's why I told Norman when we got back together last year; I didn't want to have sex anymore till we were married."

"Hhmmm . . . well that explains a lot . . ."

"What do you mean?"

"Oh I'm sorry, I should've asked – do you *really* want my opinion about all of this? I know before I was a little harsh. I promise I won't be this time around."

"Oh no, I didn't think you were harsh. Your assessment about Norman before was just a man's opinion about another man. I can appreciate that – though I will admit, you *did* catch me off guard a little bit before."

"Because you didn't expect it before . . . *now* I can call him all kinds of *MF*s since you know *now* I might go there." Lance smiles to see her reaction. Sherry frowns a little. "No, I'm just playing!"

"You're silly Lance but do tell," she says as her frown disappears.

"Well, once a man has experienced *the sex* with his woman, it's kind of hard for him to take it back; you know like suddenly not doing that once he's gotten used to it – especially if the sexual act has been going on for a year! Now I'm not saying that was the case with you, a whole year, 'cause it probably wasn't . . . but even six months; it's hard to stop . . . for a man. You know how we men are. I think it's easier for a woman to ultimately decide to apply herself more to a righteous spiritual path. It *is* easy for a woman to change her mind, right!?" Lance chuckles.

"That's for sure!" Sherry says smiling.

"It would take a *very* special and rare kind of man to willingly change his mind with you. But ultimately in the end, in my opinion, that man has to want to put himself into a more spiritual setting *within himself*, which may or may not automatically include the sexual side of his monogamous relationship. He has to be ready to do that . . . *on his own*! You can't convince anyone of something like that. Am I making any sense to you?"

The cute and heavy set waitress brings two glasses of Riesling to the table. "I should've brought the bottle with me to show you it *is* from a German vineyard."

"No dear, that's not necessary. *I know* you know what you're doing. I believe you. Thank you very much!" Lance says.

"You are *very* welcome."

Hhmmm . . . I wonder how Sherry would react if I flirted with the waitress and tried to get her number, Lance thinks to himself. "Okay Sherry, you were about to say . . . ?"

"Yes okay, what was I going to say? Oh yeah, basically you're saying that Norman wasn't ready to do the spiritual thing with me, therefore it was *easy* for him to just up and move out of state without me?"

"Yes Sherry. *Unfortunately* that's exactly what I'm saying. And truth be told, I'm not knocking Norman. I mean, from a male point of view, I didn't like the guy when I met him . . . but you're in love with this man and from what I know about *you*, there *has to be* something good in this guy that you saw."

"Lance thank you for saying that! You *really* seem very understanding of my whole situation . . . more so than before."

"Remember last year when I spoke to you about empathy . . . ? Well having *that* for my female friends as well as any women I may deal with romantically from here on out is not such a bad thing either."

"Wow . . . nice! I like the way you *say* you're going to apply something in your life and then you *actually* do it! But even last year you were a little more understanding than my so called best friend Tammy was!!"

"What happened with Tammy?"

"I don't know exactly . . . and I really don't care either at this point!!"

It surprises Lance at how angry Sherry seems when she mentions Tammy's name.

He has never seen this side of her before. Lance can see the waitress approaching out the corner of his eye. He now has his eye on her.

"Are you two ready to order appetizers and dinner now?" inquires the waitress.

"Sherry, are you ready?"

"Not quite Lance. She turns to the waitress, "May we have about five more minutes?"

"Sure no problem; take your time."

"Okay thanks," Sherry says. Lance thanks her as well, by name.

"I was sitting here contemplating if I should order this salad dish I was looking at or if I should order what I *really* want – the fish and chips! They're fried and you know I usually don't do fried food."

Lance smiles at her, "Sherry let me just say this – you're a vegetarian first of all. That in itself speaks volumes about your diet and the discipline you have within it. It's okay to let your hair down every once in a while and cheat a little bit from the *norm* . . . and I don't mean 'Nor-*man*' you love sick puppy you . . . I mean 'nor-*mal*'!!" Lance smiles to indicate to Sherry he's joking. She realizes his daring attempt at humor and smiles back.

Lance continues, "Order the fish and chips and don't worry about it. I'm here to help cheer you up . . . and so will those fish and chips!"

"You know Lance, you kind of get on my nerves when you're kind of right, you know that!?" she says.

"Yeah I know. Order the fried dish girl! Enjoy yourself!!"

Sherry laughs, "You're silly Lance! Thank you! What are you ordering?"

"Please . . . I'm *funky steak down* up in here tonight!! Hey, I ain't in the best of moods either! Tell me what happened with Tammy, before we *both* forget!"

"Oh yeah, and please *do* tell why you're not in such a good mood tonight. With Tammy though, I was talking to her about Norman one night and she suddenly *came out of a bag* on me . . . like she was jealous of me or something . . . and not just about Norman! It sounded like something had been going on inside of her, negative about me, most of our lives – for the duration of our friendship!!" Sherry doesn't mention to Lance, Tammy's apparent sexual attraction for him. While his conceited attitude about himself to most is only a slightly misguided self confidence to her, she still doesn't want to add, even to that.

Sherry continues, "As a girlfriend, especially a *best* girlfriend, I expected a little more *girlfriend* type of support from her! I don't talk to her anymore!!"

"Don't get me started on *her*. . . but she was kind of the opposite of you! That's unfortunate though, I'm sorry to hear that."

"That's okay . . ." Sherry says as she has to calm herself down. The waitress comes back again for their order. Sherry orders the fish and chips and Lance orders his "funky" steak.

"Fully cooked but not burned!! Okay dear?" he says to the waitress.

"Okay *dear* . . ." the waitress says to him. Lance doesn't notice any obvious reaction from Sherry from his slight attempt at flirting with the waitress. He figures that she probably considers it as his usual finicky preferences when eating out.

They continue their conversation about relationships in general. Lance offers his confession of trying to meet women on the internet again. She is of course amused at how often meeting people of the opposite sex can be just that; *amusing* and yet unsettling. Lance is relentless in expressing the humorous aspects of it all, just as he is in telling her the *not so* humorous aspect of who he was with a couple of hours ago – hence his not so good mood this evening.

"Believe me though Sherry, your presence here and now makes it impossible to *stay* in the bad mood I was in!"

"Thank you Lance, you're sweet. Same here," she says.

Twenty minutes later when their food arrives, Sherry is a little disgruntled about how her fish and chips turned out. They are soft in texture as if they were undercooked. She tastes one to be sure.

"Oh wow, they're really not that good," she says. "I don't know, maybe I should send them back."

"Take it from me Sherry, if you're not satisfied with your food, especially in a high end place like this, send it back," his says definitively.

"I don't know . . . they're really not *too* bad. You want to taste one?"

"Not really . . ." Lance observes her overall innocence and her wholesome, undefiled ways. It is almost pitiful to witness, if she were not so adorable . . . and so beautiful. If she somehow views complaining about her food to be an act of unkindness, Lance decides to be mean for her.

"Excuse me . . ." he says to the waitress. "The lady isn't satisfied with how her fish and chips turned out. Would you please take her dish and prepare it again or give her a menu so she can order something else – please accommodate the lady in whatever way she would like."

Lance says something on her behalf to show her it's okay to complain about her food. In the end, he wants her to feel comfortable enough to make the final decision in how it should be handled. Sherry asks for a menu and eventually orders the salad dish she had originally considered. By the time her new dish arrives, the waitress is now calling Lance by name in their courteous exchanges.

"This is very good; thank you Lance," Sherry says.

"You're welcome. I'm going to have another glass of Riesling," Lance says.

"So will I." They continue to talk nonstop, basically catching up with the happenings in each other's lives since they last spoke. The alcohol buzz for Lance is typical yet pleasing, having added a second glass of wine to the two drinks he had three hours earlier. Sherry's buzz is pleasing for her as well but a certain aspect of it stuns her.

Wait a second!! My vagina is actually *feeling a little lubricated!! This couldn't be happening!! I've always found Lance attractive but I'm certainly not ready to see* anyone *right now! What is going on!? And why do I feel so full from a salad? Is it the wine!?*

As Sherry sits slightly slouched in her bench like seat, she lifts her black top up just a little, almost unconsciously, to look at her stomach and touch it, to make sure she doesn't appear as bloated as she feels.

When Lance notices, he is completely taken by surprise . . . but he downplays it,

"Sherry, if you're wondering if your stomach is still flat after your meal, it is . . . and it looks nice too," he calmly says.

"Oh, thank you" – *Oh my God!! What am I doing!?*

Sherry doesn't excuse herself and go to the bathroom immediately because she doesn't want the guilt to show in her wanting to so badly. After five minutes pass, she can't take it any longer and does so. When she gets to the bathroom, she uses it and dabs herself with three squares of tissue as she normally does.

Surely I don't need anymore tissue than that! Whatever was going on down there has surely passed! I'm only having dinner with a friend, she thinks.

After a short pause, she considers her private area normal again and stands to pull her panties and pants back up. She goes to the sink to wash her hands and to throw a little water on her face. Afterwards, she stares in the mirror, hoping no one will come in at this very moment, *No more wine for you young lady!!* Sherry dabs her face dry with two paper towels and then tries to fling her hair back in its original position.

Meanwhile Lance is sitting at the table alone, looking at the waitress when her back is turned.

She's not really that big, he thinks. *She couldn't be more than a size 12 . . . maybe even a 10! Whatever her size, she wears it well . . . I wonder if Sherry would be jealous if I tried to get her number,* he thinks again. *I wonder if I slipped the waitress a twenty dollar bill and told her to pretend to give me her number just so I can try to make Sherry jealous because I like her . . . would that work!?*

When Sherry returns to the table, Lance smiles at her, "Are you okay sweetie?" he asks in a comical tone.

"Yes, I'm fine," she says definitively.

"You'll never guess who called while you were in the bathroom!"

"Who . . . ?"

"The female I was with earlier today. I thought she more or less understood that she and I will never *go* anywhere; I guess not! I'll have to work on that."

Lance tells Sherry this white lie as a feeble attempt to make her jealous. He knows that even though trying to get the waitress' phone number would be just a ploy, he truly doesn't have the nerve to carry through with it. He views it as a cruel betrayal towards Sherry and more importantly, a betrayal within himself and his own feelings. Lance knows that making a woman jealous is *most* effective when the other woman is desirable but the story about Arlene will have to do. Deep down though, he wants Sherry to realize on her own their potential as a future couple without having to be tricked into that realization.

When Lance walks Sherry to her SUV half an hour after coffee, he spots another attractive woman sitting in her car with a girlfriend of hers. The African American woman looks at Lance and smiles. He takes it as being indicative of her being receptive if he were to approach her.

Oh my God, she's fine, he thinks to himself. *What is going on tonight . . . ?* Of course he contemplates approaching her, either right away or seeing Sherry off before he does so. He declines both inner scenarios as he checks Sherry's tire on her vehicle. The overall innocent, wholesome and undefiled ways that truly exists within Lance's nature, dominate any potential naughty deeds that his mind wishes to carry out.

"Here, wait a minute . . . let me get my tire gauge out the car." Lance scurries over to his car, four vehicles parked away from Sherry's. He glances at the attractive woman in her car again, two aisles directly parked in front of him. He scoffs at the reality he has chosen for himself in *not* exploring the possibility of ever going out on a date with her.

When he brings the tire gauge back by Sherry's vehicle, he checks the recommended PSI on her tire's side wall and then checks the actual tire pressure with the gauge. He explains to her the concept of tires and pressure.

"Here you know what . . . take this tire gauge with you; that way you won't have to guess . . . and always keep it in the truck with you, for future situations."

"Oh Lance thank you . . . !" Sherry hugs Lance as if he has just given her a mink coat. Her enthusiasm over such a simple gesture startles him. Lance ignores it. He's not quite sure where the enthusiasm comes from or why it's occurring. As he sees her off, he yells out,

"Talk to you soon!" He hopes that "soon" is *really* soon and not a month or two from now. Even though he now remains in the parking lot alone, with only the beautiful stranger and her friend still in their car, he doesn't reconsider approaching her. He figures by now that she probably wouldn't believe that he and Sherry are just friends.

When he pulls off he scoffs again, wondering why he gives Sherry more consideration of her feelings than she probably deserves. He then takes into account his own feelings for her. Lance mentally pats himself on the back for maintaining his integrity, remaining true to himself and keeping his eye on the ultimate prize. While he's driving, he realizes that his feelings for Sherry are no longer whims of wishful thinking. She is now a legitimate single woman to be wooed, won over and had, hopefully leading to the ultimate foundation of a monogamous relationship between a man and a woman – marriage!

He now knows for certain that his feelings for Sherry have not subsided any and liking her can no longer be taken lightly. In fact, his feelings for her are probably stronger now than they've ever been before.

Lance is now in a good mood since leaving Sherry. He wants to share his good mood with someone but not as he typically would. He doesn't call Angelica to spill all about his evening; he will do that in a day or two. He doesn't call Kevin to see if he wants to have a beer or two or three. Lance wants to do something different like be around a female he hasn't seen in a long time . . . or a female he has never seen before.

While he's driving home, he calls his Caucasian acquaintance Trisha Sampson, to see if by chance she's out with her drunken girlfriends. Lance figures to "kill two birds with one stone" in getting a few more drinks in his system and finally getting to meet Trisha in person for the very first time. He wouldn't tell her about Sherry because he figures she probably wouldn't want to hear about *that* anyway. He would simply share his overall good mood with her.

When Trisha answers, she sounds a little "under the weather."

"I'm kinda getting over a cold but really, I haven't been out too much lately," she says. "I'm just trying to keep things in order around the home front ya' know – with all these kids of mine!"

"I do *still* want to meet you one day – I'm curious, ya' know what I mean?"

"I know exactly what you mean. I'm still a little curious myself, even though we started talking over the phone a year ago."

"Well I'm gonna let you go so you can get some rest. Take care of yourself, okay and I'll talk to ya' soon."

"Okay Mr. Lance, we will talk soon."

Lance gets a text message from Sherry as he's disconnecting his phone call. She thanks him for a nice and funny evening.

You put a smile on my face tonight and I really needed that! Talk to you soon.

And you, my face! Thank you too.

Lance's seven words are simple and to the point in his response, though he wanted to say more. He will let *her* determine if there actually is more.

The silly male sense of accomplishment of being in the company of different females within the same day *still* resides in him when he thinks of Lynita Everstall. He calls her but she's already out for the evening. The background noise is so extreme through his cell phone, that he can barely hear her when she tells him this.

"I want to meet you one day soon!" he screams into his cell phone to her.

"Okay, we will! I have to go . . . I can barely hear you!" she screams back.

"Okay sweetie, bye!" Lance thinks back to the attractive young lady in the mall's parking lot thirty five minutes ago. He knows that meeting *her* was a lot more obtainable and a lot more feasible than meeting the beautiful woman inside the restaurant when Sherry was on her way. He turned down both and yet he is easily willing to throw himself into a situation with women he has never seen before.

Lance wonders if there is some sort of method to his madness or if he seeks a scapegoat, so that he's free and clear to allocate all of his attention towards Sherry. He knows that if he stumbled across a woman that is undeniably attractive and she gave him "the time of day," it would make his situation with Sherry a lot more interesting *and* complicated at the same time.

As Lance parks in front of his place, he tries to convince himself that he will maintain the frame of mind of not "putting all his eggs in one basket." He reminds himself that Sherry is not a *sure thing*, just a *sure prospect*.

Lance walks into his apartment and goes straight to the refrigerator for a beer. He then goes to his computer to turn it on and anxiously wait for it to boot up so he can begin to demonstrate his new rule being in effect. While he waits, he thinks about the older rule he came up with last year – *friends first*. He wonders if he instinctively came up with this rule to strategically deal with the undesirables without conflict.

Lance has never pondered nor questioned his ability to be friends with Sherry because when he first met her, he basically had no choice. He certainly considers her worthy of the difficult task of remaining her friend, especially at this point. But he wonders as he has before, how difficult it will be to maintain the older rule, if he meets someone desirable.

When he logs on to the internet, he checks for the daily email of a few select females from the dating site he has been on as of late; the one with the tall women on it. There are five women in the email and none of them are appealing to Lance. Three of them were 5'9" and over; no surprise to Lance by now. He opens another email from the same site to reveal correspondence from a woman he met on there two days ago. They had been communicating through the website only.

Her name is Alicia Lockhart. She is single, now divorced, thirty-six years of age, has a fourteen year old daughter and is from Chicago but now resides in Atlanta, Georgia. She reminds Lance of Gladys Knight. He reads her short email and decides to send an immediate response.

Hi Alicia, how are you? I'm doing pretty good tonight. You know what . . . I would really like to talk; I have a lot to say to you. May I have your phone number?

Lance

"Hell, she's all the way in Georgia anyway so who cares," he murmurs under his breath. He goes to the refrigerator and gets another beer, then comes back to his computer to surf the web. It starts out with mostly looking up CD's and discovering new music artists and new music. An hour and a half later, when Lance is on his sixth beer, he finds himself on a brand new dating website. This one is different than any other website he's ever been on before because its protocol consists of men and women that are looking for sex only.

In caring for LJ as often as he does, Lance doesn't think about sex as often as he once did. LJ is with his mother this weekend though. The only thing that Lance is caring for on this night is each bottle that he drinks his beer from. The website lets him scroll through the different women on there for free. This particular site has a gimmick that sets communicating capabilities to a limit in the event one comes across someone that *is* desirable.

Lance comes across several and scoffs. He thinks out loud since he's alone, "Damn!! Why can't I meet women like this on the street!? Well actually, I did or had a chance to, twice yesterday evening!!" Lance looks at his watch, "Oh, it's been Sunday for a little while now . . . so I'm right . . . yesterday evening. But why can't I meet a woman and just say to her upfront, 'Look, I would love to have sex with you and that's it!! You're not completely my type but hey!' Her response would be, 'Yeah, same here on both counts!'"

Lance knows the chance of that happening precisely in that manner is slim next to none. He can recall plenty of situations in his past in which the sex was effortless to get; but he's really not into that type of thing anymore. Tonight is different though. *Tonight* Lance is drunk. He fumbles to retrieve one of his credit cards from his wallet. Five minutes later, he is a paid member of the sex only dating website.

As Lance is selecting a few of the women as favorites for future reference, he hears his incoming email indicator. When he opens the email, he is surprised to see it's from Alicia and she includes her phone number. He responds to her email.

I know it's late but may I call you right now? Just wanna hear your voice since you're up! I won't keep you . . .

Sure, give me a jingle real quick.

Lance dials her number and clears his throat while he waits for her to answer. He thinks to himself, *I must be drunk; I just dialed a woman's number the same day I got it!! Oh well, it's ringing now!*

He tells himself to speak slowly so she won't suspect he's intoxicated. It only takes him five minutes to admit to Alicia that he's had "a couple of drinks."

"You're up *this* late drinking by yourself? Are you a drunk!? She inquires without hesitating.

"No, I said a couple . . ." he says, wondering if she believes him.

"Oh . . ." she says.

They continue to "break the ice" in the usual manner that a man and a woman do when they first speak over the phone. She reveals the reason why she moved to Atlanta six years ago; her ex-husband being the culprit.

"Typical . . . and unfortunate, especially concerning his daughter. I'm sorry to hear that," Lance says.

"That's okay because the Lord has been showing me the way every since."

"Oh, you're a spiritual woman . . ."

"Very much so . . . ! I read the Bible almost everyday! My potential mate, while he doesn't have to be just like me when it comes to the Bible, has to have a certain level or foundation of spirituality. There is nothing and especially *no man* . . . that I will allow to stand in the way of my spiritual path!!"

"Bravo!!" he says in response to her declaration. He thinks to himself, "*Spiritual path*" . . . *there it is again! Why does it seem like every woman I speak to lately is talking about their spiritual path!? Is someone trying to tell me something!?*

CHAPTER 20

G ood morning Lance – Happy Friday to you! Have a good day.

This is the text message that Lance reads on his cell phone while driving like a "bat out of hell" so he won't miss his early morning train to go to work. He remembers Sherry's occasional morning gestures via telephone from a while back; so long ago that he had forgotten about them until today. Lance prefers an old fashioned telephone call versus texting but *any* type of communication that Sherry initiates on her own will certainly do. When he's on the train, he responds.

Good morning to you as well! Ditto to you on both counts!

Within the two week period since they met and had dinner together, they have spoken three times. This is a record for the two of them and Lance is determinied to make sure it continues. Lance recalls one of those conversations.

"You know what I want to do Lance . . . I want to put together and conduct a Bible study session, you know like they do in Sunday school."

"What you're trying to put together a class or something?"

"No, nothing big like that . . . just a *one on one* type of thing with a friend, maybe even two. I had a friend I used to do that with but I haven't spoken to him in a while. Would you be willing to do something like that with me?"

"Sure I would, that sounds interesting. When are you talking about trying to do this?"

"Well I guess the weekend would be the most logical time to do something like that. I know I'm tired during the week from work; how about you?"

"Yeah, I'm definitely worn out during the week, plus I'm taking care of lil' man every other day."

"How does this Saturday sound? Do you have LJ this weekend?"

"As a matter of fact I don't. He'll probably be here Saturday morning but I don't really do anything till after twelve noon anyway."

"Okay, I could call you at about two or 2:30; I'll have something put together by then."

"Wait a minute . . . you want to do this over *the phone?*"

"Yes . . . that's how my old friend and I used to do it."

"I'm ya *new* friend!!" Lance chuckles, "Seriously though, I think some things are a little too important to do over the phone. And I will admit it's been a long time since I've actually sat and read the Bible with someone." Lance doesn't tell her he's referring to thirty two plus years ago when his mother would read his children's Bible to him. "I think doing it over the phone would be just like emailing a love letter to a loved one! Kind of lacks that's personal touch . . . know what I mean?"

"Yes Lance I do. I must have forgotten who I was talking to!"

Lance takes that as a compliment and as a confidence booster, "I'll tell ya this too – I would like to see you anyway . . ." He doesn't include the word *really* because he fears it may sound mushy.

. . . Or is it my guilty conscious making me feel that way because I like her?

"We should be making up for lost time anyway," he says.

Lance smiles when he thinks of that conversation earlier in the week. He jokes with himself in imagining Sherry grabbing his hand, asking him to jump off a cliff with her and him doing it. Her influence over Lance is evident in his agreeing to sit and read the Holy Bible with her. But another part of him feels like the time has come to truly begin acknowledging and acting upon what he's been thinking for a while now – incorporating the Lord into his life more.

Later in the day while Lance is at work, he makes a phone call to Melanie, "Hey what's up! How are you?"

"I'm fine, how are you?"

"I'm good. Are we still on for six o'clock this evening?"

"Yes . . ."

"Okay, see ya then." As Lance hangs up the phone, his mind starts to wander back to a conversation he and Melanie had about a week and a half ago, resulting in their six o'clock meeting this evening.

"In mid September, I'll be going on a trip out of the country to the Bahamas and I wanted to take LJ with me," Melanie says. "I'm going out there for a little vacation and for a wedding. I'll be going with my guy Derek. You being LJ's father, I wanted to know how you feel about all of this and ask you if it's okay to take LJ with us."

"Your *'guy'* as in your *boyfriend . . . ?*" Lance inquires. His tone is calm, though on the inside he doesn't want it to be.

"Yes, my boyfriend."

"When did you get a boyfriend?"

"Well, he probably became my boyfriend last October or so. We had been dating since last July."

Last July? It probably started before then. I bet he's the guy that sent those damn roses to the house when she was still living at our place back then.

Lance calmly inquires, "Derek who . . . ?"

"Derek Smith."

"Wow! A boyfriend . . . this is a surprise to me . . . and I think you know that I'm only saying that out of concern for *who* is around our son."

"Yes, I understand that."

"Did you tell your family about your new boyfriend last year when it first transpired or shortly thereafter?"

"No . . ."

"Why not . . . ?"

"Because I didn't want them to think I was jumping into anything concerning a new relationship too soon."

So she hid this fool from the family for God knows how long . . . just like she did me a few years ago. Hhmmp! The pattern continues . . . Lance thinks.

"Do they know Derek now?" he asks.

"Oh yeah, they know Derek. Look Lance, I figured you would respond like this and that's okay. Derek really is a nice guy and you have nothing to worry about as far as me having any riff raff type of guys around your son."

"Melanie let me just say this . . . I believe you when you say that and I think I know you well enough to say that with confidence; I just wish you would've mentioned your boyfriend to me sooner . . . that's all. But what's done is done at this point. I think that even though you probably know what my answer to your original question is, I just wanna say that I appreciate you coming to me as you have, concerning your upcoming trip and all."

"Thank you for that and you're welcome."

"As long as I can meet Derek before you all leave, I don't have any problem with you going to the Bahamas with LJ in September. You know me, I ain't trying to sit down and drink a six pack with dude . . . I just wanna meet him before he accompanies you, taking my son out of the country."

"Oh that's no problem. I already told him that this trip would probably be cause for you to wanna meet him. He understands that totally."

"Okay cool, it's settled then."

Lance shakes his head with a smirk on his face sitting at his desk at work. The closer to 6:00pm it gets, the more nervous he gets. It angers him that he feels nervous *at all* about meeting Melanie's new boyfriend. But when he digs deep within himself to analyze the reason behind it, Lance realizes that Derek being an "okay" kind of guy is not the reason for his apprehensiveness . . . it's if he *isn't.*

*   *   *

Hhmmm . . . let me see just for shits and giggles if my work computer will let me access this dating website, Lance thinks to himself half an hour before his quitting time. When he clicks his curser on one particular woman's profile from his personal email account, he is delightfully surprised to have gained access.

Lance reads her profile and thinks, *Okay, her name is Sharon, she's black, thirty eight years old, 5'2", one four year old daughter, and, resides in Joliet.* He takes note of certain words that stand out to him. She is looking for a "soul mate" – "real love" isn't dead in her book – "honesty" is very important to her – and she is a "romantic." He is ecstatic to see there are pictures of her to accompany a profile that has verbally drawn his attention. The first picture is of her in a brown dress, too long to see her legs but tight enough to see an imprint of her behind from a profile.

Mmmmm . . . nice booty, he thinks. *Her hair could be a little longer for my taste . . . but she's cute!*

The second picture shows her sitting down in what appears to be the inside of a limousine. Her jeans are too big to see any form of her shape. The black leather jacket conceals *any* top side view that any man would like to see in a woman's picture. Her hair, which appears to be pinned up in the back, is a style he begs forgiveness for.

She could've kept this hairstyle! I don't think she's cute enough for the lazy ponytail. But she does have an innocent cuteness about her though . . .

The third picture shows her in another long dress, this one metallic pink with dark brown imprinted designs on it and a matching scarf tied around her head with a pink flower protruding from the right side. The brick wall she stands against in this picture matches her clothing. There is an artistic distinction to this picture in Lance's eyes, though he figures the brick wall concept was probably an accident.

On her way to church no doubt . . . her apparent innocence is on display big time in this photo. Lance clicks the "send an email" option on the website to show his interest. Just as he's logging out, his cell phone rings. The area code is *404* and lance is familiar with it.

"Mmmmm . . . it's Alicia from Atlanta," he murmurs. "Hi sweetie, how are you?"

"I'm fine sweetie, what's going on?" she says. They talk on the phone for forty minutes; while Lance is leaving work, walking to the train and riding on the train. Their exchanges are very nice for about thirty eight minutes . . . until Alicia says something that Lance doesn't like. He lets her know that he doesn't like it.

"Uhmmm . . . excuse me Alicia . . . it sounds like you're trying to tell me what to do. I don't like anyone *trying* to tell me what to do!"

"I'm not trying to tell you what to do . . . I'm just saying . . ."

"Yeah, well you *say* a lot . . . !"

"Okay well let me add to it and say this . . . I'll talk to ya whenever I talk to ya! Bye!!"

Lance doesn't bother to say goodbye. He knows he has basically been hung up on in the most cordial way he can remember. He welcomes it though because his sentiments were exactly the same. Alicia is a very outspoken type of woman. Lance doesn't mind this if a certain level of self control exists along with it; something she lacks in his opinion.

I tried to ignore her big mouth the last couple of times we spoke, he thinks. *Today though, she went too far! She's all the way in Atlanta anyway . . . so to hell with Alicia!!*

An hour later Lance sits parked in front of Melanie's apartment. Before he even thinks about placing his left hand on the door latch to open it, he goes into another one of his introspective modes.

I can't believe *this girl has been hiding this nigga from me for what . . . nine months!? She had to be hiding him; all those holidays I've been around for LJ and no Derek!! What kinda shit is that!? Thank you Melanie, for reiterating to me why I'm no longer wit'cha!! Always wearing a mask . . . always about you!! Let me get in here and get this over with!*

Lance puts his left hand on the door latch and opens it to get out. He doesn't care that his thoughts took him ten minutes past six o'clock, making him late. Melanie's place to Lance is certainly not a place he feels the need to establish as *his* territory. As far as his son is concerned, the entrenchment of being LJ's father is completely solid and a forgone conclusion – and no one can tell him any different!

Melanie opens the door for Lance and turns around to lead him up the stairs. He slowly proceeds, counting each step in his mind as if in the mode of a final few seconds of preparation. On the fourth step he thinks about Sherry.

Damn! Didn't I meet someone else's boyfriend last *year!? I'm gettin' tired of this shit!!*

On the seventh and final step, he clutches his hand into a fist, *Alright Lance, let's do this!* When he enters, Derek is not there. "You're kidding me, right!? He murmurs under his breath.

"Derek's not here yet," Melanie yells from the next room. "He should be here shortly."

"Okay . . ." Lance says as he's thinking. *Well at least I know this man is smart . . . he's late on purpose just like I am! Your territory is obviously established in your head as well. Good, 'cause brother . . . you can have it!!* As LJ walks into the room to greet his dad, the doorbell rings. *Wow! Was he parked outside waiting for me to enter first!?* When Melanie is downstairs letting Derek in, Lance hears more than one smacking sound of a kiss. *Get a room . . .* he thinks.

When Derek enters, he is calm and he is cool, "Hi Lance," he says.

"Hey, what's going on?" Lance will not call him by name until a formal introduction takes place. The length of time that Derek has been in a relationship with Melanie means nothing to Lance. The *short* length of time he has *known* about the relationship is the thing that vastly contributes to the arrogant place his mind chooses to be in.

"Derek Smith," he says while walking towards the couch with his hand extended.

Lance takes LJ off his lap and stands him up and then stands himself to greet Derek, "Lance Austin; it's nice to meet you."

"Same here . . ." As they shake hands, Lance notices that Derek's grip is stronger than his and his body is more muscular than his.

Man, I need to get back to working out, Lance thinks to himself.

"Hey lil' man . . . !" Derek says to LJ as he has a seat on a stool in the middle of the living room floor. As Lance sits on the couch again, he wonders why the stool is there. LJ turns and looks at Derek and then starts to walk towards him. Lance's heart "drops to the floor." Witnessing an interaction between Derek and his son certainly doesn't hurt in determining his worthiness to be around his son; but *it does* hurt nonetheless. Lance knows that his emotions in this situation can't be helped and deems them inevitable.

"You have a wonderful boy here Lance!" Derek says with enthusiasm.

"Thank you!" Lance says.

Melanie doesn't say a word, realizing that the two men have handled their business well regarding formal introductions. "C'mon LJ, come with Mommy in the kitchen for a minute," she says reaching for his little hand. Lance experiences a swooping transition of emotions. What had originally made him uncomfortable, suddenly felt more than tolerable.

Lance offers his reasons to Derek for wanting to meet him and he is completely understanding of those reasons, having two children of his own. He is a police officer and has been on the force for twenty six years. He's a few years older than Lance, as the excessive grays in his hair and mustache would indicate.

When Lance leaves this meeting with LJ, he is satisfied in believing that his son will be in good hands on Melanie's trip out of the country. Lance wonders though, what possible resolutions truly exist if they were needed, if his opinion about Derek had been the opposite.

I'm glad he's okay. It's not like she would leave this man alone this far into it, if I didn't think he should be around my son! I'm glad she's with a cop; probably just what she needs! I bet she won't be all up in his *face with that physical garbage of hers!! He'll knock her in the head with the barrel of his gun . . . or shoot her!!* Lance smiles at his thought but then realizes the lack of humor, *I hope not though . . . 'cause this man* is *around my son!!*

*   *   *

The next day, Lance sits in his car in the parking lot of a mini mall in Skokie. He is trying to quickly erase the irritation he feels at the moment, knowing it's showing on his face. He is fifteen minutes late arriving to meet Sherry at a book store in the area. Lance is not as familiar with the suburb of Skokie as he would like to be. This is the reason why he's late. However, the more convenient reason for his tardiness in his mind is the fact that Melanie was late picking LJ up. Lance was furious when she arrived forty minutes after their agreed time of noon, offering her nonchalant apology. He didn't express his anger though, nor did she even realize he was mad. The thought of the excellent state of their relationship where Lance, Jr. is concerned made it seemingly effortless to conceal his choler.

He wonders why he's even irritated *now*. Being honest with himself as he gets out of his car, he attributes it to how long it took Melanie to tell him she now has a boyfriend.

Even though he feels that *this* is a legitimate reason to be upset, he decides to let it go once and for all.

It's not worth it . . . he thinks as he swings the bookstore's door open. *I'm only stressing myself out . . . I met the man, he seemed humble and clean cut . . . hell he better have been; she did date* me *once!! The situation is over now . . . Move on Lance!*

A big smile comes across Lance's face as he looks around the bookstore for Sherry. When he spots a short woman in tight blue jeans with a nice shape, he thinks, *Oh boy! Here we go again with the pretty strangers* . . . The woman has on a khaki pink shirt with the sleeves rolled up and her long pretty hair is pinned up in a banana clip. *I can't tell if she's black or white . . . turn around please* . . . he says to himself. When she does, it is Sherry. He waves to get her attention.

As they approach one another, his thoughts become words, "Hi Sherry – you have a *really* nice shape! How are you?"

Sherry giggles, "Thank you – I'm doing fine; just browsing while I was waiting for *Late Lance.*"

"I'm sorry . . . I was just . . ."

Sherry interrupts, "That's okay. I was just playing with you; I don't mind." As they seat themselves, Lance's cell phone rings.

"Hey whasup Carl . . . ?"

"What's going on? Why you whisperin'!? Where you at . . . ?"

"I'm in a bookstore in Skokie."

"You in Skokie again . . . !? What female got your ass out that way every other weekend!?"

"I'll holla atcha' later on Carl . . ."

"Oh, she *must* be all that! Alright dog, I'll holla atcha'!"

Lance disconnects the call and murmurs under his breath, "He sounded jealous! Hhmmpp!"

"What did you say Lance?" Sherry inquires.

"Nothing . . . let's get started."

"Okay, write down; *Salvation.* That's our subject matter." Sherry gives Lance the first of many books, chapters, and verses of the Bible to look up so he can follow along as she reads. Lance fumbles with his Bible trying to find the first one.

He decides not to hide it, "I guess you can tell I haven't read the Bible that much in my life . . ."

"That's okay Lance . . . you're getting ready to do it now, *aren't you?*"

Once they get started, Sherry suddenly stops reading in the middle of one of the verses. They look at each other thinking similar thoughts,

"This is not working out *here*, is it?" she asks.

"No it isn't!" he says. Before they can get out of the bookstore, they are both laughing.

"Did you see that one guy that was staring at you!?" she asks.

"Yes I did and *you* were the one reading!! But he first started looking when I took that phone call."

"I thought he was going to storm over to our table, knock both of our Bibles on the floor and then do the jig on top of them! C'mon, I know a cute little coffee shop about three or four blocks from here."

Lance smiles to himself in being reminded of Sherry's sense of humor. "Okay, where's your car?"

"I *walked* over here."

"Oh, nice day for that . . . ! C'mon, I'll drive us over there." Once they arrive, Sherry treats them both to Lattes and pastries. The atmosphere in the coffee shop is much more sociable and relaxing for what they're trying to do. "Okay, so the subject matter is *How To Get To Heaven*, right?"

"Lance you are silly . . . did you really write that down!?"

"No, I'm just playing." Sherry smiles, being reminded of Lance's sense of humor.

They take turns reading Bible verses to one another, briefly discussing their interpretations of each group of passages that she selected for their meeting. While Lance is genuinely interested in what they read together, he is more *impressed* that Sherry organized this particular meeting and he is ecstatic about being the recipient of it. He likes the intellectual flow of the way she reads too . . . and how her subtle shade of lipstick gives off an enticing effect when her lips move.

When they are done two hours later, Lance shakes his head and smirks when Sherry isn't looking. His overall regard for her was *never* in question in considering her to be the "ultimate" elucidation of a lady; but now his feelings about her in that regard are ten fold.

Lance and Sherry decide to go and get a bite to eat. He initiates the inquiry to do so without thinking for once. It's as if asking her if she was hungry felt completely natural and not induced by his admiration for her; even though his feelings for her now, go way beyond just liking her. The Bible study session with Sherry took him to an inner place in his heart where he had never been before . . . with any woman.

The two of them go to a small Thai restaurant that she recommends in her area. They both order a glass of Riesling while they wait for their main course. When Sherry tastes her wine, she doesn't hesitate in expressing her dissatisfaction.

"Oh no . . . ! Lance taste your wine . . . something isn't right!" He tastes it and frowns. "It tastes like its old or something . . . okay not old!" she says. "I know alcohol gets better with age. I mean it has a stale taste to it!"

"You're right. Let's send them back!" Sherry calls the waiter over and informs him that they don't want their wine because it has an unfamiliar funny taste to it. Lance can't help but be surprised in thinking that maybe she *does* listen to him when he tries to get her to loosen up at times. Maybe he has some influence over her; a little more than he figured.

As they chat, Lance contemplates if he should tell Sherry what's *really* on his mind. When he decides to do so, finding the nerve to *actually* say it becomes an issue. With no alcohol in his system on this day, he is on his own. He remembers how it felt in grammar school when he had to stand up in front of the class and read something. The nervousness that he felt then resides in him now . . . probably even worse.

After their food arrives, Lance watches Sherry eat her food as if she hasn't eaten all day. He chuckles to himself when he realizes that his viewpoint of how she's eating is exaggerated and it is *him* that is barely eating. He picks over his food as if there's something wrong with it but there isn't.

Sherry notices, "Lance . . . is everything okay? You're not that hungry . . . ? You've barely touched your food – and that's so unlike you!"

"No, I'm really not that hungry. Well, I am actually . . . I was, but I think I spoiled my own appetite. I have something on my mind."

"You want to share . . . ? A penny for your thoughts . . ." she says with a giggle. Lance has his left elbow on the table with his fist pressed against his lips. He unclenches his fist and rubs his chin with his index finger.

"Yes I want to share . . ." he says reluctantly, though he doesn't *mean* to sound that way.

"Hhmmm . . . it sounds serious . . ."

"Sherry . . . I have *feelings* for you." Lance watches her reaction during his silent reprieve. It is subdued at best, but he can tell she didn't expect *that* to come out of his mouth. He extends both his hands on each side of his plate, laying them face down on the table as he continues, "And *please* don't misunderstand my motives in telling you this. I don't expect you to jump up and land in my lap showering me with hugs and kisses. I'm not giving you any type of ultimatum in regards to our friendship. You don't even have to say anything if you don't want to; I'm not trying to make you feel uncomfortable."

"No Lance, I don't think that at all."

"What I'm simply saying is – when I look at you and when I think about you . . . I can imagine you being *my woman* in the future. I just wanted you to know."

"That's very sweet of you to say Lance . . . but with all I've been through . . . you know with Norman and all; I'm just not ready to date anyone right now."

"I know that Sherry and I figured you would say something like that. I really just needed to say that to you . . . and I wanted you to know."

"I can understand that."

"I really do consider you a friend. I always have. I will admit though, I have felt this way about you for a while now. Did you ever suspect it?"

"Well, I kind of figured you had a crush on me for a while . . ."

"A '*crush*' huh? Well, I guess that sums it up more-or-less. I know I've taken a huge chance and this may be the last time I ever see you. I certainly hope it isn't because you really are a dear friend to me. I hope I haven't spoiled that for you."

"No Lance you haven't; you'll see me again."

"I guess that remains to be seen. So do you want coffee?" he asks as if to ease the tension that hovers over their little table. When she agrees, Lance is relieved that Sherry isn't rushing to get away from him. Deep down though, he realizes it is *him* that can't wait to leave her presence.

It's dark when they leave the Thai restaurant. Sherry tells Lance that she will walk home from where they are since she's not far from home. He won't allow it, no matter how nice her neighborhood is. Lance drives the short distance to her apartment. When they hug each other goodbye, the wishful thinking of it being a romantic hug overtakes Lance. Unfortunately he gets a vibe from Sherry that the hug is full of sorrow on her end.

"Oh Lance I'm sorry! I hope I didn't hurt your feelings," she says, confirming what he felt.

"As you now know Sherry, I care about you in more ways than one. I would *never* want you to put yourself in any kind of situation you're not ready for. That doesn't hurt me; it would hurt me *if* you *did*."

"Okay . . . I will see you later then."

"We shall see . . ." he says sarcastically.

"Why do you keep saying that Lance . . . !?"

"Honestly . . . I wonder; but I will believe it *when* I see you." When Sherry gets out of his car, Lance stares at her with mixed emotions when she's walking away. He thinks of the theory, especially in movies, that states; when a woman turns around to give one last look at the man she's walking away from, then she cares. Though his belief in this theory is strong, he dismisses its credibility just for this one night only, knowing how much he shocked her with his confession . . . and to make himself feel better in the event that she doesn't turn around; which she doesn't. Turning around and waving goodbye after she's in her doorway doesn't count as far as he's concerned.

During the drive home, his overall feelings about the situation are swirling around in his own "blender;" not quite the same way he once described her feelings as doing, but "swirling" nonetheless.

When he gets home he calls her. "Hey Sherry, I made it home okay. You know what's funny about what I told you? Well, telling you that was *very* difficult for me to do. I put it all out there on the line. What's funny is that if you should ever change your mind regarding me in not being ready to date; you'll have to do the same exact thing that I did."

CHAPTER 21

As the days go on after Lance's confession to Sherry, he starts to feel a lot better about it. He knows that having something like that all bottled up inside is no good for most and he just *did* what he had to do, despite the outcome. He also knows that because of the outcome and her decision that they remain friends only, makes it imperative that he meet someone on the internet as soon as possible, to take his mind off of what he can't *really* have.

In the past couple of days, Lance has been sharing email exchanges through one of the sites with a woman with no picture on her profile. It thoroughly disgusts him that he keeps attracting these type of females, so he doesn't take her too seriously. When she says something he likes in one of her emails, he relates it to her being intelligent and gives her his phone number in his response. Lance gets *sucked into* this every time because in his opinion, intelligent people are hard to find.

Her name is Chantal Marissa. She is single, thirty-eight years of age, resides in Chicago, and has a two year old daughter – and she's 5'9".

"Why are *all* the women on this website so *damn* tall!?" he says out loud since he's alone. "Well at least she'll be able to relate to me having a one year old boy. Hopefully she's cute and we can hit it off."

Call me tomorrow if you can.

Lance includes this statement in his responding email to her. He is trying his best to maintain the male rule of not talking to a female for the first time the same day phone numbers are exchanged. However, in giving her his number and requesting that she call him first instead of the other way around, breaks his *gentleman* rule of a man being the one that should make the first phone call to a lady. Lance doesn't care; he is now in the mode of desperation to quickly find someone to distract him from his feelings for Sherry. He doesn't admit this to himself because he doesn't analyze his actions, out of convenience of course.

Lance turns his computer off and begins to get ready for bed in his own unorthodox manner. A lot of nights, getting ready for bed for Lance is mental *only*. The physical aspect of it keeps him up two to three hours longer than the initial thought, depending on his mood and whatever's going on in his life at the time. On this particular night he finds himself sitting in the middle of his bed writing a letter to Sherry. He writes *Dear Sherry* to start it off, though he doubts he will actually ever let her see it; unless he winds up being with her the way he would like to be in the future.

As he's writing, his cell phone emits a text message signal . . . . *Too late to be Sherry – I wonder who da hell this is!? Alicia Lockhart!? Big mouth!! What da hell does she want!?*

He opens her text message and reads it. He scoffs afterwards. It is a verse from the Bible. While he doesn't mind *that*, he does wonder why she's texting him after their minor spat over the phone not so long ago. When he reads the message a second time, he then wonders if the Bible verse is meant to be inspirational or more so informative on how to better himself.

That was nice! Thank you sweetie!

Lance responds to her text out of courtesy; and he responds to it due to the abnegation he feels when trying to consider Sherry as only his friend. Lance tosses his phone on top of his night stand, not concerned that it is an unyielding surface. *You make me sick Sherry Anderson!! Hhmmpp!! I really make myself sick! When will you be ready to date someone Sherry!?*

On Wednesday evening after Bible study at her church, Sherry sits alone in her chair after everyone else has dispersed. A good friend of hers from the church, an older woman, is in the next room gathering her belongings and saying her goodbyes for the evening. She looks around and notices that Sherry is not in the room. She goes back to the room where Bible study was held and sees Sherry sitting alone with her Bible still open at the last passage that concluded their session.

"Hey girlfriend what's going on!?" the woman asks. "I'm gonna ask you what I think is an obvious question, so don't bother denying it! I have known you far too long for you to do that!! I noticed during our meeting that you seemed a lil' bit outta sorts . . . what's wrong!?"

Sherry gives her a slight chuckle, "Gladys . . . you think maybe we can talk tomorrow or something? Call me."

"My dear . . . *no*, to answer your question . . . ! Like I said . . . *my* dear . . . you are *my dear* you know! *Something* is bothering you and I want to know what it is!

You're sitting here five minutes after everyone left . . . *please*!! Up in here, we are one . . . especially you and I!!"

"Yeah Gladys, I know."

"Okay then . . . spill!! Gladys will listen – Gladys will advise – and Gladys will comfort you my sweet child!!"

"Norman *really* broke my heart . . . ya know!?"

"Sherry, we talked about that *last* Wednesday; and I know you're hurting over Norman but I think something else is bothering you!"

"That's weird that I can't hide anything from you. You're almost like my mother!"

"I *am* your mother dear . . . your *church* mother! What's wrong dear?"

"Well, there's this male friend of mine; his name is Lance and I think I may have hurt his feelings recently." Sherry explains the circumstances surrounding their friendship and the most current events involving it. Gladys is swift in her offering of advice.

"This guy Lamont sounds like a really nice person. Is that his name, Lamont?"

"No it's Lance."

"Well *Lance* sounds nice and all, but honey let me tell you something . . . you *did* hurt his feelings. No man wants to be rejected! And no man really wants to be in a platonic relationship either! Trust me when I tell you, he's *pretending* to be friends with you . . . waiting for you to come around."

"*Pretending*? I don't think he's pretending! Lance is very nice to me; he's a nice guy."

"He's nice to you because he likes you. His telling you that he has feelings for you is the first domino to fall. Next, he will start buying you gifts, and then he will start trying to touch you, if he hasn't already!"

"No, he's *never* approached me inappropriately like that."

"Well he will . . . he's gonna try to do things and say things to try and make you feel guilty for not being with him. I say stay away from him if you have no intentions of ever being with him!"

"I really truly don't know right now."

" . . . Then *stay away* from him but do it gradually so you don't upset him even more. You don't know how he'll react to you ending the friendship suddenly; he may turn into a crazed stalker or something! Does he have any kids?"

"Yes, he has a one year old."

Gladys throws her hands in the air, "Oh Lord Jesus, please watch over this child! Sherry . . . that alone is reason enough to leave him be! Even if he really *is* single, you know he's probably still having sex with the baby's mama!! You *don't* wanna put yourself in a situation like that!!"

"I don't know . . . he once told me some things about her when they were together, that weren't good at all. I *really* don't think he wants to be with *her* anymore."

"I didn't say 'be with her', I said *having sex*! Look, I know you said that you two are just friends . . . but that's right now! He's playing on your emotions; he knows you're hurting right now and he knows you're vulnerable. Is he handsome?"

"Yes he is . . ."

"Stay away from him!! He's gonna suck you in and then spit ya out!! And if you were sitting here bothered over what happened with this man last weekend, those are your gut instincts talking to you my dear. Don't ignore it!! Look, Loretta made lasagna! I'm gonna grab some for Bill and I and hurry up and get it home to him. He has to get up early tomorrow."

"Ok Gladys – and thank you."

"I'm just looking out for you my dear. You're still young; I don't wanna see you throw your life away."

Gladys leaves to go and get two servings of lasagna for her and her husband; the man that left her three years ago. Not one member of the church is aware of this. Gladys is an unhappy woman and is in denial of her true feelings regarding this situation at home. She will do tonight what she always does when she brings two servings of food home from various church meets; sit in the middle of her bed and weep, while she eats *both* servings of food.

The next evening Lance sits in the middle of his bed pretending like he's interested in what's on TV. He just got off the phone with Chantal for the first time. Their conversation was simple enough and pleasant enough. When she didn't call the next day as Lance requested, he found this to be a good indicator that her desire to date or befriend someone of the opposite sex, is not in desperation mode. He still doesn't know what she looks like though.

Lance really wants to talk to Sherry but he feels too guilty to call her because of his feelings for her and the fact that she now knows of those feelings. He considers the fact that Sherry *did* call him last, just two days after their Bible study. His revelation in the Thai restaurant on that day didn't seem to put their friendship in jeopardy.

They talked over the phone about possibly getting together to share another Bible study reading. Lance had agreed to put something together for them this time around and he had already begun to do so, during a couple of his lunch hours at work. He mentioned that he has LJ this weekend coming up but wouldn't mind bringing him.

"Lance, Jr. has really gotten big! I would love for you to see him again," Lance said to her that day.

"Okay, we'll see," she responded.

With a need for a confirmation of their plans, he no longer feels guilty about calling her; so he picks up his landline and he does so.

"Hi Sherry . . . ! How are you?"

"I'm fine Lance! How are *you?*"

"I'm doing good . . . just sitting here watching a little TV" – *and thinking about you like there's no tomorrow!!* "I'm not going to keep you – just wanted to know how we look for Saturday. I've put *some* Bible passages together and I'm almost done."

"Lance . . ."

"Uh oh . . . ! That didn't sound good at all; what's wrong, not a good day?"

"It's not that. I just . . . maybe it isn't such a good idea that we try to continue to remain friends. And it's not you! I believe you when you say I'm your friend, despite other feelings you may have. I just don't want to hurt you nor do I want to put myself in a position that could wind up being uncomfortable."

Lance is furious . . . but he doesn't let Sherry know he is. "Let me ask you this – do you feel uncomfortable *now?* Have I ruined a very nice friendship just by simply *telling* you something? It's not like I made a move on you physically or anything like that."

"I don't feel uncomfortable . . . I just don't want to hurt your feelings again or discourage you over time because you want something that I simply do not have in me to give right now. I guess in some ways it is uncomfortable to me but it's *your* feelings I'm concerned about. The guy I used to do Bible study with; he started liking me and we got into a big argument over it."

Lance is now ready to throw the phone against the big mirror on his dresser. "Sherry . . . I am *not* that guy. I will admit okay, I *was* a little disappointed last Saturday night. But as I told you, I expected you to say what you said anyway. I care about you Sherry. Wanting what I want without taking *your* feelings into consideration wouldn't be the characteristics of a *true* friend, let alone a possible future boyfriend if it ever came to that! That guy you keep mentioning to me, the one you *conveniently* want me to be just like . . . he wasn't your friend! If he *was* your friend, you two would *still* be friends. Let me rephrase my original question to you – do *I* make you feel uncomfortable and more importantly, have I *ever,* since you've known me, said something or did something that made you feel uncomfortable?"

"No Lance, you don't . . . nor have you ever. You've always been the perfect gentleman."

"Then why are we having this conversation sweetie? Look, I really appreciate you considering my feelings regarding all of this . . . but they're *my* feelings and I got this! I'm a big boy . . . I can take care of myself! I'm good!" Lance thinks about *owning* his feelings for Sherry and wonders about his opinion of his brothers *owning* their grief over their mother's death. He wonders if there is perhaps some validity to this.

"You say you care about me. *How* do you care about me? Lance . . . ? Lance, are you there?"

"Oh I'm sorry, what did you say?"

"You say you care about me. *How* do you care about me?"

Lance thinks to himself. W*hat da hell does she mean by that!?* "I care about your well being . . . I care about your happiness, no matter where you may find it . . . I care about you, as a friend. Anything beyond that is mine to own and I can handle what belongs to me. If there are no existing feelings of discomfort you can tell me about, then I have that right!"

Lance then wonders to himself. *Do my brothers even realize that I'm grieving over our mother's death, just as they are!?* He continues with Sherry, "Thank you for taking me into consideration though. So are we on for Bible study on Saturday? I really look forward to it . . ."

"My name is Sharon Warrington. I don't have a middle name. What's your full name?" the young lady says on her cell phone.

"My name is Lance D. Austin," Lance replies.

"And what does the *D* stand for?"

"Dos . . ."

"Dos . . . ? What kinda name is that? Am I pronouncing it right? '*Dos*' like the number *two* in Spanish . . . ?"

"No . . . d – o – s, as in *d*ripping *o*f *s*ex . . . ! That's what you texted me and said my voice sounded like when I left that message on your voicemail, right?"

"Right . . . !" Sharon laughs, "And if you look anything in person like you do in your pictures on the website, we *both* might be in a little trouble!"

"Slow down clown, let me meet ya first and see if you're appealing to me. If you are, *then* we can talk about *a-peelin'* my banana!'"

Sharon chuckles, "And I'm the clown . . . ? You're clowin' yourself there Mr. Lance! Ha ha!!"

"So you're at the Post Office, huh?"

"Yeah, in Bedford Park . . ."

"Oh really, and you travel all the way from Joliet to Bedford Park everyday to go to work?"

"When you hit the toll road from where I live, it's really not that far at all."

"Hhmmm, that's funny 'cause I'll be in Joliet tomorrow. I have a minor recall repair I need to get done on my car. Will you be around, say about twelve or one o'clock tomorrow?"

"Normally I would be free at that time 'cause my normal hours are from 3:00 to 11:00 . . . but I have to go in early tomorrow. I'll be getting ready around noon or so to be there by one o'clock; so tomorrow wouldn't be a good day. But don't worry Mr. Lance, we *will* meet soon enough."

The next morning Lance struggles to get himself and LJ ready for their Saturday outing. Getting his son prepared to go anywhere, even on the weekend, is something he will never get used to. He does it though; somehow, because he is LJ's father and he has to. There is nothing that Lance won't do for his son and there are no excuses that he ever makes whenever he has to do anything for him. Lance usually tries to run most of his errands when LJ isn't around but today is an exception.

They get on the highway heading to the car dealer for his car repairs. He thinks about his conversation with Sharon last night while he drives.

Wow! What a freak she is! What happened to her being 'a romantic?' What happened to her endless search for 'real love!?' False advertisement maybe . . . ? She sounds more like an easy fuck . . . something I might just need right about now!

They arrive at the car dealer. "Hi, I'm here for this recall notice for my Cadillac," Lance says, handing the technician the recall notice document. "I had an eleven o'clock appointment. It's 11:30 and I apologize for being late."

"I see you have your little one with you. Believe me, I understand; I have a three year old. How old is your lil man, one? He's adorable . . ."

"Thank you and yes he's one and a half."

"I'll tell ya what . . ." the technician says leaning closer to Lance and whispering, "I'm gonna push your car ahead of two or three others and get you outta here. I know how hectic it can be to have your one year old out running errands, especially one like this that involves a lot of waiting."

"Thank you sir, I really appreciate that!" Lance marvels at the preferential treatment he gets whenever he has LJ with him; even from men. They only wait for an hour and a half; a very short wait for *any* repairs done by the dealer. LJ is surprisingly well mannered and hassle free as he often is when either one of his parents take him out in public.

When Lance gets his car back, it is one o'clock. He has to be somewhere at four and decides on how he can waste a little time until then. He snatches his cell phone from its holster and makes a call. Afterwards he goes to buy himself some underwear because he never buys anything for himself anymore, since LJ has been in his life. He then drives a few blocks down to a doughnut shop and parks in the parking lot to sit and wait.

When Lance sees a beige mini van pull into the lot, he turns around and looks at LJ, "She's here LJ! Ooopps . . ." LJ is sound asleep. When the mini van parks right next to them, Lance looks at the driver and smiles at her. He thinks to himself,

Hhmmp! A raggedy light brown van . . . but I really expected no less. She does have six children! Am I nervous? No I'm not . . . not really . . . well maybe just a little bit.

No matter what his attitude is, nonchalant or uncaring, *friends first* mode, potential dating prospect; there is something about meeting these cyber space women for the first time in person, that gets him every time.

"So you're Trisha, huh?" Lance says to the Caucasian woman as she leans into the open window on the passenger side of his car.

"Yes I am."

"Well hi Trisha Sampson!"

"Hi Mr. Lance!"

Why is everyone calling me that all of a sudden!?

"Say, do us a favor, he says. "Grab me a large coffee, plenty of cream and sugar and whatever you want. My lil man is asleep and I don't wanna wake him." Lance hands her a *$10.00* bill.

"Okay sure, I can do that," she says.

Hhmmm, she looks a little tired . . . but what woman with six kids doesn't? She looks like she has a nice body though . . . and she definitely looks better in person than she did in her pictures, he thinks. As she walks away from his car, Lance looks at her butt through his rearview mirror. *I like the pink and white plaid shirt and the tight blue jeans. Her butt's a little flat but the hips are really nice and her thighs ain't that bad either.* Lance then asks himself if he can imagine having sex with her. His answer is affirmative.

When Trisha comes back to the car and gets in, they smile at one another. "This is really nice finally seeing you in person! We've been talking on the phone on and off for about a year, haven't we?" he asks.

"Yeah, I think so. It is nice; I didn't think I would ever meet you to tell ya the truth," she says. Their conversations over the phone were always better than the one they have today in Lance's car. His opinion of her overall is more so an empty thought than it is a rude one. Trisha hopes that Lance will ask her out as she's leaving twenty five minutes later or at least make mention of it. He really doesn't mean to neglect to do either. Lance *did* like her. It just isn't enough to be a meaningful distraction to who he really wants to be around right now – the woman he will see in an hour and a half.

Even though LJ woke up briefly during their hour and fifteen minute drive from one suburb to another, he has gotten the majority of his normal two hour nap. Lance had slipped him his bottle of milk to put him out again when he woke up to express his infant curiosity of where they were. Lance is happy about this because as usual, his son comes first.

At four o'clock on the dot, while he hangs atop his open driver's side door, he spots Sherry from about half a block away. He smiles because this is the second of three times he has actually beaten her to their meeting place. He zooms in on her with his digital camera while she's walking.

Whoa!! She looks terrible! I think it's mostly her hair. Lazy – lazy – lazy! You would think I would be used to this in her by now! Where do I have to take this girl to see her look as beautiful as I know she's capable of looking!? I better start saving my money now in case she does *become my woman, so I can buy her ten new Saturday afternoon outfits all at once!!*

Lance snaps her picture anyway, twice while she's walking. He finds it amusing that she doesn't see him, even when she gets about thirty feet away from his car.

"Hey Sherry . . . !" When she turns around, he waves. He walks half the distance towards her, "Get a table for us; the same table as before if you can. I have to wake LJ up before we come inside." When the two of them enter the familiar coffee shop, LJ is walking beside Lance hand in hand.

"Oh my . . . look at your son! He's *more* adorable now than I remember!! I'm in love!!" Sherry exclaims as they approach her.

Well that's half the battle won! Now if only I can get you to fall in love with moi the way I'm in love with you! Whoa!! Do I have D.I.D.? What did I just say to myself!?

Lance gives LJ to Sherry and takes a seat, frozen in thought momentarily. He can feel the sweat in his palms as he rests his elbow on the table and his hand clenched in a fist against his cheek. He's glad that LJ is with him at this moment. His son will not allow the time for him to dwell on any bewildering thoughts.

Sherry takes LJ with her to get in line for coffee and pastries. Her interactions with him seem a lot more natural than the first time around. Lance sits at the table fumbling with his papers and LJ's notebook, in preparing for their Bible reading. When they come back and get situated, he tells her,

"Okay, write down; *Of One's Heart.* Lance is purposely trying to speak to Sherry through the different passages he has gathered from the Bible. He doesn't feel any guilt in doing this either because in his eyes, the Holy Bible is the most sacred source of the law of life abiding material there is. He wants her to understand that choosing a mate and *even* just a friend, is a task in which the contents of one's heart should determine the birth of that relationship or otherwise.

Lance tears up for a moment when he tells Sherry that he wishes his mother could see him doing what he's doing right now. "She would really be proud of me Sherry . . . and she would have adored *you* I must admit. He turns to his son, C'mon LJ, continue to write in your notebook . . . here ya go."

Lance, Jr. is a slight distraction but not terribly. In fact, as they're winding down, LJ finds his way to a window where two twenty-something Caucasian females are sitting outside in front of the window having coffee. When Lance, Sherry and LJ leave the coffee shop, they stop by the two young women. One of them mistakes Sherry to be LJ's mother. She quickly corrects her in her assumption. Lance is embarrassed for her but just a little. He is more ecstatic about the young woman's error.

They work their way to a nearby department store in the shopping area of where they are. Sherry indicates that she and her mother are going to a religious retreat out of town next weekend and she needs to pick up a few items for their train ride to get there. Lance is more than happy to assist her with this, even offering suggestions on what they could eat on the train while they're on their journey.

Another stranger mistakes Sherry as LJ's mother while she's pushing him around in the shopping cart. She frowns a little but tries to hide it from Lance.

"Sherry, you should be flattered . . . he is a good looking boy just like you're a good looking woman."

"Thanks!" she says, hoping he won't comment further on the subject matter. Lance brings his camera in the store with them where they're shopping. He gets a picture of LJ by himself but not one of Sherry *and* LJ together as he originally planned.

"May we do that next time?" she asks innocently. " . . . I kind of look a mess! I was just chillin' today."

"Sure okay," he says. *Kind of . . . ? And just what I need, an innocent Boston girl with a Boston accent, using the word 'chillin'!*

Lance thinks that her appearance is only part of the reason why she doesn't want to take a photo with his son. He suspects a little bit of unintentional envy in her wanting a child of her own. He understands perfectly if that is the case. When he shows her the two pictures he *did* take of her upon her arrival at the coffee shop, her reaction indicates to Lance that *maybe* her appearance *is* the only reason.

When they get back to her place, it is dark and LJ is asleep. They both make their goodbyes short for his son's sake. Before she leaves though, she tells Lance something that he didn't expect to hear – Sherry is seriously considering moving to North Carolina by the end of the year.

CHAPTER 22

L ance thinks to himself while he's on the phone with Chantal.

What is wrong with our black men that justifies cause for a black woman's inner amazement when they come across one *that knows how to hold a decent conversation? Or maybe . . . I'm just meeting women on the wrong side of town . . . !*

"Lance, are you there!?" Chantal yells. "Mr. Lance . . ."

"Oh jeez . . . ! Here we go with the *Mr. Lance* stuff again . . ." he murmurs through his cell phone.

"Huh, what did you say?"

"Nothing Chantal . . . I *did* hear ya . . . I was watching TV; sorry."

Lance can tell that Chantal Marissa is hooked. She wouldn't think the same of him if she knew of his preference to be on the phone with Sherry instead. With the exception of a ten minute interruption, he has been on the phone with Chantal for an hour and a half. Lance struggles in determining if he's leading her on by talking to her for so long or if he just naturally offers lengthy conversations on an intellectual level. He knows deep down that staying on the phone with her this long only gives her something more to relish. He concludes that if he *is* leading Chantal on, it's *her* fault for allowing it; making her a front runner for the new clingy woman in his life.

Just because I'm interesting doesn't mean I'm interested, he thinks. *And as far as her maybe not being appealing to me . . . its worse* not *knowing than it is to know!* When Lance asks her to describe herself and she does, her description isn't adequate enough for him.

"Chantal, please excuse me for being blunt, okay?" He continues before she answers, "I don't particularly go for big women – what size are you?"

"What *size* am I!?" she says in a flabbergasted manner.

" . . . As in, what size do you wear?"

Chantal is taken aback, "Well I was bigger about a year ago, but I lost a lot of weight."

Uh oh! Avoiding the question . . . Lance thinks. He wants to ask her how much is 'a lot' but he doesn't. "So now you are a *size* . . . ?"

"I'm about a size *16* . . . I can wear some items in a *14* though . . ."

I should hang up the phone!!

"You're silent . . ." she says. "Is that too much for you Mr. Lance? If it is, let me know now . . . my feelings won't be hurt!"

"Well, some women can look ridiculous in a size *16* and some are capable of wearing that size very well; so I don't know, I would have to see you. Why don't you snap a picture of one of your photos with the camera on your cell phone and text it to me since you're having problems uploading on your computer." Chantal agrees and gives Lance a pleasant surprise, "Mmmmm, nice picture . . . you're kinda cute!"

"Thanks! That's a picture from when I was dancing." Chantal doesn't tell Lance that her dancing days were ten years ago. Lance doesn't tell Chantal that the chances of them ever dating are slim, even though he likes her picture. He knows her height of 5'9" will serve as a good proportioner to her size *16* weight but both of the numbers are still a little too high for him.

"Lance . . . you're silent again!" she exclaims.

"Oh I'm sorry. I was just glancing at this movie and I just realized that one of the characters in it is invisible to everyone else in the room except for one other character. He must be some kinda ghost or he's dead or both. May I call you tomorrow?"

. . . Since I ain't talking to no one else *on a daily basis!*

"Sure Lance . . . !" He gets off the phone with her and thinks about her daughter making noise in the background for the majority of their conversation. He wonders why her two year old is still up at eleven o'clock at night during the work week. He continues to watch the movie and begins to fancy it. Even though the cinematic offering is of a supernatural nature, it *is* about love.

The dead character who *is* now a ghost, suddenly becomes aware of the error of his ways concerning his wife. He tries to right those wrongs with his present widow, vicariously through a cranky dentist that he meets; the one and only character in the movie that can see him. When lance thinks of one particular woman from his past, the *woulda – coulda – shoulda* pretense of the movie resounds in his heart like the 30hz frequency of modern day music.

When the cranky dentist starts to fall for the widow, his concerted efforts to avoid his feelings reminds Lance of him regarding Sherry.

Why does everything in movies and music suddenly remind me of her all the time!? It's just like the new car you wanna buy. You hardly ever see it on the street at first. As soon as you get it, all of a sudden everyone has it!!

Lance's thoughts are disrupted when he hears a song in the movie start out with a acoustic guitar solo. A raspy yet cool and laid back male's voice begins to sing. It is a rhapsody to Lance's ears. The song lyrics profess his everlasting feelings for one particular woman and how they keep him in a state of being out of sorts. When the song is over, a tear rolls down Lance's left cheek; and then the right cheek.

Early Friday morning on the train on his way to work, Lance thinks about Sherry's trip out of town with her mother to partake in a weekend spiritual retreat. He wished her a safe excursion over the phone last night, in the typical verbal fashion that anyone would. Lance wants to do something different though, so that his well wishes stand out from all the rest. He knows that his writing ability can best furnish this courteous gesture uniquely. His mind does less thinking than his heart as the words extract from the ink of his felt tip pen, almost automatically.

"Lord – Watch over Sherry and her mother as they embark on their spiritual journey this weekend and keep them safe. May they both be enticed and enriched sevenfold with the power and the wisdom of your word."

Amen

He thinks, *yeah that's cool; I like that!*

Bow your head when you read this.

Lance begins his text message to her with this statement to let her know it's a prayer.

My mother said your words are beautiful! We both thank you!

Well at least I know that her mother knows I exist. That can be considered a good sign, he thinks. *But if she can find a new job within her field in North Carolina and it's a lateral move, it won't make a difference.*

A few weeks later, Alicia Lockhart arrives into town with her daughter all the way from Georgia to visit family and friends for the Labor Day weekend. She had mentioned to Lance before that she would possibly visit her home town for one of the upcoming holidays. There was no level of anticipation on his part though because he really didn't believe her.

Alicia calls Lance just to rub it in, "Hi Lance! I'm here; I'm in Chicago!!"

"Oh really, that's nice. So I might just meet you after all."

"For sure . . . ! I'm here for about four days. We're going back *on* Labor Day."

"Okay well tell you what . . . call me when ya got a little free time and we'll make arrangements to meet."

"Okay, I'll do that." Lance disconnects the call and thinks about Sherry as usual . . . but he only calls her a third of the times that he wants to call. This is to keep himself tamed and to not seem over zealous to her, considering that she now knows that his feelings for her go beyond the boundaries of their friendship. Lance doesn't call her because he called the *last* time he wanted to. He will try his best not to call the next time as well; to keep in line with his *one third* rule. They've never really spoken much or gotten together for holidays anyway.

The usual offerings of Labor Day activities like backyard bar-b-ques and friends getting together to go out for drinks, are extended to Lance all weekend long. He frowned over the phone at each and every invitation, male or female and turned them *all* down. Lance has always had a certain mindset about holidays in believing that the significant other should *always* come first. His wishful thinking of having a lovely lady to call his own and not having one puts him in the mood of "all or nothing."

Showing up for anything that Melanie's family has organized for any holiday is a given because his presence is for his son's sake. Melanie always invites Lance to such activities if it's his day or weekend to have LJ or not. On this Monday morning, he does not have LJ and yet he declines her invitation this time around.

Lance wonders when the day will come when Melanie will have to feel the same disquietude *he* felt when he met Derek. He could bring a platonic friend to these gatherings just to get a false sense of *ha ha – gotcha*; a momentary perfidious feeling of revenge since their relationship didn't work out. He refuses to go that route though because he knows he just won't get the same satisfaction unless the proclamation of his union with the woman he brings is real.

As far as the two female friends that contacted Lance are concerned, there are various reasons why he refused to hang out with them at this time. The reasons are insignificant to Lance right now with the constant thoughts of Sherry swarming. He simply refused their invitations and decided to ponder those issues later. The reasons concerning his male friends vary as well. One that stands out is being practically coerced into showing up at a gathering under the false pretenses of desirable women being present when they're not. Lance's stepbrother Warren, Jr. is notorious for these antics and Carl's invite in Lance's opinion was more than likely to a bar-b-que of a hoydenish nature.

Which man can beat their chest the hardest is certainly something I ain't interested in, were his thoughts on Sunday when Carl invited him to come out. *And I haven't heard from my step dad or my brothers in months, so fuck them too!! Anyway, I'm not exactly in the mood to be putting on a show for others in being a wide eyed and bushy tailed all American single father to a one year old!*

Somehow on Monday evening though, by the third conversation with Sharon Warrington while she's at work, he is 90% prepared to play the *pretend game* with her. "Hey Sharon, you know what . . . you get off at eleven o'clock, right?"

"Yeah, why . . . ?"

"I'm gonna come up to your job when you get off! Are you game? I wanna meet ya girl! Don'tcha wanna meet me too . . . !?" For some strange reason, Lance doesn't mind too much, the idea of counterfeiting an enthusiasm of his single status within the sanctum of his own mind or on his own terms.

As Alicia is on her way back home to Atlanta, she thinks about the fact that she never got back to Lance about them meeting up before she left town. Her thoughts are cavalier and it never dawns on her that a courtesy call was warranted to offer her regrets. The fact that she repeatedly told Lance she would eventually be in town, trying to build his anticipation level up, means nothing to her. While he did eagerly await her visit at one point, the thought of her on *this* holiday weekend somehow gets lost in the shuffle.

Lance only has his mind on Sharon as he drives to Bedford Park to meet her at her job when she gets off. When he gets to the Post Office and waits, the nervous anticipation of her coming out the front door starts to build but quickly subsides by the time she does ten minutes later. When Lance lays eyes on her, she is delightfully cute, daintily petite and refreshingly funny.

As Lance watches her get in her SUV, he smiles because he likes it. Her vehicle isn't raggedy like some of the other cyber space women's vehicles. He follows her to a mini mall parking lot where they can exchange pleasantries.

"Wait Lance, before you get in . . ." Sharon exclaims after they park beside one another. "Come around to my driver's side . . ." Lance wonders why and can't wait to find out as he walks around to her window. "Now turn around slowly!" He does it. "Yeah, you *do* have a nice butt! I like that! Okay, you can get in now!"

Lance gets in her SUV smiling. Her implications of a future sexual relationship turn him on. He looses sight of his true inner agenda of wanting to be in a reputable, monogamous relationship . . . and he doesn't care. The constant laughter and numerous compliments they exchange about each other's appearance, further submerges Lance into the abyss of future sexual relations – in the *near* future he suspects.

When Sharon throws her car seat back some and rests the inner part of her knees on each side of her steering wheel, her legs are wide open in a not so lady like position. The gentleman side of Lance considers it as such, even though her long blue jean dress reveals nothing; but the sexual side of him can only imagine his face being between her petite thighs with no steering wheel in sight.

Their forty minutes in Sharon's SUV is considered a successful meeting for the both of them. Lance doesn't hesitate in asking her out and Sharon doesn't hesitate in accepting his invitation. At last, Lance feels vindicated in the endless hours he has spent on the internet searching for love. He will lower his standards for the time being and reap the benefits from his hard work. As long as she shows a willingness to accept their relationship for what it seems it will turn out to be . . . Lance is okay with that.

As the days turn into weeks, Lance slowly begins to realize the messy state of mind he has allowed himself to be in regarding women. His so called inevitable quick fix with Sharon abruptly came to a screeching halt when she didn't give Lance a confirmation call on the evening they made plans. While lowering his standards in some ways just to quickly get close to her was fairly simple; allowing a woman with a lack of courtesy to be in his life is simply something he *will not* compromise.

When Alicia has the audacity to send Lance another one of her Bible verse text messages, he is reminded of her lack of courtesy on Labor Day weekend when she was in town.

Alicia – You keep sending me these Bible verses . . . how about acknowledging the ill on your part in me not hearing from you again when you were in town weeks ago! We were supposed to meet up . . . remember!?

Hey who are you!? You are insignificant when it comes to family! Family comes first in my book!!

I don't fault the philosophy of family coming first! I fault you for building up my anticipation of you coming into town and then not following through on your word – not even a phone call to show your regrets!! And your interpretation of the Bible verse you sent by the way is totally incorrect!!

You just reminded me of why I decided a long time ago, not to date light skinned men anymore!!

I'm not light skinned – I'm caramel you silly woman!!

The overall communication between Lance and Alicia comes to a close after these text messages exchanges. They are both exulted over the outcome.

With Lynita Everstall being stuck and secluded in her own little world with her dogs in Lance's opinion – Lance Austin being stuck and secluded in his own little world of vanity and self righteousness in her opinion; neither can deny that they know they will never meet.

Chantal Marissa seems to be the only bona fide dating prospect left on Lance's list; a list that has shortened truly to his satisfaction. He was starting to get confused and mixed up from talking to so many different women at once anyway. He started forgetting whom he had said *what* to. Lance thinks about Miss Marissa, with her sexy name and her sexy photo now saved on his cell phone . . . and her size *16* frame.

When he is on a four mile walk with one of his female co-workers during lunch one day, he shows her the picture of Chantal and tells her about the situation. Before long, his co-worker can't stop laughing every time he points to a female on the street and says,

"Is *she* a size *16*!?" Lance does it every few minutes, trying to convince himself that he will like what he sees when he possibly meets her in a week or so. He clings on to Chantal as his last life line so to speak, so he doesn't have to face the fact that Sherry is getting closer and closer to *actually* moving to North Carolina by the end of the year.

It was difficult enough when she first revealed this sudden change in plan for the rest of her life. It was even more of a vexatious task to hear her talk about it in detail, especially with enthusiasm, even though he detects that she is simply trying to convince herself that moving out there is the right thing to do. He's not sure if this is truly the case or if his perception is a convenient remedy to cease his own pain of hearing what he doesn't want to hear.

Sherry describes the area of Shelby, North Carolina to be a cute little town that's diverse. She proclaims to not be moving out there to be with Norman, though he is in the same state, in a town called Gastonia; only twenty five to thirty miles away from Shelby. She volunteers this information without Lance asking, yet he *doesn't* believe her.

Anyone that believes she's not *following Norman and trying to ease into the idea of relocating by actually doing it so they can eventually reunite is a fool!!*

When she reveals that she has a job interview there in the middle of next week, Lance can no longer deny that there's a good chance this move may *actually* happen. The company is paying for all the travel expenses for the duration of a twenty four hour trip. Lance realizes that each time he sees her from now on could be the last time. He has been wasting time with cyber space women that are trivial and silly in comparison to Sherry. He has let too much time go by since he's seen her last; too busy analyzing his feelings and counter analyzing them, by avoiding them.

Even Sherry seems in tune with realizing that the days of their intriguing friendship are numbered when she suggests they go to a haunted house for Halloween. Lance is more than happy to accept her invitation and do internet research as to where one is located. He will be sure to do *extensive* research on where they're going *this* time around and not do it lazily as he did two and a half years ago when they first met.

Four days later in the middle of the week, Sherry prepares to go to the airport for her flight to North Carolina. When her cell phones rings and she sees its Lance calling, she is surprised.

"Hey Lance! I can't believe *you're* calling this early! It's 6:50am! Aren't you usually rushing to get to work at this time!?"

"I guess I'm having a lucky morning . . ." It is not luck. He planned to get up early and not rush, just so he could make this phone call to her. "Are you nervous?" he asks.

"Yeah, a little . . . but I'm fine."

"Yeah, I know you will be – I'm sure of that. I just wanted to wish you a safe trip and tell you good luck on your interview today."

"Thank you Lance; that means a lot!"

"Hey that's what friends are for, right!? Do me a favor if you get a chance . . . call me at some point before the day is out to let me know you arrived safely, okay?"

"Yes I can do that." Lance doesn't really expect a phone call from her later. He figures she will have too much on her mind with such the big step she's taking in trying to move out of state . . . and Norman in particular. He gives it his best shot though, mentally leaving the situation alone, shortly afterwards.

At 6:00pm Lance is holding his phone as if he can *make* Sherry's call come through. He hates that he's doing this but he does it anyway. After a couple of minutes, he slams his cell phone on the coffee table and leaves the living room. Ten minutes later he hears the faint sound of the ring tone he assigned to Sherry long ago – a song called "C.R.U.S.H." by Ciara. He frowns at his own arrogance for being the cause of his cell phone being left in the other room instead of in its holster which is still on his belt. He scurries to the living room so he won't miss her call.

Sherry tells him that she's safe and her interview went very well. Lance is glad to hear both, though he doesn't know how he can muster up any jovial feelings for the latter of the two. He is most appreciative of the fact that her phone call separates her from all the rest – saying that she was going to do something and then actually doing it. Lance wishes her a safe trip home and smiles as he disconnects the call.

"Chantal Marissa – Chantal Marissa . . . wow! I really like her name!" Lance murmurs to himself. "Too bad this picture of her in this black leotard isn't a full body shot with just her head and shoulders. She's sexy as hell though and she looks like she may have one of those extreme feminine kinda shapes that I like."

Lance is sitting in a relatively mediocre steakhouse parking lot waiting for Chantal to show up in a small gray car. When this particular vehicle pulls up and parks some distance away, he figures she won't see him sitting in his car when she goes inside the restaurant. This way he can make a grand entrance.

When the woman walks across the parking lot, Lance is startled, "I *know* this woman that just walked to the restaurant entrance like Mr. Snuffleu . . . what was that elephant's name on "Sesame Street!?" I know that *couldn't* be Chantal!! And she had a bob haircut too!! What should I do . . . should I leave!? No I can't . . . I told her I was in a black Caddy – she may have seen me!! And how did all of *that* fit in that little ass car!? She looked like she was 6ft tall!!"

Lance's cell phone rings. He answers reluctantly, "Hello . . ."

"Lance, this is Chantal. Are you here yet? Was that you in the black Cadillac parked on the north side of the parking lot when I walked in?"

"Yes . . ." he says. *No . . .* he thinks.

"Are you on your way in?"

"Yes . . ." he says. *No . . .* he thinks. Lance hesitates when he gets out of his car. He hopes she can't see him from where she sits inside as *he* is now walking like that elephant.

His so called entrance is "shot to hell" as he walks in with total bewilderment on his face. Chantal sits at a table twenty feet from the door, depriving Lance of those few extra seconds to gather himself. He sits down with a stupid grin on his face.

"Hi . . ." he says in a dull tone.

"Hey . . . !" she says in a sharp tone. Lance looks at her and quickly determines that she looks *nothing* like her picture. The woman that sits before him is either the pictured woman's older sister . . . or her auntie he figures. Lance doesn't intentionally hold the menu up to his face when he's looking it over . . . to hide *her* face; it just happens that way.

He doesn't purposely contribute to the strain in their conversation; it just happens that way.

After twenty minutes of finally deciding what he wants to order . . . to *force* down his throat due to his spoiled appetite, Lance gets presented with the question that he fears the most.

"So what do you think about me Lance?"

Oh no . . . not again!! he thinks. "Well . . . I will admit you look a little different in person than you do in your picture."

"Well I've changed my look since then," she quickly replies.

"I see . . ." Lance wants so badly to ask her how old her photo was but he fears the answer will start an argument. After devouring his meal like a savage, he rushes to get away from his mishap of a meeting. As they are walking out the door, Lance glances at Chantal's butt. She isn't fat as he feared she would be . . . but he considers her behind to be shaped like a box; not exactly appealing in Lance's eyes. The fact that she *seems* taller than he is as they stand face to face, even though in reality she isn't, doesn't help either.

As cordial as he was in saying goodbye to her, he knows she could feel his negative vibes, not to mention the look on his face the whole time they were together. He gives a sigh of relief, knowing that she probably won't call him again. Forty minutes later, Lance's cell phone rings. He snatches it from its holster to reveal the Caller ID which reads – *Chantal Marissa.*

Unbefuckinlievable!!

CHAPTER 23

Many would find it strange that Lance likes Barbra Streisand. That is precisely one of the *many* reasons why he does, as he drives along with one of her songs playing. The song is called "Where Do You Start." It talks about the complexities of getting over someone after a recent break-up.

"Wow Lance, that was beautiful!! It almost brings tears to my eyes," Sherry says, riding in the car with Lance. "You say that's Barbra Streisand?"

"Yes. My mother liked her; you know that famous movie of hers from the 70's? My father likes her too; particularly her older music."

"You have a very wide range of musical taste!"

"Thank you Sherry." It's no accident that the words in the song were directed towards Sherry. Lance wants her to know that *he* knows how she's possibly feeling and how she's hurting over Norman. The tears that were "almost" brought to Sherry's eyes *did* actually form. She was barely able to hold them back. The song nudged the emotions inside of her, more than Lance will ever know.

The next song he plays is called "Sideways" by Citizen Cope; the song from the movie he saw a couple of months ago. Once he found out who the artist was, he went out and bought the CD immediately.

"Listen to this one Sherry . . . I think you'll like it." Lance now wants her to hear how *he's* feeling.

"Lance, I *really* like this one! I love his raspy voice!" They continue to ride around; the minutes go into a transition of hours. The original plan was for them to have dinner at an expensive crab house in Wheeling, Illinois. They are no where near Wheeling, Illinois.

"Lance, I think we went into a complete circle. We're not too far away from my apartment again. Should we go back so I can get my GPS device?"

"No, we'll be fine. I'll find it." Lance is so overtaken by the inner bliss he feels from simply being around Sherry, that he never once considers calling the GPS service that came with his car package for directions. He brought directions to the restaurant that he obtained from the internet days ago but he left the verbal part of those directions at home. The picture of the map that he *did* bring isn't zoomed in enough to actually see which way he should be going.

By the second hour of them being lost, Lance is feeling like an idiot. "You know . . . I do thank you for trusting me on this . . . but I think I've only given you false hope that we would find this restaurant. We probably should have gone back to your place for the GPS."

"It's okay Lance. I know how men are when it comes to a woman providing directions.

You wanted to figure it out on your own! I guess it just wasn't meant for us to have dinner there tonight."

"You're not upset?"

"No . . . I'm just enjoying the night scenery, the music, your company; just the drive in general. I am getting a little hungry though."

"Yeah me too . . . ! Now if we can figure out *where* we are, we can stop *somewhere* and grab a quick bite."

"I'm *really* surprised that *you* aren't upset that we're lost," she says.

"I am . . . well only to a certain extent. As far as the angry thing, I just don't let things get to me the way I used to. I chose to partake in this endeavor and I didn't succeed. There's really nothing to be upset about. However, I am regretful that I made *you* susceptible to it."

"Your overall attitude is impressive. Thank you for being so calm about all of this."

"I should be thanking you; you make it easy."

"You've heard of spontaneity, right?"

" . . . The state of being spontaneous – yes . . ."

"Well that's what *this* night is . . . it turned out to be a good night to get lost!"

"Yeah, I guess it did. I know I can think of *99* other people I would rather *not* get lost with!" Lance isn't sure if that came out right, so he looks at Sherry and smiles to let her know it was a compliment. Sherry smiles; compliment received.

"I know a place not far from here," Sherry says. "Speed up!" Sherry is first to eventually get her bearings on where they are.

'Speed up'? I know she likes speed . . . but if this woman knew how I drive when I'm by myself, she wouldn't have said that!

They wind up in Skokie again, at the back end of the same mall where they first met. They stop at a neighborhood seafood restaurant for a quick sit down since it's close to ten o'clock already.

"A glass of Riesling for you Sherry . . . ?" Lance almost calls her *darling*.

" . . . As long as it took for us to get a menu in our hands tonight . . . absolutely!! The Riesling that you serve . . . does the production of it take place in Germany?" she asks the waiter.

"Yes it does!" he replies.

"I'll have a glass then . . . and the same for the gentleman." Lance smiles. "Wha . . . ? I did it correctly, didn't I?" Lance shakes his head affirmatively. " . . . Love those white grapes from the Rhine region of Germany!"

"Ahh . . . someone's been doing a bit of research!"

"Yeah, I thought it would be fun to let you know that I knew that!" she says with a giggle.

"Speaking of research, I'm having a hard time locating a place that does the haunted house ritual . . . but don't worry, I'll find it!"

"Oh, you don't have to worry about that; I have something going on that weekend. I won't be able to make it to the haunted house. I'm sorry . . ."

"That's okay," he says. *No it's not! Damn!!* "But there is definitely one thing we'll have to do before you move . . . and that's make it to the seafood restaurant in Wheeling!"

"Yes definitely . . . that would be *nice*."

"Your birthday is next month, I'll take you then. How does that sound . . . ?"

"That sounds good!"

"Okay, we'll figure out the exact day in the upcoming weeks. Oh, remind me to give you a couple of CD's I made for you; they're in the car . . . you know, the gospel CD's you asked me about . . ."

"Oh yeah okay . . . Thank you! So tell me . . . how's your internet dating endeavors going?"

"Oh please! It's a joke! Can we talk about something else? I have something really important I need to say to you . . . and don't worry, I'm not going to propose or anything like that . . . though the idea of being married to you is *not* far fetched by any means . . ."

Sherry smiles, "What is it Lance?"

"I don't think it's a secret that I really don't want you to move to North Carolina. In my opinion, you're running away from something. Sometimes the resolutions to life that one seeks are changes that need to be made from within instead of the changing of one's surroundings. Again though, that's just my opinion. Anyhow, I do care about you enough to say *this* and mean it – if you feel that moving is what's best for you . . . as much as I'll miss you, I do support your decision 100%. I really do hope everything works out for you out there."

"I really do appreciate you saying that. I think it's safe to assume that it's difficult for you to feel that way *and* to say it?"

"Yes to both . . . but in my heart and in trying to really be a *true* friend to you, it feels right." Lance himself can't believe what he's feeling or the fact that he's verbally expressing it. The sudden alacrity to partake in a long distance relationship, if it was with Sherry, is even more shocking to him.

He thinks about what Sherry said to him before about a monogamous relationship existing under God's terms. From the perspective of his own life, Lance knows he has never been in a monogamous union under these terms. His mental state in the desires of certain women and the pursuit of them in the beginning of these relationships has lacked that certain spiritual level. He views Sherry as the perfect opportunity to change his way of thinking concerning such matters.

As they ride in his car after dinner, Lance gets another reaction from Sherry while another song is playing. Unbeknownst to her, this song too is directed towards her on purpose.

"Wow Lance, that's deep! You say this is Aimee who?" Sherry asks.

"Aimee Mann, 'Wise up.'" he says.

"Hhmmm . . . she's a little folksy but I like it." Lance isn't sure if Sherry will catch the meaning of *this* song. For him, it pertains to *her* being with Norman in the beginning, going *back* to Norman, and even now, *still* considering Norman to be the one. Though she is not admitting it, he knows that she hopes certain ways about him will change. Holding on to false hope in another person, a mate, is certainly something that Lance knows we all have done. He has had more than *his* share of this. Let Norman go and *wise up* is the message he tries to send to her through the song. Reiterating this message to himself for future reference is not a bad idea to Lance either.

When they pull up to her apartment, Lance looks at her without saying a word. His thoughts are of how pivotal their *next* meeting will be, *it* possibly being their last. He knows there will be no room for messing it up. Even something as trivial as being late to pick her up is something he will make sure doesn't happen.

Wanting to take a picture of Sherry with his son before, somehow turned into the necessity of taking the most recent picture of *her* that he could possibly get; so he brought his camera for this meeting like he did before. He is reminded of the camera in his back seat when he's reaching for the CD's he made for her.

"Thank you for the CD's!" Sherry says. "I'm sure I'll enjoy them!"

"You're welcome sweetie and you know what . . . with getting lost tonight, I guess I forgot I brought my camera. I still need a good picture of you. It's not like I don't have any good ones of you already but those were from last year."

"Oh Lance, I wish you would've remembered before; I'm at home now."

"Don't worry; I'll take one of you when you get out." Lance didn't forget he had the camera earlier as much as he was nervous about initiating the moment before now.

"Okay, if you say so . . ." When she gets out of the car, she tries to strike a pose.

"No sweetie, you're trying to force it. Just make it look natural," Lance says. When he snaps the picture and shows it to her on the camera's display, she is pleased.

"Wow! I must admit, this is kind of nice. In fact, I like it!"

"I like it too." Lance says with an inner enthusiasm of liking *her*.

"Can you get me a copy of it?"

"Yeah sure . . . ! I print *all* of my pictures from this camera at home. In fact, I included those pictures from last year in that little packet I gave you with the CD's in it. I know you don't want to be reminded of Tammy. Just try to consider those photos as memories of you and I, okay?"

"Yeah okay, that's fine . . . I can do that. Well I will see you soon Lance. Thanks again for the spontaneous evening; the lobster was wonderful, wasn't it?"

"Absolutely . . . ! Thank you too! I'll call you."

"Okay." Lance stares at her as she walks away from the car. When Sherry turns around before she gets to her front door and waves goodbye one more time, Lance is startled.

Once she disappears into the vestibule of her building, Lance pulls off but stops at the end of her block and parks. He grabs a cigarette first.

"Wow! I've wanted one of *these* for hours!!" he says aloud. Sherry is aware of his smoking habit; but he has never smoked in front of her . . . not once. Lance grabs his camera next, to pull up the picture of Sherry. She stands with her purse protruding downward from its strap hanging from both her hands clasped together. Her gray cashmere scarf and the plastic bagged contents that Lance gave to her are secured in her arms. She is looking away from the camera lens in the picture, as if she's staring off into space while in a deep train of thought. Her mouth is open, but only enough to *slightly* reveal the tops of her pearly white teeth. The look on her face is serious, yet refreshingly beautiful.

The street lights up above shine on the back of her head, giving off a marooned colored effect to her hair as it hangs down past her shoulders. Lance notices a square like shape to her face, mostly in her lower jaw area. He had never really noticed this about her until tonight; staring at the picture of the woman he is so fond of. At the moment Lance turns his camera off and pulls away, he realizes – he is *in love* with Sherry Anderson.

There is a social networking website that has grown immensely popular over the past few years. The site's main protocol is socializing in cyber space for people that already know each other. Sherry is a member of this website and she convinced Lance to become a member as well.

He really doesn't see the point of it, unless one is interested in seeing what one of their friends is doing at *any* given point throughout the day. It's like sending a text message to one person but anyone you are linked to on the site, can see that message as well. Lance mainly sees it as a way to be connected to people that you're otherwise *not* very close friends with, unless family is on there. When Sherry communicated with Lance through the site about two months ago, he was a little insulted and waited almost two months to reply. When he goes on the site on this particular evening, there is a reply to his reply, to her initial message.

You're just now replying to my message?

Yes. I prefer exchanges with you face to face!

Lance feels that people, Sherry in particular, uses social networking websites and the internet in general to hide behind. This gives them the convenience of avoiding a more personal level of communicating, like a phone call or a face to face meeting. There are all kinds of reasons why a person would want to hide behind the technology of communicating in today's world. Lance wonders to himself if any of those reasons apply to him.

When he sees Sherry has added some new photos on her page of the website, he clicks on them to view. There are some recent pictures of her at a gathering of some type and she looks as beautiful as he has always wished she would look for him. She has on a strapless brown dress with her cleavage showing more than he has ever seen before. She has on subtle applications of make-up along with the same shade of lipstick she wore for their first Bible study.

Lance wishes she would've worn her hair down like she did a little over two weeks ago the night they got lost. He also wanted to see a full length body shot of her but she didn't take any. Yet she is just as desirable as he always knew she was capable of being. When he notices the Halloween date on the pictures, the night they were suppose to go to the haunted house, Lance is furious.

Lance feels a sense of *de-ja-vu* when he considers the possible reasons as to why he wasn't invited to this affair. He takes offense to the fact that she was at this gathering with family and friends as the pictures indicate. The only friend of hers he ever met was Tammy; the out-of-towner. To Lance, she doesn't count as *true* exposure to her friends; especially with them not being friends anymore.

Lance considers replacing the picture on his wall at work, the photo he took over two weeks ago, with the picture on his monitor now. He then scoffs at that idea because he feels it's unfair that a man *has* to be her boyfriend or family, in order for her to look really nice. He questions the meaning of their friendship in her eyes.

Am I just a guilty pleasure she partakes in from time to time without anyone else ever knowing about it? Did she not invite me out of fear that someone would mistake us as dating or being a couple when we're not? Did she not invite me to this party because she doesn't like me that way or because she does?

Lance ponders over the many questions involving Halloween night and their friendship in general. Ultimately he wonders why and how he fell in love with a woman that's moving to North Carolina to pretend like she's not trying to be near a man that can't make her happy. Lance shakes his head in disgust, still staring at Sherry's picture on his monitor. He types a comment under her photo which will post and be seen by her when she opens her page on the site.

Wow! Sherry is showing some skin! Cardiac arrest!

Lance turns his computer off and goes to bed early on this night.

On the Saturday before Veteran's Day, Lance has taken a drive out to Skokie, Illinois just to familiarize himself with the area. More importantly, he drove to this area to place an order for a dozen roses for Sherry's birthday on Thursday November 12th. He goes to her area to ensure there are no problems with the delivery on that day, with her living so far away from his area.

Lance usually likes to see what he's buying but makes an exception in this case. With Sherry's birthday being five days away, he wants to make sure her flowers are fresh and slightly open. He chooses ivory colored white roses and instructs the florist to order them directly from the distributor in about three days. White roses have a meaning of purity, innocence and spirituality. Lance ordered white roses because they look sexy to him and he considers them unique and not typical as red roses are.

When Lance leaves the florist, which is only three blocks away from Sherry's apartment, he has a smirk on his face because he hopes he won't run into her. He didn't intend on winding up so close to her place but it leaves him confident that the delivery will take place without a hitch.

In some ways, Lance can hardly believe what he's doing for Sherry's birthday. His tendency to extend gestures like a *love sick puppy* is the ruler of his actions once again. Before he pulls off in his car, he grabs his cell phone and reads the text message she sent to him four days ago.

Lance, I didn't get the job. They decided to hire someone local. I am really disappointed.

Lance attributes these turn of events to his sincerity in wishing her well in regards to her moving out of state, even though he didn't want her to go. His prayers for Sherry put her wants and needs before his own. He feels like he has reached the highest plateau of empathy and is now being rewarded for it.

Lance pulls off in his car to drive the route he will take to get them to the main highway that will take them straight to the expensive seafood restaurant in Wheeling. He can't believe how easy it should have been for them to get there before, the night they got lost. Nor can he believe how far away from the place they actually were and where they ended up, as he looks at his new map directions.

He continues to drive around Skokie, learning the area to a point of being a pro. He even passes by the mall, the neighborhood seafood place where they had lobster before and the Thai restaurant where he first proclaimed his feelings for her. The fact that Sherry has decided not to move right now, gives him the utmost of confidence, that the places they've been will be pleasant memories in their future when they are together.

Lance knows that many would consider the arrangements he's made for her birthday, a dozen rose, vase and all, and dinner at an expensive restaurant, to be over the top. Lance himself agrees with this notion when he considers the status of their relationship to be *just* a friendship. The dinner he would have done for someone like his best friend Angelica, but probably not the flowers. However, Lance holds no shame and there is no self reproach in his heart. He knows he will stand out from many in her life and he celebrates from within, his capabilities to do so. He thinks with approval, about what he wrote on the small card that will accompany the flowers.

A friend is allowed to bring a smile to your face on your special day; am I not?

CHAPTER 24

The closely shaved, perfectly trimmed beard that Lance wears is periodic, depending on his mood and depending on if he feels like the daily maintenance of it. The goatee is something that has remained on his face for so many years that he can't remember when he first grew it. On this day he cuts them both off and only a small, trimmed mustache remains. After that he gets his hand held mirror to stand in front of another mirror with his clippers to cut his hair, fade and all.

An hour after that, he gets ready for his shower. It is an extended one, as if he's going on a date, yet he's not. Lance constantly reminds himself that Sherry is just a friend and their meeting later will be just two people having a nice meal together for her birthday. His overwhelming feelings for her however make his constant reminders ludicrous.

He recalls the phone call he received from Sherry several hours earlier this morning when her flowers arrived. The enthusiasm in her gratitude was quite gratifying.

"Of course you're allowed to bring a smile to my face on my birthday and they brought a really big one too!!" she says frantically. "I was *really* surprised! Thank you so much! And white roses are my favorite color; how did you know!?"

"I didn't . . ." he says tranquilly. "It just felt right for me and they seem to fit *you.*" In a couple of days when Lance will look up the meaning and the sentimental message that the color *white* roses conveys, he will shrug his shoulders and wonder how he got so lucky.

They stay on the phone for forty five minutes; an occurrence that Lance can hardly believe. There is a rhythmic flow to their conversation that he can only recall happening once before, about two months ago. The uncomfortable strain he has *always* felt with Sherry, only over the telephone, doesn't subsist on this day. It's as if there is absolutely no holding back on Sherry's part. Her offerings of trivial matters in her conversation more often than usual, gives Lance a feeling that he *can* truly *belong* in Sherry's world.

He thinks about the two birthday cards he was buying for her when he received her call. As it turns out later in the evening, after he is fully dressed and ready to go pick her up for their evening, he finds himself writing something in each of the cards at the last minute.

We have watched one another try to succeed but found ourselves in a place of failure in the category of monogamous relationships. What seemed to be pure coincidence when I came across your pretty face on the internet 2½ years ago turns out to have been I realize; God's hand in seeing that you and I met. I thank you for your part in me realizing and seeing it through, my spirituality to a higher level. It's because of you that I read the Bible on my own now; not every single day but much, much more than I ever did before. I'm glad that you're here to witness my growth in that department. There is nothing like sharing the good word with someone of a similar mindset. You are a beautiful person inside and out and I thank you for being you and I thank you for your friendship – Happy Birthday Sherry!!

With much sincerity,
Your good friend Lance

He makes sure that both of the cards and what he writes in them are purely based on friendship so she won't feel the pressure of him liking her so much. He keeps his writing to a minimum in the second card since he almost ran out of room in the first one. The birthday cards, which he will give to Sherry after dinner will be his *coup de grace* to a perfectly planned evening. Lance looks in the mirror one final time before he leaves the house.

This is not a date – this is not a date! But I look damn good though!

His hair is cut very short as always, with a perfect sheen and a perfect set of waves when he removes his du-rag. His face is about as flawless as it can possibly be, given the slightly darker discoloration on his cheeks and his neck area where he has been shaving for over half his life. His face is smooth of razor stubble though and more importantly to Lance, his face is not shining of the oils in his pours like it often does if he doesn't catch it and wipe it away.

The diamond stud earrings that the clingy woman Anitra gave to him last year, gleam in his ears like sparkles do on the 4th of July. His button down designer shirt is all white and collarless with the majority of the buttons cleverly hidden when it is buttoned. Only the two buttons at the neck area of the shirt are visible; almost giving off the effect of the Roman clerical collar on a priest. The creasing in his black slacks took him twenty minutes to iron just right and his black all leather squared toed shoes are shining just like his Cadillac outside.

As Lance is walking out the door, he double checks to make sure he has Sherry's two birthday cards and his revised map directions. He catches a glimpse of the white gold ring he has on his pinky finger and smiles with pride. His father gave him the ring when Lance, Jr. was born. Richard Austin told Lance to give the ring to *his* son, when his first child is born. The entire front base of the ring is molded into the initials – L.D.A.

Thanks Dad!!

There are two designer trench coats that hang in Lance's closet at home. One is brown and the other is ivory. He has matching Dobbs for both of them too. The perfectionism in him makes him wish he could've worn one of them tonight. But the weather is brutally cold and windy on this day after Veteran's Day. With a thirty degree temperature and a 20mph gushing wind making it feel like it's under twenty degrees, the dark beige winter coat won the battle of the coats. It *does* have a furry collar and furry cuffs, so Lance considers the coat sexy in its own right.

Lance left his apartment with plenty of time to not have to rush, so his ride out to Skokie is relaxing. He listens to Aimee Mann again, relating some of the lyrics to "Wise Up" within his own life. Lance hits the repeat button when the song is nearly done so he can hear it again. He always considered it to be about *wising up* in a failed relationship by letting it go. His interpretation of the song doesn't change but after hearing the second verse more closely referring to "having a drink," his thoughts turn to alcohol and how people use it to try and cure *more* than failed relationships.

Alcoholism is something that some people hide behind when they feel like they have too many problems to ponder when they are sober. Alcohol is certainly no stranger to Lance, with twenty five years of history involving the substance to back it up. Lance has always enjoyed drinking alcohol. He has never ever wondered or questioned *why* he does. That two and a half decade run has suddenly and surprisingly during a sober moment, come to an end.

Oh hell . . . !! I can't believe I'm having these thoughts right now . . . so close to Sherry's place! Well, I'll entertain myself with this for about three more minutes since I'm about five blocks away from her apartment. Now, there are some alcoholics that have some sense and there are some that don't!! I know I have some sense . . . and I like alcohol . . . what does that make me I wonder . . .

In being sober, Lance's thoughts are weirdly intoxicating as he pulls up to Sherry's place.

As they are on their way to the restaurant in Wheeling, Lance is confident in each left turn that he makes. His certainty is unflappable in each right that he takes.

There is a new man behind the wheel of the black Cadillac this evening. With his goatee gone, Lance looks a little younger and feels a little younger too. There is a peculiar aplomb about him on this particular evening. Within the realm of what Lance considered in showing Sherry his best before, is even better now.

He doesn't expect her to grovel at his feet in asking him to take her out on a date as soon as possible. He doesn't even anticipate Sherry to suddenly want to label their time together this evening as being an official date. Lance merely thinks that tonight will be the night she realizes he is worthy enough in her eyes to be considered *boyfriend* material. How she handles that epiphany; will be left up to her.

Lance and Sherry arrive forty five minutes prior to their reservation. He finds it very relaxing to not be in a rush mode as he usually is when it comes to keeping time in his life. After they are seated, Lance orders what he thought had become *their* favorite drink of choice whenever they are together.

"What, you're not having a glass of Riesling with me?" he asks.

"No . . ." she says. "I don't think I want to drink tonight. Well . . . maybe I should have *one* glass; it *is* my birthday."

"You know what I say . . . ? If your decision is to not drink any alcohol tonight, then be happy with your decision and stick to it. I certainly don't want you drinking on *my* account."

"Okay, I will stick with my pop then."

It never ceases to amaze me; the indecisiveness she exhibits at times over the silliest stuff!

"You're almost completely clean shaven; I like that – it looks nice on you."

"Thanks Sherry!" he says. *Mission accomplished* he thinks. "So tell me Sherry, what should I order . . . the Australian lobster tail or the South African lobster tail?"

"Whoa!!" she exclaims, " . . . *$77.00* for the *18oz.* Australian and *$39.00* for the *8oz.* South African! At least they're priced according to how much you get! But are you sure you want lobster!? Do you even know the difference in them?"

"No I don't but I intend to find out tomorrow."

"My brother was making fun of you because you eat lobster!? He said going beyond fish and shrimp is a bit much for him."

"Your brother, oh really," he says. *So she talks about me to her brother huh?*

The waitress arrives with their appetizer; one order of garlic buttered char grilled scallops for them to share. The waitress is very friendly and perky . . . to an extreme. She is quick to acknowledge Sherry's birthday by bringing her a small cupcake with a lit candle ten minutes later. The restaurant does not have a policy for the staff to sing happy birthday to the patrons but the waitress does it anyway.

When Lance snaps two pictures of Sherry holding the cupcake before she blows out the candle, the waitress joins in on that too by snapping pictures of them sitting together. Lance is jokingly ready to ask the woman to join them and have someone else serve them. He knows it's just her way of being nice though and her tip will be more than appreciative of that trait.

"Those are nice pictures, though I think I look better in *this* one from a slightly different angle," Sherry says.

Yeah, I guess so . . ." Lance knows better than to agree with her outright. In the pictures the waitress took of them, Sherry is touching Lance in both pictures. Her arm is around him in one picture and both her hands are resting on his opposite shoulder in the other photo. Lance hates to admit it but he actually looks nervous in the pictures because of this. Sherry has never been shy about touching Lance and yet there has always been wishful thinking on his part, that those touches were indicative of something more than their friendship.

After they order their main course, Sherry the Macadamia Sautéed Sea Bass and Lance the *$39.00* South African Lobster tail, she starts to talk about Norman in a repugnant tone,

"You would think that a man would be a man and go out and get some type of a job for the time being when he sees his woman is working her behind off, six or seven days a week!" Sherry says. "I was practically supporting him!!"

"That's how a lot of guys do it now-a-days unfortunately." Lance says. "He probably didn't set out to do that to you; but he did seem to get comfortably used to his unfortunate circumstances." Lance is tired of hearing about Norman. He knows each time he has to hear about the man, it is a reminder that he's *still* on her mind after all this time. But with her current status of not moving, he suspects it's only a matter of time before those thoughts and feelings start to subside.

Lance wants to give Sherry her birthday cards *before* dinner to *shut her up* but he doesn't. He wonders if she'll ever bring up the fact that she was once engaged without an engagement ring. He determines that it's too embarrassing for her to *ever* bring up, so he dare not do so, no matter how curious he is about that part of the whole story. In the end *no job* equals *no ring* and that logical assumption will just have to do.

They taste each other's food from directly out of the other's plate like they have done a few times before. By now though, this is *old* to Lance and he never gives it a second thought.

After dinner, the waitress is still "being nice" when Lance is trying to present Sherry with her birthday cards. He gives them to her when the waitress finally takes her excessive conversation to another table.

"Happy birthday Sherry . . . ! I got you *two* cards because I couldn't decide on which one to get." She reads both the cards in full length. Lance anxiously waits for her to finish the second card with the longest written passage in it.

"Oh Lance, these are beautiful! I didn't know you could write *this* well!!" Sherry gets up from her side of the booth and walks over to Lance with her arms extended outward. He turns towards her to receive her gesture. When she hugs him, it feels like it's for dear life and it is endurably long and filled with gratitude. "Oh Lance, thank you so much!!"

Lance had stopped counting the seconds of the duration of their hugs a while ago. *This* hug though, and the fact that Sherry initiated it blows him away. As much as he hates to admit that the confidence that was boiling over in him earlier has faltered a bit, it has. He can't help but wonder if the exorbitant embrace is the easing of her guilt in not liking him the way he wants her to or if the emotions in the hug are truly for him.

Lance hates that he doesn't know for sure because when it comes to women in situations like this one, he usually *does* know. Despite the fact that he has more than welcomed this *friends first* scenario with Sherry, it is still something he is unfamiliar with because he has never really done it before; not quite like this.

It would seem that Lance is going back and forth in determining if tonight will truly be the turning point of Sherry's feelings for him. One thing he *is* sure of; the comfort level is still at its highest for her, just as it was this morning when they spoke on the phone. This gives Lance his own comfort level to utilize during *some* moments throughout the evening.

As they are driving along after dinner, "Damn, I should've stayed on Milwaukee ave.; it goes all the way through back to your place you know. I remember you suggesting we take Milwaukee all the way to the restaurant the night we got lost, but I didn't listen to you."

"Oh Lance, you're still on that? Anyway, why did you want to take it going back tonight?"

"That would've been more time spent with you." Lance is surprised he let *that* slip out of his mouth . . . but he goes with it and smiles at her.

Sherry smiles back at him, "You're really sweet Lance."

"I'm not gonna lie, most of the times we've ever gone anywhere, the evening always feels rushed. I'm not blaming that on you; I know you very seldom stay up late or stay out late. I guess it's true what they say – time flies when you're having fun!"

"I enjoy your company too Lance."

"And I mean that from a friend's point of view. Never mind all that other stuff . . . not that my feelings are gone; they're not! I just don't want you to feel like I'm trying to exert any pressure on you, 'cause I'm not . . . am I talking too much!?"

"Just a little, but its okay . . . I think it's cute that . . . well maybe *cute* is the wrong word for what I'm trying to say – *cute* sounds condescending."

"Yes it does! There's nothing '*cute*' about how I feel about you Sherry – in fact . . ." Lance catches himself, *extraordinary* he thinks. "Never mind . . ." he says.

"Uh oh . . . ! Is Lance getting upset?" she says jokingly.

"No, not at all," he says in a serious tone.

"Well, what I was going to say is – I find it admirable that you're so vocal and so open with what you wrote in my birthday cards; with your feelings! Most men aren't. I remember waiting for Norman to ask me out and how long it took him."

I gotta hear about this fool again!? Well, if ya can't beat 'em, join 'em!

"Maybe he wasn't sure what your answer would've been at the time," he says, with his own present situation in mind.

"Maybe so, I dunno."

"Well anyway, I'm not most men. You do realize *that* by now, don't you?"

"Yes, as a matter of fact I do."

"Let me ask you something I've always wanted to ask you. Did you and Norman go out the same evening you and I first met at the mall for the first time way back when?"

"No, we weren't going out at that point, not yet. Why do you ask?"

"You seemed to be in a huge rush that evening, I dunno. I just always pictured you going home and fixing yourself up for *him* that night . . . plus you didn't answer the text I sent you that evening. By the way . . . you *do realize* you've come up with three different stories regarding that particular time period?"

"No I haven't; what are you talking about?"

"The *first* time we spoke on the phone in 2007, you told me you were seeing Norman. Last year you told Tammy you didn't know him yet . . . *now* you're saying you *did* know him but you two weren't dating yet. Which is it?"

Sherry notices Lance's ability to nick pick for the very first time. "Norman and I were *not* officially dating when I first went out with you," she says, slightly irritated.

Lance realizes he's in *nick pick* mode and catches himself; even though he remembers what *day* it was *and* what time it was, the first time he spoke to Sherry.

"Whatever you say Sherry; it's your life . . . you oughta know," he says.

But I know what you told me on the Sunday we first spoke two and a half years ago . . . what you told me on our date . . . and what you told Tammy last year!! It doesn't matter though . . . Norman's gone now and he ain't coming back!!

"I will admit, I didn't answer your text that one night . . . but I did think about you a couple of times after our date. I texted you a couple of times, but you never replied to them. After we *did* become friends, thanks to you, I realized that I was sending the text messages to your land line and not your cell phone. I've never admitted this to you before because I conveniently just forgot about it. I felt so silly texting someone's home phone – and I think of what *wouldn't* have happened if you didn't pick up the phone and call me again after we went out . . . none of this would have happened!"

"It's like the card says darling . . ." he says. *Oooppss* he thinks. "God put you into my life . . . and God put me into yours! It takes two to Tango. We're friends because the Lord wanted it to take place. Don't beat yourself up because you made a mistake when you were texting me. *Why* were you texting me back then anyway?"

"I thought it would be nice if we could be friends."

"Aahhh . . . *touche!* It's really funny how things work out sometimes . . ."

"Yeah it is."

"Just like our Bible studies, the two that we *did* have," he says sarcastically, "Did you expect me to say *yes* when you first inquired about us doing that together?"

"No, I didn't."

"Well surprise! See how funny life can be sometimes . . . ?"

"Yeah, just like our watching one another fail at our relationship endeavors!"

"Is it safe to assume that you haven't had sexual relations with anyone since last year? If you don't mind me asking . . ."

"Yes you're right, I haven't."

"Does your libido ever go into overdrive . . . like do you ever have a strong desire for it?" Lance grabs her hand playfully, "Do you ever *fiend* for it!?"

"Well of course I think about sex sometimes," she says sheepishly, " . . . but not like an addict or a fiend. What about you?"

"Of course I think about sex . . . about a hundred times a day! I *am* a man, right!?"

"No silly I mean, when's the last time you engaged in such activity?"

"Same as you . . . last year," Lance says proudly. "And believe me, it wasn't serious – and that was exactly the reason why I let it go. I didn't choose celibacy – it chose me! I will admit though, the more and more time that has passed since I last engaged, the less and less I think about it. With raising my son and being more set on finding a quality woman to have in my life than ever before, the easier it gets to sustain. And with my present spiritual path I'm trying to be on . . . I welcome it!"

"Yeah, I hear ya on that!" Sherry exclaims. She then changes the subject out of fear that her private area will start to lubricate unconsciously . . . without anywhere for her to escape to tend to it. "You know what I was thinking about . . . ? I don't mean to change the subject but I was looking at some nice restaurants online recently and I picked three of them that seemed really nice; I've been to one of them. I would like to treat you to one of those restaurants; which ever one you choose."

"Oh that's sweet! What are the three places you chose?" Sherry names the restaurants; he has never been to any of them. He tells her he will let her know which establishment he will choose very soon. Lance can't wait for his next meeting with Sherry, especially considering the fact that she's *not* moving to North Carolina.

As far as Mr. Lance Austin is concerned, this entire day has been a drug free high. When he puts himself in Sherry's shoes, her being the recipient of it all probably makes the day just as exhilarating for her if not more.

Even if nothing gives tonight, he thinks . . . *something will have to give eventually where Sherry is concerned.*

When they are a couple of blocks away from Sherry's apartment, Lance is telling her the story about how and when he ordered her flowers. Sherry says something that completely staggers Lance.

"Well since you never actually saw the flowers, would you like to come in and see them?"

"Sure that would be nice," he says calmly, yet feeling completely shocked that she has just extended an invitation for him to come inside her apartment for the very first time ever. He thinks back to the evening he cooked for her last year and how she had him meet her two blocks away from her place, probably because Norman still had his belongings there the first time they broke up. By the evening's end, he finally saw where she lived when he dropped her off. Lance ultimately decides *not* to read too much into her invitation when he considers it *could* be just as nonchalant an issue for her, as it was for her to drink out of the same drink glass back when they barely knew each other.

When he walks in, the first thing he notices is a big beautiful brown leather sofa, "Is that a Kipling sofa?" he asks.

"Yes – how did you know that?" she says surprisingly.

"Research of course," he says with pride. "Wow! Sherry Anderson just invited me inside her home! Break out the bottle of Merlot immediately!!" he says in a jokingly yet sarcastic kind of way. His comment will hopefully stifle the strain *he* is feeling.

Sherry smiles at him but doesn't reply to his comment, "Come around here . . . the flowers are here in the kitchen."

In the kitchen . . . ?

When Lance turns left where her kitchen is and sees the flowers, he gasps, "Wow! These are beautiful . . . who got you such a beautiful dozen of ivory roses!?"

"*You* did silly!"

"Wow, they're more beautiful than I could've ever imagined! They *really* did a good job, just like the florist said they would! Thank you for showing them to me!"

Sherry points to a picture of a white rose on her kitchen wall, "See, white *is* my favorite color rose!"

When they walk back into her living room, Lance notices a queen size mattress leaning against her wall as he has a seat on the Kipling brown leather sofa. For a quick second, he wonders why it's there. As if Sherry read his thoughts, she volunteers information about the mattress. The sound of her voice suddenly reminds Lance of how the adults sounded on the "Charlie Brown" cartoons when he was coming up.

Sherry's explanation, whatever it was, didn't include her ex-boyfriend's name in it. Lance thinks it's the mattress that Norman had to sleep on when they stopped having sex.

What man can have, probably a beautiful caramel colored naked booty pressed up against him in the night at one point in the relationship . . . and then that same woman telling him she doesn't wanna have sex again until they're married . . . still be able to sleep in the same bed with her!!? Of course that's Norman's celibate mattress!! I don't care what she's saying!

Sherry interrupts his thoughts, "You know what Lance . . . today has been a really special, unexpected day for me and I appreciate it from the bottom of my heart! I'm gonna make sure I make your birthday next year, *just as special* a day as you made mine!!"

"That's not necessary Sherry . . . it was my pleasure – but if that's what you would like to do, I *will* look forward to it!"

"That's what I want to do! Thank you so much Lance!" The living room sofa is so comfortable to Lance that he can barely remove himself from its perfectly engineered cushions. Once he's standing to get ready to excuse himself for the evening so she can get ready for work the next morning, he turns around and glances at the couch one more time. Lance will proclaim to be making sure nothing slipped out of his pockets while he was seated if she asks.

As Sherry walks him to the front door, she bestows upon him, a replica of the tight, extended hug she gave him in the restaurant. While Lance takes in the hug like a marijuana hit, he wonders to himself if he will sit on her beautiful Kipling brown leather sofa ever again.

CHAPTER 25

It is exactly one year later, November 12, 2010. Lance walks into the room and it is empty.

"I'll be there in a second! Have a seat!" the faint voice says coming from the next room.

"Okay sweetie . . . !" he says. He looks around the room noticing new pictures of art on her walls. There are also various certificates of achievement; some he has seen before, some he has not. Lance smiles because he is not surprised at her accomplishments. He turns and looks at the familiar piece of furniture.

And to think . . . I actually wondered if I would ever sit on this beautiful Kipling brown leather sofa again. How silly of me to have had that *thought, right!?*

Lance smiles again as he sits in the middle of the couch. He then kicks his shoes off feeling completely comfortable where he is. He lies across the couch to further consume its ultimate design in comfort.

"Are you nice and comfy Lance?"

"Yes I am Angelica! Do they make this Kipling in black leather? I think I'm gonna go out and get me one; everyone *else* seems to have one of these."

"I'll look it up for you in a couple of days and let you know. How are you?"

"I'm okay I guess."

"Just okay huh . . . ? Isn't today *Miss Skokie's* birthday? I remember that because it was so close to Veteran's Day . . ."

"You remember correctly."

"Did you talk to her?"

"No . . . she didn't answer so I left her a voicemail. I hate women that don't answer their cell phones on their birthday!"

"Knowing *you*, there was probably a little more relief than there was disgust that she didn't answer . . ."

"I guess . . ."

"Did she call you back?"

"Yes . . ."

"You didn't come all the way down here to my office to give me one word answers I know. What did she say?"

"Well she got *my* voicemail when she called back because subconsciously I left my cell phone in the other room after I called her. She said . . ." Lance changes his voice to a whiny female, " . . . *'Oh Lance, I'm sorry I missed your call! Thank you so much for the birthday wish! How's the little one . . . ?'* and some other shit, I dunno. She was talking too fast for me to make it out!"

"Did she sound sincere?"

"Yeah – sincere and phony . . . ! She knows she doesn't care about LJ; hell, she never even got him a gift when he was born!"

"And *when's* the last time you actually spoke to her?"

"Late January . . ."

"Hhmmp! That's *fucked up*! Oooppss . . . excuse my language."

Lance looks surprised at Angelica's choice of words, "Yeah, it *really* is, especially considering you went *there* when you very seldom curse."

"I'll tell you what . . . tell me everything that happened the night after your outing with her in Wheeling last year. I know I've heard most of this already but I also know that this whole situation is weighing heavy on your mind and you want to talk about it. Otherwise, you wouldn't have asked to see me, *especially* on this particular day. Take your time . . . I don't have anymore appointments this evening." Lance sits up. "You can remain lying down if you want."

"No, I will sit up."

"Is your sitting up indicative of you needing *a friend* rather than a psychiatrist?"

"I really don't know *what* I need in that regard Dr. Rose; but I *do* know that lying down in *this* office will give me the appearance of being weak. One thing I do know about myself is that I'm not *that*!"

"Whatever. You want a drink?"

"Excuse me . . . ?" Angelica walks over to the gigantic reddish mahogany desk and pulls out a familiar liquor bottle to Lance's surprise. "I know that's not . . ."

She interrupts, " . . . A *Very Superior Old Pale* of your favorite cognac? Yes it is."

"When did you start drinking like that . . . !?"

"Like what . . . !? A bottle of this lasts me for months! I have an occasional shot of it just to keep the edge off."

"I'm an alcoholic Angelica. You're offering an alcoholic a drink?"

Angelica looks surprised, "Lance . . . I swear . . . I have *never* heard you say that before. When did this come about?"

"Twenty five years ago!!"

"No, I mean realizing what *I've* always known and you admitting it . . ."

"I guess about a year ago."

"That's really . . . Wow! That's wonderful! I'm speechless. Here, have a shot on me. You're a big boy; you can take care of yourself – I'm sure better *now* than ever before with that beautiful two year old you're taking care of so often."

"This is true. Wow, you even thought to have snifters here!"

"Where do you think I got *that* from!? Cheers . . . !" Angelica says with a grin on her face – like *the bad little girl on the playground.*

"Cheers . . . !" Lance says – still astonished about the sudden turn of events. "You know, I spoke to Sherry on the phone about thirty five minutes after I dropped her off and she was still wide eyed and bushy tailed over the whole experience. We were talking about this movie that was coming out soon and I suggested that maybe she and I go see it. She said that going to the movies is something she only does in a dating situation. Was I suppose to ask her out then!?"

"Why, so she could throw her infamous one liner on you!? You cook dinner for her and . . ." Angelica does the same whiny voice of a female that Lance did . . . *I'm not ready to date right now* . . . 'You tell her you have feelings for her, *I'm not ready to date right now* . . . 'She sounds like a broken record!! And those same exact proclamations were made a year apart, were they not!?

"Whoa!! Why don't you tell me what you *really* think about the situation?"

"As a friend, that's exactly what I'm doing. Now, as a therapist, I *know* I'm out of line . . . but we never established in what capacity this session was to be . . . so we're gonna mix it up a little bit!"

"Boy that *shot* has got you fired up! I like it . . . okay."

"From *Sherry's* point of view, I can certainly appreciate her *not* using you to try and remedy her pain from a previous relationship. From *your* point of view, you have involved yourself with a woman that thinks she knows what's best for her but truly doesn't; not from a realistic point of view. There's this little girl fantasy of how her life should turn out! I don't knock her for that because most women have that when they're little girls, as teenagers and even in their twenties."

"I know what you're talking about. Some men fantasize about a perfect life too when they're coming up; you know, a perfect woman, perfect job, perfect home. I'm one of those men!"

"Men do it too, I know. But I'm talking about *women* in particular! Women mature faster than men do. Some women never do; and certainly some men never do! As morally sound as *this* Sherry woman presents herself to be . . . the *fantasy side* of her make up was suppose to start to subside when she reached thirty – and it didn't!!"

"*Stuck* on Norman is what you're saying, right?"

"Absolutely . . . ! You know I've always said that I thought Sherry liked you . . . but she obviously liked Norman *more* – even from the very beginning. Maybe she thinks he's more handsome than you are . . . and I *wish* I could say that she thinks he's better in bed than you are but you've never slept with her! At least *then*, the emotional instabilities of her decision making regarding you . . . would make more sense. I don't have to go into explaining the emotional turmoil that can occur when most women have sex with a man, do I?"

"Of course not . . . ! You think maybe she's just *bourgeois*!?"

"In a sense . . . yes; but not so much as I think that she's *still* trying to find the little girl fantasies that don't exist within a man or within the foundation of how she *hopes* her life will turn out. I saw a movie once recently and this middle aged woman spoke about how a *young* woman carries these notions of what is suitable in a man she should be in a relationship with, versus a man she just *settles* for. Long story short; what seems like settling at a younger age turns out to not be settling when a woman gets older. The expectations are *supposed* to become more realistic when maturity sets in. Sherry is *how* old, in her 40's like you?"

" . . . Thirty nine . . . forty one . . . something like that, I dunno . . ."

"Poor thang!! She might figure it out one day. I didn't mean to interrupt you . . . continue."

"Well, I was curious about why she asked me to do Bible study with her. It seemed like a sincere gesture at first; until I asked her if she expected me to accept her invitation to do so. She said *no*. So I figure, why ask someone to do something you don't expect them to wanna do, unless it's just to prove a point. In her case, I think it was a way to justify why Norman probably *wouldn't* do that with her. You know like the *all men are just alike* thing that some women like to hold onto."

"That's a very good deduction. I agree with you. Did you figure that out all by yourself!? We should switch seats; I could use some of your expert analysis of human behavior . . . !"

"You're silly Angelica . . . you know that!? I bet'cha all those questions at my apartment when I thought she was interviewing me for *the new boyfriend position* were all questions concerning Norman . . . not *me*!! You know, like throwing *my* answers to her questions in *his* face to make him feel guilty or jealous . . . I dunno."

"Wow! There are so many different angles you can approach all of this from . . . it's making my head spin! I know exactly what you mean though."

"You know her mother saw the beautiful roses I bought for her. I wonder what her mother had to say about me."

" . . . Probably what any smart woman her age would say; to hold on to you because you're potentially a good catch! She obviously didn't listen though; too busy stuck on stupid or maybe she just simply wasn't attracted to you. But then why keep having those intimate dinner meetings with you? Why did she even go out on a date with you in the beginning? I dunno . . . there are just too many questions concerning her! I think she was hiding something!"

"She did start acting a little weird right after her birthday last year. In fact, every time we had a *really* good outing, she would pull away from our friendship.

I wouldn't count the first time she did that, you know after our date because we officially weren't friends yet and the date was only *asi-asi* anyway."

"*Asi-asi?*"

"Yeah, *so-so* in Spanish . . ."

"That's cute, I gotta use that one."

"She said she tried to contact me via text messages after our date but I don't quite believe that."

"If I remember correctly, she disappeared right after the Reggae club outing, right?"

"Yes, your memory is correct. The second time she ran away from our friendship was after I cooked dinner for her. We had plans the week after that and she cancelled. I always figured that Norman was the reason she kept backing away from me and that's a legitimate reason. But once he was physically out of the picture last year when he moved out of state, running away from me made no sense!"

"He was *physically* out of the way, yes. *Mentally* though for her . . . his presence was probably stronger than it had ever been before. Remember, she did try to move to North Carolina to be near him, even though she never admitted it."

"Yeah that's true. You wanna hear something funny though? When we started hooking up again last year, towards the end of our nice dinner at what's-a-name in the mall, she went to the bathroom briefly. When she came back, the strangest thing had occurred . . . her face stunk!"

"Lance, *what* . . . ?"

"Have you ever smelled a person's face in the morning, like when you first get to work and there's this certain odor that comes from their face; like maybe they were rushing to get to work and somehow they forgot to wash it? Do you know what I'm talking about!?"

"Yeah, as a matter of fact I do. We *all* can have that strange odor on our face, especially in the morning."

"Yes I know. I've smelled that same odor on *my* face before; that's how I knew the strange smell was coming from *her* face!"

"Okay Lance . . ." Angelica giggles, " . . . but what does this have to do with anything?"

"Nothing . . . I was just wondering what she did in that bathroom for that odor to suddenly start coming out of her pours like that! I could even smell it outside when we were leaving the restaurant!"

"I dunno Lance. Maybe she threw some water on her face, realizing she forgot to wash it *with* a cleanser before she left home. Of course water alone is never enough . . . but can we get back to why you came here this evening . . . ?"

"Yeah sure, I'm sorry. You know about a week and half after I saw her for her birthday; I tried to get with her for a third Bible study. She said she would let me know and never did. I was so mad at her about that because it was so unlike her to say she would do something and then *not* do it. I stopped calling her for a couple of weeks after that and she actually noticed!"

"Aahhh . . . you played *the ball is in your court* game and she fell for it huh? Good for you! Us women need to be hit with that anvil every once in a while."

"One of her voice messages was, 'Are you mad at me or something . . . I haven't heard from you!?' I didn't express any anger towards her when I *did* talk to her though because it had previously always been in my nature to be argumentative. I was trying to do things differently, ya know?"

"You know *I* understand that perfectly . . . but in that case, I think you should have found a way to let her know that you demand respect, even if you had to scold her just a little bit to get your point across. Look at all you've done for her over the years! Look at all the wishy washiness you've put up with over the years. You see Lance, your history with anger is so vast, that *now* you seem to fear it a little bit. Remember, anger is just another emotion. You just continue to maintain the habitual mindset of harnessing your anger and not going overboard when you feel it and you'll be fine. Trust me when I tell you, you're doing a very good job at it. Even when you were with what's-her-name years ago you were better!"

"Who, Melanie . . . ?"

"Yeah . . . If she knew what I knew about your anger years ago . . . she would've *never* put her hands on you! But anyway, Sherry's wishy washy behavior reminds me of that funny looking girl you were dating years ago . . . what was her name, *Orange . . . Apple* . . . something stupid like that . . . !?"

"Oh, *that* woman . . . the one that picked her teeth with a steak knife in the steakhouse on Rush St; I don't even wanna *say* her name!!"

Angelica giggles, "Well I'm gonna say the poem! What did she email you one day after you told her you like to write?"

Roses are red
Violets are blue
That's you and me baby

Lance chuckles softly, "Yeah that was funny."
Angelica laughs out loud, "Funny . . . ? That was hysterical!!"
"Okay but can we get back to why I'm here . . . ?"
"Okay, I'm sorry . . ." Angelica says as she gathers her composure.
"Well it had actually gotten to a point where she started calling me and texting me more. One day she texted me around Christmas time when I was in a department store browsing and just so happened to be looking at tennis rackets and thinking about my mom."
"Right, you two used to play tennis together when you were very young."
"Right . . . I asked her if she would play tennis with me in the upcoming summer. She said she didn't know how. I said I would teach her and she said *okay*.

Well *that* never happened! I even bought her a Christmas gift out of the kindness of my heart . . . !"

" . . . You mean out of *the love* in your heart!"

"Whatever Angelica . . . ! By late January, her gift went back to the store! I had driven out to Skokie a few days before that to do some shopping . . ."

"You went out there unannounced!?"

"Yes, but I *really* was shopping out there though. Anyway I called her and left a voicemail message that I was in the area and just wanted to drop her gift off."

"She didn't call you back!?"

"Yeah she did, *three* hours later. By *then* I was on my way back home! We only spoke briefly because my cell phone battery was running low . . . and that was actually the last time I spoke to her on the phone."

"Wait a minute Lance . . . that doesn't make any sense! Well, as far as her waiting so long to call you back, maybe she was just having a lazy day and she wasn't decent."

"Oh believe me, that wouldn't have meant shit! I've seen her on her lazy days before!"

Angelica giggles, "Lance, you know what I mean. But not talking to her after that . . . I just don't understand! What happened to the three restaurants she had picked out for you to choose one of them so she could treat you!? What happened to her making *your* birthday just as special as you made hers!? She *did* say that, didn't she?"

"Yes she did. The three restaurant deal obviously never happened! As far as my birthday was concerned . . . and I don't think I ever told you this; here let me see if the text messages are still in my phone . . ."

Someone has a birthday coming up!

Yes I do.

What are you doing to celebrate your big day tomorrow?

I kinda celebrated already this past weekend.

Doing what?

Lance chuckles, "If she had *that* much to say, she should've called me instead of hiding behind the text messages! It seemed like she was trying to feel me out since it had been so long since we last spoke. When I answered two hours later that I went to dinner to celebrate, she texted me again and asked me *with who?* If the mutual understanding of our relationship was friendship, whatever I *had* planned or *did* already shouldn't have mattered! If I was seeing someone at the time or not, which I wasn't . . . shouldn't have mattered!! You know what I mean? *Make* your *fuckin'* move *already* I say!!"

"Sherry obviously grew accustomed to you re-igniting the fire so to speak in you all's friendship every time she let it go out. She expected the same when she kept texting you back in June."

"Exactly; that's why I didn't do it!! Whatever level she was trying to be on in doing something for my birthday, it was up to *her* to make that move. What was I gonna do . . . ask her out on *my* birthday!?"

"I agree totally! Sometimes one has to *step outside the box* and do what they normally wouldn't do . . . especially for the good things in life. Maybe she was scared to do that; maybe she was just scared of the whole situation, I dunno."

"I like morally sound women but *scary* women . . . I don't like scary women! They're always too afraid to wanna do anything. Some may say, *especially* the fellas, that it was *me* that was scary. I will admit that shyness can overwhelm me at times; but it never stopped me *completely* from *getting mine* so to speak . . . not for the long term. I feel like this; if I have to manipulate an indecisive woman into being in a relationship with me . . . what am I truly gaining!? Their wishy washy decision making tendencies are usually only significant in the short term of things! You don't know *which* way the wind will blow a woman like that in a month or two!"

"I definitely think that a more natural union would endure the aspect of *long term* rather than a forced one. If you were simply in it to get her sex, I could see you going all out. I can't believe you haven't dated anyone in two and a half years though!"

"Dated . . . ? That word you just used . . . *sex* . . . I haven't done *that* in two and a half years!!"

"What do you think about that?"

"I don't. Okay I *do* . . . but it's no longer a necessity in my life. I know this doesn't sound like a normal man . . . but you know me, I don't care what other people think about me. Most people are idiots to me anyway, so their opinions about me usually hold no validity!"

"I know *that* feeling in you is one thing that will *never* change about you."

"You're right, it won't!"

"You haven't had sex with *anyone* in thirty months!?"

"I haven't even *kissed* a woman in that amount of time."

"Wow!! But then again I know you. You have always been a strong willed individual and I know when you put your mind to something, it is usually etched in stone. The only things I've noticed you doing the past two and a half years are taking care of your son, improving *you* overall and driving the hell out of that Cadillac!"

"Thank you; that about sums it up . . . oh yeah and drinking my ass off and smoking cigarettes like a fool!"

"Pray on that."

"No scientific codification or rationale on how I should quit smoking?"

"What, you think I forgot who I'm talking to!? Have you even *seen* a vagina in thirty months!?"

" . . . Yes, on TV and on the internet; nothing thrilling though. I get more pleasure out of touching *myself* than looking at that crap! You know I never, not once, ever thought about Sherry while masturbating!?"

"Wait-wait-wait-wait-wait . . . we'll get to that in a sec! You said 'the internet.' You weren't on those freaky porn sites, were you?"

"The *dating* ones . . . you know, quick sex, married women looking for sex or *cyberspace* sex, something I'm not into. None of it panned out though because a lot of times the women on there don't really exist . . . *well* the fat ugly ones do . . . but the really cute ones were either links to other websites that I wasn't interested in or they were in a time zone seven hours away from ours, trying to get'cha to wire money to them! I know you've heard of those internet scams?"

"Yeah, unfortunately I have a friend that fell for that . . . more than once! So you masturbate huh? No I'm just kidding; you know that I know it's perfectly normal."

"I said that because I wonder if I ever had a sexual attraction for Sherry. Consider the fact that I fell in love with this woman without any sexual contact what-so-ever! I've never considered myself capable of falling in love with a woman in that manner. Then I thought about my spiritual path and suddenly it made sense, so I no longer questioned it. I called myself trying to find my future wife within the realm of God's rules."

"And you're *still* in love with her or else you wouldn't be here." Lance doesn't respond nor does he deny the notion internally. "I'm sure you remember my husband and I didn't have sex until we were married."

"Yeah, I remember."

"I'm sure we don't have to talk about all the *wrong* reasons that men and women engage in the activity."

"Of course not . . ."

"I will say that a lot of times, women suffer from post coital dysporia and they don't even know it."

Lance gives Angelica a look of confusion. *You know I don't know what that means . . . please tell me without me having to ask . . .*

Angelica continues as if she read his thoughts, "Oh I'm sorry! That's basically an emotional displacement after sex; depression. Even if the woman reaches orgasm it doesn't mean she actually enjoyed it. The orgasm is a retreat from other unhappy areas in her life."

"Sounds like something I've gone through *during* sex when I look at the woman and say to myself 'What am I doing?'"

"Absolutely . . . ! But of course *a man* would never admit *that* out loud."

"I would have, to someone . . . had I been familiar with the condition. Hopefully I never go through that at *this* stage in my life. I'm at the point now, that a peace of mind is better than a piece of ass!"

"That's a good one; I agree with that concept!"

"It's funny when I talk about sexual attraction concerning Sherry. I have never ever had a dream about her either."

"That doesn't insinuate a diminutive level of adoration for her. It's probably just the concept of what you're used to when you usually fall in love versus what you're trying to get used to within your spiritual path. You know the devil always has his hands in something."

"I have had a couple of strange dreams as of late Dr. Rose; not strange but unexpected."

"Do tell . . ."

CHAPTER 26

Lance hesitates in describing his dream to Angelica. "There was a beautiful . . . naked woman standing in front of my mirror in my bedroom. I've known her for a while because my thoughts were about her body being just as beautiful from head to toe as I remembered it being before. It appeared to be morning and she was about to get dressed. The woman is married in the dream and I know this because I remember thinking to try and not let it show in my demeanor. 'If it crossed *her* mind . . . ' I think, ' . . . and knowing her I'm sure it has . . . this slight inconvenience doesn't show in her demeanor either.'"

"Okay . . . the *friend* in me certainly wants to ask, *who* this woman is! However, I'm gonna switch hats for a minute and ask the *'what'* question first and save the best for last!" Angelica smiles, "Okay, so *what* does this dream mean to you?"

"Oh that's easy . . . it makes me wonder why certain situations in life often have an outcome that is opposite of what it should really be!!"

"Do you want me to answer that?"

"No I don't."

"I knew you would say that; *why* did I even ask . . . ? Okay and now the *coup de grace* . . . *who* is the woman in the dream?"

Lance hesitates for a moment, "I guess telling you she never turned around and looked at me won't *fly* with you, right Dr. Rose?"

"Right because she didn't have to turn around; you said she was in the mirror. Surely you glanced at her face for a second while you were staring at her booty!"

They both chuckle, "Okay . . . well, it was my ex; my first love . . ."

"You're shitin' me!! Okay that's it; I'm not cursing anymore this evening! You mean that funny looking girl from the 80's? The girl in that old 8' by 10" with her hand on your shoulder with the missing nail . . . !?"

"She was *not* funny lookin', she was cute!"

"Okay, wow . . . you really went back a few years with that one! You want her back!?"

"Hell nah!! I was really into her at the time though. I really don't wanna elaborate. It was the dream itself that really grabbed my attention; not her!"

"What would you like to talk about now? It seems like something's bothering you – and it has nothing to do with Sherry."

"There's no *fooling* you, is there? Here's something else you don't know . . . I had that talk with my brothers recently."

"You did . . . ? Oh my goodness how did *that* go? When did this happen?"

"A few months ago . . ."

Angelica scoffs, "A few as in *three* or a few as in *more* than three months ago!?"

"Three . . . actually about two and a half months ago – before Labor Day. I had hoped to have a more encouraging feeling afterwards but I didn't."

"That's never stopped you from telling me anything *before*. Wow, you're holding out on me!"

"Well long story short, 'cause I really don't feel like talking about this right now . . ."

"Then why'd you bring it up?"

"*Touché* . . . ! I basically came from the angle of the importance of family for my son's sake; their nephew. I know most of my years in being their big brother, if *not* all of the years from their point of view, are not very favorable. I was stand-offish for *all* of their lives when I lived with them . . . and then I just up and left; nothing to write home to mom about . . . no pun intended. We don't have to discuss the fact that I left for the sake of my son being born and his upbringing . . ."

"Of course not . . ."

"Well as we both know, they do have their issues . . . but what I also know . . . for most of my life, I have been the fuckin' king of issues. None of us have ever *broken our necks* to try and hang out or communicate on the regular . . . but what if I had been a *better* big brother to them; would that have turned out, even slightly different?"

"Lance, you're bringing me to tears . . . you said that!?"

"In so many words . . . Hhmmp! I never did find that Kool & the Gang CD for Nate!"

"Kool & the Gang . . . ?"

"Never mind . . . You know Matt & And actually came to Melanie's sister Marcy's backyard bar-b-que for Labor Day with me."

"You're kidding me . . . how did that turn out!?"

"I don't think the outcome was as monumental as them *actually* showing up. They only stayed half an hour. It certainly was awkward but I didn't expect them to put on a performance for Melanie's family and of course their one word answers kept socializing to a minimum. It was a start though."

"Sounds encouraging to me . . . You sound a little down about the whole thing; why?"

"I dunno Gel . . . I just . . . I dunno. I know your next question is why Nate didn't show up. He had to work; but he really did seem receptive of what I was saying that day the four of us talked. I kinda wanted to holla at the ol' man too but I was drained."

"I can imagine . . ."

"You know a few years ago I heard Mr. Foster on the phone *with some bitch* talking about the difference between showers and baths! They were obviously dating or whatever! Don't ask me how our telephone lines got crossed; it just happened."

"Okay, so let me ask you this – is Sherry a *bitch?*"

"No of course not . . . ! I think she's a tad bit silly for my taste at the end of the day but she's certainly not *that*! Why are you asking me that?"

"I remember a time when referring to a woman as *a bitch* for *you* was second nature, especially during one of your anger episodes. When you used the term just now, it surprised me. I haven't heard you call *any* woman that for years."

"You're right I haven't . . . but when I hear my step father on the phone talkin' crazy with *some* woman and it concerns my mother within the aspect of negativity, ANY woman is a bitch to me!!!"

"Lance, I'm really not trying to be funny . . . but I've never known you to refer to a person that is no longer with us in such a present state of mind . . . Do you wanna talk about that?"

"*Angelica* . . . I heard this *ill* conversation when my mother was *still alive*."

Angelica doesn't say anything with her mouth. She says a couple of words with her eyes.

Lance continues, "You wanna hear a funny story?"

"Yes, probably a little bit more than you wanting to tell it at this point . . . and as long as it's not about someone's face stinking!"

Lance chuckles and continues, "LJ and I were finishing up our breakfast one Sunday morning and I kept trying to wipe his mouth of the grape jelly from his toast. He wouldn't let me. I started fussing at him to let me wipe his mouth before he whined about wanting to get out of his highchair. Twenty minutes later when I was sitting in the living room drinking my coffee, I noticed something strange around the rim of my coffee cup; it was grape jelly. I was so concerned with my son wiping *his* mouth that I had neglected to wipe my own."

"Cute story . . . but don't be fussing at my lil' friend . . . !"

"You know what that is though . . . *that's* the definition of love. After forty three years of living, I have finally figured out *how* to love a woman and what it all means . . ." Lance pulls out a receipt from his wallet. The ink is almost completely faded on it. He hands it to Angelica.

"You know what that is?" he says. "That's the receipt from the Chinese food that Sherry and I had at the mall the day we first met. I had *no* idea how it was gonna come about, but I always believed from the moment I saw her, that she was *the one*. I think I put up a pretty good fight in trying to wiggle my way into her life. It was three years for the most part that I held on to that aspiration. I didn't even take her picture down from the wall at work until after I took her Christmas gift back. And you're right, I *do* still love her at this very moment . . . but I no longer consider our union to be a possibility. From a man's point of view, I know a *real woman* will only give you what ya ask for. I know I could've done some things differently; said some things differently . . . but somehow, I don't even think *that* would have made a difference. The constant conflict, her always wondering if I was trying to date her within the boundaries of our friendship made me think that she *did* wanna date me. But it created conflict within our friendship! You see the level of confusion it caused?"

"Yeah, indecisiveness and confusion are very good companions!"

"Sherry Anderson is simply not *the one* for me. I cancelled all of my memberships with the internet dating websites once and for all too; not because of Sherry but just because that part of my life is over with. When I meet my future wife, it will be face to face. Another important quality of a *real woman* – she will be able to recognize a *real man* when he's standing right in front of her." Lance hands Angelica *another* small piece of paper from his wallet.

"What's this?" she asks.

"Your phone number you gave to me the day *we* first met."

"Wow!! You still have this after all these years . . ."

"I thank God for your friendship Angelica. You have seen it all when it comes to me and I'm really surprised that you're still here. Our six and a half years together was certainly no picnic for you. Believe me when I tell you, I have *so* many regrets when I think about that."

"Lance, it wasn't *all* bad. We were both young and dumb back then. We *both* tried to love one another the best way we knew how at the time."

"I saw this movie recently and I thought about you; *woulda – coulda – shoulda!!* I'm afraid *I'm* the victim of not knowing what'cha lost till it's gone! I was *supposed* to be the man in the relationship. I was supposed to take the lead and set an example for you to follow and be the type of man you could be proud of!"

"I know this will sound cliché but I'm proud of you *now*; very proud of how you've turned out."

"But whenever you're headed home and you get there and you stick your key in the door, I will never hear it. All my dating life I've been looking for *the perfect 10* kinda woman . . . and when I had that in *you*, I was too ignorant and too selfish to see it. I didn't even comprehend it; I *never* did! I turned to a couple of other women *during* our relationship . . . when things weren't very favorable between us . . . I wasn't even a man when we were together . . . and to top it off . . . I displayed the *ultimate* state of stupidity and I let you go when I asked you to move out!! I will regret that *for the rest of my life*."

"Lance . . . I . . . I didn't expect you to say any of this. Please don't take the expressions on my face the wrong way . . ."

"I'm not. What I'm simply trying to say to you is . . . *I'm sorry, from the bottom of my heart* . . . for all the hell I put you through all those years; for all the *drinking* and the hanging out and all the verbal abuse . . . and the physical abuse especially. I was always so proud like an idiot, that I never actually hit you . . . but the grabbing and the pushing and the shoving was just as bad! You have always been the perfect red rose; you were ten years ago when we parted ways . . . and you still are!!" Your husband – God bless him; he's a very lucky schmuck!!" Angelica smiles, "I'm just kidding about the *schmuck* part," Lance says.

"I know . . ."

"Here I am proudly announcing that I would actually teach a woman how to play tennis *now* . . . but back then you dreaded *me* teaching you how to drive because of my *'F'd'* up attitude. Now here you are and you still don't know how to drive."

"You're giving up cursing all of a sudden?"

"I'm not going to answer that."

"Okay . . . I'm still mad at you about the cat; but deep down I know you did your best with Priscilla. You took care of her for what, about seven years after we broke up? I know your son was ultimately the reason why you had to give her up. Don't look at me like that, I'm being serious."

"I know you are. You know it's because of *you* that I know my way around in the kitchen. Everyone always assumes that my mother taught me how to cook; but it was you! Thank you for that. I'm sure my son will appreciate it in the years to come."

"You had to want to learn in order to master it and take it to the next level like you did over the years. And I never taught you breakfast; that was all you! Do you still make those awesome omelets!?"

"Not as often . . ."

"Good! Don't make that for *anyone* else, except your future wife . . . promise?"

"No . . . ! Well for *you*, okay, I'll think about it. You know what though . . . try sprinkling some oregano and chives on your scrambled eggs; it's the best!!"

"Where did you get *that* from . . . !? Sounds weird . . ."

"A movie actually . . . I tried the spices in the eggs *before* I scrambled them once . . . not a very attractive looking thing to eat. You have to sprinkle them on *after* you scramble them!"

"Okay, I will try that!"

"I don't know what just made me think of this . . . but ask me why I would always talk proper with Sherry and no other woman I met during, or even before I met her . . ."

"I will not! *Please* . . . give me a break! That woman got a lot more of you than she *ever* deserved!"

"One of my Hispanic co-workers said that when she looks at our overall situation and how it turned out, makes Sherry appear to be '*muy loca*'!"

"She could be right. Maybe she's bipolar; maybe *that* was her secret, who knows! But you used to talk proper with me a long time ago when we first met. After you got in good, the *thug roll* language started slipping out of your mouth! I used to think 'Oh boy; this guy is really *GH*. . .' well I'll be honest, I wasn't using the term *GH* back then . . . but I used to think you were *ghetto*, pretending to be proper. Shortly thereafter, I realized it was the opposite; you were and *are* even today, *preppy* trying to pretend like you're *ghetto*!!"

"Why you gotta use the term '*preppy*'?"

"Because I know you *hate* being described as that!"

"And its funny . . . I think that term originated in Boston. You never did tell me why you didn't come inside to LJ's baby shower . . ."

"*Please* . . . think about it, you know why! I have a hard enough time functioning in my life, possessing the physical attributes that *society* deems as desirable. I certainly wasn't going to walk into a mine field, being your ex and all!"

"I know it's kinda hard being as beautiful as you are; kinda like a blessing *and* a curse."

"I know you remember all of the incidents years ago."

"Yes I do. I also remember a certain someone once telling me that I needed to stop mistreating you . . . and if he wasn't married to my mother, he would take you away from me!!"

"You have to be *fucking* kidding me Lance!! You're gonna make me throw up!!"

"He even had poor Melanie fooled into thinking she was standing on some kinda higher plateau in comparison to me; he was trying to *fuck* her!!"

"Well good luck with giving up your profanity. By the way, is that the *last* garbage bag you're disposing of this evening!?"

"I have one more confession . . ." Angelica frowns a little bit. "It's concerning *moi*," Lance says coyly.

"Oh okay, thank goodness! What is it?"

"The dream was about *you*," he says sheepishly.

"When I open this bottom drawer, grab the cognac bottle to turn upside down and pour it *all* down my throat, you'll be satisfied then, right!? You're blowing me away this evening!!"

"I was surprised myself, and *I'm* the one that had the dream!"

"But seriously though, I kinda figured that out already . . . not being conceited or anything . . ."

"My *first love* story sounded like nonsense huh?"

"No, you kinda fooled me with that one! Actually, you called me '*Gel*' about fifteen minutes ago. You haven't called me *that* in ten years or so."

"I *did?* I didn't even realize I did that."

"I'm flattered Lance, I really am. But you know that's *all* I'm going to say on that matter, right?"

"Yes Angelica, I know that."

"Are you about ready to wrap this up?"

"Yeah, sure sweetie . . . I know you wanna get home to your hubby."

"Actually, he'll probably be a little later than I tonight. I wanna get out of here before you have me *drunk* up in here from all the earth shattering things you've been telling me tonight; good or bad! You coulda kept the bad stuff . . . from *a friend's* point of view. The good stuff though . . . Lance, thank you so much for everything . . . your friendship, your revelations and being so open about them! And you know that I *can't* forgive you today . . . I already did that years ago . . . that's why you're still here in my life as a friend; a *dear* friend!"

"Thank you Angelica. So you want my statement in summary?"

"Sure . . ."

"I feel like I truly became a man when my son was born! He's my *whole* life and I don't know where I would be right now without him! I don't know if I'll *ever* slip and have sex with a woman anytime soon and I certainly don't know who that may be *if* it does happen. It's just not on my agenda. A man thinks that just because he signed on the dotted line for the mortgage payment, he's the ruler of his castle. But only a *real man* and a *true* ruler to be followed is one of integrity within himself and empathy for others; otherwise he's only running a street corner food stand. And who wants to be the ruler of a hot dog cart with only three wheels on it!?"

"That was beautifully said Lance! Did you just make that up?"

"Yes . . ."

"One more question Lance . . ."

"Yes . . ."

"Are you depressed?"

" . . . If you're asking me within the capacity of being a psychiatrist, the answer is *no*. If you're asking me that as a friend, the answer is *yes*. What do you think?"

"As a doctor, I think you're suffering from a mild case of dysthymia and you should come back so we can talk some more. As a friend, I think you're suffering from a mild case of dysthymia and I'm not worried about you because I know you and I know you'll get the best of it before it gets the best of you!"

"Well thank you my dear *friend*. I will definitely make a note of that during my self recovery." As Lance and Angelica are near the exit to leave, she hits the light switch just as he opens the door. He turns to look at her beautiful face one more time before they depart but the lack of illumination in her office conceals it for a moment. Just as he scoffs, the light from the next room reveals what he wanted to see so badly just a mere moment before.

Wow!! Gel is just as gorgeous as she was the day I broke up with her ten years ago!! And I may never come across anyone quite like her ever again!! What a fool Lance – what a fool!!!

"You know Lance, you have always been so very talented in your writing . . . and they say writing is very cathartic. Why don't you write a book about Sherry Anderson?"

"You're silly Angelica . . . you know that!?"

CPSIA information can be obtained at www.ICGtesting.com
Printed in the USA
LVOW13s2028060214

372657LV00002B/417/P